FATHERLESS

FATHERLESS

A Novel

DR. JAMES DOBSON
AND KURT BRUNER

New York Boston Nashville

FaithWords
Hachette Book Group
237 Park Avenue
New York, NY 10017

www.faithwords.com

Printed in the United States of America

RRD-C

First trade edition: September 2013
10 9 8 7 6 5 4 3 2 1

FaithWords is a division of Hachette Book Group, Inc.
The FaithWords name and logo are trademarks of Hachette Book Group, Inc.

The Hachette Speakers Bureau provides a wide range of authors for speaking events. To find out more, go to www.hachettespeakersbureau.com or call (866) 376-6591.

The publisher is not responsible for websites (or their content) that are not owned by the publisher.

Library of Congress Cataloging-in-Publication Data

Dobson, James C., 1936-
 Fatherless : a novel / Dr. James C. Dobson and Kurt Bruner. -- 1st ed.
     p. cm.
 ISBN 978-1-4555-1311-6 (regular edition : alk. paper) -- ISBN 978-1-4555-2243-9 (large print edition : alk. paper)
 I. Bruner, Kurt D. II. Title.
 PS3604.O24F38 2013
 813'.6--dc23
                                    2012015903

ISBN 978-1-4555-1310-9 (pbk.)

In memory of the late Chuck Colson, who foresaw and warned about the ominous trends depicted in this book.

AUTHOR'S NOTE

A happy home is the highest expression of God's image on earth. And there are forces working to destroy that image, not all of them visible to human eyes. Marriage and parenthood echo heaven, something hell can't abide.

In 1969 I began serving as assistant professor of pediatrics at the University of Southern California School of Medicine and the attending staff at Children's Hospital in Los Angeles. That affiliation continued until 1983. In 1977 I founded what became a worldwide ministry dedicated to the preservation of the home that placed me in one cultural skirmish after another, unwittingly confronting forces much darker than I knew. I don't pretend to comprehend what occurs in the unseen realm. But I know that we all live in what C. S. Lewis called "enemy-occupied territory." The Scriptures tell us Satan will "go out and deceive the nations" at the end of history. A central focus of that deception will be, I believe, the final stage of an assault that began when our first parents believed a rebel's lie.

Over the past four decades I have advised US presidents and cheered exhausted moms as they engaged different fronts of the same battle. Part of my role has been to provide intelligence reports on the war against human thriving. The assignment now forces troubling questions.

What happens in a world where growing up with the protective love of a father becomes the exception rather than the norm? Today's inner-city poverty and violence give us a foretaste of how deeply and widely those ripples will extend.

What happens when the very old outnumber the very young? Demographers tell us the decline in marriage and parenthood is fueling an unprecedented drop in fertility. The growth in global population will soon end, then reverse. The human family will decline at a pace not seen since the fourteenth-century Black Death. As we are already seeing in places like Japan and Russia, economic turmoil always accompanies dwindling population as the few young and healthy are burdened with the ballooning aging and feeble. The best projections show America on a trajectory to tip downward in a few short decades.

This book series is a fictional account of what current demographic, sociological, and cultural shadows portend. But it is also a celebration of God's design for families, which retains a resilient beauty and redemptive power the most ardent forces of hell cannot destroy.

James C. Dobson, PhD

FATHERLESS

August 17, 2041

Antonio

I didn't expect the person killing me to yawn in boredom.

The small print under her name, Hannah, reads TRANSITION SPECIALIST. I recognize the title from the online permission form: she's one of the many "thoroughly trained, warm-hearted associates who provide essential services to our heroic volunteers."

She probably exhausted her warmth earlier in the day. She said I'm the fourth volunteer since noon. I counted at least three more in the reception area nervously anticipating their final moments in this very room. Hannah will be eating a late dinner tonight.

I never met the physician. I guess that's to be expected. Doctors don't take temperatures or check blood pressure. They delegate routine procedures like mine. I'm just another lame horse needing a swift, painless end to my misery. No, not a horse. Horses, at least, bring value to the farm. I've been pure expense to Mom and Jeremy for eighteen years, dead weight at a time when humanity needed all hands on deck.

Hannah lifts a dressing gown that looks like an ugly bedsheet. "We need to get you out of those clothes and into this." She speaks loudly, like I'm deaf. Or slow.

I sense Hannah's apprehension. I can tell she's never worked with someone so incapable. Most volunteers probably have a semblance of mobility. But I can't offer any help as she struggles to remove my shirt. I feel her cheek graze mine and taste the salty aroma of nervous moisture on her face as she wrestles my lifeless arm from its sleeve. Then I feel her unfastening my belt to remove my pants and underwear. She quickly covers me with the gown. It's too thin. The room turns cold and suddenly stark.

Hannah's blush diminishes as she wipes my arm with alcohol. The scent stings my nostrils. On her third attempt to locate a viable vein, she sighs at the inconvenience of such gaunt limbs. At eighteen, I'm around seven decades younger than her usual client. I'm sure she expected less aggravation. I guess every job has its little annoyances.

I feel like I should make small talk.

So, tell me about yourself.

Got a partner? Kids?

What's a good-looking girl like you doing killing a guy like me?

Laughter eases tension. But I've never made people laugh. I've always made them uneasy—like an unsightly, but harmless, bug. They instinctively back away. I suppose laughter would be out of place here anyway.

I know what Hannah's thinking. "How could any parent put a child through so much suffering?" The inverse of my question: "Why should any mom make such a sacrifice?"

And none of it necessary.

The sleepless nights.

The condemning stares.

Precious years and a small fortune spent helping me cope in a world designed for those far more capable.

Such a waste.

Hannah glances at my chart. "So, I see you just had a birthday." Her own attempt at small talk.

I wonder if she noticed that my birthday fell on the precise day demographers projected America would cross the tipping point toward depopulation. They were off by three, but that doesn't matter. The date was symbolic anyway. It's been the topic of every headline, talk show, political commentary, academic symposium, and bar stool debate this entire week. I suppose it's fitting that my transition appointment landed on the actual day. We are now officially in the same leaky boat as the rest of the developed world.

So I'm doing my part. Since I turned eighteen on Thursday I no longer need Mom's consent. Mothers have never liked it when their sons enlist. But I know I'm doing what's best.

As the first drops of yellow toxin begin seeping into my bloodstream, Hannah studies the healthy habits chart hanging on the wall over my left shoulder. Though much younger, she reminds me of Mom. Not in her features...in her movements. She carries herself with a sturdy yet motherly persistence. I want Hannah to look in my eyes. She doesn't. She can't.

I kind of wish Mom had come with me to hold my hand or rub my arm. But she never was good at this sort of thing. I remember the time she rushed me to the emergency clinic after my big brother shattered a vase, embedding long shards of glass in my foot. She willed herself to stay by my side while the nurse removed the bundled rags Jeremy had used to slow the bleeding. Then she apologized and slipped out to stand in the hallway. The nurse told me not to cry, that I would see her in a few minutes when my stitches were done.

During our farewell dinner last night Mom said her heart

ached like it did when Dad left. What else would she say? Those were hard days. That's when Jeremy told Mom he hated God. I never understood what God had to do with it. Still don't.

I can't remember Dad's face, just the scent of his aftershave. I miss his smell. Mom said she misses his playful whispers in her ear. She blushed when she said that.

I'm pretty sure Dad secretly blamed Mom for me. Like most sensible people, he wanted to stop after one child. But Mom had insisted Jeremy needed a sibling. They imagined a healthy girl. I'm neither.

They call enlisting to transition a "heroic service to the public good." In truth, I'm doing it for Mom. She deserves to have a life. Besides, I'm tired of living on the debit side of the ledger. No one has ever called me a debit directly, but the slang fits. They instead feign sympathy while mentally tabulating the costs. The latest numbers show another significant drop in the ratio of productive workers to elderly and disabled dependents. The math no longer works. People like me divert young and healthy workers from desperately needed innovation and growth. I won't let that continue. I know I'm worthless, but I have my pride.

The procedure should take "an average of forty-five minutes." The clock on the wall says I have twenty-one to go. Hannah checks her watch before retrieving a transparent mask hanging on a hook beside my right leg. She unwinds a bit of slack for the attached air tube: the next step in a tired but efficient sequence. Placing the mask over my mouth and nose, she gently stretches an elastic strap over the back of my head before typing my weight into the digital regulator.

I suppose I'm a lavish coward for choosing the optional sleeping gas. I know they've perfected the treatment to eliminate pain. I just prefer drifting into slumber to counting down final seconds like on New Year's eve. Besides, the extra fee was nominal.

"Just breathe normally." Hearing Hannah's voice brings comfort. I'm glad my transition specialist is a woman, maybe even a mom. I bet she took this job out of a maternal instinct, to create a better world for her newborn child, or perhaps a niece or cousin. She believes this is best for everyone, especially me.

I don't notice the music until a hallway disturbance interrupts its purring melody. Hannah looks away from the chart with a twinge of concern. She listens deliberately, as if hoping an intercom voice will confirm a false alarm. But the noise increases. A door opens and slams. Another slam, this time accompanied by muffled conversation.

"Please, ma'am, you need to return to the waiting room." A woman speaks with hushed intensity, like a church usher scolding an irreverently disruptive child.

Hannah appears alarmed. This has happened before.

"I don't care about your idiotic policies. I want to see Antonio!"

Mom?

Hannah moves toward the door and reaches for the lock. Too late. It swings inward, knocking her off balance toward my bed. I feel a slight prick from the jolted needle. No harm, just the embarrassment of a mother interrupting my first and only act of independence.

"Ms. Santos?" Hannah asks, regaining her professional composure. "I must insist that you leave. We've entered a delicate phase of this procedure and…"

Hannah's voice and body freeze. Twelve inches from the tip of her nose a small, razor-thin scalpel threatens. At the other end of the knife I see Mom's trembling, extended arm.

"Stop this right now! I've changed my mind." An odd thing to say since she never consented.

I'm surprised to see Mom with a scalpel. She must have grabbed it from another transition room. I had forgotten about the organ donation process. They'll extract my useful parts from this very bed.

Over Mom's shoulder I see the blue shirt of the building security guard arriving on the scene, short of breath and winded from the urgent, three-story climb. The scene unfolding before me feels sluggish, like a film in slow motion. I notice the twenty on the clock become twenty-one. Nineteen minutes left.

"Please, ma'am." The guard looks young and sounds frazzled. "Let me just…can I please walk you back?"

Our eyes meet. In a fraction of a second Mom and I silently converse through forming tears.

"Let me go, Mom. You deserve this."

"I don't want you to leave."

"You know it's best. I'm a burden for you, Jeremy, everyone."

"You're part of me. Part of us."

"I want to go."

"No."

The look in her eyes tells me this is more than last-minute theatrics of regret. It is an act of sturdy, motherly persistence.

Mom waves the scalpel toward the needle and the mask. "Please. Remove these now." A tender plea from one woman to another that is also a nonnegotiable demand.

"I can't do that," Hannah says sternly. "A portion of the solution has already entered his system. If I cut it off now your son could suffer a slow, painful death."

"But he…"

"The treatment is cumulative," Hannah interrupts. "Even a small dose is fatal. The more he receives, the quicker the process."

"I don't believe you!"

"Please hear me, Ms. Santos. It's too late. Give your son this one mercy."

The words sting. A clear indictment. "*How could any parent put a child through so much suffering?*" Mom failed to screen out genetic defects. She forced me to live imprisoned in a twisted, sickly body. Must she also profane my final moments, my heroic act?

Our eyes meet again.

"Forgive me, Antonio."

"Of course."

"I did what I thought was best."

"I know. I understand. Now let me go."

I feel woozy, struggle to keep my eyes open. A long blink before forcing them back. Sixteen minutes remain.

Sensing his opportunity, the rumpled blue shirt lurches forward, awkwardly wrapping itself around my mother from behind. The guard tries to force her arms downward and knock the scalpel loose, but the surprise causes her body to react instinctively. The knife lunges forward, grazing the lower right side of Hannah's jaw.

Both the guard and Mom fall forward, disappearing from sight. I hear a brutal thud and feel the force of crushing skull against the metal edge of my bed. I see Mom's convulsing body topple into view.

Is an act still heroic when it kills the person you were trying to free?

I can no longer open my eyes. I don't want to.

I sense commotion and shouting, but the noise fades.

I submit to approaching waves of slumber.

PART ONE

CHAPTER ONE

Julia Davidson took a sip from her second glass of ice water. Pretending to study the lunch specials, she tried piecing together her transformation from rising star to plunging rock. Was it a specific story? The inevitable shift in reader tastes? Or had she lost her edge? A few years ago editors eagerly accommodated her busy schedule rather than the other way around. Now only one even returned her calls.

Paul Daugherty's manicured hand gently squeezed Julia's shoulder from behind. "Sorry, Jewel. Couldn't get away. Been waiting long?" Fiftyish and impeccably groomed, Paul had a pudgy frame that reeked of freshly applied cologne, overpowering the smell of warm garlic bread and a passing pasta dish. The fragrance, like the man, seemed indiscreet.

"I just arrived myself," she lied. "Thanks for carving out the time."

"Don't be silly. I'm always eager to see my favorite journalist."

Former favorite, she thought. Just that morning Julia had read another sloppy piece by Paul's new go-to gal, Monica Garcia.

"Don't you mean *columnist*?" Julia jabbed to remind him of her diminished post.

Paul waved his index finger at the naughty comment. "Shame on you. I know dozens of great writers who would kill for the top RAP column."

A compliment or threat? she wondered.

"And your numbers remain respectable by any network's standards."

"Respectable"? Is that like "a nice personality"?

"Thanks, Paul. And I appreciate all you've done to make that happen." A bit of flattery, even if undeserved, seemed judicious.

"What can I say? Our target demographic loves your stuff. And you can still turn a phrase like nobody else."

Still? Past my prime at thirty-four.

"Welcome back, sir," the waitress interrupted. "Shall I have the chef prepare your usual?"

"That would be lovely, Debra." Paul was more loyal to a pasta dish than he was to the woman who had propelled his career. Before acquiring Julia, Paul had sat in a cubicle suffering the mindless tedium of copyediting. Now he managed features and columns for the second-largest media company on the planet.

"Let me guess." Paul dug deep to remember Julia's favorite. "Salmon salad?"

"Please," Julia said to the waitress, who retrieved her menu.

"Got a man in your life yet?" Paul's usual question.

"Nothing steady." She disliked small talk. "I'm meeting another one of Maria's friends at the theater tonight."

"Promising?" Paul prodded.

"I have low expectations."

Both smiled as Paul turned to business. "You'll be pleased to know that I come bearing gifts."

"I hope they're better than your last gift."

"Hush," Paul said, raising a finger to his pursed lips. "I think you're going to like this one. It could be a big story."

"Feature story?"

"That depends on what you find."

"Find?" Julia swallowed back rising indignation. There was a time when Paul's team had delivered the material she needed for a feature.

"Just listen, Jewel. We've contacted the plaintiff who initiated a wrongful death lawsuit against NEXT Inc."

Nothing connected. "I don't follow."

"You wouldn't yet. It was a small story that ran about seven months back. Some eighteen-year-old debit scheduled himself for a transition. His mother freaked out and attacked a clinic employee."

Paul paused to receive his glass of diet soda. Winking a thanks while sipping from the straw, he waited for Debra's departure before leaning into Julia. "Anyway, the woman died."

"The employee?"

"No, the mom. Get this. She slipped during the attack and smashed her head against her own son's transition bed!" He leaned back, smiling at the comic irony.

"Who initiated the lawsuit?"

Paul seemed irritated at Julia's anemic sense of humor. "That's the really interesting part. The invalid boy had an older brother who blames the clinic for both deaths."

"Both deaths?"

"Yeah. The older brother said the appointment was made three days before the kid's birthday. He was eighteen for the actual transition, but they accepted his online registration while he was still a minor."

Julia took an unnecessary drink while considering the story's potential. It was uncommon for someone that young to transition, but not unprecedented. And there were a thousand cases of distraught loved ones or religious nuts trying to interrupt transition deaths at the last minute.

"And?"

"And we want the boy's story," Paul explained.

"I thought the boy was dead."

"Not the debit kid, the brother." Paul moved slightly back so the waitress could slide his hot dish onto the table. Eyeing it eagerly, he continued. "We want to portray him as a pawn of greedy lawyers."

"Greedy?"

"Sure. Every other transition dispute has been settled out of court. This one went all the way, even demanding punitive damages. NEXT plans to appeal, of course."

"Look, Paul, I'm not sure—"

"I know what you're thinking, love," Paul interrupted. "But I really think this could be interesting. And our editorial board considers it very important. There are people who will try to misuse this story. You can imagine the headlines, *Youth Initiative Causes Teen Suicide* or *Distressed Mother Killed During Illegal Child Transition*." Paul sniffed in contempt. "We need to get ahead of this story before some crusading reporter plays it wrong."

"So they want the brother demonized?"

"In the most fair and balanced manner possible," Paul said wryly.

Julia took a bite of salmon to buy herself a moment to think. She doubted the story could hit big; just another seemingly frivolous lawsuit against one of the most respected nonprofit organizations in the nation. Transition clinics enjoyed a stellar reputation. Most readers would quickly scan the headline before moving on to more significant topics, the kind Paul had been assigning to Monica Garcia. But she couldn't risk refusal.

"OK, Paul," Julia began. "I'll do it."

"Great!"

"But on one condition."

"Condition?"

She breathed deeply. *Here goes.*

"I want the next big exclusive."

"This *is* the next big—"

"Then why didn't you assign it to Monica?"

A lingering silence shifted power to her side of the table.

"Don't look at me like that, Jewel." Paul reacted like a boy caught with his hand in the cookie jar. "You know I wouldn't hold back on you."

Three words exposed his ruse. "*Return to Guyland.*"

Paul had given the story to Monica. He had pirated the title from Julia's Pulitzer-winning feature *Guylanders*, the very story that had catapulted Julia and Paul to the top of RAP Media Syndicate.

"She did a good job on that piece," he said sheepishly.

"You leveraged my reputation and my prior research to give her a big break."

"I never…" Paul stopped short. He had lost this argument before. He owed her, plain and simple.

"Please, Paul. Don't make me beg. You know I need this."

"OK, Jewel. You win. Take the lawsuit story and you'll get the next big feature."

"Thank you, Paul." She meant it. Her window was closing fast. If she didn't release a major piece soon she would find herself tumbling all the way to the rocky bottom, where feature writers and columnists became story consultants and research assistants.

He pulled a card from his coat pocket and slid it across the table. A name, Jeremy Santos, along with a phone number and address. "He's expecting you at noon tomorrow."

"You already said I'd interview him? But I just—"

Paul flashed a scheming grin and winked. It reminded her of the old days.

Julia took another bite of her salad, this time enjoying the taste. She glanced around the restaurant, noticing the admiring gaze of a handsome young man seated at a distant table. He seemed embarrassed as he forced his eyes back onto the menu.

She felt a long overdue flicker of confidence.

CHAPTER TWO

"Are you serious?" Kevin Tolbert felt the pit of his stomach land somewhere between *This could be big* and *Don't say anything stupid*. "Here? Today?"

"That's the rumor," Troy's voice continued through the phone. "They say he plans to make a surprise visit to the summit this afternoon. And get this, no press allowed."

"Franklin? No press? Wonders never cease…" Kevin's voice trailed off as he gazed out the panoramic window overlooking natural red rock formations surrounding the Camelback Resort. He hesitated. "A reliable source?"

"Excuse me?" Troy snipped, his words followed by a low growl.

"I know. I know. You wouldn't include it in my daily briefing unless the source was solid. Sorry." Kevin appreciated the thousand-mile protection afforded by Troy's decision to remain in Washington, DC, to mind the office. Troy had been taller and stronger since the two met at Littleton Middle School in 2019, giving him the perfect angle to rub Kevin's head in a sandpaper motion whenever irritated with his "little buddy." The routine began when Kevin accidentally spilled Troy's carton of chocolate milk all over the prettiest girls in seventh grade. Troy avenged the girls the only way a junior high boy knows, through physical violence.

The head-rub had remained Troy's go-to attack ever since. Their new roles as congressman and chief of staff only relegated the practice to places hidden from public eye. Neither had been willing to give up the most intimate sign of a friendship that had spanned high school, college, three successful business ventures, and their recent victory over four-term congressional incumbent Nicolas Long.

Kevin changed the subject while gently patting his own head. "What else have you got?"

"Ever hear of NEXT Inc.?"

"It rings a bell. Transition services?"

"That's the one," Troy said. "They got nailed in a high-profile lawsuit. Wrongful death."

Troy paused to let the pieces assemble in Kevin's mind. He had always admired his best friend's ability to connect dots and anticipate the next move. Troy's role, the years had confirmed, was to provide straw that Kevin could weave into gold: trade convention rumors, market trend analysis, financial projections on declining small businesses poised for turnaround. Once Kevin understood the landscape and opportunity, Troy's role shifted to that of a loyal general who could protect and implement.

Nothing much had changed since the move to Washington. The same alliance that had built a successful investment enterprise now sought to influence the national debate. Troy's role as campaign manager and then chief of staff fit like a glove. Kevin Tolbert possessed the brains and charisma needed to debate in Congress, woo donors, and charm the press. Troy Simmons had the heads-down determination and street-smart radar required to keep his little buddy on track and away from trouble. Each needed the other. Both knew it.

"How many transition lawsuits have been settled out of court?"

Troy had anticipated the question. "So far, all of them."

"What makes this one different?"

"Two deaths, a young man and his mom."

"A double transition?" Kevin asked.

"No. The mother tried to stop the procedure. She died from a severe blow to the head. The clinic claims it happened when she slipped and fell during an attack."

"And the son?"

"He scheduled his appointment while a minor, a pretty clear violation of the age and non-compulsion guidelines established three years back."

Kevin noticed several summit participants reclaiming their seats around the conference table, carrying small plates of cookies or fresh fruit.

"Looks like round two is about to start," Kevin alerted Troy. "Give me the bottom line on this one."

"I have a hunch the case could be important no matter which way it goes. A small chink in the armor?"

"Unlikely," Kevin said dismissively. "Too soon, anyway. I don't think this group will entertain further restrictions on transitions during a budget battle. We've already cut into the bone."

Kevin felt a tap on his shoulder, Congresswoman Nicole Florea silently reprimanding her last straggler.

"Gotta go." Kevin bought patience with an apologetic nod and just-one-more-second gesture.

"Kevin," Troy scolded, "don't forget why we're here."

"I know why we're here, Troy. But we need to pick our battles. Or at least fight them in a sequence that might give us a chance. We agreed. The deficit comes first."

"You know as well as I do that the deficit will get worse, not better."

The room's noisy chatter dwindled as the group quieted for the next item on the summit agenda. "I hear you, Troy," Kevin whispered. "We'll talk about it later."

The call ended, freeing Kevin to attempt an inconspicuous reentry. Approaching his spot at the conference table, he winked effortlessly at anyone who happened to notice the late arrival, one of many small habits that made Kevin easy to like.

Easy for everyone but the hostess.

"Thank you for gracing us with your presence, Mr. Tolbert." Nicole Florea of Nevada would have preferred it if Kevin had declined her reluctant invitation to the summit. For more than two decades she had been the de facto leader of the Western State Caucus, a respected fixture in the political establishment with a gift for melding the group's diverse opinions into a generally unified front. Kevin's youth and independence made her uneasy. So did his popularity among the nearly three dozen congressional leaders attending the summit.

A handsome thirty-six years, Kevin Tolbert carried himself with poised confidence that fell sufficiently shy of conceit. His blond hair and trim, athletic build suggested a high school letter in tennis or wrestling. It had actually been soccer, lining him up for a full-ride scholarship to the University of Colorado, where he had graduated with honors one week before marrying his high school sweetheart. "Any man who could snag Angie Greer can do anything!" Troy had said during the best-man toast. Few acquaintances were surprised to learn of Kevin Tolbert's election as sixth district representative for the state of Colorado. Most of them had donated money and volunteered time to make it happen.

Kevin glanced at the next item on the agenda. *Census briefing.*

The group had tackled relatively simple topics before lunch, like taxes. Only two in the group supported Nicole Florea's proposal to eliminate what remained of the dependent tax break, meager as it was.

"Desperate times call for desperate measures," she had argued and lost.

Kevin's persuasive opposition shifted the momentum, in part due to the cute picture of his own growing brood. "Look at these adorable faces," he playfully pled. "Do you want to make it harder for me to create the next generation of taxpayers and politicians?" The warm laughter handed him control. It also foretold Florea's decline.

"If I can draw your attention to the top of page three, you will see our preliminary estimates." Kyle Journeyman appeared nervous, like a child trying to explain a report card filled with D's and F's to parents he had assured would see A's and B's. He told the group he had given the same confidential briefing to five other Washington groups in his role as a strategy consultant to fiscal conservatives. The reaction must have been less than positive. "I should emphasize that these calculations will likely change as we fine-tune the numbers."

They had come to expect caveats and qualifiers from political consultants. Everyone knew that a string of overly optimistic projections had deepened the present crisis by blindsiding party leaders with a staggering deficit increase. Six years earlier the Western State Alliance had supported the president's domestic spending agenda, expecting marked improvement. But they had used flawed projections. The party now found itself in damage control mode, trying to salvage what little credibility remained among angry voters fearing America could become the next economic domino to fall. The president had assured them they could avert the kind of trouble engulfing the rest of the world through courageous fiscal austerity. He had even managed to implement most of the controversial "Youth Initiative" proposals he promised would create a million jobs while reducing swelling entitlement spending. But none of it had been enough. The deficit snowball continued to grow.

Kevin reached for the bound blue notebook that had been distributed during the break.

CONFIDENTIAL BRIEFING
PRELIMINARY REVISIONS FROM THE 2040 CENSUS

As he flipped past the cover and introductory remarks his eyes landed on the chart embedded in the executive summary on page three. As Journeyman braced himself for reactions, Kevin joined the others absorbing the data with periodic outbursts of disbelief.

"This can't be right!"

"Am I reading this correctly?"

Solitary comments swelled into whispered commotion as the bewildered delegates leaned toward one another to unpack the implications of numbers more sobering than any had anticipated.

Florea slowly rose from her chair, walking toward the podium with page three of the report still open before her wagging head. "Ladies and gentlemen," she began, "please direct any questions to Mr. Journeyman and hold your comments for now. We have scheduled a solutions brainstorm session later this afternoon."

"Solutions?" muttered an older congressman from Arizona on the opposite end of the room. "Moving deck chairs on the *Titanic*."

"If I may?" Journeyman continued. "I'd like to draw your attention to several underlying trends that could prove useful as you explore policy options."

"Yes, please," Florea responded eagerly.

"We are all alarmed by the revised trend lines. New data coming out of the census office forced us to revise earlier projections. The president's numbers were based upon 2030 data."

"And it took two years to disclose it?" someone objected.

Of course it took two years, Kevin thought. *Bad news travels slowly in Washington.*

"We now know that the fertility cliff has been steeper than expected," Journeyman was saying, "which will lower projected tax revenue starting in 2048. We also adjusted upward end-of-life management expenses as a percentage of GDP, which wipes out all of the savings gained from the severe cuts approved in 2038. Please flip to the data summarized on page nine and you'll see that…"

Tuning out of the formal presentation, Kevin began reading through the full report. He trusted his own interpretation of the data more than a political consultant's script.

The situation looked grim. Four years after the launch of the president's controversial programs the aging population curve showed no sign of flattening. It now matched levels seen in Europe and Asia ten years earlier, just before their financial implosions. It appeared a century of declining birth rates had finally driven the United States past the same irreversible tipping point.

Kevin knew the data would force both political parties to finally address realities no one wanted to face. For nearly fifty years demographers had been predicting the devastating economic and social consequences of a decreasing pool of young people burdened by the needs of a rapidly aging population. Few had heeded those warnings or paid attention to what was happening in places like China. No one had noticed the erosion beneath the feet of a billion workers flexing their collective economic muscles. How quickly the tables had turned.

Japan had seen it first, offering generous tax credits for every kid born. But a few thousand yen can't offset eighteen years of child-rearing expenses. Japan now laid claim to the oldest average citizen on the planet.

Even Russia's signing bonuses for prospective immigrants hadn't made much of a dent. Why invest three mandatory years working an elder-care job when America remained a land of relative prosperity and opportunity? So they came in droves, buying the United States an extra decade of growth.

Growth turned to stagnation in 2024, the year Kevin graduated from high school. Virtually every segment of the population, including the once-fertile immigrants, was reproducing at far below replacement level. The economic pyramid flipped and began to teeter and strain under a top-heavy load. By the time Kevin graduated from college the social safety net had begun to rip.

"This year the youngest of the nearly sixty million baby boomers turned seventy-eight." Journeyman's comment reclaimed Kevin's attention. "The oldest, four million of them, turned ninety-six. These seniors hold most of the nation's wealth and are twice as likely to vote as any other segment of the population. As you know, few of those votes come our way."

"The bottom line, ladies and gentlemen, is that we are getting squeezed from both directions. The cost to care for our oldest citizens continues to rise while the pool of working, taxpaying citizens continues to shrink. These new trend lines require a downward tax revenue adjustment of about eighteen percent over the coming decade."

"But that's almost a trillion dollars in lost revenue annually!" objected someone seated to Kevin's left.

"One point two trillion," Journeyman clarified. "Keep in mind, only a fraction of those sixty million boomers generate any productive economic activity. The few who can afford it pay about ninety thousand dollars per year in medical and care expenses to remain independent. The rest rely on their kids, diverting another thirty million people from working a full-time job or building a profitable business. The combined GDP hit runs about five trillion per year."

The door flew open. Senator Josh Franklin entered the room as if on cue, two aides trailing closely behind.

Nicole Florea leaped toward the podium like a tail-wagging puppy delighted by a master's homecoming. She knew, along with everyone else in the room, that recent polls made Franklin the party favorite for a potential 2044 presidential run.

"Ladies and gentlemen, it appears we have the great honor—"

"Please, Nicole," Franklin interrupted in self-effacing deference, "don't let me disrupt the agenda. Carry on with what you were doing, we'll just take a seat in the back and—"

"Don't be silly, Senator Franklin," she objected. "We can come back to this presentation later. Please, do us the honor of sharing a few words."

Feigning reluctance, the senator bowed in assent before filling the space Kyle Journeyman had occupied moments earlier. The consultant stepped backward, timidly extending his arm to shake hands with the potential future president, the man donors had been urging to form an exploratory committee because they hoped Franklin's popularity among young and minority voters might pull the party out of political quicksand. Few believed they could retain the White House without Franklin on top of the ticket.

"Thank you, Nicole, everyone," the senator began. "I apologize for the intrusion. But when I heard you would receive a briefing similar to the one I received last week I wanted to join your gathering as a fly on the wall to explore how we might lead this nation back toward prosperity." Kevin was impressed. With just two sentences Franklin had managed to lift the summit mood from gloomy despair to determined optimism. He reminded Kevin of the legendarily upbeat Ronald Reagan, who had ridden into town to rouse a disheartened people. Only this time the nation's problems were more severe and the economic hole much deeper.

"I understand you've seen the dismal demographic forecast. Clearly, the days of head-in-the-sand denial are behind us. In just a few weeks this information will be released and the public will know that we face very serious challenges. But they are challenges I'm convinced we can meet." Franklin paused, as if expecting a crowd to cheer in adoring approval.

Kevin recalled a quotation from someone. *He who brings hope brings leadership.*

"I stopped by today to tell you of my plan to form a task force that will partner with innovative leaders from both the private and public sectors to propose bold new strategies for tackling the deficit." The senator looked directly at Kevin, nodding like a teacher acknowledging the presence of a favorite student. Kevin felt a knot in his gut. Troy had said Franklin planned to form a fiscal austerity coalition. He had said it would include promising young House and Senate leaders. "Mark my words, Kevin," he had predicted. "Franklin will need someone from the Western States Alliance. He wants a dream team, a proving ground for potential cabinet appointments."

Kevin returned the senator's nod, hoping Nicole Florea hadn't noticed their silent exchange. Her seething told him she had.

He then sent a quick message to Troy.

RIGHT AGAIN. FRANKLIN SPEAKING NOW.

Seconds later, Troy's silent reply appeared on the tablet.

DOUBTING ME = ONE HEAD RUB.

CHAPTER THREE

Julia reached toward the jarring noise, grateful for rescue from a restless sleep. The dream had held her captive until the rattling clatter of a vintage alarm clock announced her parole. Hitting OFF instead of the snooze button, she pulled back the sheets, which were slightly damp from perspiration and tears, and slid out of bed. Pulling her knees against a shivering body, Julia grabbed the pen and pad sitting on the nightstand. She had been able to remember scant details of the countless earlier dreams beyond a paralyzing dread mixed with a deep, lingering sorrow. She hurriedly added to her growing list of words before the murky images could evaporate again.

MAN
SHADOW
FEAR
ANGER

She only saw his silhouette, but the man's figure seemed what she had always imagined her father might be—tall, strong, and kind. Of course, the shadow could have just as easily been cast by a crazed killer stalking his next victim.

No. Julia somehow knew that he posed no threat.

But if he wasn't dangerous, why so much fear? If kind, why the intense anger?

The dream's vapor dissipated mid-thought. Her weary mind reached for more as Julia stared at the pad. Several minutes passed. Nothing came.

Exhaling deeply, she pulled her legs tighter, offering herself a comfort Jonathan might have given had he accepted her invitation to spend the night.

Oh well. It's a start.

Julia gave herself the same pep talk on those rare days when writer's block put her behind schedule. She hoped the same pattern of determination and optimism that had brought journalistic honors would get her past this nocturnal crisis.

Ever since her sophomore English teacher invited Julia to blog for the high school opinion journal, words had been her driving passion. They had also been her therapist, helping her sort through private pain and troubling questions. Maria called writing Julia's defense mechanism, a harmless but secretly annoying dig at her big sister's driven personality.

Julia and Maria shared a house on the outskirts of Denver, only a few miles from the suburban high school they had attended one grade apart. To this day they didn't agree on who had cast the bigger shadow. Julia had graduated valedictorian and received countless scholarship offers from top universities. But Maria had received eleven invitations to the senior prom.

Things hadn't changed much. Despite declining readership, Julia remained a fixture among the journalistic elite. Maria still enjoyed the company of immature guys, ensnaring Julia in several unwelcome double dates.

Happily, Jonathan seemed different from Maria's other friends.

He held a steady job, read the right books, and drank the best wine. He talked about culture and politics instead of video games, and she found herself strongly attracted to his distinguished demeanor. That's why she'd done something out of character by inviting him to the house. Actually, Maria had made the invitation with her usual tact. "I bet Julia would love to show you her Pulitzer medal. It hangs on the wall in her bedroom." This time, rather than laugh off the suggestion and make excuses about a pressing deadline or an early interview, Julia hesitated—hoping for a slight tug on the line. When Jonathan remained silent, she took a risk.

"What do you say? Can I interest you in a nightcap?"

Now, standing alone in front of her bathroom mirror, Julia felt foolish. She glanced at the cocktail dress and one-inch heels lying on the floor where she'd left them eight hours earlier. Maybe Maria was right.

"Why don't you change outfits?" she had asked. "Guys don't want pretty sophistication. They want alluring fun!"

Alluring and fun seemed to work for Maria with her endless variety of hairstyles, sassy outfits that filled two closets, and a magnetic, perky bounce that made her impossible to snub. Julia, by contrast, wore her jet-black hair at shoulder length and stylishly cut, just as in college. Her tailored wardrobe embodied knee-length elegance rather than slit-skirt seduction. Friends called her stunningly beautiful, even slightly intimidating. So she wondered why Jonathan found her so easy to resist.

By the time Julia entered the kitchen Maria was already rushing to start her day.

"You look tired. Another dream?" One sight of Julia prompted genuine concern despite the distraction of trying to scrape off the slightly charred edges of Jared's bagel.

"Same as before."

"Did you make an appointment with Dr. Moreland like I told you to?"

"Eleven today."

"Finally! You'll like her."

"I'm fine."

Jared entered the room, frantically searching for his tablet. Both sisters silently pointed him toward a table beside the living room sofa.

Maria resumed the conversation. "I think Jonathan really liked you. I bet he spent all night thinking about what might have been." A mischievous smile.

"Not funny."

"He had all the symptoms."

"All guys have symptoms around you." Julia regretted the words immediately.

Maria's jaw dropped. "You don't think—" She stopped herself. "You can't blame me this time. I barely talked to him all night. I even set you up at the net for an easy spike, for heaven's sake!"

"You could have worn something a bit less"—Julia reached for the right words—"*fuel-on-the-fire*."

"Why didn't you wear something less *call-for-an-appointment*?"

A brief silence told both to retreat.

"Can we please just change the subject?" asked Julia. "What do you have going today?"

Lowering both hands from her hips, Maria resumed her chaotic preparation process. "Jared's teacher wants to meet with me after work. Something about a few missing assignments." Maria glanced around the kitchen before her eyes landed on the stack of napkins. "I think it's just an excuse to see me again. I don't mind. He's kind of cute."

Julia rolled her eyes in mock disgust, prompting another playful grin from Maria.

"Any chance you can make sure Jared gets started on his homework tonight? I'll need to head to the school right from work."

"That's fine," Julia said while settling in at the table, placing her empty cereal bowl beside a digital pad awaiting her attention.

Julia's eyes settled on the YOUR MESSAGES section of her tablet.

FROM JONATHAN SOWELL: *Enjoyed the show last night. Sorry I couldn't stay over. Busy days. Let's keep in touch.*

Maria's verdict overturned. Unlike Julia, Jonathan seemed to have slept just fine.

Pouring Fiber Crunch and fat-free milk into her bowl, Julia continued her digital ramp-up routine, scanning the next message.

FROM PAUL DAUGHERTY: *Hi Jewel. Read today's White House and Franklin clips. I have another idea brewing. I'll call next week.*

Julia waved out of her messages to review the day's headlines.

- White House responds to census data
- Rare auto accident prompts safety study
- Home vacancy rates rise again
- Spring fashions will turn heads
- Franklin proposes further cuts

Maria and Jared were putting on their coats while juggling bagel-filled napkins by the time Julia clicked MORE on the first headline.

"We're off!" came a brief interruption. "See you tonight."

"OK. Have a good day," Julia said, already midway through the lead story in search of the golden nuggets Paul would want to discuss. She had trained herself to quickly spot key phrases that told the larger story.

The latest US census report...an average 1.4 births per woman of childbearing years...nearly three decades since 2.1 needed to stabilize population...undermining confidence in America's long-term fiscal health...further emboldens critics claiming the president's signature "Youth Initiative" is too little, too late...

Julia dragged the SAVE COPY icon into her PENDING COLUMNS folder before scanning the other headlines. Skipping past the auto-accident and home-vacancy stories, she glanced at the pictures embedded in the fashion story. Too risqué for her. She forwarded the link to Maria before raising another spoonful of now-soggy cereal. Spotting the Franklin story, she expected nothing useful, since budget battles made big news, but boring columns.

A leading voice on Capitol Hill...Franklin gained popularity among younger voters when he sponsored an app that makes it easy to review federal program allocations and vote "Thumbs Up" or "Thumbs Down"...latest cuts could impact epigenetics research grant...widely anticipated treatment for age-related dementia...affects over 9 percent of the population...

"Another daft attack on scientific progress," she mused while saving the link. "Mindless Neanderthal!"

Backing out of the news app, Julia noticed two new messages.

FROM MARIA DAVIDSON: *Don't forget about helping Jared tonight. Love u Sis!*
FROM ANGIE TOLBERT: *Hi Julia. Did Jared's gift arrive?*

She smiled at Maria's reminder before feeling her stomach tense at the note from Angie.

I asked Jared to send Angie a thank-you text last week, she recalled. *That would have ended the dialogue until his next birthday.*

Instead, Julia felt obligated to send a response, which required searching her contact history to retrieve the name of Angie and Kevin's latest baby. She remembered signing a congratulations note Maria had put in front of her several months earlier, but couldn't recall the kid's sex or name to save her life.

Moments later, Julia had the tidbit of information needed to draft a quick reply.

Hi Angie. The package arrived safe and sound. Jared loved it. Very thoughtful of you and Kevin! I hope little Leah is doing well. Stay in touch.

She reached for the send now button, but paused, choosing instead to schedule delivery for later in the evening. No reason to let Angie know she might be available to chat.

Noticing the time, Julia grabbed her bowl and moved toward the sink. She felt a tad light-headed. The restless nights were taking a toll. Steadying herself for a moment, she considered postponing the counseling appointment so she could lie down on the sofa. But she knew it wouldn't help. Dreams don't sleep.

CHAPTER FOUR

Angie Tolbert froze in mid-stride, her body stiffening as she watched the plastic Minnie Mouse cup fly downward toward the kitchen floor. There was nothing she could do. The dancing sequence of bounces would wake the baby, who had finally fallen asleep a mere thirty minutes earlier.

She had managed to tiptoe through the breakfast routine, successfully shushing five-year-old Tommy and two-year-old Joy through their meal in hopes of settling them in front of a video while she took a much-needed nap. But then it happened. Joy stretched out her chubby little arm in an unspoken request for more apple juice. Always in tune with his sister's needs, Tommy decided to lend a hand. Something went wrong in the handoff, launching Minnie from the side of the counter into an impressive acrobatic spin.

After the sixth noisy hop the cup decided to settle itself against the far cabinet, ushering in eight seconds of hope-filled silence. Then Angie's heart sank as she heard the same erupting cry that had kept her awake for seven of the past nine hours.

"Sorry, Mommy." Tommy took the rap. "It was an accident."

"Don't worry, sweetheart," Angie said. "Thank you for trying to help your sister."

Angie was so ready for Kevin to get home, desperate for a good night's rest. Proud as she was of his growing influence in the Western State Alliance, she found herself resenting the additional travel required.

*Kevin enjoys adult conversations over steak while I eat boxed mac and cheese with the kids. He gets a wake-up call from a friendly hotel service. I never get to sleep due to endless screaming from a fussy baby…*She caught herself in mid-complaint. Nothing good would come from another pity party.

While placing the cup in the sink Angie noticed that both Tommy and Joy had climbed down from their counter stools. Joy trailed her brother as they ascended the staircase on a quest to rescue their baby sister from solitary confinement.

As Joy reached the tenth step she giggled at the sound of Angie's approach from behind. Both knew what would happen next.

"I'm gonna get you!" came Mommy's threatening promise. "You better hurry!"

As usual, Joy did the opposite. She held still, eagerly anticipating Angie's scooping her up and burying her face in the space between Joy's pudgy cheek and lower neck.

Joy squealed with delight at each nibbling attack. Angie let herself enjoy a somewhat delirious laugh.

As they approached the nursery, Angie noticed the baby's cry calming into a whimper, then a contented coo. Mysteriously, Tommy's presence had soothed little Leah's bouncing-cup-induced trauma. She stood in the doorway and quietly watched as big brother gently caressed baby sister's cheek with the back of his hand, while baby sister curled her tiny fist around big brother's index finger.

The phone rang.

"I only know one person who would call us at nine thirty in the morning!" Angie exclaimed. "I bet it's your daddy!"

Midway down the stairs Angie realized her mistake as she heard the digital butler announce, "Call from Dr. Martha Chapman, pediatrician."

"Oh no!"

Between the chaos of life without Kevin and the exhaustion of sleepless nights, Angie had completely forgotten about the nine a.m. appointment. Not good, considering the doctor's long scheduling backlog.

"Ms. Tolbert?" came the office assistant's voice.

"I'm so sorry," Angie began. "I bet you called to say I missed Leah's appointment."

"No, ma'am. Your appointment is tomorrow."

Angie sighed in relief.

"I was actually calling to confirm whether you and Mr. Tolbert can attend together."

Angie felt a rush of fear. No pediatrician had ever asked whether Kevin could join a child's appointment before.

"My husband will be out of town tomorrow. But I'll be—"

"Ms. Tolbert," the nameless voice interrupted. "Dr. Chapman thinks it would be best if you both attend."

"Is something wrong with Leah?"

"I can't discuss particulars over the phone, Ms. Tolbert."

"*Mrs.* Tolbert," Angie corrected.

"Yes, ma'am. Dr. Chapman just wants to walk you through the results of the baby's genome sequencing."

"We received summaries for both Tommy and Joy in our message box. Why can't you do the same with Leah's results?"

"When parents opt out of prescreening the doctor is required—"

"I know what the law requires." Angie surprised herself with her intensity. "We've expected a genetic sequence overview. But why do we need a face-to-face appointment? Is something wrong with our daughter?"

Several possibilities raced through her mind.

Asthma?

Diabetes?

"Please, can you tell me anything?" Angie pleaded.

Leukemia?

Bone cancer?

"Mrs. Tolbert, when is the soonest the doctor can meet with you and Mr. Tolbert together?"

CHAPTER FIVE

The office looked not at all as Julia had imagined. The desk held no stack of confidential patient files. Beautiful paintings hung where she had envisioned tacky posters of cats playfully depicting overused feel-good sentiments. The window blinds were open to invite sunlit warmth rather than closed to conceal embarrassing confessions. Even Dr. Linda Moreland fell short of the stereotype, comfortably crossing her legs while stealing a sip of Earl Grey tea, her eyes fixed on Julia rather than staring at a notepad in detached scrutiny.

Julia had convinced herself to schedule one appointment with Maria's therapist as a favor to her sister. *I don't need some mushy-headed psychologist probing my mind for clues explaining insomnia.* To her surprise, Dr. Moreland neither looked nor sounded mushy. She seemed formidable, like a dear friend who cared too much to cut her any slack.

"So you've had this same dream for seven months," the invasion began. "Every night?"

"Only recently. When they started in the summer they came

once every few weeks. But they gradually became more frequent."

"Anything unique about that time frame?"

"Not that I remember." Julia paused, reluctant to lower her
guard any further. "I was hoping you could prescribe something
to relax my mind at night. I'm sure this is all stress-induced."

"What kind of stress?"

"Mostly work, I suppose. I'm in a bit of a decline." Julia felt
exposed voicing aloud what she had been feeling.

"Is it causing financial problems?"

"Oh no," Julia said too quickly. "I make a very good living."

"Then what kind of decline?"

Julia paused to consider her answer. She had felt herself spiral-
ing downward in more than her career. Jonathan's rejection had
not been the first. But she decided to stick to the script. *One humiliation at a time.*

"I guess the best way to describe it would be a loss in stature."
Hearing her own words made her feel trifling. "That's not what
I mean. How can I describe it? It's just that for the first time in
my life I sense myself sliding down instead of climbing up. Yesterday's news."

"I understand," Linda sympathized.

Did she? Julia wondered. An elegant fifty, Dr. Moreland carried
herself with a grace that evoked calm confidence. A visual tour of
the office suggested Linda's practice had been thriving for many
years. No sign of any downward plunges.

"I did get a new assignment earlier this week," Julia continued. "Probably nothing like I've done in the past, but it could
open more doors and put me back on track."

"Let's hope so." Linda's soft smile failed to conceal her skep-
ticism.

As nine ticks of the clock bellowed over the silence, Julia
wondered what Linda was thinking. Dr. Moreland had no doubt

heard far more serious problems. *She probably thinks I'm a prima donna with a bruised ego.*

Julia wanted the session to end.

"What can you tell me about your father?"

"My father?" The question surprised Julia.

"Yes. You said the man in the dream made you think of your father."

Julia relaxed some. "Right. He did. Well, at least how I've imagined him."

"In his face?"

"No. I can't see his face, only his shadow. Never his face."

"How then?" Linda probed.

"I guess in his presence. He seems strong and kind."

"But you wake up frightened?"

"More frightened than I've ever felt before," Julia continued. "But I don't think I'm afraid of the man as much as what's happening, like we're both caught up in something dreadful."

"What can you tell me about your father?" Linda asked.

"Just what my mom told my sister and me. There was an affair. He left when I was little."

"Has either of you ever tried to contact him?"

"Never had the chance. He died when we were five and four. End of story."

"And you can't recall any other details from the dream?"

"None. It almost feels like entering the most intense scene of a long movie. I know something bigger is happening, but I've walked into the theater just when the conflict peaks. I sense the danger, but I have no idea what's going on."

Julia stopped. She had never attempted to describe her dream to anyone before, keeping it buried beneath a solitary facade. Linda's attention, like a reader's subscription, had given the experience validation. Perhaps even purpose.

"Anyway," she said, hoping to retake the reins. "Do you think you can prescribe something to help me sleep better?"

Dr. Moreland grinned, revealing a gentle patience likely acquired working with clients far more high-strung than Julia. "I'm afraid I don't make a habit of writing prescriptions during the first thirty minutes of meeting a new patient."

"Of course. I'm sorry."

Still in command, Linda launched the second wave of her invasion. "Tell me about your love life. Are you in a relationship?"

"Nothing steady. But I date." The question triggered defensive feelings in Julia similar to those felt during college dorm life. Girls sized one another up based upon their latest sexual conquests. She'd hated the demeaning game, even when winning.

"So there has been no breakup?"

If only my relationships lasted long enough to break, Julia thought. "Not since college."

"Recent rejections?"

"I'm thirty-four. Let's just say I don't get as many invitations as in the past. But men still find me attractive."

Distant, but attractive.

"I have no question about that. You're a lovely woman."

Julia smiled uneasily.

Linda's eyes moved away for a peek at the clock. "I'm so sorry, Julia," she said, "but I need to wrap up our conversation to prepare for my next appointment."

"Yes. I understand. Thank you for squeezing me in on such short notice."

"Perhaps next time we can schedule a full hour. That would give me more time to unpack your experience."

"I'd like that," Julia lied, eager to check *Tried therapy* off her list.

"I can say this much, Julia. I'm fairly confident medication won't solve the problem. I'm not even convinced the dreams *are* a problem."

Of course they're a problem, Julia thought. *I need rest.*

"I'm not a dream specialist," Linda continued. "But I think your subconscious may be urging you toward something important."

"Something important? Like what?"

"I don't know," Linda confessed. "But I imagine it has something to do with your dad."

"I told you, my dad was never part of my life. Besides, he's dead and gone."

"Exactly."

CHAPTER SIX

Thirty minutes later Julia stood in a dimly lit hallway opposite a peephole through which Jeremy Santos could peer to check the identity of his guest.

She continued probing the assignment Dr. Moreland had given. *Talk to someone who can help fill in your father's face.*

What did she mean? Her father's absence had never caused strange dreams before. Why should it be causing them now? Julia hated the idea of wasting time and energy coddling silly insecurities. What she needed was the welcome distraction of hard work on an important assignment.

As the door opened, Julia smiled at the skinny, pale young man who seemed surprised by her appearance. "Mr. Santos? I'm Julia Davidson. Paul Daugherty arranged for us to meet. Is this still a good time?"

"Yes. Welcome. Please come in."

The small apartment felt more cramped than its size required. It contained typical signs of bachelorhood: piles of empty pizza boxes, unwashed dishes stacked in the sink, and the slight musty smell of fermenting laundry. Her eyes landed on an assortment of mechanical devices gathering dust in the space traditionally occupied by a sofa and end table. At first glance they looked like neglected exercise equipment. Closer scrutiny, however, offered a heartrending image of how difficult life for Jeremy's younger brother Antonio must have been.

"Won't you sit down?"

Approaching a chair beside the kitchen table, Julia noticed other signs of life before Antonio's transition: a lift harness visible through the open bedroom door, the corner desk surface higher than normal to enable wheelchair access, and a high-end blender well suited for turning solid foods into soft puree.

Retrieving a portable digital recorder and touch-screen notepad from her purse, Julia asked if he would allow her to record the conversation.

"Of course," he agreed.

Hitting the record button, Julia felt a tiny rush of adrenaline, a sensation she had missed. The rewards of writing opinion columns paled in comparison to the thrill of investigative reporting. Each story was a new puzzle to solve, problem to decipher, or secret to expose. You never knew what you might uncover while asking questions, following leads, chasing obscure details. And then the best part: selecting the perfect ingredients to prepare a delicious entrée of journalistic prose.

"First," Julia began, "I want to extend my condolences on the loss of your mother and Antonio."

"Oh. Yes. Thank you." Jeremy seemed genuinely surprised by the sentiment. Months of litigation had probably demanded an unnatural detachment. Lawyers needed facts, not feelings.

"I hope telling your story can help others avoid what you've endured." It was the right thing to say, even if only half true. "Can you start by describing what happened last August and why you initiated the suit against NEXT Transition Services?"

The look in his eyes told her she had been too abrupt.

"I'll do that," he said. "But I want to show you something first."

Two pictures. The first contained a man who looked remarkably like Jeremy holding a three-year-old boy laughing in delight. Beside them a lovely young woman knelt beside a stroller carrying a toddler. Jeremy's intact family.

"This was us in 2025. As you can probably tell, my dad and mom were crazy about each other."

"They seem to be a lovely couple."

Julia braced herself for the second picture.

"This is us last August at Antonio's farewell dinner."

The image contained three people rather than four. Jeremy wore a staged grin, an emotional hostage turned reluctant accessory. His mother's face showed wearied relief mixed with guilt and indignation. Only Antonio beamed in self-congratulating pride, his twisted body restraining bold resolution while his eyes provided the smile weak facial muscles could no longer raise.

"Your father?" Julia asked.

"He left shortly after Antonio's diagnosis. Longer than most would stay I suppose." Jeremy's resentment remained palpable. "He said he would visit, send money. You know how that story ends."

Julia felt anger welling up inside. Against her own social politics, she could not escape the expectation fathers should protect and provide. Her hand instinctively reached toward Jeremy's arm.

He pulled back. "I didn't show you the pictures for pity."

"Of course. I'm sorry, I didn't mean—"

"I wanted you to see them so that you'll remember that this story is not about a lawsuit. It's about real people. Lots of them."

"I understand that."

Neither spoke for a moment. Jeremy examined Julia's face, trying to find her soul. Against journalistic protocol and personal impulse, she let him look deeply. Fifteen seconds passed. He decided to trust her.

"I'll send you a set of the pictures, along with these." He tapped the digital pad to open a new folder before sliding the pad in front of Julia.

A list of documents. She opened the first, dated August 19, 2023. Her eyes widened, and then softened. "Your mother's journal?"

"Parts of it. I copied the sections where she writes about Antonio." He paused. "She did the same for me. I didn't know about it until we retrieved her digital library after the cremation. I'm keeping those entries private. You understand."

"Of course."

"Other entries came from Antonio. At first he used a voice transcription application. It got harder for him the last few years when his speech became weaker and more distorted. The most recent entries were typed one pinky finger movement at a time. A single sentence could take him an hour to complete. He was a persistent guy," Jeremy said with a warmhearted laugh. "A lot stronger than I'll ever be."

"I can tell you loved them both very much."

"She never did anything for herself," he reminisced. "She deserved better."

"I look forward to reading her journal, getting to know her. And your brother."

He didn't hear her. "His disease was similar to the one that famous physicist had. What was his name?"

"Hawking?" she offered.

"That's it. Stephen Hawking."

Julia remembered seeing pictures of the brilliant cosmologist from Oxford, his distorted body held captive in a mobilized wheelchair. She looked again at the unused equipment in the adjoining room.

Jeremy proceeded to describe the events surrounding his brother's transition day: an unexpected visit from a police officer delivering very bad news, the drive to the clinic to formally identify his mother's lifeless body, Antonio's cold corpse lying beside a visibly shaken woman wearing a fresh bandage across the side of her face and the dark redness of coagulated blood on her blouse.

"They told you your mother slipped and fell while attacking the nurse?"

"Transition specialist," he corrected. "Yeah, they said Mom fell during a violent episode trying to stop Antonio's procedure."

"But you don't believe that?" Julia asked.

"I believe it."

Julia looked up from her list of prepared questions.

"I never thought anyone intentionally killed my mother. Why would they do that?"

"Then what prompted the lawsuit?" she asked.

"NEXT will say I'm just after money."

Julia remembered Paul's marching orders. *Portray the kid as a pawn of greedy lawyers.* "Are you?" she asked.

"Listen, if I just wanted money I would have accepted their third offer to settle the case."

"You've had three settlement offers?" Julia's eyebrows lifted in surprise.

"My lawyer says I can't tell anyone the amount. But he said it was more than we're likely to net pushing this boulder all the way up the judicial mountain."

She looked into Jeremy's weary eyes. He seemed ready to move on with his life and be done with the whole mess.

"Did you know that my brother scheduled his appointment as a minor?" Jeremy asked. "I didn't realize it until my lawyer showed me a copy of Antonio's application. He applied a few days before his birthday. Mom never approved it."

"Do you think that's why they offered to settle?"

He didn't.

Julia had expected the answer. Paul had explained that out of nearly three hundred thousand transitions involving minors, only fifteen had failed to obtain parental permission. Each of those incidents had led to a mere slap on the wrist, a small fine for inadequate procedural oversight, and modest compensation to the families. Nothing significant enough to motivate such large settlement offers to Jeremy.

"Help me understand, Mr. Santos. You knew NEXT wasn't worried about your case due to Antonio's age?"

"Yep," he replied.

"And you believe your mom's death was an accident?"

"That's right."

"And you've turned down large financial offers?"

"Correct."

"Then what motivated this lawsuit?"

"Hannah."

Julia had no recollection of anyone by that name associated with the case. "Who's Hannah?"

"Hannah Walker, Antonio's transition specialist," he explained. "She called me a few months after the incident. Told me she had quit her job and wanted to meet me for coffee."

Stumbling onto an odd-shaped puzzle piece, Julia felt another surge of adrenaline.

CHAPTER SEVEN

"Earth to Kevin. Are you with us, boss?" Troy asked as a congressional intern shifted nervously in the chair beside him.

"Yeah, I'm fine," the congressman replied. "Sorry, Troy. The largest donation ever received. Got it."

"I guess I expected a bit more enthusiasm. You do remember that it will take money to run another campaign?"

"Of course." He forced his thoughts away from Angie's anxious face and the baby-powder scent of little Leah. He had gently squeezed them both before heading to the office. "I just have a lot on my mind."

"Do you want to talk about it?" Troy asked. The intern made a slight move toward the door, but Kevin waved him back to his seat.

"No. I'm fine." He saw no reason to discuss Leah's situation until they knew something concrete. *It could be nothing. Stay positive.* He was struggling to heed the advice he had given Angie.

"OK. As I was saying, he's a first-time donor. We checked the database and then I asked everyone on the team. No one has record of any prior communications or meetings."

"Name?" Kevin asked.

"Dimitri. Evan Dimitri."

"Doesn't ring a bell with me either. What do you know about him?"

"He owns a majority share in an equity investment company. I asked around and learned he has donated to other campaigns, mostly on the right. Still, he may be trying to cover bases on something. That's all I know at the moment."

"So there's no cause for concern?"

Kevin's loyal guardian shook his head. "I don't know. It feels odd. No prior gifts or connections. It doesn't usually work like that."

"We can't afford to look a gift horse in the mouth, Troy. Schedule a lunch so I can thank him."

"Already set," Troy replied. "I've also asked Shaun here to research his company and associations."

The intern grinned at the mention of his name. "We'll update you before you meet the guy," he said.

The door opened. "Excuse me, Congressman. It's time to head to your ten o'clock appointment in Senator Franklin's office."

"Thanks, Renee. Tell the driver I'll be right down."

"Driver?" Troy said. "Since when can we afford a driver?"

"We can't. Franklin offered his."

Troy gave Kevin a *be careful* frown before raising his *way to go* eyebrow. "Make us proud, Congressman."

◆

Sliding into the long leather seat of the senator's limo, Kevin remembered the first rule in courting power brokers: *They believe their own good press, so be sure you've read it.* He opened his tablet to scan for any news items referencing Franklin. One story surfaced.

EPI-GENOMIC FUNDING QUESTIONED

A leading voice on Capitol Hill has raised questions about the value of further epi-genomic research, citing a series of inconclusive findings despite billions in federal spending. Senator Joshua Franklin gained popularity among younger voters after launching a mobile app that invites registered voters to review every federal budget allocation before dragging it into a "Thumbs Up" or "Thumbs Down" bin. The most recent item recommended for elimination is a request for additional R & D funding by the widely respected Epigen Inc., a company working with several leading research universities on an effort it claims could "eradicate many age-related diseases and associated dementia." But Franklin's constituents don't buy it. In his words, "We have yet to see any serious breakthroughs on the epigenetic front. We simply can't afford to keep throwing the dice."

Scanning the rest of the article, Kevin found a link to Franklin's SLASH citizen network. The running tally at the top indicated more than a trillion dollars had been categorized as "unworthy spending" by users, every one of them a registered voter in someone's district. Another number revealed how many of the proposed cuts had made it through Congress to date, 64 percent. The app had created enormous austerity momentum in Washington. It had become political suicide to oppose any Franklin cost-reduction proposal.

Five minutes later, Kevin found himself standing in a large office complex being greeted by a cheerful receptionist. One look around the bustling room reminded Kevin of his place in the political food chain. Franklin lived a very different reality, including assistants who had assistants, drivers and pilots, and a long line of lobbyists jockeying for five minutes of time with the most popular fiscal conservative on Capitol Hill. The significant donation

Kevin had received that morning would have been a mere rounding error in Senator Franklin's campaign budget.

"Kevin!" The senator extended his right hand while lifting the other toward his guest's shoulder. "Thank you for taking time to meet on such a hectic morning. I bet your staff greeted you with a laundry list of urgent decisions the moment you got back from the summit."

The comment was another reminder of Kevin's lesser world. Troy's list of "urgent decisions" that morning had taken less than fifteen minutes to discuss.

"Thank you for the invitation, Senator. I'm honored." Kevin meant it. He admired Joshua Franklin, a man many described as a political genius. "Congratulations on the epi-genome story. The *Journal* seemed upbeat."

"We only need to find a few trillion more to make a dent!" the senator huffed in mock dissatisfaction. "Please, have a seat."

As Kevin settled into a chair he noticed a young woman poke her head inside the office. "Excuse me, Senator, I'm afraid they've initiated roll call."

The senator cursed. "I'm sorry, Kevin. We're trying to rush through another austerity cut before the break. You know the drill."

"Shall I bring Congressman Tolbert a drink while he waits?" The young woman smiled at Kevin in a way that made him slightly uncomfortable. Rumors about Franklin's "intern harem" were probably exaggerated, but Kevin preferred denying his imagination any room for mischief.

"You don't mind walking with me, do you, Kevin?" Franklin asked. "I don't want to waste your time. I think we can settle our business on the fly."

Our business? Kevin wondered. "That's fine. Lead the way."

"Two issues," Franklin began as they paced quickly down the hall toward a waiting car. He raised a single finger. "First, I want you to play a key role in the coalition I'm forming. Like I said in Scottsdale, we need to get ahead of this budget revision fallout before it hits the public."

Kevin had expected the request, but tried to appear surprised. "Thank you, sir. Although I'm not sure I'm the most qualified—"

"No need for false humility, Kevin," Franklin interrupted. "You and I both know the Western State mantle is shifting from Nicole to you."

"I'm not so sure about that," Kevin protested.

The senator stopped. "Yes, you are," he said while looking into Kevin's eyes. "And so is she. Let's face it. Old is out of style, and Nicole has definitely passed her sell-by date."

Kevin paused. There was only one thing to say. "Thank you for the invitation. I'm honored."

"Good," Franklin said as he resumed walking while raising another finger. "Second, I need every member of my coalition to support phase two of the Youth Initiative."

Kevin froze in his tracks. Had Franklin surmised Kevin's covert opposition to the program? He had very intentionally remained under the radar to avoid being labeled disloyal—or worse, naïve. *The budget comes first.* He and Troy had agreed.

"Senator Franklin, sir," Kevin responded. "I don't think I can form an opinion on that one yet since we haven't seen the specific—"

The senator cut him off. "Listen, Kevin, I know you'll need to hold your nose on this one. Lots of us will. I'll be the first to admit it's not a perfect solution."

"I'm not sure it's a solution at all," Kevin heard himself say.

The senator forced a patient smile. "I understand your opposition, and I respect your religious convictions." He seemed to be reading a script. "But we can't sacrifice the savings it generates. This fiscal hole is deep enough already. I'm not aware of any other way to cut as much from entitlement spending. Are you?"

Kevin held his tongue. He knew he could not afford to blow this opportunity. Franklin could open doors he would never walk through on his own. An appointment to Franklin's coalition could provide the ideal platform to propose changes, give him leverage no freshman representative from a midsize district could hope to attain in isolation.

"Listen to me, Kevin." Franklin's tone and demeanor softened, transforming him from power-wielding strategist to affectionate uncle. "In a matter of weeks the entire nation will know that what we've done so far isn't working. The markets will panic. Voters will get angry. I need leaders ready to articulate workable solutions. You're smart and you're popular. I really want you on the team."

"Can you give me a few days to think it over?"

"Afraid not. We've already prepared two versions of the press release. One has your name and the other Congresswoman Florea's."

"Has she already agreed?" Kevin asked.

"I haven't spoken to her yet. We're having lunch today. She wants this pretty bad, and I'll need at least one player from the Western coalition. I had planned to tell her the role has been filled by a sharp young leader who will represent the Western states with reasoned, fiscally viable recommendations."

Kevin heard the approaching clack-clack of a woman's heels running to catch the senator from behind. The young aid from Franklin's office positioned a signature screen before the advancing senator, offering a stylus pen and pointing him to the right location on the screen. The interruption gave Kevin a welcome moment to gather his wits.

The deficit first. That's how we gain credibility, he reminded himself.

Franklin finished signing as they approached the car doors. "What do you say?"

"I'm in."

"And the Youth Initiative?" Franklin pressed.

"I'm not sure I can support it, but I promise to withhold criticism until we find something better."

"Not likely," the senator scoffed while extending his hand to Kevin's. "Deal. Welcome to the team, Congressman Tolbert."

"Thank you, Senator Franklin."

As Kevin watched the senator's limo pull away from the curb he felt surges of elation and trepidation collide within.

CHAPTER EIGHT

Julia drove through the neighborhood well below the posted fifteen miles per hour, giving herself ample time to envy each house more than the last: three-car garages, perfectly manicured lawns, white stone facades, double oak doors situated behind enormous front porches at the ends of rosebush-lined walkways. She wondered how much time and money each resident of the Mountain Springs Resort Community spent trying to outdo the next.

"Arriving on right," announced a friendly dashboard voice. Julia pulled into a long driveway that encircled an ensemble of red boulders positioned in front of what she guessed to be a five-bedroom, four-thousand-square-foot residence. The only thing missing from the picturesque scene was a tree swing blowing casually in the wind or a kid's scooter leaning delinquently against the side of the house. Like the eighteen other neighborhood homes she had passed since turning onto Summerhill Lane, this address showed no signs of children.

Pressing the doorbell prompted an echo of orchestral chimes followed by the faint *yip-yip* of a tiny dog eager to defend its master against Julia's invasion. Several minutes passed, the pooch growling threateningly while Julia checked her schedule. She definitely had the right time.

Through the window Julia noticed a fortyish woman tying her waist sash while rushing toward the entryway. "Shush, Teddy!" she ordered before opening the door. Hannah Walker retained a natural beauty, a hint of gray at her roots and a mature figure in a lovely Asian silk robe.

"Ms. Walker? I'm Julia Davidson. We exchanged texts last evening."

The dog retreated in deference to his queen.

"Yes, of course. I'm sorry. Please come in." Hannah appeared flushed, as if she had hurriedly splashed and toweled her face to wash away tears.

A lovely interior reflected a woman who enjoyed spacious, ordered beauty. The contrast to the crowded, disheveled Santos apartment could not have been more stark. It seemed lawsuits had the power to link disparate worlds. Julia thought of the awkward grieving rituals that occur at funerals between distant cousins who no longer send Christmas cards. Something similar united Jeremy Santos and Hannah Walker.

Julia and her hostess endured polite small talk as Hannah offered and poured fresh-brewed tea, delaying the conversation she seemed reluctant to begin. It was one thing to anonymously feed information to Jeremy Santos's lawyers; it was another thing entirely to go on the record with a prominent journalist.

Hannah finally summoned the courage to ease into the topic Julia had come to discuss. "I've read your columns."

Julia waited as Hannah bolstered apparently waning courage with a sip of tea. The scar across her jaw showed itself for the first time.

"You're wrong, you know," she continued.

"Wrong? About what?"

"About the volunteers." Hannah paused, pressing herself to finish what she had started. "They aren't heroes."

Julia took immediate offense. Not for herself. For millions of others. What could be more heroic than transitioning your resources to loved ones rather than wasting them on costly end-of-life expenditures? "I'm sorry?" she heard herself say.

"They aren't heroes. They're sheep."

"How can you say such a thing?"

"Have you ever participated in a transition, Ms. Davidson?"

The question silenced Julia. Her column had repeatedly celebrated the transition industry. She had defended its virtue against religious extremists. But she had never actually witnessed the procedure firsthand. *Who had?*

"Ever spoken to someone just before they enter a transition room?"

Silence again.

"I didn't think so," Hannah continued. "There was a time I read your column to convince myself that what I was doing was good, something important for the economy and best for the volunteers." She stopped, remembering her manners. "Forgive me. I hope this doesn't sound like I'm being critical of you."

"Don't worry." Julia's professionalism conquered her offense. "You need thick skin in my line of work."

Hannah offered a polite laugh before continuing. "To be honest, what you wrote probably motivated me to continue the job longer than I might have."

"Are you thanking me or blaming me?" Julia asked.

"Neither. I just think you should know that what you write has an impact. That's why I'm trusting you with my part of this story. Only a tiny fraction of the population knows anything about the Youth Initiative beyond headlines touting budget savings or mocking religious nuts."

Julia felt her conscience prick her. Hannah seemed eager

to expose a dark side to the industry that had left a scar on her formerly perfect world. Like Jeremy, she saw Julia as a sympathetic ally in her pursuit of revenge. Julia had let them think it.

She recalled Paul's words. *"We need to get ahead of this story before some crusading reporter plays it wrong."* Attacking NEXT or the Youth Initiative would definitely violate RAP Syndicate's editorial agenda, not to mention undermine her own journalistic credibility.

Julia began the formal interview. "I understand you quit your job after the Antonio Santos incident."

"I was given an extended medical leave to recover from this." Her hand gently caressed a faint line across her jaw. "At least that was the official reason. I certainly didn't need six months. My doctor removed the stitches after a few weeks."

"Employer generosity?"

"More like employer anxiety," Hannah mocked. "They didn't want me at the clinic when the police began asking questions."

"Police? What kind of questions?"

"I don't know. I assume they didn't want anyone around who might veer off the official script."

"Would you have?" Julia asked.

"No. I've seen their report. Pretty accurate," Hannah explained. "The irony is that giving me such a long leave ended up creating more problems for them."

"Because?"

"I'd been fighting feelings of depression for nearly a year. The time away from work gave me an opportunity to reflect." Hannah stared out the window for a moment, appearing to reach for distant memories of better days. "I had always been a fairly upbeat person. My husband used to call me his little joy bubble." She turned slightly red at the admission. "He hasn't used that nickname in a while."

"We all have ups and downs." Julia realized the comment sounded tactlessly glib. Hannah didn't seem to notice.

"I found myself becoming short with Philip, more irritable, much more difficult to be around. At first I assumed normal hormonal swings. But I never swung back. And then the dreams began."

Julia's eyes widened. "Dreams?"

"A sequence of faces."

"A man?" Julia asked.

The question surprised Hannah. "Sometimes. There are lots of faces. They haunt me."

"Who haunts you? The boy? Antonio?"

"No. I don't remember his face. I had stopped looking them in the eyes long before his appointment." Her voice broke. "I'm sorry. This is hard to talk about."

Julia sat in silence while Hannah reached for a tissue.

"They're sheep to the slaughter," she continued.

"But transitioning is a voluntary activity," Julia defended. "Sheep don't volunteer."

"They don't resist either." Hannah paused for another sip of tea. "Before they realize what's happening, a knife slits their throat, turning them into a meal for the people they had trusted to protect them."

Julia showed disapproval at the analogy.

"That bothers you, doesn't it?" Hannah pressed. "I don't like to think about it in such naked terms either. But it's true. Where do the assets go?"

"I suppose to loved ones or a charity of the volunteer's choice," Julia guessed.

"Seventy percent goes to family members who, in the past, would have been saddled with the cost of care."

"Of course. Who wants to burden their kids with—"

"Any idea where the other thirty percent goes?" Hannah interrupted.

"I don't know. The cost of the procedure?"

"A small portion. The rest funds Youth Initiative advocacy programs. Last year alone the transition tax contributed nearly thirty billion in new revenue to the federal bottom line. But that pales when compared to reduced entitlement spending. Fewer beneficiaries in 2041 translated into about two hundred billion in savings, an amount that will accumulate year over year."

Julia's eyebrows lifted at numbers more impressive than she had realized.

"I can't tell you how often I repeated those statistics to myself, trying to connect what I was doing to some greater good. Everyone wins, right?"

"Don't they?"

"Maybe. But someone has to hold their shaking hands, wipe their dejected tears, calm their quiet panic." Hannah looked Julia in the eyes. "Slit their outstretched necks."

Julia flinched at the analogy.

"It wears on you," Hannah continued. "Pep talks work for a while. Affirming columns like yours and employer perks only carry you so far. I convinced myself they were something less than fellow human beings."

"Sheep offering themselves in sacrifice?" Julia filled in the blank.

Hannah nodded slowly. Shamefully.

Nervous about the direction of the conversation, Julia's tone altered from that of confidential confessor to that of suspicious reporter. "What's your stake in the Santos lawsuit?"

"My stake?" Hannah seemed to notice the change in her guest's tone.

"Are you a co-litigant? Do you stand to receive any payment if Jeremy wins?"

"He has won."

"I mean if he wins the appeal process."

"No. I have no financial stake in the case whatsoever," Hannah defended herself. "In fact, my husband could lose his biggest client when this story breaks. That's why I've tried to remain anonymous."

"What does Philip do?"

"He's a process efficiency consultant for NEXT clinics."

Julia sat in silence, absorbing the revelation.

"He knows what you've done? Knows you've been helping Jeremy?"

"Of course," Hannah replied. "He agrees with what the suit demands."

"Demands?"

"Have you read the details of the case, Ms. Davidson?"

"Most," Julia bluffed.

"Then you know about the gaping hole in the permissions process. It's easier to schedule someone for a transition than it is to book an airline ticket."

"And?"

"The current procedures don't protect volunteers from coercion," Hannah explained. "I estimate two-thirds of my clients participated against their will."

"They sign an approval form, usually in the presence of a spouse, child, or parent. That seems like adequate protection to me."

"You mean the person exhausted from managing their care? The person likely to inherit their assets? The one who has put his or her life on hold to help a parent delay the inevitable?" Hannah looked like a teacher scolding a lazy student. "Do you honestly expect that person to discourage a parent's transition?"

The possibility of such subtle coercion had never occurred to Julia.

"Would you put your career on hold if your parents needed your full attention for who knows how long?" Hannah continued.

"What would you do if given the option of keeping yourself alive for another five years or freeing the money to fund a grandchild's college education? How would you feel being called a debit, knowing others consider you a liability rather than an asset? Yes, they grant permission. What else can they do?"

Sheep to the slaughter, Julia remembered.

The Antonio Santos case involved much more than a distraught mother's accidental death or a clerical slipup in the massive transition machine. This story was not about a minor casualty, but the fate of a program contributing hundreds of billions of dollars in revenue to the federal bottom line.

It was more than Julia wanted to know.

CHAPTER NINE

A haggard woman looked up slowly from her screen at the same impatient man standing in front of her receptionist window. "Once again, Mr. Tolbert, we will call your name when the doctor is available to see you."

For the third time in an hour, Kevin returned to the waiting room chair beside his wife Angie. Neither his charm nor his influence could overcome the reality of physician shortages that had turned doctor visits into an all-day outing.

"Welcome to my world," Angie said, gently poking her husband in the side. "You'll just need to learn some patience, Mr. Congressman."

It was a virtue Kevin had rarely required. He had grown accustomed to making things happen quickly, squeezing a two-year MBA program into eighteen months, acquiring and selling three successful businesses before turning thirty, and winning national office after a single campaign. Like a driver hitting a dozen consecutive green lights, he had almost forgotten how to use the brakes.

"I don't do patience well," Kevin reminded his wife needlessly. "Is it always like this?"

"No." Angie smiled feebly. "Only on the rare occasions I can actually get an appointment."

The door opened and a nurse holding a tablet read the next name. A woman on the other side of the room gratefully lifted her hand like a schoolgirl timidly seeking permission to use the restroom. Moving an infant from her lap to her shoulder, the mother inched through the door as Kevin watched the light once again turn red.

Kevin noticed Angie looking down at Leah, who was still sleeping in her carrying seat. He could sense the anxiety she had shelved long enough to ready the other kids for their playdate at a friend's house. Angie had apparently used the sudden quiet to indulge another fear.

"Do you hear a difference in Leah's cough?" she asked hesitantly. "It seems deeper than I remember in Tommy or Joy."

"Angie," Kevin answered in the kindest tone he could muster, "we agreed to avoid speculation until we know something." She had never actually agreed, only adjusted herself to his inability to talk about the one thing that had been on her mind for the past four days.

In truth, the same questions tormented them both.

He felt she needed a new distraction. "Troy sent me an interesting analysis of the census data. I think he found something important."

Angie forced her usual cheer. "That's great, sweetheart."

He sensed her veiled indifference, but continued to avert silence. "There appear to be needles of economic strength buried in the haystack of dismal trends. Troy calls them bright spots."

"As in optimistic?"

"Sort of. He borrowed the phrase from a case study we both read during grad school. About fifty years ago a nonprofit group was given six months to solve child malnourishment in poor Vietnamese villages. A crazy deadline since experts had identified a complex range of systemic problems intertwining to cause the epidemic."

The look in Angie's eyes told Kevin her mind had already started to drift.

"Anyway, one guy decided to cut through the complexity that had paralyzed the experts. He researched what the mothers of the few healthy kids were doing differently from everyone else in the villages. He figured if some kids thrive despite identical poverty, then there might be hope for the other kids."

The words *hope* and *kids* pulled Angie back.

"They discovered several simple habits among those families that made a huge difference."

"Like?" Angie asked.

"Like mothers dividing their children's daily rations into four meals instead of two. They also violated cultural norms by feeding their kids certain types of food that society deemed low-class." Kevin's excitement peaked as he came to the punch line. "A book by Chip and Dan Heath called these families *bright spots* because their success became a model for large-scale solutions."

"Always trust moms over the experts," Angie teased.

"You're more right than you know. If Troy's analysis is accurate, moms will be the key to solving our long-term deficit problem."

Her confused expression nudged Kevin to the bottom line.

"It looks like the pockets of economic stability and growth are the areas with the highest fertility. We seem to have found our nation's bright spots. We just need to find out what they do that's different from everyone else."

"Leah Tolbert." The interruption reminded Kevin of his impatience.

"Finally," he voiced too loudly.

"The doctor can see you now." The nurse held the door open as Angie reached for Leah.

"I've got her," Kevin insisted.

♦

Leah whimpered on cue, as if understanding the doctor's diagnosis better than either parent could.

Kevin reached deep but could not recall ever having heard of a disorder labeled *fragile X syndrome*. "I don't know what that is."

"Not many do these days," the doctor continued. "In the old days a small percentage of the population had something they called intellectual disability. Your grandparents would have called it mental retardation. But the disorder has become extremely rare."

"So it can be cured?" Angie asked expectantly.

Dr. Chapman paused. It must have been many years since she last discussed such a disheartening diagnosis with uninformed parents. Genetic prescreening had virtually eradicated fragile X from the population in developed nations; it surfaced only in extremely religious families who bypassed a process that kept defective eggs from implantation. But neither Angie nor Kevin seemed the extremely religious type.

"Can I ask why you were unable to do genetic prescreening on this pregnancy?" Dr. Chapman asked Angie.

"Why do you ask?" Kevin intercepted, hoping to absorb the predictable assault.

"Well, it's highly unusual to decline the procedure."

They had heard the speech before. Screening promised to eliminate the most severe genetic defects, allowing parents to produce offspring that inherited only their most attractive features and least vexing defects. Apparently this disorder, whatever it was, fell in the latter category.

"We consider life a gift to receive rather than a product to select." Angie's intensity surprised Kevin. He had used the same words with her six years earlier when they decided to start a family. She seemed excited about genetic screening as described by her obstetrician. Common sense and practice said, "Do it." Kevin's upbringing said, "Don't." One argument and two sleepless nights later she relented, which had resulted in now-five-year-old Tommy, whom Angie wouldn't trade for any genetically optimized kid on the planet.

The doctor's expression fell short of condemnation, landing on pity. "I meant no offense." She returned to Angie's question. "No, it can't be cured."

The words hit hard.

"But you said it had become extremely rare…" Kevin's own realization cut his comment short. *None survive the screening process.*

Caressing Leah's tiny fingers, Angie breathed deeply. In that moment, all her anxiety seemed to dissipate into clear, motherly resolve. "Tell us what we need to know."

"The effects vary a great deal from person to person," Dr. Chapman explained. "I've only seen two cases myself, both in adults. Your daughter may display irregular physical characteristics."

Both Kevin and Angie looked in Leah's direction. Neither knew what to notice. They turned back to the doctor.

"Most likely peculiar facial features that may become more pronounced as she ages, including an elongated face and slightly enlarged ears."

The doctor glanced down at the cheat sheet on her digital pad. "Is she crawling yet?"

"Some," Angie replied hopefully.

"Well, she probably won't walk as early as normal kids. And there will most certainly be mental impairment. We'll want to measure Leah's cognitive abilities when she's older, but most fragile X children possess about half the average IQ."

Angie and Kevin looked at each other.

"Will she be able to attend school?" Kevin wondered aloud, willing himself to remain strong for Angie's sake.

"Possibly, although you'll be hard-pressed to find a competent program since the disorder has become so rare. Public schools cut special education funding back in the early twenties."

"Marriage and family?" Angie asked.

"Unlikely. But I see nothing to prevent your daughter from enjoying a vibrant sex life."

Both Kevin and Angie winced at the suggestion.

The doctor continued, but neither heard the rest of her summary. Kevin and Angie would take time to understand the details of Leah's disability in days to come. For now, they tried to absorb one simple reality: *Our daughter will never have a normal life.*

Neither would they.

CHAPTER TEN

Julia reached frantically toward the silhouette of a hand as it withdrew from her extending fingers. Despite a vivid brightness that seared the vision of her sleeping eyes, she noticed only shadows. A dark, masculine form appeared stretched and diluted. Its comforting presence ebbed away while something mysterious pulled her downward toward a brutal, merciless place.

She inhaled violently like a child desperate to break free from an outbound ocean current, then screamed at the shadow drifting from view.

"Where are you going? How can you leave me like this? Help me!"

She heard a voice.

"It's OK, sweetie. Wake up. You're all right."

Julia's eyes opened to the welcome sight of Maria. Overpowering her confused anxiety, she quickly grasped what had happened. Maria had heard the screams from the next room, startling her into action. Julia's relief met embarrassment. She reluctantly accepted her sister's nurturing embrace.

Moments later, Julia sat propped against her pillow, hugging both legs tightly against her chest. She habitually retrieved the pen and pad she had used in the past.

MAN
SHADOW
FEAR
ANGER

She added a single word.

ABANDONED

PART TWO

CHAPTER ELEVEN

"I can't keep taking you to the doctor, Mom!" Matthew Adams barked after reviewing the $1,152 bill for three visits to treat what had turned out to be phantom ailments.

"I think she likes the attention," the nurse had explained.

Seeing tears form in his mother's eyes made Matthew feel like a heel. He reached across the table to rub her frail arm while handing her a partially used tissue.

"Here you go." He hated making her cry. But he didn't know what else to do. He was losing his battle to protect her dwindling assets.

"I'm sorry, Matthew," she said.

"The doctor said there's nothing wrong with you, Mom," he continued gently. "Just remember to take your pills and everything will be fine."

But he knew she would not remember her pills any more than she could remember other important details. She became confused over the simplest tasks, like trying to recall the two-word voice command that would dial his number. It caused her to panic whenever he left for work or to run errands.

The sound of two quick raps at the door announced Donny's arrival. "Sorry I'm late," he said while letting himself in. He began removing a coat. "Low on gas. Had to stop on the way."

"No worries." Matthew was just grateful Donny had kept his promise. "Thanks for coming early. I really need to snag some extra hours."

In truth, Matthew needed a break. That's why he'd spent the money to hire a second part-time parent-sitter, even though competition for senior-care workers had driven hourly rates to an all-time high. The income from Grandpa's life insurance covered essentials like rent, utilities, groceries, and basic digital access. But it didn't cover extra help. Last month he'd paid a portion of her prescription expenses out of his own paycheck. A waste, he thought, since she seemed to be getting worse instead of better.

"Enroll in college," his mom used to say. "Use the money for tuition. My son should be a professor."

She knew he could do it.

He no longer even hoped.

Before heading to work, Matthew began a morning ritual his mother had come to expect. Retrieving a set of rosary beads from the kitchen counter, he placed them carefully in her left palm. Engulfing her tiny fist with his own, he knelt down in front of her and looked in her eyes. "I'll see you soon, OK, Mom?"

Peering warily at Donny, she concentrated long enough to recognize the former stranger. She gave her son a hesitant but reassuring smile.

"I'll be back around four thirty," Matthew informed Donny on his way out the door.

◆

By the time Matthew arrived at work about a dozen students were already sipping drinks while scanning the day's assignments or reading social media updates. He slid past a sofa and three tables, placing his backpack behind the pastry counter before starting another day retrieving empty mugs and tossing coffee-stained napkins.

Glancing around the room, Matthew recognized three of the eleven students: nameless acquaintances who acknowledged his presence with a silent nod the way actors condescend to greet a helpful stagehand. He knew that his role, like those of the librarian and cafeteria workers, was trivial compared to those of the tuition-paying students and tenure-earning faculty. A quick mental tabulation said the room represented nearly six hundred thousand dollars in annual tuition, not including room and board, tech access fees, or specialty drinks.

Slow day, he thought.

"Hi, Matt," came Sarah's warm but apologetic greeting. "There were seven or eight frat parties last night. I think it's gonna be slow all morning. Would you mind waiting to sign in until your regular shift? Or maybe even third-period rush? Kelly and I have it covered."

Just like that, his income dropped; it was the third time this month a shift manager had casually reduced his hours. Sure, he would work the guaranteed twenty hours this week, but he needed more.

"I'll make extra income to cover an additional sitter," he'd told himself in October. He had yet to make good on the promise.

Never one to show his disappointment, especially to Sarah, Matthew glanced at the clock. Ninety minutes until third period.

"Mind if I camp out at my usual table until then?" He didn't need to ask, but wanted to keep the conversation going. "I can catch up on research for my project."

Both Sarah and Matthew knew that he had long since abandoned his formal education. It had been three years since he completed his fifth and sixth community college courses, environmental studies and a comparative religions class called Our Spiritual Impulse. His "project" nibbled around the edges of both by reading this and that tidbit to become a self-appointed expert in the nonexistent field of "spiritual environmentalism."

"No problem!" came Sarah's reply. "Need to borrow my access code?" The offer meant she felt bad and wanted to make it up to him. A promising sign.

"That'd be great."

Seconds later Sarah reached over Matthew's shoulder to swipe her finger across a ten-inch screen embedded in the table surface. Her fingerprint opened a window to the collective wisdom of humanity thanks to a gold-tier tech access subscription he could no longer afford. His own fingerprint gave access only to free, public domain content.

Matthew resisted the urge to move closer to Sarah's body, but couldn't help breathing in her fresh, feminine scent. He felt bad for secretly enjoying the pleasure of her presence. Unlike the lurid images of seductive women that populated his virtual games, girls like Sarah incited feelings just as exciting, but more wholesome. He couldn't describe the sensation, even to himself. She offered a mysterious healing from the diminished manhood his porn habit seemed to breed. But she was far too young, not to mention way out of his league.

After a brief security scan, the screen came alive. Six taps on the digital keyboard presented Matthew with familiar icons conveniently sequenced in use-frequency order:

GAMES

GUY STUFF

INTERESTS

DAILY SYNOPSIS

ACTIVE PROJECTS

Knowing Sarah or Kelly might walk by at any time, he chose the safest icon on the screen.

Matthew's Daily Synopsis—April 26, 2042

- <u>YOUR DAY</u>:

  - 9 a.m. = Start Work

- <u>YOUR MESSAGES</u>:

  - TROLLMASTER: "You gotta see this one. Hot!"
  - GAIMGOD: "I just got accepted into Zilla Clan. Eat your heart out!"

- <u>YOUR NEWS</u>:

  - Release of *Planet Battle VI* exceeds game industry expectations

- <u>YOUR MONEY</u>:

  - $578 monthly prescription fee charged on 4/14/2042 to Visa account
  - $3200 from Campus Grinds deposit scheduled to Chase account on 4/15/42

Matthew waved out of DAILY SYNOPSIS and selected the INTERESTS icon in search of something to occupy himself until the usual third-period rush. He went in and out of five recommended links that seemed promising, but none held his attention.

"Here you go." The singsong interruption startled Matthew. "Your usual poison, on the house."

"Wow. Thanks, Sarah." He savored the unexpected attention.

"You bet!" came her casual reply. "Enjoy."

After taking a cautious drink to avoid burning his top lip, Matthew returned to the screen and tapped the ACTIVE PROJECTS icon to initiate the research genie, hoping Sarah's clearance would generate more useful links than his own. Seconds later, two new items appeared: a report in *Green World Journal* describing disproportionate environmental impact from larger households and a news brief quoting the director of epigenetic research saying something about reversing age-related dementia.

Matthew browsed the second item. Skipping over the medical lingo, he found the article's bottom line.

Dr. Wayne Galliger sounded optimistic about the team's initial findings, suggesting the project could yield practical treatment options for age-related dementia as early as fall of 2044.

"That's another two and a half years!" Matthew said aloud, prompting a confused glance from the student sitting at the next table. Shushing himself, Matthew scanned the rest of the article for a more optimistic crumb. Nothing.

I don't think I can handle another thirty months of lost keys, forgotten names, repeated conversations, and bathroom mishaps.

Noticing the strain of his own clenched fists, Matthew decided to change the subject. It had been awhile since he last explored new pictures and updates from fellow Littleton High School graduates. Over the past three years nearly every former cheerleader had approved his "Secret Admirer" status request, giving him anonymous access to an occasional "Secret Surprise" they might post for their mysterious followers. But one prize remained, the only girl he had ever mustered up enough courage to ask to the prom. Although she had rejected him, he had never lost his fascination with her.

Typing DAVIDSON into the search field, Matthew expected to find another perky picture of Maria. He instead saw a professional press photo beside the latest column written by her older sister—the former valedictorian.

A quick glance at the clock told Matthew he had plenty of time to kill. He began reading…

FREE TO THRIVE
By Julia Davidson (RAP Syndicate)

A friend of mine recently informed me she wants to have a child. She's not religious, but her parents are devout Catholics. They have an opinion on the matter. Actually, two opinions.

First, they want their daughter to find a partner (*husband* to use their word) before becoming a mom—something less than 25% of women do for good reasons I've covered in earlier columns. (Why do religious fundamentalists criticize our generation for avoiding parenthood yet complain when single women choose motherhood?)

Second, my friend's parents disapprove of a practice that has become standard medical procedure, even among heterosexual domestic partners. In vitro selection (IVS) brings enormous benefits to parents, children and society. But they've cautioned their daughter against "engineering her child" by vetting common genetic imperfections. They believe IVS puts humans in the place of God and fear we have become "picky shoppers" rather than "grateful recipients" when it comes to the "gift of life."

Caving to parental pressure, my friend postponed her selection appointment. I suppose I should celebrate the decision. One fewer carbon footprint polluting the planet. But I hate to see her give up something she wants just because her parents view technology as a moral bogeyman.

These are the facts. Eight out of ten women who wish to have a child use in vitro selection, otherwise known as common sense. In our day and age, why would anyone risk giving birth to children with costly health challenges? Women no longer have to fear receiving bad news after the birth of a child due to unforeseen disabilities and complications. Only children born to parents who opt out of the genetic vetting process risk the heartache, burden and expenses associated with the most common disabilities and age-related illness. Those expenses, by the way, will end up hitting federal and state budgets as "faith children" survive their well-intentioned but misguided parents. You and I will inherit costly care and medical obligations on top of the massive care and medical obligations associated with our aging parents and grandparents.

If my friend decides to have a child, I hope she will give the baby the freedom to thrive by eliminating the risk of unnecessary disease and disability. I only wish we could give the same freedom to those of us already burdened by both.

Taking another sip from his mug, Matthew reread the final paragraph. Then he read it again, this time mentally selecting and rearranging seven words to give them their due.

Give those burdened the freedom to thrive.

Making a note to explore other columns by Maria's sister, Matthew opened a journal page filled with previous entries. Up popped seemingly random phrases, references, and concepts he had been capturing for months. Scanning the list, he found the item he was looking for.

SPIRIT GOOD. BODY BAD. (4th Century Manichaeism)

Taking one final sip of his cooling mocha, he glanced out the window toward nothing in particular. Looking back at the screen, he typed a missing piece into his project puzzle.

FREE TO THRIVE (Julia Davidson)

Two minutes later, Matthew shot off a request to meet with the chairman of the University's Religious Studies Department.

CHAPTER TWELVE

"I don't like it," Troy whispered into his friend's ear. "Near as I can figure, you'll start with a five-stroke handicap. Maybe more."

Only seven of the twelve other faces in the room looked familiar to Kevin Tolbert, many of them rising stars in other congressional regions. Like Kevin, each had been invited to join the closed-door session of Senator Franklin's austerity coalition in an effort to stack the political deck in favor of whatever recommendations emerged. All of them were strong fiscal conservatives who had voted to support phase one of the president's agenda. None of them would be easily convinced.

He also recognized Trisha. Who didn't? Every bit as striking as her magazine cover shots, Trisha Sayers seemed out of place at any gathering of corporate and congressional titans. But she qualified, especially since trading her "Trisha Delisha" pop-icon status to launch what had become the nation's leading chain of fashion outlet stores. It only elevated her first-name-only renown, especially among women who admired the model-turned-recording-artist-turned-retail-entrepreneur. They spent hundreds of millions annually to mimic her empowering, form-fitted beauty at an affordable price. Six years earlier Trisha had given the president credibility among female voters when she endorsed his campaign. She remained a favorite face of the new, trendier conservative movement.

"I'll give you ten to one Franklin uses Trisha as press liaison for this coalition," Troy said softly, clearly troubled by the prospect.

Kevin nodded silently. Despite his concern, he had to admire the senator's political savvy. "She's definitely easy on the eyes," he quipped. "Let's just hope she goes easy on our proposals."

"Don't count on it." Troy handed Kevin a tablet containing his presentation slides and a page with a short bio on every attendee, complete with photos he could use to connect faces to competing agendas.

The host called the meeting to order as Troy spotted a seat behind Kevin reserved for support staff and aides. He patted his friend on the shoulder. "Make us proud, Congressman."

"Welcome, ladies and gentlemen," Brent Anderson began. "I'd like to once again thank you for accepting our invitation to help tackle some pretty big issues in a very short time frame."

Anderson had been the senator's most important companion since their corporate days, long before Franklin had pursued his first public office. The architect of the SLASH application, Anderson proudly wore his corresponding nickname, *the Scalpel*. He had proven himself capable of cutting through government fat to find substantial savings. As chairman of the austerity coalition, Anderson would bring the same tough-minded tenacity to finding proactive strategies to present when revised budget projections went public. With less than two weeks to go, he hoped to solidify agreement on the most promising proposals first.

"I'm going to assume you have all read the executive summary sent out yesterday," Anderson continued. "We won't take time to review the agenda other than to emphasize our goal of identifying big-boulder opportunities."

Kevin liked Anderson's style. Jump right to the bottom line to avoid wasting time. Why mess with a hundred pebbles and miss the two or three large rocks?

The agenda listed several fast-fire presentations. Each had been allocated fifteen minutes to summarize the big idea and another fifteen for group discussion. Over the next four hours members of the coalition would present, debate, and rank the most promising options. Kevin was up first.

"Congressman Tolbert." The terse introduction started the clock.

"Thank you, Mr. Anderson," Kevin began. "I appreciate the opportunity to present ideas that should, in my opinion, inform any solutions we propose."

With a swipe of his hand Kevin's first slide appeared on a transparent board behind him. Across the bottom of a graph ran a sequence of decade markers starting with 1950.

"This chart shows population trends in China over the past century."

Brent Anderson rose to his feet. "Mr. Tolbert, a reminder that each presentation must be short. Are you sure you want to waste part of yours talking about China? They aren't our challenge at the moment."

"But they are an important reference point, Mr. Anderson," Kevin said. "Their economy is in a free fall after decades of rapid expansion. Their decline will shed light on our own."

"Very well."

"The black line tracks population. You'll notice a gradual leveling off that started in 2022, about two parenting cycles after China implemented the most far-reaching population control measures ever devised. Fears over feeding their massive populace led to policies that created a very different problem."

Another wave of Kevin's hand caused a second line to appear.

"The green line shows total gross domestic product for China by decade. We see a bubble of growth from about 1995 through 2017 as they took advantage of lower dependency ratios. With one child per couple, women entered the workforce like never before, dramatically expanding their economy. They grew at lightning speed, for a while. As you know, that growth slowed and then stopped about fifteen years after their population peak. They've been shrinking ever since."

A third line appeared.

"This blue line shows the percentage of the Chinese population over the age of seventy, the highest ever recorded. The low dependency ratio that had been fueling growth turned on its head. Instead of one dependent child per couple, they now have two dependent parents per child. They find themselves paying the piper for the decades spent making money instead of raising kids. Today they don't have enough young adults to fuel an economic engine pulling a pretty heavy load of nonworking passengers named Mom, Dad, Grandma, and Grandpa."

A sequence of identically shaped graphs with similar trend lines appeared on the screen in rapid succession, each with a different title:

JAPAN

KOREA

AUSTRALIA

NETHERLANDS

SWEDEN

CANADA

FRANCE

RUSSIA

GERMANY

ENGLAND

"As you can see," Kevin explained as the series of charts continued, "every other developed nation in the world has been experiencing the same phenomena thanks to a combination of declining fertility and senior longevity."

The dominos stopped on a graph labeled USA. "And we now find ourselves in the same situation. The black line reflects actual and projected population in the United States as reported by the Census Bureau since World War Two." A consistent but decelerating climb, from a 1950 start of one hundred and fifty million to a 2050 peak of four hundred million. "As you know, we will never reach the growth levels predicted in 2030, leading us to our present financial crisis. This year marks the first year we will see net population decline. Based upon current trends, our pool of working-age adults will continue to shrink."

Kevin looked at the clock. Five of his fifteen minutes had passed and he had said nothing the group didn't already know. He hurried on.

"We looked beneath the surface of the data hoping to find bright spots in this overall cloudy picture." A color-coded map of the United States appeared, various regions bearing different shades of red toward light pink. A few appeared in pure white.

"What do the circled white regions represent?" asked someone seated to Kevin's left.

"I'm glad you asked, Mr. McGurn," Kevin replied after a quick glance at Troy's pictorial cheat sheet. "We call them bright spots. They are subregions of the country that show consistent economic growth even during down cycles. Our goal was to identify any common characteristics as a shortcut to finding effective turnaround strategies."

"Did you?"

"We did. Two." Kevin looked at Troy, who offered a slight nod of affirmation. The moment of truth had arrived. In the next five minutes Kevin would make the most important and risky pitch of his political career.

Troy jumped to his feet to distribute twelve copies of the supporting research document as Kevin advanced to his next slide.

"Ladies and gentlemen, the regions with the strongest and most consistent economic output share two simple characteristics."

Kevin swallowed hard.

"First, they have much higher rates of fertility, more than twice the national average." Kevin paused to let one unlikely reality settle before revealing a second.

Here goes, he thought.

"They also have the fewest transition volunteers."

At that moment, every bit of oxygen left the room.

CHAPTER THIRTEEN

"Thank you both for seeing me." Angie's voice was slightly higher than usual, anxiety restricting her vocal cords. "I didn't know who else to call."

The pastor's wife, Talia, moved toward their nervous guest to offer a reaffirming embrace. Angie clung possessively to the elegant, dark-skinned woman. After a few seconds, she released her hostess with a blush. It was not the kind of first impression Angie had intended to make.

"I'm sorry," she said. "I guess I needed that more than I knew."

"Please, don't apologize." Both women looked at Reverend Mubar, the white of his smile lifting the mood. "We're glad you came."

The pastor spoke with the faint echo of an accent neither Kevin nor Angie had been able to peg despite six months of competitive speculation. His light ebony complexion and deliberately articulate vocabulary suggested childhood immigration from an African state. Kevin had guessed Uganda while Angie supposed Ethiopia. Both assumed Reverend Mubar had come to the United States between the ages of seven and nine, since his speech retained scant traces of his mother tongue.

The minister ushered his wife and Angie toward the counseling section of his office. Angie accepted one of two chairs opposite the sofa positioned behind a glass coffee table displaying an assortment of scones next to a small teapot with matching cups on saucers. The presence of delicate china made Angie even more grateful the pastor's assistant had offered to occupy the children in the nursery during the session.

Talia sat beside her husband and began pouring tea. Angie watched quietly, wondering how to begin. She had never met with the pastor before and wondered why his wife had joined the discussion. She took a small sip of tea while wondering who should speak first.

"I hope you don't mind that I invited my wife to sit with us," Pastor Mubar said, breaking the silence. "Talia joins me whenever I meet with a female parishioner."

"Not at all." In truth, Talia's presence comforted Angie. "That seems like a wise policy."

"It protects everyone. Besides, the Scriptures tell the older women to instruct the younger. I know I'm not qualified." He gave himself a slight courtesy laugh.

"Who are you calling old?" Talia winked while flashing a playful smile that further lightened the mood. The pastor's wife had no discernable accent. Perhaps the northern Midwest? Chicago? Or Detroit? Probably in her late thirties, Talia Mubar did not seem much older than Angie.

"Reverend Mubar, can I ask a personal question?"

"Please, call me Seth," he corrected.

"My husband Kevin and I have been attending Apostles' Church since moving to DC. We both love your teaching ministry." She paused to let the compliment sink in before asking him to resolve a trivial dispute. "But we have a running debate over your background. Were you born in America?"

Seth chuckled at a question he seemed to have answered many times before. "My parents immigrated from Egypt to the United States when I was seven years old. My father was a civil engineer until he fled during what they now call the Arab Spring."

"Fled from what?" Angie wondered aloud.

"My parents belonged to the Egypt Orthodox Church, which made them second-class citizens amid the Muslim majority. After the revolution my father feared things would become much worse for believers in Egypt. He wanted to give my sister and me a better life, so he came to America. If you know anything about the plight of Christians in Egypt today, you will understand why I remain very grateful."

"Egypt Orthodox. Is that like our church?"

"Yes and no. They don't have many Protestants in Egypt. Most believers attend either a Coptic or Orthodox church where they use ancient liturgies few in America would recognize. But we affirm the same basic creeds defended by the early Church fathers."

Angie nodded politely at matters far removed from her present concern.

"But that's enough about my background," Seth said. "Let's talk about your situation."

Placing her saucer and cup on the table, Angie took a deep breath in preparation for her dive.

"Two days ago my husband and I met with our daughter Leah's pediatrician." The doctor's accusing face invaded her memory, stirring defensive feelings she thought had been purged. "We learned that our baby's genetic profile revealed irregularities."

Seth gave Talia a knowing glance.

Angie's voice broke as she spoke the words aloud for the first time. "She told us Leah has something called fragile X syndrome. It's a rare disorder that causes physical and mental—"

"We know the disorder," Seth interrupted. "A former member of Apostles' Church had it also."

For a brief moment Angie felt less alone. "Former member?"

"Yes. She died shortly after her mother. A very sad situation." Seth assumed a reflective posture. "Between genetic screening and transitions very few believers ever meet a disabled individual, let alone serve one."

Angie continued. "Our doctor asked why we skipped the genetic screening process before Leah's conception." Her head fell as if she had exposed a mortal sin.

Angie's eyes darted between her two confessors in anticipation of condemning glares. To her surprise, both glowed like parents genuinely pleased by a child's Crayola mess.

"I felt—" Angie began.

"She made you feel foolish?" Talia asked.

Angie nodded. "And irresponsible. The doctor said the only parents who skip the genetic screening process are religious extremists."

Seth started to speak, but Talia squeezed his leg in pain-inducing punishment. He obediently bit his tongue to let Angie continue.

"We've never considered ourselves to be extremists." She was trying to convince herself. "We just never felt comfortable with the whole designer-baby thing. Now I'm not so sure."

Talia loosened the grip on Seth's leg, releasing his tongue.

"You are extreme." Talia's grip clamped again. Seth's reaction struck Angie as funny, causing her to smile at the couple's wordless banter.

"I mean to say, most people will consider your choice extreme." He removed Talia's hand in self-defense. "Even most of the people who attend this church opt for genetic screening. No one seems to question the procedure since it's become the new normal."

Angie felt abnormal. She recalled the label *blind conception* to mock mothers who rejected prescreening, mothers who wanted to conceive babies through the beauty of intimate passion with their husbands rather than the clinical proficiency of in vitro selection.

"But normal is not the same as good," Seth continued. "Or heroic."

Angie reacted with curious surprise. "Heroic?"

"Angie, sweetheart." Talia took over. "Describe what you felt the moment you learned something was wrong with your little girl."

Angie remembered the call from the pediatrician's office insisting Kevin attend Leah's genetic profile appointment. "I was terrified."

"I bet you held Leah extra tight that evening," Talia continued.

She had.

"I imagine you felt an intense urge to protect her, even though you had no idea what you needed to protect her from."

A single tear on Angie's cheek confirmed the suggestion.

"Did you resent Leah?"

The question jolted Angie. "Resent Leah? Why would I resent her?"

"She'll be a major burden to you and your family," Seth interjected.

"But that isn't her fault."

"Whose fault is it?" he asked.

"Nobody's. Maybe mine. But certainly not hers," Angie said with indignation.

"How about God?" Not a question she had expected from her pastor. "Shouldn't he have protected Leah from disability? Protected you from this burden?"

No one spoke as the interrogation served its purpose.

"Your heart yearns to protect your daughter," Seth explained. "You defend her instead of resent her, accept her as a gift instead of criticize God for a faulty design."

Talia moved from the sofa to kneel beside Angie's chair and placed her dark fingers onto Angie's milky-white arm. "In a world that treats human life like a commodity to use and discard, many would call you extreme. Extremely heroic."

♦

After a therapeutic sob, Angie gratefully accepted her second cup of tea and a cinnamon-almond scone. Her appetite finally released from days of stomach knots, the simple pleasure seemed a soothing tonic to her soul. So were the pastor's words.

"The Christian faith views children as a gift from the Lord. It understands that every human being is made in the image of God himself and so has inherent worth and dignity. Leah's value isn't based upon her capacity to make money, enter the Olympics, or win glamour pageants. Although I know she's a beautiful baby."

Angie felt her heart swell.

"She has infinite value because she reflects the image of her maker. Just like your other two children, Leah is a masterpiece in God's gallery of family portraits. He reveals part of himself through every child or adult who has ever received his breath of life."

Seth drank from his cup as his wife read Angie's face. More needed to be said.

Talia jumped in. "But Leah will be a tremendous amount of work and expense to raise. She might cause embarrassment when you take her out in public. She may become a source of tension in your marriage. You've already seen how some people will react, questioning the wisdom of your choice."

Seth appeared agitated at his wife's negativity. But Angie understood. Mothers need more than inspiring truth. They must brace themselves for hard realities.

"Your daughter will be called a debit," Talia continued as Seth visibly reacted to her offensive slang. "Leah will never fit in. She'll always be seen as an expensive burden and as damaged goods. You and Kevin will ask why this had to happen to your child, why it invaded the life you imagined for yourself."

They were Angie's very thoughts. Unspoken. Stifled. Guilt-ridden.

Seth could no longer remain silent. "Angie, we don't know why bad things happen to good people. We live in a fallen world that includes a whole lot of sickness, death, and heartache, but very few answers."

"I know."

"All I can tell you is that you and Kevin made the right choice by becoming tools in the artist's hands. Now comes the hard work of putting God's little masterpiece on display."

A noise caused Angie to turn.

"I'm sorry, Pastor." It was his assistant peering through the door. "I hate to interrupt. But I think someone needs her mommy."

Angie heard Leah's whimper of discontent. The sound intensified the pain in her breasts. Feeding time had passed.

"I should probably go," Angie said as she placed her empty teacup beside the plate containing the remains of a scone. "There's nothing damaged about her hunger clock. Every bit as inconvenient as Tommy's or Joy's was."

Accepting Leah into her arms, Angie cradled her daughter with a gentle swinging motion. An immediate tranquility overtook both child and mother.

Seth and Talia leaned back on the sofa, quietly observing the holy reunion.

CHAPTER FOURTEEN

Troy scanned the faces around the room to gauge reactions. Kevin would land his formal presentation one minute early, an impressive first. Opinions were now forming. Political calculations made. Sides chosen.

Reviewing his hastily crafted tally, Troy confirmed five in the Against column, Trisha Sayers most visibly of all. Only three appeared warm to Kevin's proposals. He optimistically marked them For. He presumed the remaining poker faces Undecided, including the ever-pragmatic Brent Anderson, who rose from his chair to moderate fifteen minutes of questions and debate.

"Thank you, Congressman Tolbert." Anderson visually sized up the same mix of faces. He momentarily studied his handwritten notes. "Before we begin discussion I want to make sure we clearly understand your proposals. Can you please return to the earlier slide titled *A Better Path*?"

"You bet." Kevin waved back to a page displaying two items.

PROPOSAL A: ELDER-CARE TAX EXEMPTION FOR PARENTS

PROPOSAL B: ALL TRANSITION BENEFITS TO CHARITY

"That's it. Thank you." Anderson allowed a moment for the slide to refresh memories. "As I understand them, both of your recommendations would reduce two large revenue streams."

"Not reduce. Reinvest," Kevin clarified. "Let me explain Proposal A first. Our present system indirectly penalizes parents trying to raise future workers. Future taxpayers. Curbing downward population trends by even a small amount will generate long-term revenues that dwarf the short-term investment."

"How do we penalize parents?" Anderson asked. "Elder-care tax rates are the same for everyone."

"The average parent spends around three hundred thousand dollars over a lifetime to raise each child. As adults, those kids get jobs, buy homes, and launch businesses. Each will generate an average of one point six million dollars in lifetime GDP. But, as you said, parents investing to raise future workers pay the identical elder-care tax as childless individuals who spend the same three hundred thousand dollars on themselves."

Kevin paused. Few in the room had ever thought about child-rearing as an investment in future economic growth. When it appeared everyone was still with him, he continued.

"Fast-forward to age seventy. The childless citizen, the one who spent three hundred thousand dollars on himself, has no sons or daughters paying into the system to offset his own withdrawals. He will receive the identical elder-care benefits as a parent who spent decades investing to replace himself with one, two, or more younger workers now paying into the system."

"So you think childless citizens should receive lower benefits?" Anderson asked.

"No. But I do think we should ease some of the burden on those creating our future tax base."

"Are you suggesting we subsidize lifestyle choices?" Trisha Sayers appeared to take personal offense. "Give favorable treatment just because someone spawns offspring?"

"Fewer citizens are spawning offspring, to use your words, than ever in our history," Kevin replied. "Which is exactly why we face a declining tax base amid skyrocketing elder-care expenses. Our incentives have pushed both of those trend lines in the wrong direction."

"Our charter is to close the deficit gap," Anderson interrupted. "Cutting sources of tax revenue will make that much more difficult."

"Not cutting. Reinvesting," Kevin corrected again. "If we shift the incentives in the right direction we encourage more bright spot behaviors, which will actually increase revenue."

"That might help us over the long haul. But what will it do to our short-term projections?" Anderson appeared highly skeptical.

"I won't kid you. They will look worse at first," Kevin confessed. "But after a few years they will improve sharply. Do you remember the bright spot regions? The average household generates significantly higher GDP and spends far less on elder care."

"How can parents generate more wealth when they spend so much to raise kids?" Anderson probed. "And how can communities with fewer transitions spend less on the elderly?"

"Remember, necessity is the mother of invention," Kevin continued with a wink. "Kids motivate everyone in the family to make different choices than they would otherwise have made. Dads take extra shifts and second jobs. Moms scan coupons and launch home-based businesses. Grandparents buy birthday presents and watch grandkids, providing cheaper and better child care while giving them something better to do than rot away in retirement villages. The average married father, for example, earns seventy percent more lifetime income than the average single man."

"That can't be right," Trisha objected.

"It is right. For a thousand reasons, children give young adults incentive to work, save, and invest. They also give older adults positive purpose. The numbers don't lie. Our brightest economic regions have more kids and fewer transitions."

"Have you run the projections on these proposals?" an Undecided asked, eagerly flipping through the supporting document.

"We have," Kevin answered. "You'll find them on page seven. A net gain after ten years. If we could affect a ten percent shift over two decades we would generate six trillion dollars in additional GDP while reducing end-of-life expenses by two trillion more."

Troy noticed a slight rise in one of Anderson's eyebrows. A budding For?

"And all on the backs of women!" Trisha erupted.

"Excuse me?" Kevin replied.

"The regions you call bright spots, Mr. Tolbert, look more like a retreat to the Dark Ages." She glanced down briefly to confirm her hunch. "I'm looking at a map of store placement for my company. It's interesting how few of our outlets show up in the areas you've highlighted."

She stopped, assuming her point self-evident. The blank stares around the room prompted a reluctant explanation of the obvious. "Our stores serve professional women. We have lots of outlets in Mr. Tolbert's dark red regions. Almost none in his so-called bright spots."

Troy quickly connected the dots. Trisha's fashions accentuated ladder-climbing gals, not diaper-changing moms. Women purchased her clothes to make presentations, not to burp babies.

"Who do you think wipes the noses of all of those future taxpayers, Mr. Tolbert? Certainly not the fathers."

Troy sensed trouble. He had seen the strongest, most decisive men shrink in the face of an offended female, especially one as attractive and articulate as Trisha Sayers.

"Raising children requires enormous sacrifice from both parents," Kevin countered.

"Am I correct to assume you have children, Mr. Tolbert?" Trisha asked.

"Three," he replied. "Would you like to see pictures?" The comment prompted the intended laughter, shifting momentum back in Kevin's direction.

"Where are they now?"

"With my wife Angie."

"What about when she goes to work?"

Kevin anticipated the end of her line of questions. "Ms. Sayers, my wife decided to put her career on hold after becoming pregnant with our third child. Your point?"

"My point, Mr. Tolbert, is that higher fertility comes with a price tag."

"Which is why we should stop penalizing those willing to pay it," Kevin retorted.

"I mean that women give up far more than men when couples have kids."

Anderson stepped in. "As much as we'd love to relive the battle of the sexes, Ms. Sayers, we don't have time for that debate today."

An assortment of masculine chuckles peppered the room. Trisha leaned back in her chair and assumed a seething posture.

"But I'm sympathetic to Ms. Sayers's position," Anderson continued. "After all, it will be necessary to sell our plans to a skeptical public. It might be political suicide to propose fertility incentives. But we can debate the specifics later. Right now we need to decide whether we consider this idea a big-boulder option for further exploration."

"Then I'll state my first proposal plainly." Kevin quickly retook the floor. "I want to re-incentivize growth by granting one elder-care tax exemption for each minor dependent in a household. We project a slight dip in net revenue for four years followed by offsetting growth thereafter. No net increase to the ten-year deficit projection."

"And Proposal B?" Anderson asked, prompting Kevin to highlight his second bullet:

PROPOSAL B: ALL TRANSITION BENEFITS TO CHARITY

"Another significant revenue hit," Anderson observed. "Only a small fraction of transition volunteers currently use the charity option. Most want to help a partner, child, or significant other by transitioning the estate. If forced to give those assets to charity we could see a significant drop in volunteers."

Troy's eyes met Kevin's as Anderson finished making his point.

"Do you have any idea how much we save on entitlement spending with each transition?"

"About two hundred thousand," Kevin said with calm confidence. "Plus about thirty thousand from the federal share of each estate."

A moment of uncomfortable silence.

"Will you be writing a personal check in the amount of a quarter trillion to make up the difference?" Anderson mocked. Even those in the For column joined the laugher.

"You won't lose one hundred percent of transition volunteers," Kevin explained in good-natured irritation. "And the increase in charity donations would give the nonprofit sector desperately needed capital to meet the demands our tattered social safety net has created."

Several nods around the room confirmed Troy's earlier advice: "Shifting big-government programs to the private and nonprofit sector plays well with fiscal conservatives."

"Again, this is a growth strategy," Kevin continued. "Seniors in bright spot communities work seven years longer on average than those in high-transition regions. That's seven more years of tax revenue. They also cost less. We spend half as much on the elderly who are parents as we do on the elderly childless."

"Half?" Anderson reacted. "How is that possible?"

"Partly because those with kids and grandkids stay healthier, probably because they have a greater sense of purpose. But mainly because grown children provide free assistance to their aging parents instead of costly nursing home care."

Kevin looked at the rapidly advancing clock.

"I could go on, but I've hit the highlights. I'd like to conclude by saying I think it's time we found ways to grow our long-term revenue base. Both of these proposals will do just that."

His fifteen minutes ended. The time to vote had arrived.

"If you don't mind, Mr. Tolbert, I think we should consider your proposals separately rather than as a pair," Anderson insisted, calling for the first vote before Kevin could react. "By show of hands, who supports forming a subcommittee to explore the first Bright Spots proposal, elder-care tax exemptions for parents?"

Five hands went up immediately, then a hesitant sixth. One shy of a clear majority.

"Opposed?"

The five hands Troy had predicted joined Trisha Sayers's simmering opposition.

Troy looked toward the host, who now held the tiebreaking vote. Brent Anderson's eyes vacillated between Kevin Tolbert's onscreen summary and the fashion diva's threatening glower.

"Approved," Anderson announced without raising his hand.

Troy began circling names to serve on a subcommittee as Anderson derailed item two. "Does anyone support the idea of banning transition volunteers from leaving an inheritance to their partners and children?"

Kevin started to correct Anderson's phraseology, but stopped when he noticed Troy's head moving from side to side in a quiet effort to temper his boss's enthusiasm. As much as both men hated the transition industry, they shouldn't risk alienating Franklin's right-hand man. The first proposal had been accepted. The second would not be. Par at the end of round one.

CHAPTER FIFTEEN

Julia turned sideways to inspect her full-body profile before leaving the ladies' locker room. Though it had been two weeks since her last workout, the glance boosted her confidence for the stroll past the free-weight room where, as usual, a crew of testosterone-laden guys would conspicuously size her up against every other passing woman. Despite taking offense at the ritual, she was more worried about losing the competition. Today she would score well above average.

The sounds of whirring elliptical machines and clanking barbells welcomed Julia back to her increasingly sporadic exercise routine: a five-minute stretch, a two-mile treadmill run while watching her custom selection of news topics, and twenty minutes of resistance training to strengthen her upper arms and torso. Just what she needed to push past a growing exhaustion incited by her latest dreams.

Breathing the musky odor of masculine sweat prompted Julia to look toward her panel of judges, five pairs of eyes already appreciating the view. Before she could relish the moment, however, Julia noticed a sixth man straining to curl his fifty-pound dumbbell. It was Jonathan Sowell who, as during their recent date, seemed indifferent to her presence.

He probably didn't see me, she hoped, quickening her pace to avoid reliving her recent humiliation.

Guylanders! She thought. It was the title of her Pulitzer-winning feature critiquing the dominant male culture. Many considered Julia the foremost authority on modern guys. Not men. Few of those, eager to pursue a long-term relationship, existed anymore. Guys, by contrast, preferred the never-never land of boyhood delights. Fewer and fewer chose the headaches of marriage or the sacrifices of fatherhood, half as many as their parents' generation. A quarter of their grandparents'. In the 1960s almost 70 percent of men were married with kids by age thirty. Two generations later, less than 20 percent. Julia would lay odds all five of her free-weight oglers worked part-time jobs and shared apartments with fellow gamers, partiers, and bodybuilders. Each of them played the field of willing ladies rather than trying to meet the expectations of a single life partner.

She knew for certain Jonathan Sowell had no interest in a serious relationship.

Finding an open mat on the opposite side of the facility, Julia sat down to begin the torture of stretching. Her hand reached toward toes once easily grasped, settling for an ankle. Forcing her head downward, she positioned her nose just above a kneecap despite fierce protests from her lower back.

"Julia?"

The masculine voice startled her.

"I thought that was you."

No!

"Hello, Jonathan." It was all she intended to say.

"How are you? You look great."

The flattery worked. "You too," she replied with a slight smile. "Great show the other night!"

Great show? Not great time together?

"How's Maria?" he asked. No surprise.

"She's fine. What've you been up to?"

"Work mostly," he responded, eyes momentarily distracted by the tall blonde bouncing on a nearby treadmill. "You?"

"Been pretty busy working on a new feature for RAP." It felt good to remind him of her professional stature, even though she felt he was intimidated by her success. Few male egos could handle female strength. At least that's what she chose to believe over the alternative.

A moment passed.

"Well, I'll let you get back to your workout," Jonathan said. "It was really good to see you again."

Liar!

"You too. Stay in touch."

Not likely.

Julia consoled herself by abandoning the stretching pad for a stress-crushing run. The only open treadmill stood beside the bouncing blonde. Placing a water bottle in one cup-holder and her phone in the other, Julia hit START while nodding at the stranger. She felt slightly less confident running beside a woman who undoubtedly held the gym's glamour title.

Just as Julia reached her usual pace she noticed the illumined vibration of her phone. Glancing up, she saw that the clock on the machine said 12:32 p.m.

She answered after tapping a tiny wireless speaker in her ear. "Hi, Paul. Can you hear me OK?"

"Fine," he replied. "You sound a bit winded. Bad time?"

"At the gym. Now is fine," she explained.

"Staying trim for the gentlemen?"

"Something like that." If only he knew the joke.

Paul got right to business. "I'll make this quick. You can hit pause on the debit story I assigned last Monday."

Julia felt a mix of relief and disappointment.

"I'll toss that piece to Monica so that you can focus on what has the potential of becoming a major feature."

"No need. I'm sure I can handle both." Monica Garcia was the last person to whom Julia wanted to hand over her notes.

"I don't know, Jewel. This one's pretty big," Paul countered.

"Just tell me what you've got and I'll decide."

"Suit yourself, love. Do you have access to a tablet?"

She waved out of the news clip screen embedded in the treadmill to access a search field. "Sure do. What do you want me to find?"

The neighboring blonde looked toward Julia, clearly impressed by a woman capable of three-way multitasking. Julia nodded casually, claiming superiority on her own turf.

"Search 'bright spots' and 'Franklin.'"

"As in Josh Franklin?" Julia asked.

"None other. I think he's up to something, but I can't quite connect the dots."

"What dots?"

"He formed a covert team of young fiscal conservatives," Paul explained. "They've been meeting behind closed doors for a few days now."

"Meeting about what?"

"That's the problem. I don't know. But I have a confidential lead that says it has something to do with an upcoming revision from the Congressional Budget Office."

"The budget?" Julia protested. "Come on, Paul. You promised a big feature."

"Hear me out, Jewel. My sources tell me the trend lines look bad. Very bad."

Taking a sip from her water bottle, Julia lowered the pace of her jog to make it easier to type BRIGHT SPOTS into the digital keyboard. Nothing of note surfaced until she added the name Franklin.

"Got it," she said as she started to read. Only her accelerated breathing filled the silence on the line. "A short rumor piece about a subcommittee of Franklin's team researching something they call bright spots. But no details."

"I want you to get the details," Paul explained. "My sources tell me the guy behind this Bright Spots proposal falls in the breeder camp."

"Got a name?"

"Tolbert. A young buck with three kids. Can you believe it? Three!"

Julia hit the treadmill's pause button. "Did you say Tolbert?"

"T-O-L-B..."

"I know how to spell it. I'm just surprised."

"You know him?"

"Kevin Tolbert. His wife and I were close during high school. We keep in touch, but the friendship drifted."

"Get close again, fast," Paul ordered. "We need inside information on what Franklin plans to do. The editorial board wants us to be proactive on this one. The budget revision has everyone nervous. We think Franklin wants to capitalize on the situation."

"To do what?" Julia asked. "I thought he supported the Youth Initiative."

"He did. But we don't yet have access to the revised numbers. If public sentiment turns against the president, I wouldn't put it past that power-grabbing Franklin to jump ship, even if it requires entering the breeder asylum."

Julia vaguely recalled a story in the alternative press predicting growing influence from a block of voters motivated by breeder ideology. After decades disregarding warnings of ecological disaster, these families tended to have more than the sensible one or two kids. A stark contrast to women like Julia or the citizens of Guyland. The story suggested radical fundamentalists were the only people who had been having enough kids to create pockets of population growth. They had become a rather large voting bloc, tilting political clout in their favor. Tens of millions of their kids had reached voting age, most echoing their parents' quirky politics. The shift was a bewildering nuisance to enlightened progressives like Paul and Julia, not to mention their employer, RAP Syndicate.

"What do you want me to do?" Julia asked.

"Find out what this bright spot thing is all about. I don't want Franklin or his pals catching us flat-footed. We need to be ready to discredit any extreme ideas before they gain traction."

"Deadline?"

"Not sure, but soon. We'll want to run something before the CBO releases their revised numbers, and we don't know when that will be."

"I'm on it."

Julia ended the call to restart her run.

Glancing at her nubile competitor's treadmill she noticed the pace, level five. Julia set hers to level six.

CHAPTER SIXTEEN

"Where have you been, girl?" Maria waved her hand to shoo her sister out of range while plugging her nose in mock disgust. "You smell like a ditch digger!"

Her workout clothes damp with perspiration, Julia still felt the adrenaline high of her vigorous run. Or was it the excitement of a new feature assignment? Either way, she was in a great mood no verbal abuse could alter.

"They ran out of towels at the gym so I decided to shower at home." Julia paused. Something was not quite right. "Since when do you fix dinner wearing heels? And what's with the robe?"

Maria stopped chopping carrots to look in Julia's eyes. Her doleful expression said she needed an inconvenient favor.

Julia cut to the chase. "Let me guess, you're going out."

"Remember the other day when I met with Jared's teacher?"

"OK."

"OK what?" Maria asked.

"OK I'll stay with Jared tonight so you can go out with the professor." Julia didn't want to waste part of her evening negotiating.

Maria leaped in delight. "Thanks, Sis. You're the best."

Julia agreed.

Fifteen minutes later Julia joined Jared at the table, her wet hair wrapped swami-style in a towel, the foul aroma of sweat replaced by the feminine scent of freshly applied body lotion. Jared picked at the carrots in his salad while Maria danced her way from the kitchen with a pitcher of water to fill Julia's glass.

"Don't worry about me," Julia insisted. "Go finish getting ready. We'll be fine. Right, Jared?"

He said nothing.

"Up for a chess rematch?"

He quietly lifted a single leaf to his mouth and nibbled its edge. Not a word.

"Jared, baby," Maria pleaded. "Don't be like that."

"Like what?" he huffed.

"Punishing me by ignoring Julia."

Defiantly glaring into his mother's eyes, Jared placed his fork on the table, got up, and walked to his room. As soon as he closed the door Maria looked at Julia with a shrug.

"I take it he disapproves of you dating his teacher," Julia guessed.

"I think he'd prefer I became a nun." Both sisters burst into laughter at the suggestion.

The doorbell rang.

"That'll be Fin," Maria said as she hurried toward her bedroom. "Be a doll and let him know I'll be right out. I need to put on my dress."

"His name is Fin?"

"Mr. Finelson to Jared. He told me to call him Fin."

No first name. It figures!

Removing her swami towel, Julia opened the door to greet her sister's latest conquest. He looked at least five years younger than Maria. Possibly more. Did he even shave yet?

"Hello. You must be Fin."

"And you must be Julia," he replied. "I'm here to pick up your sister."

Fin's boyish face tempted Julia to ask if he wanted Jared to come out and play hide-and-seek. She restrained herself. "She'll be right out. Please come in."

He did, gently sliding his shoes across the mat before entering.

"Is Jared around?" he asked. "I'd love to say hi while I'm here."

"I'm not sure where Jared is at the moment," she lied. "I'll let him know you asked about him."

"Great." His voice squeaked.

"Big plans tonight?"

"I hope so," he said with a sly grin.

Julia turned away to roll her eyes at the not-so-subtle implication just in time to see Maria approaching in an even less subtle dress. Julia remembered the outfit from the article she had forwarded to her sister about risqué fashion trends.

Moments later, Julia waved and wished the eager couple a good time. Returning to the kitchen, she began stacking the dishes in the sink while considering her options. Curl up with a good e-book or coax Jared out of adolescent apathy?

Jared cast his vote by opening the bedroom door. "She gone?"

"Like the wind." Her usual description of Maria's getaways. "Game of chess?"

"I guess so."

"Don't do me any favors," Julia taunted.

"No, I want to play. I'm just…" Jared seemed thoughtful, searching for the right words. He gave up. "I'm white this time."

"I'll make the popcorn."

She did, along with root beer floats capable of frothing away the deepest sorrow.

The screen taps began, moving 3-D chess pieces in a familiar opening sequence.

King's pawn to king's three.

Julia's knight jumped its pawn to queen's rook three.

White king's bishop to queen's bishop four.

Anticipating Jared's favorite speed-game opening, Julia placed a finger on her king's knight, offering her opponent a false glimmer of hope. Jared's face fell as she shifted her hand and tapped the queen's pawn to move it forward, blocking his bishop's future checkmate move.

"You really didn't think I'd fall for that sequence again, did you?"

A frustrated Jared concentrated to conceive an alternative strategy, stealing a spoonful of melting ice cream from his mug to help him mentally regroup. Julia chose the moment to ease into a conversation her nephew needed but might resent.

"It bothers you, doesn't it?"

"Nope. I'm still gonna win," Jared responded, a trickle of dark foam escaping the side of his mouth.

"I mean your mom and Mr. Finelson."

After a long silence, the eleven-year-old kid tried to express an age-old quandary. "Why does she have to…you know…be like that?"

Julia heard more than the words. Jared hated to see his mother throw herself at one man after another. It distressed him when she wore clothes that made his hormonal buddies stare or make crude comments about her body. He might have been a boy, but he couldn't suppress the desire to protect a virtue his mom didn't care to keep.

"It's embarrassing," Jared continued. "Somebody will see them together and the stories will fly. Every time kids see Mr. Fin take a call they'll jab me and hoot like they do when they watch porn."

"Porn? Really?" Julia hadn't considered Jared old enough for such things.

Surprised by her naïveté Jared looked away, embarrassed about saying so much to his aunt.

Julia took a single piece of popcorn to nibble while considering the boy's feelings.

"Your mother is a very attractive and spontaneous woman, Jared," she began. "And she deserves to be happy."

Jared stiffened. "She's not."

"Not what?"

"Happy," he explained. "At least not the way Calvin's mom is happy."

"Who's Calvin?"

"A friend of mine. We sit by each other. I go to his house on Thursdays whenever Mom needs to work late. Mrs. Nowell picks us up from school."

"And she seems happier than your mom?"

"I don't know. Maybe not happier." He reached for the right words. "Calmer. More secure. Less show-offish."

"Is *show-offish* a word?" Julia wondered aloud.

"You know what I mean."

She did. Julia knew that Maria's appeal had a dark side, an insatiable craving for male attention. Julia considered her sister's countless romantic sprees a sign of weakness. Why depend on guys to feel good about yourself? But then she recalled the sting she had felt over Jonathan Sowell's apathy. Julia too had unmet needs.

"So what makes Calvin's mom different?"

"Well, she's really pretty," Jared explained. "And she smells terrific. But none of the guys talk about her like they do Mom."

"Does she have a partner?"

"Calvin's dad, Mr. Nowell. He's great!"

Another piece of the puzzle slid into place. "Great how?"

He smiled at some unspoken recollection as he tapped a pawn on the screen to launch a modified assault. "Just great. He tells lame jokes during dinner. Nobody laughs. It's hilarious!"

Julia had never considered what it was like for a boy to grow up with two women. Jared had never met his father, a fly-by-night encounter Maria hadn't bothered to tell about the pregnancy. Nor had Jared spent any time with a fisherman grandpa or backslapping uncle. She remembered eating dinner with Angie's family as a girl. Julia knew what it was to covet a friend's daddy.

"My dad left our family when I was little," Julia said. "Four maybe. I don't remember much. Only saw him twice after the divorce, once as a flower girl in his wedding. His fiancée thought I would be the perfect adornment for the ceremony. But I got nervous and threw up on the bouquet. Turned out to be a bad omen for the marriage."

"You barfed?" Jared exclaimed. "Cool!"

"My mother loved telling that story. I don't actually remember the day. But I have seen a picture of me in the dress. I looked darling."

Julia mindlessly moved her other knight.

"Did your dad ever call?" Jared asked. "Did he write?"

Julia surprised herself by feeling a slight swell of anger. *After all this time?* she mused.

"Never heard from him again."

Two fatherless children shared a moment of isolation.

"He never contacted your mom either," Julia felt it important to add.

Both took a handful of popcorn to fill the silence.

Five moves and a checkmate later, Jared broke his string of losses and declared himself household champion. They finished the popcorn and floats while watching television before calling it a night.

After slipping into her nightgown Julia tried to ignore a nagging memory. Going home with Angie to have dinner at her house. Watching her dive into her daddy's open arms, feeling her own paternal poverty. She decided to type a quick message to the girl she had loved and envied as a child.

HI ANGIE: *I have a meeting in DC a week from Monday. If I fly in a few days early could we connect to catch up?*

Before hitting SEND, she recalled Paul's demand. "Get close again, fast."

She added one more line to the message.

I've missed you.

CHAPTER SEVENTEEN

"**An astute** observation, Miss Arrasmith," Matthew heard while slipping into the back of a large classroom where five dozen sophomores yawned their way through life's most profound questions. Only one, a vivacious brunette seated in the front row, seemed remotely interested in the topic: "Christian heresies reconsidered." On second look, however, Matthew sensed the girl was less enamored with the lecture than with the speaker, Dr. Thomas Vincent.

In his early forties, Dr. Vincent had flowing gray hair and a lean vigor that seemed fitting for a man who had renounced his vow of chastity and exchanged administering holy sacraments for evaluating doctoral dissertations.

Vincent winked in affirmation to the student, who appeared to be his favorite for reasons beyond academic initiative. "If you can remain after class for a few moments, I'd like to discuss your perspective further."

The girl smiled as two boys seated in the back nudged one another with a snigger.

Having arrived thirty minutes before his scheduled appointment, Matthew had decided to catch part of the professor's lecture. He had hoped to audit the entire semester, but paying the additional parent-sitting fees was out of the question. Walking into the classroom stirred Matthew's resentment at a vague target. Whom could he blame? Certainly not his mother. She hadn't chosen to get sick. His dad? How could you blame an unspecified sperm-bank donor for failing to support a nameless recipient? Himself? What else could he do? Mom only had one child and there was no one else to help her. His oppressor remained anonymous.

Matthew found an empty chair and settled in, eager to glean from an intellect few in the room seemed clever or disciplined enough to appreciate.

"Rosalyn raises an important point," the professor continued. "While we often see church history as those in power defending their territory, it's an oversimplification to say all church leaders were corrupt or all motives impure."

Matthew admired Dr. Vincent's balanced handling of the church fathers. His book did not paint them as villains, just mistaken. During all three brief conversations the two had shared in the coffee shop Matthew had sensed philosophical alignment, possibly rooted in their lingering respect for a church both had left.

"Don't be afraid to give credit to the Christian ideals where credit is due. Denying the good things that came from the church won't nullify their dogma. It will just make you appear ignorant."

A hand raised. "I thought you said the evils of the Inquisition can be blamed on church dogma."

"Close. I said trying to enforce compliance with church orthodoxy led its leaders to betray Jesus's teachings. He never advocated killing pagans and infidels. He taught his followers to love their enemies."

"But he also said he came to bring a sword." The student raised the stakes.

"The Gospel of Matthew, chapter ten, verse thirty-four. Very good, Mr. Fuller." The boy's thumbs stretched invisible suspenders in self-congratulation. "But we need to observe what Jesus *did* to properly understand what he *said*."

"Meaning?"

"Meaning he told his followers to put away their swords at the very moment they tried to protect him. Meaning he, like Socrates, chose suicide over betraying his ideals. Meaning, Mr. Fuller, that he demonstrated the ultimate purpose of life."

"Which is?" the student asked.

"Transcending oneself."

The answer skimmed classroom heads like a stone skipping along the water before sinking in for Matthew. *Free them to thrive.*

"What the church fathers missed," Dr. Vincent continued, "was the purpose of Jesus's martyrdom. They created the myth of a bodily resurrection to portray him as a death-conquering deity. In reality, he discarded his body as a death-embracing mystic."

"I can think of much better things to do with my body!" The comment came from a sneering hedonist in the back row. Dr. Vincent's disarming smile released a sprinkling of macho guffaws.

"Like every great prophet from Moses to the Dalai Lama," he continued, "Jesus modeled a path to fulfillment much more intense than anything even Mr. Thurman's body can give."

Laughter swelled as the girls cheered the counterpunch.

"Better than sex?" a guy seated immediately in front of Matthew asked.

Dr. Vincent glanced at his watch. "Different from sex. But we'll unpack that after you finish the assigned reading covering the first church council. Come ready next time to discuss chapter three, 'Arius Reconsidered.'"

A chorus of slothful groans reminded Matthew that he deserved college more than most of those enrolled.

"I'll see you next week." Dr. Vincent discharged his prisoners as the brunette sprang forward to relish his personal attention.

Matthew's approach seemed an unwelcome distraction from Rosalyn's admiring gaze. Dr. Vincent had apparently forgotten their appointment. *Understandable*, Matthew thought as he ogled the professor's groupie.

"Hello, Matthew," Thomas said while hastily scratching out a handwritten note. "I'll be with you in a second."

Matthew remained just out of range, unable to decipher the writing. *A book title? A lecture podcast? The name of a hotel?* Regardless, the words denoted a life Matthew envied and, if he believed his mother, deserved.

◆

Fifteen minutes later Matthew and the professor entered the vestibule of a gothic building that had once held a steady stream of people lighting candles for deceased parents, struggling children, or world peace. More like a museum than a church, St. Thomas Aquinas University Parish now served as the place Dr. Vincent reflected in solitude or hosted rare chats with those students curious about the ideas explored in his classes.

"I see what you mean," Matthew said. "Very tranquil."

"I like it," Thomas said while removing his scarf. "I've done some of my best thinking in that pew right over there." He pointed to a row next to last. "Far away from the presence of Christ, but not as far as I could be."

Both smiled.

"How's your mother?" The question surprised Matthew. He had only mentioned her once to the professor, nearly two months before.

"She's fine, I guess," he responded. "It's thoughtful of you to remember."

"Dementia?"

"That's right. She has good days and bad. More bad lately."

"I'm sorry."

A brief silence.

"So, what's on your mind, Matthew Adams?"

Matthew retrieved a digital tablet from his coat pocket. It woke with a ping. The sound seemed out of place amid icons and relics from a bygone era.

"I've been doing some reading and I want to ask you about an idea I think has merit."

"I love discussing ideas of merit," Thomas replied. "Shoot."

"Have you ever heard of something called Manichaean philosophy?" Matthew sounded doubtful. "I'm not sure of the right pronunciation."

"You got it right," Thomas affirmed. "And yes, I have. St. Augustine was schooled in Manichaean philosophy prior to his Christian conversion."

"That's it. What's your opinion of it?"

"Do you mean my opinion of the philosophy or my opinion of its being labeled heresy?"

"I suppose both," Matthew responded.

Thomas grinned. Nothing kindled his passion like an eager, open mind. "How much of today's lecture did you hear?"

"None really. Just a few questions at the end where you touched on the true meaning of Christ's martyrdom."

"Why the fascination with Manichaean philosophy? It's not exactly recreational reading."

"I'm working on a thesis about spiritual environmentalism." The statement fell flat, less impressive than it had sounded to his coffee shop colleagues. "I should say, I'd like to develop the idea if I ever go to grad school."

"You'll get there," Thomas said with well-meaning condescension.

Matthew felt both affirmed and put in his place.

"As I started to say during class today, the early church missed the point of Jesus's death. Manichaean philosophers offered something that I think came closer to Jesus's intentions."

"Is that what you meant by understanding Jesus's words in light of his actions?"

"Nice to know someone was listening."

"I think I know what you meant about Jesus's martyrdom."

Thomas appeared pleased. "Do you? Let's hear it then."

"The church presented Jesus's death as an act of sacrifice for sin. But what he really did was demonstrate what it means to abandon the body for a purely spiritual existence."

"Very good, Matthew. Hence, Manichaean philosophy. I think Augustine had it right before he submitted to church dogma about Jesus. The Manichaeans taught that the physical body is evil, a prison cell keeping us from our true nature."

Spirit good. Body bad, Matthew recalled.

"They rejected the idea that Jesus was God in the flesh because God, pure spirit, would never defile himself by becoming a material being," Thomas explained further.

"So freeing ourselves from the prison of flesh is the ultimate meaning of Jesus's life and teachings?"

"I think so. That's why I left the priesthood. Official church teachings demand the celebration of Christ's incarnation and affirmation of a bodily resurrection. I could no longer do either."

"What changed your mind?" Matthew asked.

"My spirit changed before my mind changed," Thomas admitted. "My conversion, pardon the expression, began in the confession booth."

"Confession booth?"

"You may laugh, but my journey out of orthodox Christianity began with the body odor and bad breath of my parishioners."

Matthew thought of his mother. Her soft beauty had become harsh and haggard, her clear mind confused. And yes, her fresh scent had been overcome by smells of stale perspiration and dehydrated urine. "I think I understand."

"We decay, Matthew. Why would a good God create a decaying masterpiece?" Thomas paused to let the question stew. "I don't think he or she would do that. The Manichaeans, like the ancient pagans, including Plato, understood what the church fathers missed. So did Arius."

"Arius?" Matthew reached to recall the context of the name he had seen in Dr. Vincent's book.

"Fourth century. The Gnostics influenced him. Like the Manichaeans, they saw God as ultimate goodness that could not become matter since matter itself was considered evil. Every major controversy of early church history came back to the same question. 'Did God, who is pure and perfect spirit, defile his purity by becoming a material being?'"

"The doctrine of the incarnation!"

"Exactly. God becoming man suggested good becoming evil. In short, they didn't think God could have bad breath."

Matthew sat quietly for a moment, hesitant to admit what remained hidden beneath the surface of his questions.

"My mom is deteriorating quickly. She needs me more than ever. She's unhappy. So am I."

The comments splashed cold water in Dr. Vincent's face, jarring him from the abstract world of ideas he loved to the gritty reality of Matthew's here-and-now dilemma. He said the only thing he could. "We decay."

Decay...

Decay...

Decay...

The word bounced off the distant walls with fading repetition. Matthew turned to survey a hollow building once alive with rituals celebrating a creed he hoped false. He wanted to escape the images and ideas that continued to make him feel tentative, even guilty, for wanting to liberate his mother.

Give those burdened the freedom to thrive, he thought, resentment and relief flowering within.

"Do you ever read a columnist named Julia Davidson?" Matthew asked.

"Sometimes. Pretty on target, I think. Why?"

"She used a phrase I found interesting in a piece on genetic screening." Matthew tapped his tablet screen to recover a highlighted quotation before handing it to his unwitting mentor.

I hope she will give the baby the freedom to thrive by eliminating the risk of unnecessary disease and disability. I only wish we could give the same freedom to those of us already burdened by both.

Thomas returned the device with apprehension. "Matthew. What's this about?"

Matthew wanted to say more, to trust Thomas Vincent with his moral quandary.

Tell him what you want to do.

He'll understand.

He might even approve.

"Thank you, Father…" Matthew blushed at the mistake. "I mean *Dr.* Vincent. You've been a big help."

CHAPTER EIGHTEEN

"I'm afraid you only have two choices," the elderly woman squeezed through grinding teeth, her thinning patience on overtime. "Keep the seat you've been assigned or wait for the next flight later this afternoon."

Julia's brow furrowed at both options. Booking at the last minute had forced the humiliation of a middle seat in coach, probably cramped between two armrest hogs. Despite her gold status with the airline, she couldn't get an upgrade to either first or business class. But Angie Tolbert expected her to arrive before six o'clock. The later flight wouldn't depart Denver International Airport until four thirty, landing in DC after eight p.m. East Coast time.

She checked her bag and headed toward a security line much longer than usual while opening the airline app on her tablet. Twenty-three minutes and seventeen, sixteen, fifteen, fourteen seconds until takeoff. There were twelve impatient travelers between her and the body scanner, each glaring at the front of the line, where a pregnant mother awkwardly removed her squirming toddler from a stroller while her husband scolded an older brother. The kid had climbed onto the baggage treadmill, hoping to ride one of the personal belongings tubs through the X-ray machine.

"Breeders!" Julia heard someone say with a sneer.

"Sure hope they aren't on my flight," added another.

After three unsuccessful attempts to move through the scanner, the unruly clan finally cleared security thanks to a supervisor who overruled an entry-level officer trying to validate his existence. Nineteen minutes and fifty-three, fifty-two, fifty-one seconds remained for twelve others to pass before Julia could sprint to her gate. Still too close to call.

Julia pulled up Angie's message to consider her options should she miss the flight.

HI JULIA: *I'd love to reconnect! Kevin suggested that we plan a girls' getaway. Let me know if you can arrive by 6 p.m. and I'll reserve dinner at Ruth's Chris and then we can stay at the Four Seasons to enjoy morning pampering in the spa. Our guest room is yours if you want to stay at the house Saturday and Sunday. I can't wait to see you! I need a break, and a friend.*

Julia smiled, then panicked. She hadn't intended to spend the entire weekend with Angie. One evening would have been more than enough. But she had accepted the offer anyway. Time with the family might prove helpful. Who better to gain access to Kevin's bright spots coalition than his wife's former, renewed best friend?

◆

The cabin door closed moments after Julia found a space to stuff her carry-on bag. The flight attendant seemed eager to get his final passenger seated before the last two minutes and forty-one seconds drained from the on-time-departure countdown clock. A heavyset woman shimmied herself out of the aisle seat, clearly disappointed by Julia's arrival.

Julia looked beyond her temporary torture chamber to see her other tormentor, an ornery looking five-year-old boy freshly incensed by a father's tongue-lashing—the same kid who had delayed the security line to turn the X-ray machine into an amusement park ride. Noticing the child's flustered parents and baby sister seated across the adjoining aisle, Julia decided to take a shot. "Want to sit in the middle seat to be closer to your mommy and daddy?"

"I wanna look out the window!"

Of course.

Buckling her belt while the large woman squeezed back into her seat, Julia breathed a sigh of relief over having made the flight.

"Welcome aboard American United Flight two-five-five to Washington, DC," the voice said with haste. Julia tuned out the captain to plan her next three hours. She needed to act preemptively before either seatmate could initiate conversation. Remembering the journal files Jeremy Santos had given her a few days before, she reached for the tablet buried in the shoulder bag she had stuffed in the space beneath her feet. A quick retrieval provided the ideal excuse to lock herself behind an invisible wall of solitary confinement.

"My name is Tyler. What's yours?"

In no mood to chat, Julia placed her index finger over her lips to imply the captain expected silence from every passenger.

"Can I play a game?" the boy asked, after glancing to make sure his parents weren't listening to his hushed request. "My daddy lets me play games on his tablet in the car."

Ignoring the question, Julia searched her bag for an age-appropriate consolation prize. "Would you like a breath mint?"

The boy nodded eagerly before forcing a mock gag at the wintergreen scent.

The lights dimmed for the video safety instructions. Seven minutes later Julia opened the Santos folder while the kid admired his bird's-eye view of the snowcapped mountains below.

The folder contained two icons. The first, labeled SYLVIA SANTOS'S JOURNAL, contained files sequenced from August of 2023 through a final entry entered the morning of Antonio's transition. The second, titled ANTONIO'S MUSINGS, contained less than half as many files.

Julia chose the mother's journal. Tempted to read the last date first, she decided to start at the beginning out of respect for Jeremy's intent.

<u>August 19, 2023</u>: Last week we brought Antonio home from the hospital. He's a perfect little gentleman, never crying except when hungry. Last night he slept through the night. Jeremy didn't do that for months. Ramon seemed relieved. He's been on edge over the responsibility of another child. Seems we're off to a good start. Thank you, God, for another beautiful boy!

<u>August 30, 2023</u>: I'm finally feeling rested enough to journal again. Nina took the boys last night to give Ramon and me a break from diapers and the feeding schedule. I've healed up pretty well so we made love for the first time since seven months pregnant. Probably a mistake since I haven't had my episiotomy follow-up exam. I'm a bit sore this morning. But neither of us could stop ourselves. I think it relieved some of Ramon's stress. Mine too.

<u>September 5, 2023</u>: I nearly had a heart attack today when Jeremy dropped Antonio on his tiny head. He insisted he was strong enough to hold his brother. My heart melted when he bent over to kiss Antonio's hairless forehead. It happened when I left them for a second to grab the camera. I'm such an idiot!

I'm grateful he fell on the rug instead of hitting the end table. I would never forgive myself if I let something like that happen. I wasn't going to tell Ramon, but Jeremy blurted out "Antonio fell on his head!" as soon as Daddy walked in the door. The lack of fear in Ramon's eyes scared me. The baby is fine, but I'm a bit shaken.

The further Julia read the larger the gaps became, once or twice per week at the beginning dwindling down to once every few months toward the end. Either Sylvia Santos lacked journaling discipline or, more likely, Jeremy had screened and selected specific entries to reveal a central narrative. Julia scanned through the newborn years, trying to piece together the main plot of Act One.

Scene One: A young wife tries to preserve her sexually charged marriage despite a husband who resents the interruption of two kids.

Scene Two: Sex becomes infrequent as she becomes less available to him and he seems less interested in her.

Scene Three: The husband becomes more patient with their waning passion. Too patient. She fears he has been having his needs met elsewhere but is too frightened to risk confrontation.

Scene Four: Early signs something is wrong with Antonio trump concerns about the marriage. Mom hides her worries and avoids genetic testing because she doesn't want to further disenchant an increasingly detached dad.

After nearly thirty minutes of reading, Julia noticed a long gap between the next two journal dates. She clicked the first, which was much longer than prior entries. The start of Act Two.

September 12, 2026: I've been crying most of the past two days. My worst fears are true. The doctor said Antonio's slow development is caused by a motor neuron disease. I can't remember the initials or what they stand for. All I know is that he won't get better. The doctor said he will most likely get worse over time. He wouldn't say how much worse since the disease has usually infected adults. Infected is the wrong word. Inherited. He said Antonio has a genetic disorder that could have been screened out.

I feel so guilty.

How am I going to tell Ramon? I'm glad he's out of town. I need to think.

Nina and Marcos said they would pray for healing. They go to a church where people do that sort of thing. They said I needed to have faith. But the doctor told me Antonio would gradually lose all use of his limbs and his voice. Dear God! Why my son? Why anyone?

Julia opened the next journal entry, propelling her more than six months forward in time.

<u>March 21, 2027</u>: Ramon is gone. He walked into the house after driving home from the airport yesterday and said we needed to talk. He looked slumpish, like a kid forced to tell the neighbor he smashed his window with a baseball. I knew something was wrong when I noticed him carrying a large, new suitcase instead of the travel bag he'd taken three days earlier. I asked him to wait a minute because I was in the middle of bathing Antonio. He started to fidget, like I was messing up his perfect plan. I didn't know the other woman was in the car impatiently waiting for him to wrap up the last-minute detail of his marriage and family.

He slunk into our room to pack his clothes. He found Jeremy hiding in the closet.

"Close the door, Daddy," he said. "I'm playing hide-and-seek with Mommy!" I had forgotten about the search.

The bastard told Jeremy first. I learned of my divorce eavesdropping on a little boy's nightmare.

"You have to go where?"

"Don't worry, buddy. I'll visit you all the time. I just can't live with your mommy anymore."

Holding Antonio in a towel at the door, I started to cry. Not for me. For Jeremy. I saw the panic in his face, a five-year-old desperately trying to think of how he might prevent his daddy's exile. He looked at me, pleading with his eyes. "Do something to make it all right."

I should have listened to Nina. She suspected an affair. I got mad at her, partly because I knew she was right. Ramon had been pretending for more than a year. I had been tiptoeing around his agitation and apathy ever since receiving Antonio's genetic profile.

Ramon said he needs more than I can give. He's right. I miss the days he couldn't keep his hands off me. Kids change things, especially one like Antonio. I guess it's my own fault. I fell for the red-hot lover instead of a plain-vanilla guy like Nina's husband. I think Marcos has hugged Antonio more often than Ramon has. I've known Antonio was doomed to grow up without his father's affection. Now Jeremy will too.

God forgive me.

God help me.

A tap on her wrist startled Julia, reminding her of her imprisonment. She looked up to notice the flight attendant handing her a small carton of chocolate milk.

"Would you pass this, please?"

She handed the drink to the eager child. He punched the tab and took his first sip, a tiny trickle of brown escaping the side of his mouth. It dripped onto the corner of a half-finished coloring book page.

Julia studied the boy's carefree face, trying to imagine him in place of another five-year-old watching a father pack, weeping after another cancellation of a promised visit, pleading with his mother to let Daddy come back home. She turned and looked across the aisle at Tyler's father, a plain-vanilla husband rubbing his wife's arm as she stole a nap while their baby gulped a bottle of juice.

The kind of man her sister Maria would never notice, let alone date.

The kind of breeder her best editorials scorned.

The kind of daddy the boy seated beside her would kiss good night.

CHAPTER NINETEEN

The eighth and final pretzel clung stubbornly to the bottom of a tiny plastic bag, resisting Julia's attempt to secure one last tease of nourishment. She should have eaten before boarding the plane but had failed to account for the two-hour time difference. Landing in DC at one o'clock eastern meant flying right through her usual lunch. A diet soda and mini carb packet couldn't compete with the aroma of a turkey-and-salami sandwich her plump seatmate pulled from a large lap purse or the apple slices Tyler had consumed between sips of chocolate milk. Her stomach growled beneath the hum of jet engines propelling 350 passengers toward the most powerful city on earth.

With more than an hour remaining on the flight Julia debated between reading more of the Santos journals and compiling a list of questions for her upcoming interviews. Despite the human drama of the Santos story, her career depended on understanding and exposing the cryptic Bright Spots proposal. She closed the journal folder to open her calendar, where she found two Monday appointments.

10:30 A.M.: NEVADA CONGRESSWOMAN NICOLE FLOREA (CAPITOL BUILDING)
3:00 P.M.: TRISHA SAYERS, CEO OF HER LOOK INC. (101 WATERSIDE COURT NEAR NATIONAL HARBOR OFFICE COMPLEX)

Paul had arranged the interviews with both longtime acquaintances. He had said Nicole Florea would be a great voice to counter any anti–Youth Initiative rhetoric. Florea was a respected fiscal conservative, so she would be difficult for anyone on the radical right to marginalize. Trisha Sayers, a heroine of capitalism who embodied the dramatic ascent of the fairer sex, could bring celebrity and glamour to the debate. Together they would provide a strong voice for progressive ideas. That was the easy part. Getting inside the mind of anti-progressives would likely prove much more difficult.

Before drafting a list of interview questions, Julia immersed herself in the topic. She had compiled a CliffsNotes version of the Youth Initiative controversy starting with the 2036 presidential election cycle.

It was the heyday of the new conservative movement that won elections in landslides by promising an economic utopia. It took credit for curtailing restrictive governmental regulations on the burgeoning genetic technologies industry. Nearly a hundred thousand ideas had been filed with the global patent office since 2031, when the movement had managed to pass the Genomic Frontier legislation removing many restrictive ethical safeguards from university and corporate scientists. Most inventions had attracted massive infusions of research and development funding from aging venture capitalists hoping to cash in on a gold rush of health-care and life-enhancement innovations.

Julia recalled one of her earliest editorials. She had been a young journalist at the time. She reluctantly praised fiscal conservatives who had courageously defied their religiously rigid base. "It's high time level heads started to find common ground with social progressives," she had written.

RAP Syndicate ran a daily feature in the Life and Tech department highlighting some of the most promising new developments. She recalled several headlines.

CANCER EXTINCT IN FIVE YEARS?
HORMONE GLAND REFURBISHED IN 90-YEAR-OLD MAN
WILL ARTIFICIAL WOMBS SAVE US FROM STRETCH MARKS?
OBESITY ON THE RUN AS NANO-BOTS DEVOUR FAT CELLS
DOUBLE-SIZE CORN HUSKS YIELD CHEAPER BIOFUEL

Lance Lowman rode a wave of optimistic speculation into the White House in 2036, his party ushering in what some described as a return to Camelot: no wars, terrorist attacks in decline, and stock markets soaring. Within a few short years, said common wisdom, decades-old deficits would evaporate in the wake of unprecedented economic growth.

Then the bubble burst. Too few patents delivered on their promises, causing skittish seniors to pull out of stocks to salvage what remained of their dwindling retirement savings. The few genetic advances that turned a profit did so on the backs of taxpayers because they served the federally subsidized senior-care industry. Federal and state entitlement spending mushroomed. The boom brought very little of the new growth that had been projected. A bullish gen-tech stock boom turned bearish overnight, losing nearly half of its value in less than a month.

The crusading radicals on the far right seemed to gloat. "Demographics control destiny," they chided, claiming falling fertility had undercut what little growth had come from all those seniors' investing in their own longevity. "More 80-year-olds performing in bed can't mask our true impotence," wrote a particularly obnoxious columnist. "We are paying the price for neglecting to produce a new crop of entrepreneurs and taxpayers."

Whatever the reason, optimistic growth projections slammed into the wall of massive spending increases, leaving the president's fiscal conservatives holding the gun at the very moment people wondered who had killed the economy.

To his credit, the president took decisive action. He proposed a solution that angered his far-right-wing supporters but that united the far left and moderate elements of both political parties. The Youth Initiative seemed based on a commonsense and compassionate idea: to give seniors and other dependent adults the right to transition resources to the younger generation rather than hoard it for their own preservation. Rejecting the failed policies of other developed nations with aging populations, the president said, "America should chart a boldly different course that continues our unique legacy of individual autonomy and concern for the common welfare." In other words, reduce entitlement spending and incentivize wealth transfer from those draining the economy.

The proposal passed both houses of Congress with a two-thirds majority. If even 5 percent of ailing seniors opted for transition, projected the Congressional Budget Office, the initiative could reduce federal entitlement spending by hundreds of billions per year. It would also improve the economic situation for millions of younger workers while generating a healthy revenue stream that would keep the program in the black. A win-win-win.

Not surprisingly, however, some religious leaders expressed moral outrage and called the Youth Initiative "a Nazi-like solution that diminishes the dignity of human life."

Julia had never understood their objections. She wondered how letting each person choose his or her expiration date takes away dignity. Wasn't personal autonomy a great American value? Why would anyone want to stop a sickly, aging senior from giving scarce resources to others by transitioning?

But, unbelievably, many protested. The usual suspects: religious zealots who would rather thump Bibles than solve problems, frumpy moms who would rather pollute the planet than use birth control, and patriarchal men who thought the only good female was a pregnant one. This same backward thinking had come to inform growing opposition to the transition industry.

Opening a blank document file, Julia proceeded to capture questions that could steer interviewees toward the expectations of one person, Paul Daugherty. It was his view, not theirs, that would dominate the feature. It was his opinion alone that would determine her professional fate. It was his agenda, not the facts, that would dictate success.

Five minutes later a friendly voice asked all those on board to return their seats to the upright position and place digital devices in safe mode. Julia quickly scanned her work. Satisfied, she powered down the tablet and returned it to the bag at her feet.

Peering through the small gap of window above Tyler's glass-pressed face, she saw the outskirts of the nation's capital. Adrenaline surged as she anticipated walking the halls of power. The boy turned, extending his right index finger toward Julia.

"What should I do with this?"

As she searched frantically for a tissue, a man's hand appeared from across the aisle. It was Tyler's father passing an airline-branded napkin he must have saved for just such an occasion.

CHAPTER TWENTY

"Kevin?" Julia was momentarily startled at the sight of the man opening the door to greet her. This wasn't Kevin Tolbert, Angie's hunky high school sweetheart. Nor was it the jeans-wearing entrepreneur who had made his mark before turning thirty. This was Congressman Tolbert, clean-shaven face above a slightly loosened necktie. He had unfastened the top button of his classic white dress shirt, but his dark suit still conveyed an air of authority she found impressively out of place on her friend's adolescent heartthrob.

"That's what they name us..." he began, pausing for effect.

"And soon we'll be famous!" Julia joined him in unison while rolling her eyes at the recollection of Kevin's annoying signature line. Not as much had changed as it had appeared.

Both extended arms for the kind of embrace estranged relatives give at holiday gatherings when they don't know what to say. Slightly rigid and awkward, but better than a simple handshake, which would not have fit the occasion of Angie and Julia's long-overdue reunion.

"Good to see you, Julia." He seemed to mean it. "Angie's pretty excited about this weekend."

"Yeah. Me too," she lied with overdone enthusiasm.

"Let me take your bag." His extended hand stopped short. "Wait. I guess you'll need it at the hotel tonight?"

Julia wondered who should make the next move, guest or host.

The faint sound of a plop and a splash came from around the corner, followed by the ascending whimper of a panicky toddler. Kevin winced.

"Ugh! I forgot the sippy cup lid again!" The dashing power broker morphed into a plain-vanilla daddy on cleanup duty.

"Do what you need to do," Julia said eagerly. "I'll be fine."

"Angie's in the bedroom packing," Kevin said, as he moved toward the dining room. "Third door on the left."

Reaching the hallway, Julia noticed several picture frames hanging on the wall. She paused, taking advantage of the moment to connect baby announcement names with gallery faces.

The five-year-old version of Kevin had to be Tommy, the spitting image of his daddy. Especially in his bright-eyed smile eager to befriend a world full of waiting adventures.

Joy looked about two and a half. She seemed graced with a hint of Angie's delicate beauty. The photo of mom and daughter in matching dresses seconded the motion.

Leah was harder to place. Her picture, taken at about six months old, offered few maternal or paternal clues. Hardly an expert on childhood development patterns, Julia assumed the baby's features were simply too young to resemble either parent's.

While mentally preparing herself to knock on Angie's door Julia paused in front of a series of pictures assembled in a single frame. None included the kids; most likely they had been taken during various romantic escapes or anniversary trips.

Angie the bikini model beside a slightly thinner Kevin on

the beach. Despite sunglasses and the white sand beneath a clear blue sky in the background, neither appeared to have been spending much time in the sun.

Their honeymoon in Cancún, Julia remembered.

The happy couple sitting in what must have been a five-star restaurant beside a bottle of Californian zinfandel. He was flashing a wide grin while pointing to a thin strip of white paper with a blue dot.

Dinner celebrating the discovery Angie is pregnant with Tommy.

Kevin in a tux beside a very pregnant Angie wearing an elegant black cocktail dress and heels. They stood in front of a *Les Misérables* marquee next to a stretch limousine. She appeared very uncomfortable. He appeared madly in love.

Thirteenth anniversary trip? she guessed after counting fingers from their 2027 wedding year and calculating Leah's delivery date.

The thought of two people she'd known in high school celebrating thirteen years of marriage and spawning three kids prompted Julia to wag her head in disbelief. Few of her other friends had long-term monogamous partners, let alone more than a single offspring.

Here goes, she thought while gently tapping a closed bedroom door.

◆

They hugged, awkwardly at first, before either said a word. Their embrace released the familiar scent of Angie's favorite perfume. Julia felt at once accepted…and suddenly ashamed. She was the one who had eased away from the friendship, made excuses to cancel trips, forgotten to send birthday cards. Angie had never stopped missing, inviting, and accepting her teen companion. Standing face-to-face after nearly five years of avoidance tactics, Julia searched Angie's eyes for signs of a well-deserved rebuke.

Angie spoke first. "I'm so glad you came."

A pile of discarded clothes beside the partially full suitcase suggested she had been playing musical chairs with her closet, modeling one outfit after another, hoping to look her best without appearing to have tried.

"I really need my friend."

The comment surprised Julia as much as Angie's apparent unease. This was the gorgeous cheerleader who had attracted guys like flies to honey just before her strict religious beliefs shooed them away. If not for a purity fetish, she might have beat Maria's record for most requests to the senior prom. Angie had always held her head high regardless of what anyone else thought. Always seemed secure in who she was. Julia had always admired her friend's grounded confidence. Had something changed?

Julia noticed the silence between them. It was her turn to say something. Anything. She had decided not to script this moment, intending to pick up the friendship where they had left off, two girls separated by time and space who still shared a unique history. The same teachers, favorite movies, and inside jokes. She had imagined Angie saying something to offer instant reconnection to their former intimacy. But that task now fell to Julia. She reached deeply. Nothing came.

"You look wonderful," Julia said at last.

Angie stepped away to give Julia the once-over. "Well. You certainly haven't changed a bit!"

Julia blushed slightly at the reference to her size-two figure, the same as it had been when they'd last seen one another. Was the comment sincere flattery from a friend or jealous envy from a woman who had matured into a less girlish size eight?

"You're still absolutely beautiful."

Julia scolded herself. *Why did I say "still"?*

The sound of tiny footsteps approached from the hallway, followed by Kevin's distant voice. "Come back here, Tommy. Leave Mommy alone, she needs—"

It was too late. Tommy interrupted the first moments of the reunion, much to Julia's relief.

"Well, who have we here?" Julia said, bending down to admire Angie's first. "I bet your name is Tommy."

He froze and nodded, unaccustomed to seeing another mommy in his parents' room.

"What's your name?" he asked, like a cop about to arrest a trespassing criminal.

"This is my very good friend, Ms. Davidson," Angie said.

He lowered his guard on the word of the character witness.

"You can call me Aunt Julia."

The offer drew a beaming grin. "I have anothew aunt?"

"You do now," Julia said. "And I get to stay at your house after your mommy and I get back home!"

Another officer scowl. "Back? Mommy, are you weaving?"

"Ms. Davidson…I mean Aunt Julia and I are going out to dinner and staying at a hotel tonight, but we'll be back tomorrow afternoon."

He turned and ran from the room, apparently to report Mommy's pending escape to Officer Daddy.

"Did I blow your plan?" Julia asked.

"Kevin suggested keeping it secret from the kids until I was gone to avoid a scene. I told him it wouldn't work, but he insisted."

The sounds of Joy's wail turned Angie's prediction into Kevin's crisis.

"They don't like it when I'm gone, which is part of the reason I need to go." She paused to correct the impression. "I'm crazy about the kids, but I need a few hours of uninterrupted adult conversation."

After tossing a swimsuit and toiletries into the open bag Angie latched her suitcase and playfully grabbed her accomplice by the arm.

"Let's make a getaway while we can!"

CHAPTER TWENTY-ONE

Angie didn't know what to expect from the dinner with Julia. Catching up on the latest news from each other's lives, laughing at shared memories of high school mishaps, or perhaps providing girl-to-girl advice on skin-care products. Anything but a massive assault on her sense of significance.

Julia meant no harm. She probably wasn't even aware of what caused the offense, making Angie feel even more pathetic.

The first affront came when Angie noticed half of the restaurant's eyes following Julia as she returned to the table after visiting the ladies' room. When they were young, Angie had attracted most of the attention. Back then guys appreciated Julia for her brains instead of her body, despite the fact that she was one of the prettiest girls on campus. Angie rebuked herself for such a silly reaction. She was a happily married mother of three. Still, it stung knowing she had gone largely unnoticed.

The second surfaced when a series of innocent questions constricted air from Angie's suffocating ego.

Had Angie continued her part-time nursing job?

Did they maintain their Colorado residence?

How often did they get to ski since moving to DC?

Had Kevin met the president?

Did she like the latest film by some foreign director whose name Angie didn't recognize?

After an hour of conversation Julia had failed to ask a single question about the central focus of Angie's existence, her children. The friend in whom Angie had hoped to confide, from whom she had intended to seek comfort over Leah's condition, had not come. Julia, like nearly every other adult in her life, was engrossed in what she considered far more significant affairs.

The third affront occurred when Julia finally recognized the past five years of Angie's existence.

"So, three kids. What's that like?"

It wasn't really a question. More a reprimand mixed with bewildered curiosity, as from a child whose sibling had caved in to parental pressure by actually eating the steamed broccoli. Angie held her tongue, trying to come up with a response that would give Julia the benefit of the doubt.

That's when Julia added insult to injury. "I don't think I could do it."

"Do what? Have children?" Angie forced a lilt, but still sounded defensive.

The air thickened as Julia rummaged for words that might rescue the conversation. "Well, yes. I mean, no. I guess I'm just amazed by what you're doing."

Julia lifted her glass to take a sip of iced tea, apparently hoping the condescending compliment had soothed any offense.

"Like what?"

"Excuse me?" Julia asked.

"What's amazing about it?" Angie wasn't fishing for a compliment. She was calling a bluff.

"I don't know. The whole thing."

Angie stared silently, allowing her friend a moment to think.

Julia started to mention specifics but stopped short, clearly at a loss.

"Do you mean like giving up a perfect figure and paycheck in order to remove the crust from peanut butter sandwiches and read the same bedtime story every night for a month?"

Julia laughed more than the comment deserved, then stopped when it became clear Angie was not making a joke. "Did I say something wrong?"

The question alerted Angie to her own intensity. "No. I'm sorry. I guess I'm just..." She paused. "It's been a difficult month. I'm feeling a bit on edge. Like I said, I need my friend."

Both smiled at the temporary truce.

"Do you want to talk about it?" Julia asked.

Tempted by the offer, Angie decided no. "Maybe later. Let's order dessert."

Another mistake. They "shared" the Ruth's Chris infamous "simply sinful" chocolate layer cake. After one small bite Julia instinctively slid her fork aside. Angie reluctantly did the same.

Opening the door to her third-floor hotel room, Angie felt more alone than ever. While exiting the elevator at floor two, Julia had claimed exhaustion from a long day as an excuse to skip the Jacuzzi. Angie had been searching for an excuse herself, hoping for a reprieve from cautiously stilted conversation. Girls' night out had turned out quite different from what she had scripted.

Julia was supposed to gush over Tommy, Joy, and Leah. Especially Leah.

She was supposed to admire Angie's role in Kevin's influence and success rather than view her as an unemployed nurse demoted to baby factory.

They were supposed to talk about books they'd read, causes they'd supported, dreams they'd shared, and memories they cherished.

But both had changed. Life had created a gulf between them.

They lived in different worlds. Worse, on opposing sides. But opposing sides of what? Even the most innocent topics seemed to fall in the firing line of some conflict Angie could not write off to mere differences of opinion.

Much of the conversation had focused on Julia's career or Kevin's agenda, giving Angie an inkling of the chasm neither seemed able to bridge.

"Do you ever read my column?" Julia had asked.

Angie stretched the truth. "When I'm able." She had let her subscription lapse while pregnant with Tommy. Most of Julia's readers were childless singles. Angie was neither. In a sincere effort to catch up on her friend's writing career she asked Julia for the titles and dates of the five feature articles or columns she felt best about. Angie quickly jotted down titles. The closest things her friend had to children.

#1: *Guylanders* from spring of 2034. No surprise. It was Julia's most celebrated work to date. Angie and Kevin had both agreed with Julia's take on the growing pool of immature men.

#2: *Paternal Good Riddance* from February 2036.

#3: *What's Conception Got to Do with It?* from October 2039.

#4: *Mommy Knows Better* from May 2040.

#5: *Free to Thrive* from the previous week.

The final title seemed safe territory. "Last week's column?" Angie asked.

"I wrote it after a conversation with a mutual friend of ours, Molly Carson."

"Jolly Molly?" Angie smiled in recollection of the heavyset class comedian. "I haven't heard from her in years. I'm pretty sure her parents still attend the church I grew up in. How is she?"

Julia's reply seemed cryptic, as if she hoped to protect Molly from Angie's expected disapproval. "She's fine. Trying to have a baby."

"Molly? When did she get married?" Angie corrected herself to avoid causing offense. "I mean. Does she have a partner?"

"The column is about Molly's decision to have a baby on her own," Julia explained. "Although I didn't use her name, of course." She then seemed to start quoting portions of her own writing. "Her parents disapprove. They want her to find a partner before becoming a mom. They also caution her against engineering her child by vetting for common genetic imperfections."

Angie was not sure she wanted to know the answer, but asked anyway. "What did she decide?"

"She hit the brakes. But I think she'll go ahead once she works through the conflict with her folks. She's a pretty levelheaded gal."

Levelheaded, Angie thought. *As opposed to knuckleheaded religious types who choose marriage and natural conception.*

That's when Angie decided against discussing Leah's diagnosis. It was also when she felt most alone.

Angie returned to unpacking her suitcase. Moments later, she called home.

"Hi, Mommy!" Tommy always beat Daddy to the draw.

"Hi, sweetheart. How's my favorite little boy?"

"Mommy. I'm your only wittow boy!" Their usual exchange of affection.

"What's Daddy doing?"

"He's working at his desk. He said I could have another bowl of ice cweam," Tommy seemed relieved to confess.

"He did?" It was then that she noticed the clock. Thirty minutes past Tommy's bedtime.

"Let me speak to him, please."

"Hey babe!" Kevin sounded equally ready to confess. "Uh…he said he couldn't sleep."

"I understand," she said with a smile, but a sudden commotion on the other end of the line seemed to trump her pardon.

"I'm sorry, babe. There's someone at the door. Can I call you right back?"

The phone went dead before Angie could agree.

CHAPTER TWENTY-TWO

"Good evening, Congressman." It was Franklin's aide, the woman Kevin had intentionally avoided thinking about since their brief encounter in the senator's office. "I'm Kari Samson. Josh Franklin asked me to stop by with a confidential memo. Is this a good time?"

It wasn't. With Angie away, he disliked the idea of an attractive woman entering the house. "Is it urgent?" he asked.

Of course it's urgent! Why else would the senator make her stop by my home on a Friday night?

Kevin corrected himself. "Please, step in from the cold."

She noticed Tommy's forehead and eyes peering around the corner. "Hello there!"

Tommy fled the scene, eager to finish his ice cream before Dad's "fifteen more minutes" extension expired.

"When the cat's away?" she asked.

How would she know the cat's away? he wondered. "Cat?"

"I assume your wife is out of town," Kari replied. "Little boys don't usually have a chocolate ice cream-mustache this late at night."

A single, nervous chuckle confirmed her suspicion. "Oh, right. My wife went to dinner with a friend." Kevin didn't mention Angie's plans to stay at the hotel. "In fact, we were just talking." It felt right mentioning the call. "I should call back. Will this take long?"

Before he could finish the question Kevin noticed Kari removing her coat. She appeared to have come from some sort of party, her short skirt and heels more suitable for after-hours flirting than congressional business. He took the jacket, walking it to the living room, where he placed it on the recliner. He turned back and was surprised to see she had followed closely behind. Kevin took a step backward.

She said nothing and handed Kevin a folder marked CONFIDENTIAL.

He broke the seal, curious to discover what was urgent enough to interrupt an aide's weekend plans and so important it couldn't be sent digitally.

Good evening Kevin,

I apologize for interrupting your weekend, but I just learned that someone violated the confidentiality agreement of our coalition meetings. Word is out that you are spearheading a key subcommittee labeled Bright Spots.

Key subcommittee? Apparently someone was taking his ideas seriously enough to dislike them. He continued reading to the bottom of the page.

As you know, any premature leak of pending proposals will undermine our strategy. Timing is everything on this thing. We simply can't let any details out of the bag before the revised budget numbers go public. Please speak to every member of your sub before Monday to get assurances none will speak to the press or anyone else outside the team.

Josh Franklin

Who would talk? Kevin wondered, consulting a mental checklist of the people on his subcommittee. None fit. But whoever it was knew enough to leak the bright spots label.

He instinctively moved toward his desk to alert Troy to the development. Before he could take a step, however, he felt Kari's hand gently restrain his forearm. She took the page from his hand and turned it over to reveal a brief postscript.

I have assigned Kari to you for tonight.
She is very good.

Kevin looked up from the page. The woman stood a few inches closer, a single finger lingering on his arm.

The phone sounded a familiar ringtone.

Seconds later Kevin heard his son's voice. "Hi, Mommy!"

Tommy walked into the living room toward Kevin, who was grateful for the interruption. As his son approached, Kevin heard the faint echo of Angie's interrogation. "Why are you still out of bed? What's your daddy doing?"

Tommy replied before Kevin could grab the phone. "Daddy's talking to a pretty lady."

Three minutes later Kevin was explaining the situation to his wife on the other end of the line, describing Franklin's note after apologizing for Tommy's broken curfew. He mentioned nothing about Kari's appearance or advance, content to say one of the senator's staff had dropped off the urgent document on the way home from the office.

"She just left," he said dismissively before quickly changing the subject. "So, how's the reunion going?"

There was silence on the line, followed by the sound of futilely suppressed crying.

"Babe? What's wrong?" He recognized the sound distressingly similar to that of the flood unleashed during their appointment with the pediatrician. "Did something happen?"

The sound of a tissue muffling sniffles. "Not really."

"Do you wanna talk about it?"

A brief pause. "Am I wasting my life?"

"What?" he said much more loudly than intended. "You can't be serious. You have the most non-wasteful life of any person I know!"

The last bit of Angie's sniffle submitted to a rising laughter of relief. For reasons Kevin did not understand, she needed his assurances every bit as much as he needed hers.

"Is this about Julia?" he asked.

"She seems so together. So successful and connected. Did you know she has nine million readers?"

"And you have a husband and three kids. I call that pretty successful!"

The doorbell rang. Kevin noticed Kari's jacket still draped across the living room chair.

"Don't hang up, Angie. I'll be right back." He wanted his wife on the line. *Take no chances.*

Placing the phone down on the end table, Kevin turned the handle to make a quick handoff. But Kari stood three feet away from the door. As soon as she saw Kevin, she spun around in an unspoken invitation for him to place the coat over her shivering shoulders.

He did.

"Thank you, Mr. Congressman," she said, turning back with a wink. "Are you sure you don't need anything else tonight?"

Kevin closed the door without a word, grabbed the phone, and peered out the front window to confirm Kari's departure.

"I'm back," he said, clutching the phone-shaped life preserver. "Where were we?"

"You were talking about my non-wasteful life."

"Right," he said with a sigh of relief.

CHAPTER TWENTY-THREE

Julia flipped through a never-ending menu of options, hoping to find something that might distract her from feelings she was trying unsuccessfully to ignore. Despite her having the entire history of film and television production available at the tap of a remote, nothing held her attention. She muted the sound and kept the screen on for company. A jaded-looking professor appeared to be presenting a drowsy lecture. He was speaking to an unseen universe of college students enduring a Who Cares 101 course from the comfort of their living rooms or digital tablets. The icon on the bottom of the screen told Julia she had landed on IQTV, the network of choice for trade school and junior college students on the bottom rung of the tuition budget ladder.

She feared she might be experiencing a mild panic attack. The trembling in her hands and pounding in her heart began the moment she stepped off the elevator. Maybe she had too successfully contained her anger, forcing her body to express its rage by other means. Or maybe she was just tired from a long day of travel. Regardless, Julia wanted to get her mind off two mutually exclusive thoughts the past few hours had spawned.

1. Angie embodied everything Julia scorned.
2. Angie had everything Julia wanted.

Stupid insecurities! she rebuked herself while tapping a digit on her phone.

"Hi, Sis." Maria's voice was missing its usual chirp, but still offered Julia a lifeline.

"Just checking in." A lie. She needed someone to talk to. "You OK? You don't sound yourself."

"I'm fine," Maria said. "Just another fight with Jared."

"Anything to do with you dating Fin?"

"No. Well, not exactly."

Julia waited, knowing more would come.

"I told him I don't think I'll be seeing Mr. Finelson socially again."

Seeing him socially? Julia admired the description of their one-night romp.

"Too young?"

"No!" Offense taken. "Well, sort of."

Maria seemed more evasive than her usual tell-all self. "Spill it, Maria. It's me you're talking to," Julia prodded.

"Sorry. I guess I'm still trying to figure it out myself."

Julia waited again.

"We had fun. You know. But I think I'm ready for a change."

"Ready for a change? One date and you want to move on?"

"I don't mean a change from Fin, per se. More like a change to someone more..." Maria paused to find the right words.

"Mature?"

"No!" Offense taken again. "Well, maybe. Someone Jared might, like, admire. Or at least accept."

Julia was speechless. In the two decades she'd served as her kid sister's love-life confidante she had never sensed anything remotely resembling remorse.

"He's pretty upset?" Julia guessed.

"Livid," Maria confirmed. "He called me some pretty awful names."

"Hmm."

"Actually, they are the names his friends call me," Maria explained. "Jared said he had been taking the jokes in stride until today. One of the boys sent a message labeled MR. FIN'S FAVORITE PARENT CONFERENCE. It included a doctored picture. My face on a nude woman's body. Fin's face on a flounder fish. You can probably guess their posture."

"I'm sorry," Julia offered while recalling a similar incident after Maria's prom. They never had figured out who sent the image. She would never forget the humiliation on her sister's face.

"Anyway, he was pretty upset. I apologized. Note to self, 'Don't date Jared's teachers.' "

"Probably a good idea," Julia said, knowing Jared wished for more than a teacher moratorium.

"Hey, I thought you were going out with Angie Tolbert tonight. Why the call?"

"Just back from dinner. Got a second?"

"Of course. The only thing on my agenda is fishing popcorn and M&M's out of the sofa."

"What?"

"Jared threw the bowl across the room," Maria explained. "He lost interest in the movie we were watching."

A momentary pause.

"How well do you remember Kevin Tolbert?" Julia asked.

"We never dated, if that's what you're wondering. He was cute. But he was a senior when I was a freshman. A different universe. Besides, he and Angie were already an item. Did you see him?"

"Just for a minute. I met Angie at their house before we went to dinner tonight."

"How is Angie-Pangie?"

"She always hated when you called her that."

"That's why I did it. Why have a big sister if you can't irritate her best friend?"

"She seems fine. Three kids." She anticipated Maria's gasp in reaction to the size of Angie's brood, forgetting that Maria was the official household librarian of such details.

"How's little Leah?"

Julia thought for a moment. She must have seen the baby, but failed to recall anything of note. "How should she be?"

"Please tell me you at least pretended to fawn."

She hadn't.

"You're hopeless!"

"We were in a hurry."

Maria's silence sent an invisible scowl. "Why did you ask about Kevin?" she said to end Julia's banishment.

"I don't know. I'm trying to connect the dots between what he and Angie have become and what they were."

"Become?"

"You know," Julia hesitated. "Breeders."

Saying the word felt wrong. Julia prided herself on open-minded acceptance of any and every lifestyle choice. So why did Angie's choices upset her enough to warrant a belittling label?

"I can't say I'm surprised," Maria said. "Angie's family was pretty uptight growing up. Remember the time she invited us to church?"

Julia recalled many.

"It always felt, I don't know, weird. Like she was in a bizarre cult or something."

"I went with her a few times," Julia said. "But I don't remember Kevin going to church. In fact, I remember thinking he might help balance Angie a bit. Her parents were pretty upset when she started dating Kevin in her junior year. They wanted her to date a nice religious boy, not a good-looking jock."

"Maybe she balanced him instead."

Julia ran through a mental checklist. *Three kids. Radical religious views. Mom giving up her career. Anti–Youth Initiative. Probably even opposed to in vitro selection.*

"I wouldn't use the word *balanced*," she replied. "I hate to sound judgmental. But they do fit the stereotype."

Julia had become one of the most popular columnists in America by articulating a philosophy that was the polar opposite of what breeders valued. No wonder Angie seemed insecure and defensive. No wonder Julia felt irate rather than relaxed after dinner with her friend.

"It was awkward," Julia confessed. "We spent the whole evening trying to avoid conversational land mines. I think we both lost a few limbs in the process."

"Some friendships work best from a distance," Maria suggested.

"I guess so."

I just need to grin through the weekend and get an interview with Kevin, Julia thought. *Then we can go back to comfortable estrangement.*

"Will you and Jared be OK?"

"We'll be fine."

Julia started to say goodbye, but Maria interrupted.

"You'll never guess who called today."

"Who?" she asked without interest.

Maria took a second longer to answer than she should. "Jonathan Sowell."

Julia felt a slight flutter. *Maybe playing hard to get can work after all.* "And?"

Momentary reticence.

"Come on, Maria. What did he say?"

"He asked if I'd like to go out tomorrow night."

A long silence.

"Sorry, Sis."

CHAPTER TWENTY-FOUR

The sound would have been imperceptible to anyone else. But to Matthew Adams it had become unbearable, drowning out the quiet hum of an aging refrigerator and the faint rush of water moving through household pipes toward a summoning rinse cycle.

Crunch. Smack.

Crunch. Smack.

He tried to ignore the distraction, concentrating on the spreadsheet displayed on the tablet before him. The numbers, remarkably similar to those he reviewed on the last Saturday of every month, presented more than enough to occupy his weary mind:

CAMPUS GRINDS INCOME: $6325

MONTHLY EXPENSES TO DATE: $5945

OUTSTANDING BILLS: $1273

Another occasion to rob the Peter of his mother's dwindling savings to pay the Paul of his mother's ailing body.

Crunch. Smack.

Crunch. Smack.

Matthew glared at his mom. He said nothing, instead taking his glass of orange juice in one hand and the digital pad in the other to move toward the other end of the table, out of range.

He returned to his analysis. Which bills would get paid this week? Which could wait until after payday? He remembered his reduced hours. The next check would fall short. He cursed aloud.

Crunch. Smack.

Crunch. Smack.

"Mom!" Enough was enough. "Would you please stop that?"

She returned his glare with a confused expression.

"Does the whole neighborhood have to hear you chew?" He slid her half-empty cereal bowl toward the middle of the table. "I need quiet if I'm going to figure out this mess!"

"I'm sorry, Son." She formed a tear, a child shaken by sudden discipline for an obscure offense.

Matthew slid the bowl back to his mother while placing a hand on her arm. "Never mind."

She resumed her breakfast.

Crunch. Smack.

"I'll be in my room," he said on his way out of the kitchen.

Matthew disliked his shortening fuse. He and his mother had had a very close relationship, especially when he was young. But the woman who had once provided the wind beneath his wings now felt like an exasperating anchor.

He halted, suddenly turning back toward the table. "Did you remember your pre-breakfast pills?"

Her eyes darted back and forth as they searched an inner file cabinet. Matthew knew immediately that she could not recall, sentencing him to a scavenger hunt across her bathroom counter, where he would find and then count the remaining pills. It was their usual routine to prevent missing or doubling her daily dose.

Thirty minutes later Matthew situated his now-dressed

mother in her favorite reading chair in a cramped living room containing one too many pieces of furniture for comfortable navigation. Handing her a digital book device, he tapped the start button. An actor's voice commenced reading as she attempted to follow the text scrolling on the screen.

"You good?" he asked.

"Fine." She patted his hand gratefully. "You go ahead."

He retreated to the sanctuary of a bedroom with walls displaying relics of a life he had intended to live.

A framed acceptance letter from the university he still hoped to attend.

A poster of the virtual game he still planned to beat.

A high school graduation cap converted into a picture frame holding his favorite snapshot, Matthew seated beside Maria Davidson in her cheerleader outfit. He had clipped the image from their high school annual. A yearbook photographer had snapped it during one of the three opportunities Matthew had taken to sit with Maria at lunch. Discovering the image had been the highlight of his senior year, a reminder of what might have been had she accepted his invitation to the prom.

Plopping himself on the bed, Matthew grabbed the remote sitting on his nightstand to wake a giant screen that filled the opposite wall. His portable tablet instantly became a steering wheel from which he could navigate a range of media options. The conversation with Dr. Vincent fresh on his mind, he searched and found two related documentaries.

AUGUSTINE: SINNER TO SAINT—An exploration of the life of St. Augustine, a fifth-century bishop who had an enormous influence on the theology of the Christian West.

GOOD VS. EVIL—During the third century AD Manichaeism emerged as a religion melding ideas from ancient paganism and the rapidly growing Christian cult. A Gnostic faith, Manichaeism taught that God is pure spirit who did not create the evil of a material world that it attributed to the lord of darkness, Satan.

Spirit good. Body bad, Matthew recalled, choosing the second program. The screen refused his command, instead displaying text that reminded him of his financial inferiority.

SELECTED PROGRAM NOT AVAILABLE TO PUBLIC DOMAIN SUBSCRIBERS. UPGRADE NOW!

Matthew decided against the additional expense, choosing instead to navigate to his default entertainment option, viewing the latest posts from fellow 2027 graduates of Littleton High. There were four updates since his last view.

Roberto Ortega announced his recent promotion to district sales manager for a line of specialty foods. The picture showed him and his girlfriend celebrating with margaritas and a plate of onion rings.

Cynthia Beal boasted about another published article in *The New England Journal of Medicine.* There was no picture, only a link that Matthew could not access due to his peasant subscription status.

Colin Smith said one of his songs was climbing the charts, breaking into the rare air of the top 200 downloads. A picture showed Colin sitting in a studio beside Bret Reese, a rising new country star. Colin had always been a gifted musician, voted most likely to live in Nashville by his fellow graduates. Matthew remembered Colin's goal of becoming a recording artist performing his own material. Apparently writing for top artists paid better than the wedding-and-bar-mitzvah circuit.

Kanisha Wood had posted a picture next to her ten-year-old daughter holding up a ribbon won during a recent swim meet.

The daughter resembled his former classmate more than a now-plump Kanisha resembled her former self. Both had the same sparkling smile.

Matthew reviewed the most recent date on his own profile. It had been months since his last post, since anything had happened worth sharing.

MATTHEW ADAMS: "Closing in on a first draft of my thesis."

He had included a picture of himself standing in front of the UC Department of Philosophy building to make the lie seem more authentic. Did anyone believe the post? Had anyone even read it?

"Matthew!" The shout seemed a cry for help.

"Mom?" Matthew leaped out of the bed toward the door. "Where are you? What's wrong?"

Rushing to the living room he noticed the empty reading chair. He quickly peered around the corner to scan the kitchen floor, half expecting to see her holding a sprained ankle or bleeding head.

"Matthew!" she yelled from behind a closed door, this time more urgently than before. "I'm in here."

Matthew turned the doorknob to reveal an all-too-familiar scene.

"Not again!" he groaned.

Another bathroom mishap.

CHAPTER TWENTY-FIVE

"Yes I'm sure!" Julia used the most enthusiastic voice she could muster. Even so, Angie seemed reluctant. She and Kevin had not gone on a proper date in months, but she felt guilty accepting Julia's offer to watch the kids for the evening.

"Come on, Angie. How often do I get to be someone's Aunt Julia?" Remembering her nephew, Julia added, "Jared doesn't count. He doesn't think I'm cool anymore."

It was all Angie needed. "Well, maybe we'll grab a quick bite out and get back in time to put the kids to bed."

"No deal," Julia said. "Either you stay out until after they're asleep or I withdraw the offer."

Angie could no longer restrain her enthusiasm, a giant smile overtaking her adorable face. "Kevin will be so surprised!"

The accepted offer magically ended the awkward tennis match of stilted comments that had been masquerading as conversation. They resumed their stroll through the crowded shopping mall in comfortable silence, reluctant combatants momentarily restored to fast friends.

Noticing the mall directory, Julia slid her arm under Angie's like a schoolgirl eager to share the latest gossip. "I've got an idea."

Julia accelerated her pace, dragging Angie toward the directory. She stopped to scan the list of stores with the tip of her index finger.

"It has to be here somewhere."

Angie seemed to enjoy the sudden mystery. "What are we looking for?"

Julia threw in the towel, deciding to ask the voice-activated directory for guidance. "Show me women's lingerie stores."

She turned to Angie with a sly smile as a list of lingerie shops appeared on the screen before them.

"I think you should really surprise Kevin."

Angie blushed. Then she nodded.

"You should reserve tonight at the hotel," Julia suggested. "I'm sure I can handle both bedtime and breakfast."

Angie's eyes brightened, then fell. "Oh, that would be wonderful."

"But?"

"We have obligations at church in the morning."

Julia felt her stomach tighten. "I see."

"In fact—"

Here it comes, Julia thought.

"—I was going to ask if you would be interested in joining us."

The last time Julia had set foot in a church was for her cousin's wedding five years earlier. It had been much longer since she had attended an actual Sunday-morning service.

"I know you had a bad experience at Littleton Assembly."

The comment refreshed Julia's memory. Her last Sunday service had been a few years after graduating from college. She had just returned to Littleton to share a house with Maria, who needed support with newborn Jared. Angie had been the culprit then also.

"The church we attend here is different from my home church. You might like it."

Unlikely.

"I'd love to," Julia lied.

Angie appeared surprised, as if she had scripted a longer conversation suddenly cut short.

"Really? Great! It's a bit of an ordeal getting the kids ready in the morning. We leave around ten to make it in time for the ten thirty liturgy."

Liturgy? Julia had never heard Angie use that word in connection with her old church.

"I'll tell you what," Angie continued. "We'll stay out until after you put the kids to bed and slip in unnoticed. Believe me, Kevin will enjoy the surprise just as much at home as at a hotel."

"Deal," Julia agreed.

Angie slipped her arm under Julia's as they headed toward the lingerie store.

♦

Four hours later Julia felt the weight of two-year-old Joy's body pressing against her own, an occasional quiver the last remnants of the tantrum thrown when Kevin and Angie walked out the front door. Missing one's mommy for twenty-four hours was bad enough. But to see her leave with daddy after a brief reunion would push most toddlers toward traumatic stress syndrome. Having survived the thirty-minute ordeal calming a hysterical child, Julia enjoyed the feel of Joy's rapid sniffles, machine-gun fires of recovery every fifteen to twenty seconds.

Julia remembered similar moments when Jared was little. It seemed like yesterday, and like a hundred years ago.

"Aunt Juwia." The voice startled an exhausted Joy.

"Yes Tommy," Julia whispered.

"Weah did it."

"Leah did what?" She noticed Tommy pinching his own nose. "Oh. Does she need a new diaper?"

A vigorous nod.

"I'll be right there."

Tommy walked back to the kitchen table, where a stack of Legos awaited his return.

Julia started to lift Joy's body in hopes of placing her on the sofa, where she might continue the drift toward slumber. It didn't work. The rising sounds of a tantrum sequel prompted Julia to pull Joy close again. Noticing the deposit of mucus and drool on her left sleeve, she reached for the box of tissues. Empty.

"I'm hungwy!" Tommy summoned from the center of his own universe. "Can I have a banana?"

Leah's voice came next, a slight sigh of relief mixed with a whimper of discomfort.

Three against one. Momentary paralysis. One sniff of the air, however, ended the indecision. With Joy still draped over her shoulder, Julia approached Leah who was seated in her high chair beside Tommy's burgeoning Lego cityscape.

Removing the tray and unlatching Leah's high chair strap with one hand proved too difficult. Julia had no choice but to place Joy on a seat beside Tommy, trying to move quickly to calm Leah's escalating cry.

"Can I have a banana?" Tommy repeated, extended tongue held strategically in place by his pressed lips, apparently to help him focus on a crucial step in the construction process.

Realizing she had been abandoned in favor of Leah, Joy morphed from comfort-starved toddler to revenge-driven tyrant. She stood up on the chair to scan Tommy's miniature town in search of the perfect weapon. Seconds later, a ten-inch-high skyscraper flew past Julia's shoulder toward the wall, where it rebounded to become fifteen scattered blocks on the floor.

From relative peace to three crying children in less than sixty seconds! Julia thought.

After rescuing Joy from Tommy's intended retaliation, she swept Leah from the scene and headed toward the nursery, where a supply of fresh wipes, diapers, and pajamas could resolve one-third of the crisis. It was her first opportunity to focus on the baby since the commotion of pushing Angie and Kevin out the door.

Something seemed wrong, or at least different. Leah was more quiet and sedate than Julia had expected. She tried to remember Jared at the same age. Hadn't he been squirmier? She recalled her nephew's army crawl at seven months old. He had found and broken one of Julia's matching vases filled with fresh-cut flowers. At nearly eleven months Leah seemed far too passive to attack innocent decorations.

"Leah," Julia heard herself say in a gentle, melodic pitch while rubbing fresh powder onto the baby's naked belly. "Are you a happy girl? Huh? Are you a happy little girl?"

The answer came in the form of a tiny smile that forced her tongue farther forward and eye slits nearly closed.

"You did it wong!" Tommy the engineer turned Tommy the Leah-care critic.

"Did what wrong?" Julia asked.

"You're supposed to use the wotion first."

Julia noticed the unopened bottle of baby lotion sitting on the changing table. "Got it! How's this?"

"That's wight," Tommy approved.

Two more little eyes peered around the corner as Joy joined the baby-admiration party.

CHAPTER TWENTY-SIX

Kevin was still in a shock. In less than two hours he had been promoted from spit-up and peanut butter and jelly duty with the kids to sitting in a five-star restaurant across from the most beautiful woman in the world.

"You look gorgeous." Kevin raised a glass to his wife's most flattering dress. "And I still can't believe you pulled this off."

"Thank Julia," she insisted.

Gently tapping their drink glasses, they took a sip before opening their menus.

"Are you feeling better today?" Kevin remembered Angie's phone call dripping with self-doubt.

"A little. Julia and I had a much better time together today. I think I was just a bit tense last night. You know, seeing her for the first time in nearly five years."

"Has she changed?"

"Not really. That's part of the problem. I'm a different person than I was when we were young. You know, the kids and all. But she's just the same."

"You look better than ever," Kevin said.

Angie paused long enough to offer an appreciative smile.

"Julia seems to view the whole world, including me, through different lenses. I get the feeling she pities me, like I'm a senseless girl who's made one wrong turn after another."

"From what I remember of Julia I'm sure she considers us both bad drivers," Kevin said. "She probably comes down on the other side of nearly every issue we care about."

Angie nodded. "And nearly every choice I've made. She's always been left of left, even when we were in school. I don't know what I thought would happen. Maybe that time and maturity would magically bring her around. Kind of silly, I guess. Still, I love her. She's the oldest friend I've got."

Kevin huffed, pretending to take offense.

"I said oldest friend, not best friend," she said, placing her hand on his. "Anyway, she accepted my invitation to attend church tomorrow. Didn't even put up a fight. Who knows?"

Kevin waited a moment, allowing sufficient space in the conversation to change the subject. "Can we talk about Leah?"

She smiled as if she had hoped he would raise the subject.

"I did some research this week," he said.

"On what?"

"Treatment options." Kevin tried to decipher Angie's body language.

"You heard the doctor, Kevin. Fragile X syndrome can't be cured."

"I wasn't looking for a cure, just something that might give her a moderately normal life."

Angie waited without saying a word, her eyes suggesting a rising indignation.

"I know what you're thinking, babe," he said in a hurry. "But hear me out."

"I'm thinking you want to fix her," Angie said severely, halting his advance. "I know you, Kevin Tolbert. One of the things I love is your ability to make things happen. Get things done. But Leah isn't a failing business that needs a turnaround strategy. You can't fix this."

"I know I can't fix it. But I can't sit back and do nothing, either. I'm her father, for God's sake."

His voice broke, prompting an instinctive touch from Angie. Kevin took a sip of water to regain his composure.

"Is it wrong for me to try whatever I can?"

"No. It's not wrong," Angie said, squeezing her husband's hand. "Nothing could be more right. But she's not broken. She's just...different."

"Let me at least tell you what I've learned," he insisted. "Then we can decide together whether we want to look into it further."

He took her silence as consent.

"Troy knows a guy who works with the director of epigenetic research at a leading research laboratory near Richmond." Kevin pulled a tablet out of his jacket to read the details Troy had included in his daily briefing. "Here it is. Dr. Wayne Galliger. Anyway, they've been accepting applications for an experimental treatment for those with mental disabilities like—"

"Can I tell you about what I learned this week?"

The interruption told him Angie had no interest in experimental treatments, as he'd feared. He slid the device back into his pocket and assumed a listening posture.

"Go ahead."

"Normal doesn't mean good," Angie began.

A look of confusion on Kevin's face. "What does that mean?"

"It's something Pastor Seth said during our meeting this week."

"When did you meet with Pastor?"

"Thursday. I needed someone to talk to. His wife Talia joined us for a chat. A sweet lady."

"Is she from Uganda too?" He forced a competitive grin in an effort to lighten the mood.

"He's not from Uganda," Angie said with an air of triumph.

"Don't tell me he's from Ethiopia."

"No," she confessed. "He's from Egypt. His family moved here when he was seven to flee persecution. But Talia was born in Chicago."

"What did he mean when he said normal isn't good?"

"Normal isn't *always* good," she corrected. "Most people would consider us abnormal for the choices we've made. Julia certainly does. But sometimes abnormal is good."

How could anyone call Leah's problem good? Kevin wondered.

"Talia said that in a world where human beings are treated like a commodity, people who raise disabled kids are heroic."

"Come on, Angie!" Passive acceptance had never been part of Kevin's DNA. "Of course we'll love and care for Leah. But that doesn't mean we should ignore opportunities to help her overcome her disabilities. We both had laser eye surgery so we can see normally. Did that make us unheroic?"

Angie pursed her lips, as if reluctantly absorbing Kevin's question.

"I'm sorry, babe," he said. "But I think we would be wrong to ignore any options for Leah. That doesn't mean I'm trying to fix a broken child…" His voice cracked again. "It might just mean helping her see more clearly."

The waiter arrived with the soup of the day, reminding the couple they were on a date.

"What do you say we give ourselves a few more days to absorb the news about Leah before discussing options?" Kevin asked.

"Maybe we could meet with Pastor Seth together?" she asked.

"I'd like that. But for now, I'd like to celebrate."

Anticipation crossed Angie's face, exposing the single dimple Kevin had always found irresistible. "Celebrate? Celebrate what?"

He lifted a spoonful of hot clam chowder, inviting Angie to join him in a toast. She quickly scooped from her own bowl and met his spoon mid-table. A slight spill from both spoons prompted a playful laugh.

"To our three children. Gifts from above," he offered.

"To a break from their incessant demands," Angie countered with a sigh.

"To the prettiest wife on planet Earth," Kevin added.

"And to the handsome congressman from Colorado who's going to change the world!"

Each tasted the soup while Angie rubbed her shoeless toes up her husband's thigh.

CHAPTER TWENTY-SEVEN

"Are you sure about that?" Julia asked.

Tommy's eyes widened like those of a witness caught perjuring himself.

"I'm pretty sure your mommy said you should only have one cup of water so you don't wet the bed."

"Daddy wets me have two." His last-ditch effort to delay the inevitability of night-light solitude.

Julia was eager for Tommy to join Joy and Leah in dreamland but couldn't find the strength to stand her ground. "Half a cup," she conceded. "And then you have to fall asleep. Deal?"

"Deawl!"

Twenty minutes later Julia sneaked into Tommy's room to confirm he had fulfilled his end of the bargain. She wanted the kids fast asleep before hiding away in the guest room to give Angie and Kevin the next best thing to a romantic hotel rendezvous.

Leaving her door slightly ajar, Julia changed into her nightgown and propped herself with pillows behind her tablet. Her fatigue put up a brief protest before submitting to a tiny surge of adrenaline sparked by Julia's tap on the digital screen. Two messages appeared, both of which had arrived during the flying Lego calamity. *Where did three hours go?*

FROM JARED DAVIDSON: *When are you coming home? I need to talk to you.*

The fight over Fin must have been more intense than Maria had implied. Jared almost never asked Julia to talk. It was his aunt's job to smooth things over, to cajole Jared from hiding behind the protective shell of his locked bedroom door. Glancing at the time she decided to wait until morning to call. She opened the second message.

FROM PAUL DAUGHERTY: *Have an idea for the feature. Give me a call tonight no matter how late.*

Julia tapped Paul's image. She heard a single ring followed by a stew of pounding music and laughing crowd chatter.

"Hi, Jewel!" Paul shouted. "Hold on a sec while I find a quiet spot."

Moments later the background noise dipped, along with the volume of Paul's voice.

"There we go," he began. "Great party at the Funky Buddha. Wish you were here!"

"I'm in DC. I got your message. Is now good for you?"

"Now's great. I might be hungover in the morning!" He laughed more than the joke deserved.

"What's up?"

"The editorial board is pressing me pretty hard on this bright spots controversy. They want something soon."

Julia felt a mix of exhilaration and alarm. RAP editorial board mandates generally meant top story billing. They also meant walking the journalistic high wire without a net.

"How's it going, by the way?"

"Making great progress. I'm interviewing Congresswoman Florea and Trisha Sayers on Monday."

He didn't react.

Remembering that he had arranged both meetings, she quickly added, "And you'll never guess where I am right now."

"You told me. DC."

"I'm in the Washington residence of Congressman Kevin Tolbert." She let the name sink in.

"Good Lord, girl! You do move fast!" He seemed both impressed and mistaken.

"Not like that!" she said hastily. "I'm in the guest room after spending a day with Kevin's wife Angie. You remember. I told you we were high school friends."

"Right." He sounded disappointed and intrigued. "Any openings?"

"I think so." She thought of her agreement to attend church. "I plan to meet several of his associates tomorrow morning."

"Perfect."

A brief intermission.

"You said you had an idea for the feature?" she reminded him.

"Oh yeah. A soft-think idea you can take or leave."

Julia knew that Paul's "soft-think" suggestions were actually nonnegotiable edicts. "Great. Let me hear it."

"I want to position this story as your next *Guylanders*."

Another surge of adrenaline.

"I don't follow." But she did hope.

"Think about it, Jewel," he continued. "You became a legend by exposing the downside of a major demographic shift. You gave women everywhere a vocabulary for describing their angst."

He was right. Her *Guylanders* feature had struck a major cultural chord. For decades two trend lines had been moving in opposite directions. Women were on the rise, earning most of the college and graduate degrees and filling most openings in the more lucrative professions. In a few short decades, American girls managed to overtake centuries of boy's-club bias and patriarchy to become the most affluent, independent females in history.

Over the same period, however, another trend had emerged. American boys were more than happy to hand over the reins to assertive gals. Unlike their grandfathers, more and more guys inhabited the comfortable borders of Guyland, where they formed clans of rent-sharing roommates and worked part-time jobs to protect time for climbing virtual-world ladders and sampling the endless supply of young women offering no-strings-attached pleasure.

Many said the trends of guy passivity and gal advancement had fueled the innovations that created the multibillion-dollar in vitro selection industry. As age ambushed millions of women, they now sought something no Guylander seemed willing to provide. A child, rather than a mate, became the life partner of choice.

Girls on top.

Boys having fun.

Every child a wanted child.

The perfect world.

But getting what one wants does not guarantee liking it. Julia's feature was the first mainstream story to overtly associate a decline in male achievement with a rise in female depression. She compared the phenomenon to separation anxiety after centuries of male domination. Like abused children taken from parents to foster-care safety, oppressed women needed time to adjust to a better existence.

Medicate the depression, she had written. *Don't abandon the dream.*

"I think you can do it again," Paul continued. "I've already decided on a title for the feature."

A feature I haven't even outlined? she thought.

"*The Breeders*." He paused for impact. "What do you think?

Clear. Simple. A short title like *Guylanders*. It has your name written all over it, pardon the pun."

"I'm not sure. I mean, *Guylanders* wasn't an offensive word. But *Breeders* is used, you know, like an ethnic slur."

Momentary silence suggested Paul hadn't thought of that. He protested anyway. "Apples and oranges. You can't equate offending religious nuts with demeaning an entire race."

Glancing at the family photo hanging on Angie's guest room wall, Julia wasn't so sure. But she went along anyway. "What do you have in mind?"

"You need to get inside Tolbert's head. Spend time with his coalition. I promise you'll find more than enough to characterize the bright spots agenda as radical breeder nonsense."

"I'll do my best," she said pensively.

A rhythmic thump resurfaced on the other end of the line, accompanied by what sounded like a sea of humanity shouting over one another. Someone must have opened whatever door Paul had hid behind to take Julia's call.

"There you are!" The faint voice sounded vaguely familiar. "Come on, Paul. You're missing the table dance contest!"

Julia resisted the urge to ask, choosing instead to end the call. "Go back to your party. I'll touch base with you in a few days."

"Do," Paul shouted. "Bye, love!"

Julia set her tablet aside and reached for a decorative pillow sitting on the undisturbed half of the bedspread. She held it close while sorting a half dozen thoughts and feelings.

The thrill of journalistic resurgence.

The challenge of a big idea.

The pressure of a tight deadline.

The determination to win at all costs.

Hushed voices interrupted her sorting. Angie and Kevin had arrived home. Quickly slipping out from under the covers, Julia quietly pulled her door closed.

CHAPTER TWENTY-EIGHT

Kevin gazed at Leah slightly longer than he had at Tommy or Joy, the final stop on his promised round of inspections before joining Angie in the bedroom. All three were blessedly asleep. He glanced at the floor beneath the guest room door. No light. Julia was out after what must have been an exhausting night of a job well done.

The phone in his jacket vibrated. Reaching into his pocket, Kevin congratulated himself on the silence, recalling too many opportunities for intimacy derailed by an ill-timed ring that woke one or more of the kids. He decided to ignore the message, turning instead toward the kitchen, where he retrieved two glasses. He checked for orange juice, without which he could not mix fresh mimosas, Angie's favorite indulgence when accompanied by fresh strawberries.

Moments later he arrived at their bedroom door, one hand awkwardly balancing the glasses while the other held a small plate.

Another vibration. Two instant messages in rapid sequence

piqued his curiosity. It had to be Troy burning the midnight oil again. He slid into the kids' bathroom to free a hand by placing the strawberries on the sink counter.

FROM TROY: *See attached. Press interview I just approved for Monday afternoon.*

There was nothing particularly noteworthy about the message, the kind Kevin received routinely whenever Troy had screened a request and determined a meeting advantageous and safe. He ignored the attachment, confident in Troy's judgment. But then he read the second message.

FROM TROY: *BTW—Who is Julia Davidson?*

He immediately opened the attachment: an interview request from Julia sent to his office in-box a mere six minutes earlier.

Dear Congressman: *I hope you and Angie had a great date. Your kids are terrific! Any chance you would return the favor by granting me an exclusive interview? I'll be in DC through Tuesday afternoon. (Julia Davidson, RAP Syndicate)*

Kevin smiled. Apparently, Julia was not as soundly asleep as she had made it appear.

Angie had already lit the bedroom candles by the time Kevin arrived. Eyes still adjusting to the diminished light, he heard her voice before he saw her.

"Are they asleep?"

"Like rocks," he assured her.

"Julia?"

"No sign of life." True, if you discount messages intended to be read on Monday.

"Good," she said, stepping from the shadows into the warm glow of a dancing flame.

Kevin's heart began to race as it had on countless occasions since their wedding night as he anticipated opening the same favorite gift in new wrapping paper.

Flowing lace in precisely the right locations.

A single finger summoning him to draw closer.

An alluring grin that enticed him back into everything they had known together: the flirty glances of a teenage crush, the tingling thrill of gently held hands, the sweet taste of a first stolen kiss, the breathless wonder of caressing her honeymoon body.

He smiled gratefully for a fifteen-year discovery of pleasures both had come to crave.

"I told you I had a surprise." She blushed at his greedy gaze. "Do you like it?"

He approached, delightfully conflicted between a desire to satisfy her and anticipation of his own culminating release.

"You're amazing." He brushed his lips across hers. "Thank you."

♦

Angie and Kevin lay on top of their bedspread gently caressing one another's arms. The intensity of their union had both exhausted and refreshed. Still catching his breath, Kevin sensed himself being renewed, as if a mysterious tailor were repairing his frayed edges. He turned his head to look into his wife's contented eyes. He wondered if she felt the same. Had he been for her what she had been for him, a brush in the hands of a gentle artist adding yet another finishing touch?

She rolled onto her side while pulling his arm around her relaxed body from behind. They held one another silently for several more minutes.

Kevin felt himself drifting into sleep until Angie's voice pulled him back.

"What are you thinking?" she asked.

He forced his eyes open. "Thinking?"

Angie giggled. "I forgot. Your mind ceases to function after we make love."

She was more right than she knew. "My mind is in perfect working order. Although I'll admit not as perfect as other parts!"

She giggled again. "I was thinking about Julia."

He ignored the bruise to his ego. "What about her?"

"I was trying to imagine what it's like for her. You know, no husband or kids. Having sex instead of making love. I couldn't live her life."

"I certainly hope not!" he teased.

She slapped his hand, then raised it to her lips for a gentle kiss. "You know what I mean."

"She probably can't imagine living your life either." He immediately disagreed with himself. "I don't know, maybe she can. After all, she was made for it."

"Made for what?"

"Family."

"She'd beg to differ."

"Sure. But she'd also know it's true." He said it as if launching a political speech. "Do you remember what God said after making Adam before Eve?"

"'Just kidding'?"

He moved his hand to her naked side to threaten tickle retaliation.

"Don't you dare!"

He moved his hand back, receiving another peck. "God said it wasn't good for Adam to be alone. After describing everything else he made as good, he called something he made not good."

"I never thought of that."

"I told you. My mind is in perfect working order," he continued. "He couldn't have meant that Adam was bad. He must have meant Adam was incomplete. You know, unfinished."

"Makes sense."

"Men and women are two halves of a whole. I bet Julia has moments when she feels incomplete."

"She certainly doesn't show it. I've never met a more confident woman."

"I have," he said.

She turned her head in his direction. "Who?"

He propped himself up on this right elbow to kiss Angie on the cheek. "I know a woman who is confident enough to volunteer for the most important job on earth, a job very few of her girlfriends would even consider."

She turned toward Kevin's eyes as he continued.

"I know a woman so courageous that she quit a successful career in order to give three kids the kind of love and security no other person in the world could provide."

Her hand rose to his face in an invitation to kiss her fingertips before saying more.

"I know a woman who stood up to an arrogant pediatrician and defended the dignity of a little girl whom God entrusted to our care."

Kevin used his palm to intercept a single tear leaking from Angie's eye before it could reach the pillow.

"And I know a woman whom every guy in high school wanted to date, but who wisely chose to become Kevin Tolbert's better half."

Angie burst into moist laughter as she mashed her face against her husband's.

"I love you," she said through a flood of tears.

"I love you too."

They lay side by side to resume their gentle caresses. After a few minutes Angie's hand moved lower, surprising Kevin with an invitation to a second round of intimacy.

CHAPTER TWENTY-NINE

The building appeared to have been constructed with a capacity for five hundred worshippers, six counting the small balcony located above the entry door at the back of the room. It possessed all the markings of a traditional East Coast church circa 1950, when the iconic Billy Graham had dominated headlines and personified the growing evangelical movement. Countless fire-and-brimstone sermons must have been heard between these walls before Protestant congregations found a new audience using a simpler, more user-friendly message about God's love, man's sin, and Christ's gift to all willing recipients.

The walls and pews retained the faint aroma of sweaty week-night revival meetings ending with an invitation for sinners to stream forward and accept salvation. A large woman would have been playing soft hymns on an upright piano while the minister extended his hand to the congregation, asking reluctant stragglers, "Won't you come?"

The church, like so many others, had suffered a gradual death during the years when another style of evangelicalism took center stage. Before the turn of the century, pianos and organs lost ground to guitars and drums. Pulpit-pounding appeals were replaced by conversational teaching. Hardwood benches, like the one Julia occupied now, had been replaced by padded theater seats in front of large-screen projection units. The style had created some of the largest congregations in Christian history by appealing to the huge baby boom population during its child-rearing years. The early twenty-first century had seen churches from various denominations in every large city boast weekly attendance in the thousands or even tens of thousands. But that movement also died when a new generation of kids started yawning at their parents' favorite songs and teachers.

From the first moment of the sermon Julia sensed something quite different. The minister seemed to lack the bohemian-casual persona of Angie's high school and college pastors. Perhaps Reverend Mubar had flunked the seminary course on coffee shop posture and trendy lingo. Maybe he had assumed his slight African accent would doom all attempts at cool. Regardless, Julia found his dignified solemnity absorbing as he invited the congregation into hushed reverence at the start of its weekly litany.

Like the lift of a maestro's baton to call an orchestra to the ready, the pastor's move toward a small podium summoned all two hundred worshippers back to their seats. Moments earlier they had been lifting their hands while singing melodies and words Julia didn't know with a passion she didn't share. Killer shows by her favorite recording artists had never stirred her to tears as a few simple songs had stirred Angie and other members of Apostles' Church. One guy with a guitar, his voice barely on pitch, seemed to elicit more emotion than a platinum-album-selling band with massive projection systems and thousands of screaming fans.

Julia wondered whether the low-key style represented Angie's reaction against her own parents' brand of church. No big screen or coffee shop. No cool band. Not even a conversational teacher, which became abundantly clear when Pastor Mubar transitioned them from "a season of worship" into a talk he read rather than presented to his flock.

"Peace be to you," he began.

"And also to you," the congregation responded.

"This morning's text comes from the Gospel of Saint Luke, chapter twenty-four."

Julia heard the sound of mass movement. She noticed Kevin retrieving a Bible from the slot in front of them. She did the same.

"Jesus Himself stood in the midst of them, and said to them, "'Peace to you.'"

Kevin and the other listeners managed to locate the passage in time to read along. After a momentary effort to find some sort of index, Julia forgot the name of the page she was supposed to find. She held the book open toward the middle and ignored the print in order to listen to the reading.

"But they were terrified and frightened, and supposed they had seen a spirit," the pastor continued. "And He said to them, 'Why are you troubled? And why do doubts arise in your hearts? Behold My hands and My feet, that it is I Myself. Handle Me and see, for a spirit does not have flesh and bones as you see I have.' When He had said this, He showed them His hands and His feet."

Sensing he had finished reading the Bible passage, Julia looked toward the pastor, whose eyes remained fixed on the page before him.

"Our Lord appeared to literally hundreds of eyewitnesses after his resurrection. But this may be the most important of all appearances, as we consider what C. S. Lewis called the grand miracle of the Christian faith, the bodily incarnation and resurrection of our Lord. These very disciples and their descendants would soon face false teachers claiming that Christ came to free us from the evil of material existence. In one council after another the church rightfully condemned a heresy known as Gnosticism, the belief that spirit is good but body is bad. Yet God himself became a body, a human body, to restore the full goodness of what it means to be human—one made in God's very image. It is our enemy, Satan, who hates the flesh. It is Jesus, our Savior, who sits at the right hand of the Father in a human body. Notice his words, 'Behold My hands and My feet…a spirit does not have flesh and bones as you see I have.'"

Julia did not remember any of Angie's former pastors using a word like *heresy*. She did, however, recall them talking about Jesus's death on a cross and emphasizing his resurrection.

"The Scriptures make a very strong emphasis on this point. Saint Luke goes on to describe Jesus asking for a piece of broiled fish and sweet honeycomb to eat in their presence. His empty plate would become further evidence of his physical reality if they later assumed their eyes had played tricks."

Another pause. Julia glanced around to see if others were as underwhelmed by the sermon as she. Apparently not, eyes scanning open Bibles to confirm what must have been an important realization.

"Years later Saint John, an eyewitness to this moment, described it in his First Epistle when he said 'That which was from the beginning, which we have heard, which we have seen with our eyes, which we have looked upon, and our hands have handled…we declare to you…that your joy may be full.' He says it is the bodily resurrection of Christ that brings fullness of joy. Although I do wonder why he forgot to mention the fish and honey part."

The pastor looked up from his page, apparently pleased by the playful ad lib. No one laughed with him, although Julia could not help smiling at him.

"Saint Paul, while not an eyewitness to this moment, did write to the church at Corinth that if Christ did not rise bodily from the grave then the Christian faith is completely empty. In fact, all of the apostles confirmed, many by their own martyr deaths, that the bodily incarnation and resurrection of Christ are essential doctrines of the Christian faith."

Throughout the rest of the sermon Julia tried to follow a train of thought important enough to warrant half of a Sunday service.

God became flesh. Jesus rose bodily. Lots of people saw and touched him. Religious leaders said he never rose, that his disciples removed the body. Christians were killed for saying otherwise. False teachers said he rose, but only in spirit, to show the supremacy of spirit over body. Seven major church councils defended both the deity and the humanity of Jesus Christ.

So what? she wondered. *What does an ancient debate over body and spirit have to do with life in the twenty-first century?*

Pastor Mubar concluded his remarks and took a step away from the podium. Everyone stood. Julia was grateful, assuming the service had reached the end. It hadn't.

The doors at the back of the chapel opened. A long train of toddlers and preschool children trailed a teenage girl leading them into the room. Another teen followed behind, corralling any stragglers. Each child's eyes darted to and fro around the room, trying to locate a welcoming mom or dad. The scattered crowd of two hundred suddenly mushroomed into a packed auditorium of hushed parent-child reunions. Julia could not recall ever seeing such a high ratio of kids to parents. A quick guess suggested households two or three times the national average.

"I believe in one God, the Father, the Almighty, Creator of heaven and earth..." the minister began. Julia noticed everyone rising, most families holding hands as they began reciting the same words in unison.

"...And of all things visible and invisible. And in one Lord,

Jesus Christ, the only-begotten Son of God, begotten of the Father before all ages…"

She looked at Angie and Kevin, both mouths in sync. She started to move her own lips ever so slightly, hoping to appear on cue and on script.

"Light of light, true God of true God, begotten, not created, of one essence with the Father, through whom all things were made…"

Julia recognized a few words from the next sentence from a verse Angie had often quoted when they were younger, something about God loving the world and giving his only begotten Son and about believers living forever. Julia always had a bad feeling about the emphasis on forever-livers and pagan perishers. Apparently Angie's new church was not as different as it had seemed.

"Who for us and for our salvation came down from the heavens and was incarnate by the Holy Spirit and the Virgin Mary, and became man…"

Julia sensed the volume starting to rise like a song approaching everyone's favorite phrase. She looked back at Angie, whose eyes were closed. She looked back toward Pastor Mubar. His were also.

"Crucified for us under Pontius Pilate, he suffered and was buried…" The voices swelled even higher. "Rising on the third day according to the Scriptures, and ascending into the heavens, he is seated at the right hand of the Father…"

Julia saw more tears, this time inspired by a toneless unison of ordinary people reciting memorized words. No guitar strum or mediocre vocalist to work its magic. The emotion, she realized, must be rooted in the ideas conveyed through both song and script. She listened more attentively.

"And coming again in glory to judge the living and the dead, His kingdom shall have no end…"

Judge? I thought Jesus was about love.

The rest flowed quickly. A Holy Spirit giving life, proceeding from the Father, and speaking through prophets. Then a quick reference to "one, holy, apostolic catholic church."

Is that why they called it Apostles' Church? Had Angie and Kevin joined the Roman Catholics, a church infamous for its virulent opposition to both in vitro selection and the transition industry?

"I acknowledge one baptism for the remission of sins; I expect the resurrection of the dead and the life of the age to come. Amen."

The final word served as an audible period, declaring the prolonged recitation complete. Neither Angie nor Kevin joined the half of the crowd that crossed themselves. Then all returned to the discomfort of their bench seats. Julia perceived a change in the air, like a sense of anticipation that occurs when the lights dim at the movie theater.

"Those who affirm that creed as their own may now partake."

Partake of what? Julia wondered.

A family of five seated near the front stood. Julia began to lift herself until she realized everyone else had remained seated. The pastor stepped out from behind his podium and moved around to the front, where a table Julia hadn't noticed held a saucer-shaped tray and several mugs with no handles. The family approached, the minister handing the father a piece of bread and one of the cups.

"The body and blood of Christ, sacrificed for you," he said.

The father took a bite of the bread and a tiny sip before handing both to his wife, a woman who appeared miserably pregnant with number four. Each child mimicked Mom and then the father took what remained of the bread and cup and returned it to the table. The pastor was already serving a different group, a couple with their own brood of three gangly kids.

The process continued for several minutes, one row after the next leaving their seats to participate in a ritual Julia perceived to be the culminating event of the service. When the family seated in the row in front of her own rose to their feet, Julia felt a knot in her stomach. Was she supposed to join Angie's clan at the front? She did not, as the pastor expected, agree with the script they had recited. Was she supposed to participate anyway, or was the purpose to make outsiders feel second-class?

Angie leaned toward Julia. "Do you want me to stay here with you?"

Question answered. Julia would remain seated, her sweet friend abstaining if necessary to prevent embarrassment.

"I'm fine," Julia whispered back. "You go ahead."

Moments later, Angie joined Kevin and the kids at the front of the chapel. But Julia realized she was not the only person seated. Across the aisle sat another solitary figure. He had remained behind when the family sitting in his row walked forward. Slightly older than Julia, he appeared equally uncomfortable despite greater familiarity with the routine. His face seemed kind, yet alluringly rugged—as if he were a soldier on leave from dangerous duty willingly accepted to protect those he loved.

Their eyes met. He gave a slight smile and a nod. He wasn't flirting, more like a chivalrous knight reassuring a damsel in distress.

The man's name, Julia would soon learn, was Troy Simmons. Kevin Tolbert's best friend and chief of staff.

CHAPTER THIRTY

Troy stood out of range while Kevin spoke to the pastor. He noticed Angie re-bundling Tommy's coat and little Leah absorbing the admiration of four teenage groupies watching her every move. But his eyes settled on the mysterious visitor brushing a strand of lovely dark hair from her face with one hand while awkwardly helping Joy rewrap an unwieldy scarf with the other.

Before he could offer the woman his assistance Troy noticed a miniature Eskimo lumbering in his direction.

"Hi Uncle Twoy!" a boy's voice hollered.

"Is that Tommy?" Troy removed the parka hood in search of the oldest Tolbert child. "It sure is! How's my favorite little buddy doing this fine Sunday morning?"

"I'm gweat! Are you going wif us?"

"With you where?" Troy's eyes shifted to Angie, who had caught up with her escaped son.

"Out for a quick lunch. Can you join us?"

Troy raised his eyebrows in mock amazement. "Out to lunch on Sunday?"

"Kevin and I had a late night." A slight blush. "So we told the kids we would go out instead of the usual meal at home. You'll come?"

"Pwease!" Tommy insisted.

"You bet I'll come!"

"Gweat!" Tommy cheered.

"Joy-Joy!" Troy stooped to look the two-year-old in the eyes. "What a lovely scarf you're wearing today. Very becoming!"

A bashful grin.

"Hello," he said, standing upright. "I'm Troy Simmons."

Julia extended her hand for Troy to accept with a light shake. Her soft skin fit the elegant beauty he had been admiring with quick glances for the past ninety minutes.

"I'm so sorry," Angie reacted. "Where are my manners? I forgot you two never met back in the day. This is my longtime friend Julia Davidson."

The name rang a bell. He remembered the message containing a media interview request.

"Julia Davidson from RAP Syndicate?" he said without thinking. *So much for first impressions*, he thought, exposing himself as the work-obsessed friend who spends Saturday nights reading office messages because he has no life.

"That's right. You've read my column?"

He hadn't. But she seemed pleased by the possibility. He decided to lie without words.

"I work with Kevin. It's part of my job to know who's who in the media." He made a mental note to scan a few of her columns on the way to the restaurant.

"I didn't realize Kevin had a brother," Julia said.

The comment puzzled Troy.

"Tommy called you Uncle Troy."

"Oh, that!" He smiled. "That's what the kids call me. But we're just longtime friends."

A knowing nod from Aunt Julia.

"Do you live in DC?" he asked.

"Denver. I'm here for Monday interviews and decided to come early for some girl time with Angie."

"Very nice," he said, looking in her eyes two and a half seconds longer than he should have. She appeared uncomfortable. He looked away quickly, spotting Kevin heading in their direction along with the pastor.

"I see you've met Julia." Kevin announced the obvious. "Join us for lunch?"

"Do I have to keep minutes of the meeting?"

A polite laugh. "Not if you'll pay the bill."

"Stop it!" Angie said, gently slapping her husband's chest. "He already accepted Tommy's unconditional invitation."

Julia extended her hand toward Pastor Mubar. "Hello, Father," she began. "Thank you for the service today. Or do you call it Mass?"

"We call it worship. And you can call me Pastor Seth," he replied. "Thank you for visiting with us today."

He began to walk away but Julia retained him. "May I ask you a question?" She sounded like a reporter wanting facts more than a parishioner seeking answers. "It's about something you said today."

"Of course," he replied.

"Actually, it was something everyone said during that group recitation."

"The creed," he clarified.

"Right. I heard something about the one apostolic church. Is this church Catholic?"

"'I believe in one, holy, apostolic catholic church,'" he repeated the precise wording. "The answer to your question is yes and no."

She waited for more.

"Christians started reciting the creed long before any divisions existed in the church. We use the word *catholic* as they meant it. We are catholic with a small *c* because we join all believers in all generations affirming the reality of Christ's incarnation, death, and resurrection. But we do not belong to the Roman Catholic denomination—which is probably what you are asking."

"I see." She seemed to have anticipated a different answer to set up her second question. "So do you hold similar views on issues?"

"Issues such as?" he asked.

"Such as the Youth Initiative?"

The question raised Troy's antennae. It felt improper in the one place and time he retreated from the kind of political acrimony that defined his existence the rest of the week.

The pastor glanced at Kevin before answering. "We believe all human life has dignity because it reflects the image of God himself, if that's what you want to know."

"I see," she said again, her journalistic curiosity appearing satisfied.

An uncomfortable silence followed the exchange as a caution light went on in Troy's mind. He wondered whether the lovely guest from Colorado supported or opposed the president's agenda. What would she think of Kevin's Bright Spots counterproposal? He made another mental note to look into whether she had written anything on the topic.

"A wonderful message today, Pastor Seth." Angie to the rescue. "I never considered the connection between Christ's incarnation and marital intimacy."

The comment surprised Troy. Where had he been during that part of the sermon?

"'I speak concerning Christ and the Church,'" the pastor said, reminding Troy of the brief mention. "St. Paul called it a mystery." He placed one hand on Kevin's shoulder and the other on Angie's. "But I think these two understand some of what he meant."

The statement seemed to be directed at Troy, another playful jab at his lonely bachelor status.

"Once again, I'm in the dark," Troy said in self-deprecation. "You'll need to pray for me, Pastor Seth. Ask God to bring me a woman who can open my eyes."

His usual defense.

"The Scriptures say he who finds a wife finds a good thing. One must search if he is going to find. God won't do for you what he told you to do yourself!"

The pastor's usual retort.

Kevin punched Troy's arm, his version of a playful nudge.

Angie patted the pastor's hand resting on her shoulder, her way of accepting the subtle compliment.

Julia looked down and reached for Joy's hand, her diversion from an awkward moment.

CHAPTER THIRTY-ONE

There were about twenty or thirty vehicles on the lot, three or four hundred fewer than would have been seen a quarter century earlier. The pavement showed signs of neglect, and lines of paint that once distinguished parking spots had faded, replaced by patches of resilient weeds reaching toward a sky no longer obstructed by packed minivans and sport utility vehicles.

There was a time when this same campus hosted a beehive of Sunday-morning activity. Friendly parking attendants waved visitors into special spaces reserved for a sure stream of first-time guests. Smiling greeters held doors for throngs of worshippers scurrying into the building two minutes after services began. Young couples watched the first set of songs on a flat-screen television conveniently mounted by the coffee bar before entering the auditorium just in time to miss the passing offering plate and catch the pastor's message in a place they called The Chapel.

The cars parked this Sunday morning didn't belong to commuting parishioners. They belonged to attending staff and the handful of residents still sharp enough to drive and clever enough to protect their licenses from confiscation.

The Chapel continued holding services in a scaled-down version of the auditorium, using a time-delay video feed from Pastor Skip Gregory. His image appeared immediately after thirty minutes of music specifically chosen to suit the worship-style preferences of nearly two hundred elderly baby boomers, most of whom lived a short walk down the hall.

It had been nearly ten years since the sign had been changed. The text beneath CHAPEL HILLS CHURCH had once read COMMUNITY WORSHIP CENTER. It now said RESIDENTIAL COMMUNITY, code for an elder-care facility. Even eighty- and ninety-year-old baby boomers hated the notion of getting old.

A nurse's station dispensing daily medications now stood where the coffee bar had served caramel lattes and nonfat mochas. The indoor playground had been converted into a comfortable sitting area where it had been assumed grandchildren would share details of the latest school grades earned or peewee sports trophies won. Most of the space previously designated for small group classrooms, a student center, an infant nursery, and the brightly colored "Kid Village" had been gutted and remodeled to accommodate the building's growing population of senior citizens in various stages of despondency, debilitation, deterioration, or death.

As soon as he entered the building Matthew recognized a familiar image on the wall, an ancient icon of Christ holding a book in his left hand while the tips of three fingers pressed together on his right. If memory served, it had originated in the fifth or sixth century. Before he could place the date, however, the picture changed. A thousand tiny digital shifts morphed the icon into a less familiar religious symbol, a cartoon dove spreading its white wings against a baby blue background. It seemed modern, like a relic of the late-twentieth-century charismatic movement. Then another change, to Jesus dying on a cross. It reminded him of the crucifix that had hung behind the altar at the church his mother attended while still limber enough to kneel and lucid enough to remember the Sabbath. Next came the silhouette of hands raised in worship, facing a brightly lit stage.

Matthew noticed the receptionist just in time to escape another image change. He walked toward the middle-aged woman seated behind the kind of desk likely occupied by a security guard during weekday visiting hours. The sign-in list told Matthew he would be the first of the weekend. From all appearances, guards didn't keep a flood of intruders from getting in. They prevented residents from wandering out.

"I'm here to see Richard Tomberlin," Matthew explained. The woman appeared alarmed, frantically searching the desk for a volunteer manual explaining what to do if an actual visitor came by during her shift as a hospitality hostess. After thirty seconds of panic she remembered her manners.

"I'm sorry. Welcome to Chapel Hills. Did you enjoy the service?"

"Excuse me?" Matthew asked.

"Did you enjoy the worship service? It's so nice when loved ones attend with the residents. They get quite lonely."

"No, ma'am. I'm not related to any of the residents."

She looked over Matthew's shoulder to peer at a clock on the wall. "Of course. I'm sorry. The service doesn't end for another fifteen minutes."

He stood quietly.

"How can I help you, then?"

"Richard Tomberlin?" he repeated.

"Oh. You wish to see a resident?"

"No, ma'am. I'd like to see Richard Tomberlin. He works here."

"Is he a doctor?"

"A priest. Or rather, a retired priest. I forget his title, but I think he's some sort of counselor."

Five minutes later the flustered hostess located the information Matthew needed and sent him on his way to find room 122—which, she explained, could be found just beyond the auditorium entrance. Approaching the doors, he heard an amplified voice within. The service was still in progress, but someone pushed the doors open nonetheless. A smattering of attendees walked or wheeled out in an apparent effort to beat the crowd to a lunchroom where, he would soon discover, everyone was simultaneously served.

Noticing an emaciated woman trying to navigate her wheelchair through the narrow passage, Matthew rushed over to hold the door for her. She moved past him without acknowledging his presence. He looked in her eyes, noticing the same forlorn gaze he detected in the other passing residents, a look increasingly evident on his mother's face.

He remembered the words of Professor Vincent. *We decay, Matthew*. All the genetic screening and medical advancements in the world had not reversed a process that had been vexing the human race since the dawn of time. His mother would not improve. He too would age. He too would decay.

SPIRIT GOOD. BODY BAD.

"Matthew?" The voice sounded familiar. "Matthew Adams?"

Father Tomberlin looked much older, reminding Matthew how long it had been since he had taken his mother to Mass. Having received first communion and attended St. Joseph's Parochial School during his elementary and junior high years made Matthew technically a Roman Catholic. But he was sure he had passed some sort of expiration date after nearly two decades avoiding church. Still, he had always liked Father Richard, his mother's favorite priest, turned Matthew's favorite teacher, turned whatever role he now served at Chapel Hills Residential Community.

"Father Richard?"

"Just Rick. That's what everyone else calls me these days. Wonderful to see you again, my boy!"

Matthew smiled at the reminder of Father Richard's pet handle for every student at St. Joseph's. They had all been his boys, each craving affirmation from the closest thing most had had to a flesh-and-blood father.

"I appreciate you taking time for me." He meant it. Dr. Vincent had a keen mind. But he might also have a damned soul. Father Richard, by contrast, still wore a clerical collar. Wrestling with a profoundly spiritual question had incited Matthew to seek a priestly perspective on the off chance God really did speak through the church.

"Let's pop over to the dining hall before we get trampled in slow motion." Music began in the background, signaling the benediction of a service that must end at noon. "I hope you like creamed corn and tapioca pudding!"

The priest's laughter sparked fond memories for Matthew, who tended to take himself too seriously. When teaching junior high Father Richard had often cracked himself up in the middle of his lectures on topics like the imagination of J. R. R. Tolkien or the wit of G. K. Chesterton. None of the students got their teacher's humor, but all of them relished his snorting guffaws.

During the fifty-yard stroll toward lunch Matthew caught up on Father Richard's life. His retirement from St. Joseph's. His year in Vatican City. His return to Colorado, where he was asked to provide specialized counseling to ailing seniors disguised as carefree retired church members. Because the facility housed residents from a broad spectrum of religious traditions, the Chapel needed a man who could cater to the particular spiritual needs of Roman Catholics. As it turned out, residents of any and every religious persuasion came to see him. All of them needed someone to talk to about the question that haunted anyone past seventy. The same question that had prompted Matthew's visit.

"How's your mother?" Father Richard asked as they took their seats at one of the small tables near the outer window.

"Not good."

"Does she still attend Mass at Our Lady?"

Matthew had been refusing her requests for years. He felt an urge to confess his negligence. "When she can. Not often."

Father Richard looked deeply into his former student's eyes as if reading a story, requiring mere seconds to discern the plot. "Dementia?"

"Yes, sir. Worse by the day." Matthew glanced around the room, spotting the wheelchair-bound woman he had helped at the door. He pointed. "Sort of like her."

"How old now?"

"Seventy-seven next month."

"Still living at home?"

A nod followed by a long silence. "I'm tired."

"So you're considering putting her here?" Father Richard assumed aloud.

"Oh no." The possibility had never occurred to Matthew. "She doesn't have that kind of money. I hire a parent-sitter when I can. We manage."

"But?"

"But I think there's a better option." He hesitated.

"What kind of better option?" the priest prodded.

"We're considering a transition."

It was the first time Matthew had spoken the words to another human being. It felt simultaneously shameful and liberating, as when he had confessed impure adolescent thoughts to the same man two decades earlier. Now, as then, he hoped to receive absolution for what he knew was wrong but couldn't help.

"She wants me to finish college. To become a professor." The words rushed out as if trying to overtake the sin with validity.

Father Richard's eyes narrowed at the thickening plot. "She wants to end her life?"

Matthew disliked the sound of the question. Too much clarity for a complicated decision.

"I think so."

"You think?" No letup. "What did she say?"

Another urge to confess bullied by rationalization. "She said she wants me to teach college, to use what money remains for tuition."

Two plates of unappetizing food invaded their privacy. Priest and confessor raised their forks, the sound of chewing filling the silence as Matthew awaited advice he hadn't requested. He swallowed hard, opened his mouth to speak, then took another bite.

Father Richard turned his eyes toward something specific on the other side of the room. "Do you see the woman over there in the red dress?"

Matthew searched and found. "I do."

"Her name is Carolyn. She came into my office last week after attending a transition consultation with her daughter. She closed the door and began weeping like a baby. I guess the family has hit upon some pretty hard financial times. I think her son-in-law lost a job. Something like that."

Matthew looked back across the table. "She seems pretty healthy. Why would the daughter want her to transition?"

"It wasn't the daughter who made the appointment. It was Carolyn. She wants to help them out by preserving as much of her estate as possible. She came to my office upset over her daughter's reaction."

"Was the daughter mad?"

"At first. They've always been very close. The daughter hated discussing the possibility of her mother's death. But Carolyn insisted, so they made the appointment just to gather information, no immediate intentions of exploring the possibility. More like a remote contingency option in case Carolyn's health deteriorated and elder-care expenses became cost-prohibitive."

"Sounds reasonable."

"Does it?" A slight edge invaded Father Richard's customarily playful voice.

"Isn't it wise to know your options?" Matthew asked.

"I'll let you decide after hearing the rest of the story. Carolyn wept in my office because of what happened once her daughter better understood the transition option."

He had Matthew's undivided attention.

"Long story short, the daughter did a one-eighty. She saw Carolyn's interest in a transition as the answer to a whole bunch of problems like mounting debt that threatened their ability to pay the mortgage. Not to mention her husband's depression over the lack of decent job opportunities."

"So the daughter changed her mind?"

"She did. But so did Carolyn." Father Richard leaned back in his chair. "The daughter now seemed eager for Carolyn to transition. She thanked her mom for being willing to make such a heroic offer at the same moment Carolyn got a knot in her stomach like a condemned prisoner touring the gallows."

"Wow." It was all Matthew could think to say.

The priest took another bite of food to let the scene sink in.

"Carolyn wanted my advice. But she mostly wanted a shoulder to cry on. Imagine how she felt, her beloved daughter suddenly eager for Mom's demise."

"What'd you say?"

"I mostly listened while handing her an entire box of tissues one at a time. She grew up attending the Chapel so she wasn't Catholic, but I read her what the catechism says anyway: 'Being in the image of God the human individual possesses the dignity of a person, who is not just something, but someone.'"

"Isn't her dignity the point?"

"Yes, it is."

Matthew sensed they were on different wavelengths. "What I mean is, doesn't it grant the highest dignity to a spiritual being to free him or her from a decaying body? You know, go to heaven and all that."

"Have you so quickly forgotten what I taught you in catechism class, my boy?"

Apparently he had.

"I quote the catechism again. 'The human body shares in the dignity of "the image of God": it is a human body precisely because it is animated by a spiritual soul, and it is the whole human person that is intended to become a temple of the Spirit.'"

Matthew looked around the room. "Temple of the Spirit? More like a collection of shacks."

He felt a warm hand on his forearm. "Look at me, son," Father Richard said earnestly. "You need to convince your mother that a transition is not the answer. Tell her what I told Carolyn, that our heavenly Father feeds the birds of the air. I'm sure he can take care of an overdue mortgage payment or two." A slight pause. "He can also fund a young man's college ambitions."

Matthew tried to hide his annoyance at the implication and give Father Richard the benefit of the doubt. Perhaps the priest was ignorant, unlikely as it seemed, of the teachings of ancient Gnostics and modern professors like Dr. Vincent. Maybe he had been so busy tending parishioners and preparing high school lesson plans that he had overlooked a form of spirituality offering freedom from rather than imprisonment within failing bodies.

"I don't know," Matthew began. "I mean, she is deteriorating pretty fast. I'm not sure I can..."

"You can," Father Richard interrupted. "You must. Transitions are nothing more than suicide by a different name. A mortal sin. Satan's attack on the very image of God."

It was then that Matthew realized his mistake. He should not have sought the advice of Father Richard Tomberlin.

CHAPTER THIRTY-TWO

Julia retreated to the guest room, eager to recover from one of the few fast-food meals she had eaten since graduating from college. She felt a rumble in her stomach, not from the grease, but from the conversation with Troy Simmons. It had been quite some time since an attractive man showed genuine interest in her that wasn't motivated by alcohol or overheated hormones. She reprimanded herself for a spark of chemistry she could not allow.

You could never be with a man like that! Or could she?

Troy is another Kevin, stuck in the Dark Ages with archaic views of masculinity. Or was he?

Of course he is! How else could he attend a church filled with breeders and mindlessly parrot a creed written back when women were treated like property?

And yet she found herself mysteriously drawn to his quiet strength. Troy Simmons carried himself with an unforced, natural authority that invited a sense of belonging and safety Julia remembered feeling around Angie's dad when they were teenagers.

Their conversation included none of the smooth one-liners or cocky self-obsession she had endured with other men. Troy had seemed more like an apprehensive adolescent trying to avoid missteps while talking to a cute girl. She found herself flattered by his nervous attempts, like the question he asked while they sat at the table waiting for Kevin and Angie to order their food.

"Do they harass you about being single too?"

"Who?"

"You," he said inadequately. "I mean, your friends and family. Do they prod you toward marriage?"

"I don't have a *partner*, if that's what you're wondering," she answered, emphasizing the more acceptable word.

"Partner. Right. Sorry."

The word *marriage* had fallen out of favor, especially in the glossary used by Julia's editors, ever since cohabitation became the new normal. The mistake seemed to make Troy even more tongue-tied as he tried to make small talk with someone who held very different assumptions about love and sex.

Julia decided to ease the tension. "I don't get much prodding. Although a few rogue readers have asked me to soften my critique of traditional unions."

"Traditional unions?" he repeated. "You mean like Kevin and Angie's?"

"I guess."

"What, specifically, do you dislike about it…er…them? About marriage?"

And so it went. During their early conversation Troy seemed to tangle or butcher most of his sentences. She found it infuriatingly charming.

Things got worse and better when Angie suggested Julia stand in line with Troy to retrieve three junior ice-cream cones, a task he could easily have handled alone. Despite Julia's glower, Angie winked at her not-so-subtle matchmaking effort.

"I noticed you stayed seated during that last bit in the service." Julia felt she owed him her thanks. "I couldn't parrot the mantra so assumed I didn't qualify. You?"

Troy winced at her choice of words. "I try to recite the creed, but I don't have it down like Kevin, Angie, or the other members."

"Have it down?"

"I usually stumble somewhere between 'Crucified for us under Pontius Pilate' and 'right hand of the Father.' And once I mess up the cadence I can never find an easy reentry."

Julia heard herself laugh, happy to learn she had not been the only one faking it during the service. "But you believe it?" she asked.

"Most of the time," he confessed. "I'm pretty new to Christianity."

Julia reacted in surprise. She hadn't expected Kevin's closest friend to be a lapsed pagan. "How new?"

"You might say I'm still kicking the tires. I started attending Apostles' Church with the Tolberts when I came to DC." He looked quickly at his watch, mentally calculating backward. "About a year now. It's quite different from the churches I visited with my grandma as a kid."

"Tell me about it!" she agreed. "I expected something more like the church Angie bribed me into attending with her during high school."

"I never took to Christianity before." He looked away for a moment. "Wish I had."

"Had what?"

"Wish I had taken to it. You know, went all-in. It might have helped me make better choices." His voice sagged, the sound of a man living with regrets he would rather not describe. "How about you?"

"I've never wished I had," she admitted. "My mom didn't take us to church, and most of my churchgoing friends outgrew religion. To be honest, I was surprised that a bright, popular kid like Angie stuck with it. She seems more religious now than she was then."

"More how?"

Julia thought for a moment. "I don't know. I get the feeling she lets her religion spill over."

Troy looked intrigued. "Spill over?"

"It's hard to explain. The times I attended church with her she got pretty emotional. I remember how it would weird me out, all the singing and tears and praying for this and that. But Angie was a very caring person. She was never ashamed that she cried at the drop of a hat."

"That's Angie all right," he agreed.

"I figured church was part of a package that included taking in stray cats and befriending lonely kids. I never expected religion to spill onto her choices about"—Julia stopped short of mentioning motherhood—"real-world matters."

"Were you one of those lonely kids she befriended?" Kevin asked.

The question smacked Julia's memory. In truth, she had been. A brainy girl with no figure invited into the popular crowd by a curvy cheerleader who seemed too eager to invite her to church but also too kind to let her eat alone in the cafeteria. Julia was the fatherless girl who borrowed confidence from her friend's daddy whenever invited to stay for a dinnertime ritual unknown in her own house.

"How was your day, Julia?" Angie's father always asked.

"You'll do great," he encouraged.

"Hold hands for grace," he decreed.

Those were the fleeting moments of her youth when Julia felt at home. But they were also the times she resented whatever God hadn't cared enough to give her what he or she had given Angie. A God who she decided probably didn't exist.

"Wasn't every kid lonely at one time or another?" she answered.

"I guess so. I know I was," Troy confessed.

"Anyway, like I said, I've never wished I were religious."

The entire conversation lasted the time it took a pimply-faced teen to prepare three ice-cream cones. Julia received two of the treats, grateful for the interruption. They walked toward the table, where Kevin was holding Leah while Angie relished a mischievous smile.

Julia's eyes shot a wipe-that-matchmaker-look-off-your-face warning toward Angie. Then she noticed her beckoning phone.

"Excuse me a second," she said to Troy while tapping the glowing screen.

"Hi, Aunt Julia."

"Jared? Is something wrong?"

"I need to talk to you," he began.

She remembered his message. "Oh, Jared, I'm so sorry. I got your message late last night. I intended to call first thing this morning but...well...it doesn't matter. Are you OK?"

Troy appeared embarrassed, standing too close to avoid eavesdropping.

Julia muted the call. "Sorry. My nephew. Minor domestic crisis."

He nodded.

"Go on, I'm listening," she said into the phone.

For the next sixty seconds Jared vented into Julia's ear, prompting the occasional tidbit of perspective or wisdom he would only take from his aunt.

"You don't hate your mother, Jared. You're just upset...She does care. She probably wasn't thinking. Nothing more...You know that's not true. And what does it matter what they say anyway?...I promise to talk to her about that when I get home.

OK?…Everything's gonna be fine, you'll see…Listen, I've gotta run. We'll talk when I get home. Your mom loves you, Jared. So do I."

She ended the call.

"You seemed to handle that well," Troy said, reminding Julia he had been listening. "You must be a terrific aunt."

"Oh, thanks," she said with some embarrassment. Julia raised her phone. "Julia's crisis hotline, at your service."

She felt admiration through his smile.

During the rest of the meal Julia managed to direct the conversation toward clues that might prove useful to her feature story. Kevin let slip something about a Tuesday-afternoon subcommittee meeting. Troy cryptically mentioned a first-draft report that would be on the congressman's desk in the morning. No title was mentioned, just that it included "revised projections that look better than expected." For the most part, however, the conversation steered clear of politics or religion in order for the adults to attend to cones threatening to drip and children needing a nap.

◆

The house was wonderfully quiet as the Tolbert clan enjoyed its Sunday afternoon siesta. Julia debated whether to rest or read. She chose both, slipping under the sheets with her tablet in hopes of drifting off between pages. She opened the Santos journal. The next entry Jeremy had included picked up the story five years after Antonio's diagnosis.

> <u>August 29, 2031</u>: I just got Antonio to sleep. He's been crying all afternoon and evening. Last night he was so excited about today. But when I arrived at the school they told me he couldn't attend, that the budget for special student assistance had been slashed in a late round of cuts. They blamed conservatives who voted to reduce education funding.

Jeremy was four and a half when he started prekindergarten, so we expected Antonio to go the year before last. They told me then that the kindergarten program could not accommodate his needs, that I should wait another year. I've been holding on by my fingertips ever since, the hope of Antonio spending six hours per day in a classroom motivating me to scrape our way through another twelve months.

I guess I'll need to find another source of hope. Quitting isn't an option.

I called Nina. She said she could continue coming to the house at 2 p.m. when I leave for my shift at the store. She'll stay until Jeremy gets home from school. I know I'm abusing her goodwill, that she and Marcos could use her second income. I don't know what I'd do without my sister's support.

Tomorrow I'll research remote education programs for Antonio. He's really smart and wants to learn things Nina and I can't teach. I only hope today's news doesn't crush his spirit.

Julia thought about her nephew and Maria back home. What hope would Jared have if he were told he couldn't attend school? How would her sister have managed a career if Julia had not been her backup during Jared's early years? What if Jared had required twenty-four-hour attention year after year after year?

She continued reading, noting the next entry included a picture link, which she tapped. It was a shot of Sylvia and Jeremy standing behind eight-year-old Antonio sitting in a tinsel-strewn wheelchair. Another woman knelt beside Antonio, probably Aunt Nina.

December 25, 2031: I'm sitting next to our small tree enjoying the flicker of lights. Jeremy and Antonio are still sound asleep. They didn't get to bed until nearly one o'clock in the morning when we returned from midnight Mass.

Julia paused her reading, wondering why on earth a woman in Sylvia's situation would go through the hassle of dragging two boys to church at midnight on Christmas eve.

I expect Jeremy to wake soon and, remembering the day, shake his brother. I told Jeremy Santa might bring a very special gift for Antonio this year. He begged me to say what it was, but I told him I couldn't since Santa doesn't make guarantees. Truth is, I didn't receive confirmation until last night when our priest showed me the chair. He said he finally found a donor. I suspect it was Father Mark himself, but know he'll never say.

We no longer hope that Antonio will be able to walk, and he has become too heavy for me to continue carrying everywhere. More importantly, he needs some sort of independence. He will be so excited! Finally able to steer himself around unaided. This particular unit includes an upgrade option for when Antonio's deterioration continues, an attachment that would let him control the chair with a single finger using a tiny touchpad that works with both hands or either. It can also interface with a tablet in case Antonio loses his speech.

A few months ago I brought my son to the school where we were both reminded of his defects. Today he will receive a small measure of dignity. It may not be the kind of healing Nina has prayed for, but I gratefully take what we can get. This is going to be a wonderful day!

While other kids got the latest digital toy, Antonio got a wheelchair. Hardly a moment Julia would call wonderful. Certainly not one for which she would express gratitude!

No longer sleepy, Julia continued reading confessions from a woman's life that could not have been more different from her own. For the next hour the years flew.

2032: Sylvia lands a slightly higher-paying job doing cleanup work for a start-up research lab funded by a federal grant for genetic technology. Jeremy earns mostly B's and C's in sixth grade, which Mom considers outstanding in light of the time he spends helping Antonio every weekday afternoon. Nine-year-old Antonio has become a voracious reader, devouring every article and e-book he can find on dinosaurs or robots. Especially robots.

2033: Antonio's medical needs intensify after he loses movement in both legs and much of his left arm. A concerned doctor tries to encourage Sylvia by telling her about a recent court decision expanding the scope of those eligible for assisted suicide to disabled minors. Father Mark blows his stack when he finds out. Antonio spends his days fiddling around with an outdated robotics software program he received from a member of their parish, a retired engineer who learned of Antonio's interest.

2034: Sylvia worries about Jeremy as his grades drop and his attitude sours. Marcos and Nina try taking him to their church, introducing him to the youth minister, and praying for him. Nothing seems to help. Father Mark says it's normal for teen boys to push away from their mothers, that they need a strong male influence to help them navigate body changes and build a masculine identity.

2035: Antonio finds a free online program he can do from home to reach his goal of completing seventh-grade material a full year ahead of his eleven- and twelve-year-old peers. But he loses most of his capacity for speech. They can't find a donor to fund an auxiliary voice device in such difficult economic times.

2036: A great year. Sylvia receives a pay increase after her company goes public and receives an infusion of research funding. She and the boys get involved in the Lowman presidential campaign, even volunteering to provide basic e-marketing labor from home. Antonio becomes proficient at single-finger-motion typing. He starts a journal labeled ANTONIO'S MUSINGS. Despite declining mobility he seems in good spirits, especially on election night, when he feels like a small part of history.

2037: Sylvia loses her job after the gen-tech market crash. The Santoses are forced to move in with Nina and Marcos for six months while she pieces together part-time work. Thankfully, the store where she used to work creates an opening to hire her back. The income drop forces Sylvia to move into a low-rent apartment in an even less affluent school district. Jeremy hates his new school and is nearly suspended for fighting. He claims self-defense, so only receives a warning.

2038: The economic downturn hits the Santos family hard prompting another move. Sylvia receives some help from a fellow parishioner she dates now and again, a retired engineer who has taken an interest in Antonio's education. She wants the relationship to become more serious but understands his reluctance to take on a disabled adolescent and an angry Jeremy trying his best to flunk out of high school. They remain friends, however, and he helps on occasion when the month outlasts her paycheck. He also keeps Antonio stocked with a series of dated software licenses.

2039: Congress responds to the economic crisis by passing the president's Youth Initiative. Sixteen-year-old Antonio, losing interest in his studies and robotics, shifts his focus to economics. He follows the national debate with great interest, becoming visibly angry when religious conservatives criticize the president's motives. Sylvia wishes Antonio would spend his time on more productive concerns, apply his impressive intellect to learning a useful trade. She knows he is capable of making a great contribution to the world despite his physical limitations. He ignores her pleas, says she's just a biased mom. True. But she still worries. Meanwhile, Jeremy takes a job in the same store as his mother after a near-miss graduation from high school. Minimum wage, but better than nothing.

2040: Sylvia becomes serious with another man. With Jeremy picking up part of the financial burden she is able to cut back from sixty to fifty hours per week, giving her a small margin for social activities. She had almost forgotten the rejuvenating effect of simple pleasures like eating out, watching a movie, and holding a man's hand. But it all ends abruptly when the man honors Antonio's request for a ride to the brand-new transition clinic that has opened up a mile down the road. Antonio returns from the consultation eager to play his part, serve the common welfare, and give his mom a life. Sylvia refuses to ever see the gentleman again.

As Julia swiped the screen to read Sylvia's last few entries she heard a timid knock on the door, followed by the sound of a child's voice coming through the gap at the floor.

"Aunt Juwia. You awake?" Tommy in search of a playmate.

She pulled back the sheets and moved toward the opening door.

"Yes Tommy, I'm awake. Are you?"

He didn't know how to answer.

"Give me a minute, OK?"

He nodded eagerly.

The Tolbert household was coming back to life and inviting Julia to emerge from her cocoon.

CHAPTER THIRTY-THREE

"The congresswoman will see you now." The receptionist appeared to be in his late twenties. As he opened the door for Julia she breathed deeply for one last scent of the cologne that had been teasing her senses throughout the five-minute wait. Julia had stolen a dozen glances at the man's form-fitted suit and alluringly perfect smile. She wondered whether he had been hired as eye candy to give the ten-term representative something to look forward to each morning before facing a barrage of lobbyist pitches and mind-numbing debates with fellow congressional blowhards.

"Julia Davidson!" Nicole Florea was already standing. "To what do I owe the honor of meeting one of my favorite columnists?"

It hadn't occurred to Julia that a member of the Western State Coalition might be a fan. But then she remembered the relationship with her editor. Any friend of Paul's must also be an advocate of progressive ideas regardless of party affiliation.

"The honor is mine, Madame Florea," Julia began.

"Please, call me Nicole."

Julia had seen still pictures and press conference footage of the congresswoman for years. Standing close, however, she appeared much older. Any publicist worth his salt would have carefully screened photos and clips to release only the most flattering images of a woman who had passed her prime a decade or two earlier. Even a dramatically older population considered aging taboo, especially for women. Repeated cosmetic surgeries and a costly hair enhancement routine could not hide a slightly arched stature or a voice diminished from what it had been when the now-seventy-one-year-old politician took the political world by storm.

After the usual pleasantries Julia asked permission to record their conversation. It was a journalistic courtesy that, if refused, would either banish a politician from much-needed coverage or free the reporter to speculate on why he or she had declined to comment on whatever issue dominated the day's news wire. Nicole readily agreed.

"I understand you want to discuss Kevin Tolbert."

The question surprised Julia. She hadn't mentioned Kevin, nor had she intended to. Had Paul given the congresswoman a heads-up?

"Well, actually, I wanted to get your thoughts on Senator Franklin's fiscal austerity coalition," Julia explained. "They've been pretty secretive, but we've heard something about pending proposals that seem—"

"Crazy?" Nicole interjected. "That's why I mentioned Kevin Tolbert. He's the ringleader, and I don't like the direction he seems to be taking things."

Her intensity surprised Julia. Nicole Florea had always come across as consummately evenhanded, as one willing to hear all sides before drawing conclusions or giving public comment. In this instance, however, she seemed thirsty for blood in the water.

"He's inexperienced and arrogant," Nicole continued, "and

he has no business contributing to such an effort, let alone leading it."

"I thought Senator Franklin was leading the coalition." Julia tapped her tablet screen to find the specific quote. "Here it is. 'He claims to have invited a variety of leading voices into a dialogue in order to surface the best solutions to our mounting fiscal crisis.'"

"Humph."

"I'm surprised you aren't one of the participants," Julia said, altering Nicole's expression from one of angst-filled resentment to one of ego-massaged satisfaction.

"Too much on my plate already," she said. "I don't have time for secret meetings that are unlikely to surface any new solutions."

"Can I ask why you're concerned about Congressman Tolbert?"

"Like I said, his ideas are crazy!"

"I know what you mean." Julia pretended to know more than she did in hopes of opening the congresswoman's spigot. "Do you think he's got a breeder agenda?"

"Without question," she nearly shouted. "Don't get me wrong. I'm not party to the specifics, but I know a renegade when I see one. Kevin Tolbert is a renegade."

"If you don't mind, I'd like to understand a bit about your part in getting the president's agenda passed."

"My part? In all modesty, I played the quarterback," she boasted. "Ask anyone in this town and they'll tell you. The Youth Initiative was dead in the water before I got the Western State Coalition on board. The Eastern and Northern states supported the concept immediately. But the Southern states mounted a pretty ugly attack, accusing President Lowman of sacrificing human dignity on the altar of financial stability, trying to save his own political neck by lynching senior citizens, blah, blah, blah. You know the script."

"Forgive my ignorance, but can you explain which elements of the initiative they most disliked?"

"Some of them hated the whole thing on religious grounds," Nicole explained. "Human life is sacred. Suicide is a sin. That kind of thing. We quickly waved off those objections like annoying flies. Separation of church and state."

Julia recalled pictures of offensive protest signs held by a small gathering of religious zealots outside the White House. They depicted President Lowman in a tiny black mustache beside the faces of famous senior citizens superimposed onto skeletal corpses from World War II concentration camps like Dachau and Auschwitz.

"Others played the compassion card," Nicole continued. "Much harder to ignore. They claimed the Youth Initiative snubbed the wishes of immediate family members, and demanded a provision requiring co-approval before any transition could proceed. Of course, that would have cut the estimated savings by at least half."

"Half?"

"More. Think about it, it's not like cosigning a credit card application. Putting your John Hancock next to the name of Mom, Dad, or your partner would be like throwing the switch on an electric chair. Even if they wanted to transition, the final say remains with you. So we pushed back pretty hard against that amendment."

"How did you win?"

"Simple math. Remember, every member of Congress was facing an angry constituency demanding something dramatic be done to stop the fiscal meltdown. All we had to do was show them the difference between likely transition savings with co-approvals versus the savings without. The Youth Initiative has generated over one trillion dollars in entitlement savings over the past four years. Do you know how hard it would have been to vote against that kind of savings?"

Julia sat silently remembering Jeremy Santos's words. He said this story is about real people. She calculated backward to figure out exactly how many of those *real people* it would have taken to reach the trillion-dollar figure. At least four million.

"I'm absolutely convinced we did the right thing. The compassionate thing."

"Why compassionate?" Julia wondered aloud.

"Because we compromised by including the loved-one approval stipulation for all minors and mentally impaired individuals. We also required that every application recommend transition volunteers discuss their decision with loved ones before making a final decision. It usually shows up in the fine print, but it's always in there."

Julia must have appeared unconvinced, prompting Nicole to continue.

"But the main reason the final version is more compassionate is that it protects vulnerable family members from harming themselves."

"Harming themselves how?"

"Let's face it. Lots of people will undermine their own financial stability, not to mention drain the larger economy, out of a religious or emotional resistance to a loved one's death. Our critics called preventing family member intervention cruel. We convinced them it's the most compassionate approach. Sure, family members grieve the loss. But the transition inheritance eases the pain. They very quickly see the folly of wasting perfectly useful assets on a completely pointless existence."

Julia felt a sudden shiver as she recalled her own columns written during the height of the Youth Initiative debate. She had said individual autonomy should trump family wishes, that transitions must remain a personal decision rather than a group argument, and that limited resources should be freed up from debit-care expenses to invest in future growth.

The Santos family came to mind, prompting Julia's next question. "Do you worry about the potential impact of the NEXT lawsuit?"

"I do," Nicole replied. "I can't believe they got hit with a wrongful death judgment. If that decision isn't reversed on appeal then all bets are off. Mark my words, that kid is nothing but a pawn in the hands of shark lawyers who taste money in the water."

Julia feigned a blank stare of ignorance.

"The last thing we need right now is—" Nicole stopped short, as if realizing she had said too much, then redirected. "The transition industry can't afford a black eye right now, especially when naïve freshmen like Kevin Tolbert want to take us back to the Dark Ages."

"Dark Ages?" Julia asked. "How?"

"As I told your associate—"

Associate?

"—I expect Tolbert to recommend breeder tax credits or similar rubbish. I can tell he dislikes the Youth Initiative on religious grounds. But he's clever. He'll attack it on a less obvious front. I still can't believe anyone in this town would oppose the one program we've managed to implement that's helping us claw our way back toward financial stability."

The sound of an opening door and the delicious scent of the receptionist's cologne interrupted the moment.

"Madame Florea." He said nothing more.

"Thank you, Jeffrey. Wrapping up now." The door closed as Nicole's demeanor altered from that of hardened political operative to that of a dirty old lady. "Isn't he something? Hired him right out of modeling school. Great front office decoration. Too bad he plays for the other team, if you know what I mean."

"He's lovely." Julia didn't know what else to say.

Nicole rose to her feet, signaling Julia to do the same. "I wish you well on the story. I really do hope it will head this bright spots nonsense off at the pass. Call Jeffrey if you have any further questions and we'll do what we can to help."

As the door closed behind her, Julia remembered Nicole's brief reference to an associate. She approached the pleasant aroma seated behind his desk.

"Excuse me, is it Jeffrey?"

"Yes, ma'am."

"A quick question, Jeffrey. Has anyone else from RAP Syndicate been to see Madame Florea lately? Perhaps a Mr. Paul Daugherty?"

"Just a second while I check." He tapped a calendar icon on his screen before scrolling through recent appointment notes.

"No record of a Daugherty or RAP Syndicate. Sorry."

"OK. Well, thank you for checking." She turned to go.

"I do have a record of a phone interview with a Ms. Garcia this past Friday afternoon."

Julia halted her advance.

"But there's no indication of her affiliation," Jeffrey continued.

"Monica Garcia?" Julia knew the answer already.

"That's right. Monica Garcia."

A volcano of wrath threatened to explode as Julia realized her editor had hedged his bets. He had assigned the same story to two journalists without telling either, or at least without telling her. The realization immediately cooled Julia's fury behind a chilly flood of insecurity.

CHAPTER THIRTY-FOUR

Kevin sorted and deleted a sequence of inane Monday-morning messages while listening to Troy's daily briefing: the usual rundown of subcommittee sessions and scheduled meetings with lobbyists to hear, allies to thank, and opponents to woo. But he heard nothing about the one item he really cared to know about.

"Anything on the revised projections?"

"Nothing yet," Troy said. "We just made the latest round of changes to the proposal in Thursday's session and our guy in the budget office promised to number-crunch all weekend. I'm hoping to get something this afternoon."

"I have to know that what we're selling can be sold before tomorrow's presentation," Kevin said apprehensively.

Troy looked up from his notes to silently rebuke his boss for stating the obvious.

"Sorry." Kevin shielded his head in mock defense against his friend's favorite form of revenge.

"You'll also want to know that I plan to speak personally with each member of the subcommittee today. Every one of them will deny leaks. But you know as well as I do that it could be any of them, or a spouse, or a staff member, or the friend of a friend who heard something from someone who promised not to say anything to anyone else. Rumors and speculation will happen right up until the moment Franklin goes public with the proposals. So don't sweat it. You're doing everything you can."

"I know," Kevin said with a hint of resignation. "Anything else?"

Troy took two steps backward to open the door. "One more thing." An intern entered carrying his tablet at an awkward distance, like a child inching toward the table with an overfilled cup of milk. Afraid of spilling the biggest assignment of his tenure, the young man appeared eager to finally hand over whatever information he had gathered.

"Relax, Shaun." Troy placed his hand on a tense shoulder. "Just tell us what you found."

"Yes, sir." Shaun stood at attention, a habit difficult to break after four years in the Texas A&M Corps of Cadets.

"At ease, son," Kevin jibed. "Let's hear what you've got."

"As you'll recall we received the largest reelection campaign donation to date last week. Mr. Simmons here asked me to learn what I could about the donor and update you before today's lunch meeting with Mr. Evan Dimitri."

Kevin and Troy shared a smile. The lad's voice matched his stiff posture.

"Mr. Dimitri has a long history of supporting fiscal conservatives, but very few of his donations come close to the amount he donated to Congressman Tolbert's campaign."

"What was the donation amount again?" Kevin could not recall details of a conversation held on the heels of learning about Leah's condition.

"A quarter million," said Troy.

"Only two others have received as much from Mr. Dimitri," Shaun continued. "Including Senator Josh Franklin."

Kevin accepted the news as a compliment. "Really? Franklin?"

The look on Troy's face deflated the moment.

"What's wrong?" Kevin asked.

"Nothing." Troy tried sounding upbeat. "I just want to withhold judgment until we know more."

"What's more to know?" Kevin pressed. "It makes sense that a Franklin supporter who backs fiscal conservatives would support a congressman the senator invited to chair an important subcommittee addressing economic challenges."

"Yes, it would."

"Weren't you the one who predicted Franklin's coalition is a proving ground for potential cabinet appointments if he wins the White House?"

Troy still sounded hesitant. "Yes, I was."

"But?"

"But we received the donation a day before Franklin asked you to serve."

"May I continue, sir?" Shaun still seemed worried about spilling the milk.

"Go on," Troy said.

"The only other person to receive such a large donation was Congresswoman Nicole Florea."

"Wasn't it Nicole Florea who chaired the retreat Franklin interrupted in Scottsdale?" Troy asked. "The one who has given you the evil eye every time she's seen you since Franklin invited you onto his team?"

"I get it," Kevin replied, copying Troy's folded arms in a show of reserve-judgment solidarity.

"Thank you, Shaun," Troy said to dismiss the aide. "Well done."

"Yeah, great job, Shaun," Kevin added.

Kevin followed Troy out of the office to begin his trek toward his next meeting. When they reached the stairs Kevin placed a hand firmly on his friend's shoulder to halt their advance. "One last thing."

"Shoot."

"I need a report on one other matter."

Troy appeared puzzled. "What other matter?"

"A certain Angie Tolbert expects a briefing on your assessment of Julia Davidson."

"Excuse me? What about Julia Davidson?"

"My guess is she wants an explanation for the way you were looking at her."

Troy shook his head. "Can't a guy enjoy an attractive woman's company without his friends assuming—"

"No, he can't. Nor can you send me home to a curious wife without a shred of intelligence. Angie senses you're falling for Julia. My job is to fill in details."

"I just met the woman!"

"And?" Kevin pressed.

Troy's brow made a show of resistance.

Kevin glanced at the time. "You have exactly sixty seconds to give me something or you can kiss our friendship goodbye. I refuse to sleep on the sofa tonight!"

Troy rolled his eyes at the threat. "She won't make you sleep on the sofa."

"One sound bite. That's all I need. Come on, Troy, don't leave me hanging."

Troy laughed. Then he reached for a suitable nugget. "OK. I've got something," he said. "I overheard a phone conversation between Julia and her nephew."

"I think Angie wants something about you and Julia, not Julia and her nephew."

"Just let me finish," Troy said. "During the conversation with her nephew I sensed a maternal warmth that surprised me."

Kevin appeared intrigued. "Hmm. That's good. Would you say *pleasantly* surprised you?"

"OK. Pleasantly surprised me," he conceded.

"Better." Kevin winked.

"Julia portrays herself as a competitive, cutthroat journalist," Troy continued. "But I saw something in her eyes and heard something in her voice during that call that told me there's more to Julia Davidson than a pretty face with an impressive portfolio."

"Such as?"

Troy hesitated, as if embarrassed to say any more.

"Come on Troy. You know Angie will want the punch line."

"OK," he relented. "I sensed a hint of what I see when Angie is with the kids."

Kevin understood. And, more importantly, he had what he needed. "Perfect! She'll love that. Thanks, pal. You've kept me off the couch tonight!"

Troy punched his friend's arm. "You better get moving. You don't want to be late."

◆

An hour later Kevin extended his hand to the mysterious Evan Dimitri, who had already been seated in the congressional dining hall.

"It's an honor to meet you, Mr. Dimitri." His usual warmth and enthusiasm concealed a lingering apprehension. "I hope you haven't been waiting long."

"Fifteen minutes." A rebuke.

Kevin looked at his watch for confirmation that he had indeed arrived early. To remind his guest of their scheduled time would lack decorum. To apologize for an unspecified mix-up would show weakness.

"Well, thank you for taking time to meet."

"It worked out. I had several other meetings on the Hill this afternoon," Dimitri explained flatly.

Kevin took a chair across from the man who squeezed congressmen into his day. His solid frame matched a strong jaw beneath a full head of thick gray hair. He wore a black, mousy suit that gave him the appearance of an accountant who played rugby. He had apparently developed his social skills while banging heads with opponents on a muddy field.

"I wanted to express my appreciation for your generous donation to my reelection campaign." Kevin dove right into his only agenda item. "As you probably know, the next election cycle should prove tough in light of our economic challenges and—"

"Save the speech for campaigning," Dimitri interrupted. "Elections are only tough when the other guy has more cash to spend marketing himself. Consider my gift a down payment on what should be a very aggressive campaign."

Kevin felt both flattered and uneasy, like a kid receiving a side-armed hug from the school bully who had selected him as his new sidekick.

"We've been watching you, Mr. Tolbert," Dimitri continued. "We think you have great potential."

"We?"

"Let's just say you've been the topic of conversation among friends who have the means to give you a bright future in Washington. We like what we've seen thus far. A solid fiscal conservative with the brains to come up with innovative ideas and the will to run toward rather than away from tough issues."

Kevin remained quiet, waiting for the other shoe to drop.

"You remind me of Nicole Florea when she was younger."

Kevin repressed any show of taking offense at the comparison. "Really. How's that?"

"People liked her. Trusted her instincts. And when her influence was needed most she rallied the troops."

"Rallied them for what?"

The question prompted a sardonic laugh. "What else?" He

looked around for their waiter, impatient after nearly three minutes without attention. Then he noticed the hostess escorting a couple to a table twenty feet away and gave a summoning motion. "Two soups of the day," Dimitri ordered without bothering to check with Kevin. "And more bread."

He turned back. "The most important austerity measure ever enacted happened thanks to the political skill of Nicole Florea. If she hadn't managed to get the Western states on board, Lowman's agenda would have gone down in flames. More importantly, our financial crisis would be even worse than it is now."

"Are you sure about that?"

Dimitri ignored the question. "You know as well as I do that things are about to get much more severe. We will need new, younger voices with bold ideas like the one you plan to propose tomorrow."

"Tomorrow?" Kevin tried to sound surprised.

"At the austerity team meeting where you'll present the Bright Spots proposal."

Is he fishing? Kevin wondered. "I'm not at liberty to discuss—"

"Have you cashed it?" Dimitri interrupted.

"Excuse me?"

"Have you cashed my donation check?"

"I suppose it's been deposited. Why do you ask?"

"Then you're at liberty to discuss, Mr. Congressman." The rugby player's tone changed from patronizing to lecturing. "You plan to propose incentives that will make it easier and more likely for citizens to have and raise kids. You'll show the annual economic impact of each worker to demonstrate why creating a new crop of taxpayers is essential to our long-term financial stability. Am I right?"

Kevin gave a reluctant nod. "Among other ideas, yes."

"Good. I like it." He sounded like an architect approving one last detail on an intricate blueprint.

"I'm glad," Kevin replied. "But can I ask how you know so much about my proposal? Every member of our subcommittee pledged to hold our sessions in strict confidence. Who's been talking?"

Dimitri waved off the question. "Don't worry. I don't have many details, just broad strokes. Enough to know you'll be an important player when Franklin makes his move. Your proposal will round out a nice package."

"Round out?"

"It adds a long-term strategy to the short-term measures we'll need if we're going to avoid a meltdown."

The pieces of the Evan Dimitri puzzle began to assemble themselves in Kevin's mind. A big player among political action committee donors. A man who backed fiscally conservative candidates, reviewed confidential economic forecasts, and received briefings on Senator Franklin's secret austerity coalition. Kevin was having lunch with a man accustomed to pulling the strings of various insider puppets.

A fresh basket of bread and two bowls of soup appeared on the table. Kevin hadn't noticed the waiter's arrival.

Dimitri spoke slowly as he concentrated on spreading a slab of butter across a hunk of the warm loaf. "Listen, Congressman. You wanted to have lunch to say thanks for my donation. I get that, and you're welcome. Consider the gift an expression of my appreciation for what you're doing to help this nation avoid economic collapse. It comes with no expectations."

Kevin braced himself.

"But it does come with a request. I ask you to think both/and rather than either/or. Use your growing influence to advance new ideas without undermining existing, proven austerity measures. Trust me, kid, that approach will take you far."

Evan Dimitri had apparently selected his next useful marionette and made a first tug on the strings. In the middle of spooning his soup Kevin felt a sudden loss of appetite.

CHAPTER THIRTY-FIVE

Julia took one last look in the mirror hanging above the ladies' room sink to inspect the renovation of her face and hair. The brisk trek along Independence Avenue had subjected her uncovered head to brisk April winds only partially blocked by the Longworth Building, situated between the Cannon and Rayburn Buildings. The walk had done her good, cooling more than her now-rosy cheeks. It had helped her simmer down after the galling realization that Paul had given Monica Garcia equal access to Congresswoman Florea and, Julia assumed, to Trisha Sayers.

Her shaken confidence had been bolstered as soon as Julia stepped into the building that held Kevin Tolbert's office. She assured herself that Monica could not possibly have similar access to a bright spots insider, a disadvantage impossible for the younger journalist to overcome.

"Julia?"

Startled to hear her own name seconds after entering the hallway, Julia turned toward the voice. Troy Simmons smiled in her direction from thirty feet away.

"Hello, Troy." Julia surprised herself by the slight lilt in her voice.

"We didn't expect you for at least another hour."

"I just left a meeting at the Cannon Building." She chose not to mention Nicole Florea. "It ended early. Since I had some extra time I thought I'd pop over to make sure I could find Kevin's office."

"I'm heading there now. May I escort you?" He offered an arm.

"Lead the way." She pretended not to notice his courtly gesture.

He quickly retrieved the extended arm to salvage his injured pride, then gestured with his open palm toward office number 202 just down the hall.

Kevin Tolbert's suite was the second-smallest in the Rayburn House Office Building. It held a few tiny desks occupied by fresh-faced interns in front of two enclosed rooms occupied by the congressman and his chief of staff. Freshmen were at the bottom of the congressional pecking order, accepting whatever meager facilities remained after veteran representatives had finished vying for larger accommodations vacated by retiring or ousted colleagues. A very different world from the more elaborate offices of Nicole Florea, who had steadily increased square footage by winning several rounds of musical chairs. Julia found the cramped space and functional arrangement of the congressman's complex highly unimpressive.

"Welcome to Tolberton!" Troy announced.

"Tolberton?"

"As in Hobbiton," he said proudly.

She didn't follow.

"Come on. Middle-earth? The Shire? 'In a hole in the ground there lived a hobbit'?"

Nothing connected.

"We merged Tolkien's world with Kevin's last name and came

up with 'Tolberton' as an apt label for our hole-in-the-ground dwelling."

"I see," she said indifferently.

"Anyway, I expect Kevin to return from his lunch meeting soon. He has an important call at one thirty before your interview." Julia followed Troy ten steps, into his hobbit hole. He quickly removed a stack of folders sitting on top of the room's only vacant chair. "You're more than welcome to wait in my office if you'd like."

Julia glanced at her watch. Over an hour to kill.

"Or"—Troy seized on her apparent hesitation—"we could pop across the street. Have you been to the Botanic Garden?"

She hadn't.

"A much better way to spend an hour than sitting in this dreary office," he said.

"I wouldn't want to impose. You have work to do and—"

"Are you kidding?" he interrupted. "I'll get twice as much done if I recharge the old batteries. Besides, I need to get over there before they level the place for the new office building. I've never visited. But I'm still sad to see it go."

Every instinct told Julia to refuse. An internal tennis match ensued.

Don't do it. You could give him the wrong idea.

But you might learn more about the Bright Spots proposal.

He'll become a distraction.

He seems so sweet.

"That actually sounds kind of nice," she said with too much enthusiasm.

"Great!"

The next sixty minutes flew by quickly as they chatted casually while admiring the oasis of deep green and floral colors on display throughout the glass building.

"So you've known Kevin for a long time?" Julia asked.

"Met the first day of seventh grade," Troy mused. "Both new to town and each condemned to lunchroom solitary confinement. He noticed me first and joined my table. From that moment on we were pals, two self-doubting boys yearning to become insecure teens."

She laughed at the truism. "And look at you now. Obviously you helped one another along."

"A little."

"A little? I don't know many men who have accomplished as much. You certainly found some measure of confidence."

"That would be Kevin. Confidence found him."

"How so?" she asked.

"Angie."

Julia's surprised reaction halted their stroll.

"He started seeing her the year I moved across town. He couldn't stop talking about this amazing girl I'd never met. Kevin will tell you she made him into the self-assured man you see today. I've just been lucky enough to glean the scraps."

She flashed a quizzical expression. "What does that mean?"

He thought for a moment. "Ever hear of a rainmaker?"

"Someone who lands the big deal?" Julia guessed.

"That works. You could call Kevin the rainmaker, the guy who makes things happen."

"So what does that make you?"

"I guess I'm Sam Gamgee." He seemed proud of the label.

A blank stare. "Sam Gam-what?"

"Sorry. Another Tolkien reference. Sam Gamgee. My favorite of his characters."

"I guess I should read *The Hobbit*."

"You should. But Sam Gamgee shows up in Tolkien's longer work, *The Lord of the Rings*."

She waited for further explanation.

"To make a thousand pages short, Frodo Baggins is given an

enormous assignment to save Middle-earth from certain doom. Sam goes along to support, encourage, and protect his friend. Without Sam, Frodo would have failed in his quest. But without Frodo, Sam would have lived without adventure."

Julia sensed Troy's pride in his identity as Kevin's right-hand man. "I admire that. Not many men have such calm confidence."

"Kind of you to say, my lady," he said playfully.

"Have you ever wanted to switch roles? You know, grab the limelight. Have Kevin defer to you instead of the other way around?"

"Sure. But that's not my calling."

"Calling?"

"My assignment. The unique contribution only I can make," he explained. "I could no more fill Kevin's shoes than he could fill mine."

Julia felt a twinge of indignation on Troy's behalf. "But why should he get all the attention? Give all the orders? You seem every bit as sharp, articulate, and successful as Kevin."

"You forgot handsome," Troy jibed.

"Definitely as handsome!" Julia agreed with a slight blush.

"More handsome," he added with a wink.

"I guess I don't know many people who are content sitting in the second chair." She wasn't sure whether she found the trait admirable or weak. "Isn't that—"she reached for a word besides *demeaning* "—difficult?"

"Sometimes," Troy confessed. "But I draw inspiration watching Angie. She's pretty amazing, like a Sam Gamgee who can have babies."

Julia clenched her teeth as she tried to suppress offense at the blatantly sexist comment. She waited a moment to allow three elderly ladies to pass. "So Kevin puts Angie in the second chair? 'Take care of the kids while I conquer the world'?"

Troy appeared startled by the reaction. "Not at all. The only place I've ever seen Kevin place Angie is on a pedestal. Angie puts herself in the second chair."

"Why would she do that?"

"Do what?"

"You know. Sell herself short. She's a smart woman who could do anything she put her mind to. Why would she throw away her dreams so that Kevin can—"

"She said that?" Troy asked.

Julia went silent.

"Did Angie say she threw away her dreams to support Kevin?"

"Well, not exactly," Julia confessed. "We had dinner the other night and she seemed, I don't know, less confident than when we were younger. She was never like that before. I guess I just assumed—"

"You assumed no intelligent woman would choose to raise kids or give up a career to support her husband?" Troy interjected.

"Well, yes," she answered.

The faint sound of ventilating mist filled the tense silence as surrounding plants received an early afternoon spray of refreshment. Julia felt an urge to quote from a long line of her own columns.

The days of patriarchal dominance are dead.

Our generation of women can see an endless horizon because we stand on the shoulders of our courageous grandmothers.

Show me a home with more than two kids and I'll show you an oppressed woman.

"Can I ask you a question?" Troy asked tentatively.

"Of course."

"Why does my second chair imply calm confidence but Angie's implies weakness?"

Julia realized her unintended offense. "I didn't mean to imply—"

"Listen, Julia. Angie is the strongest woman I've ever met," he continued. "It takes great courage and dignity to serve."

Julia felt another flare of anger. "Serve? Like a slave?"

"A slave is not better than his master," Troy replied.

"Meaning?"

"It's something Jesus said, that he came to serve rather than to be served. Like I said yesterday, I'm still new to this whole Christianity thing. But that's one of the ideas I find very appealing. Imagine a world of people trying to out-serve, out-love, out-sacrifice, and out-honor one another. Sure beats a world of people trying to outdo and outsmart one another. Don't you think?"

Monica Garcia came to mind instantly. Then Paul Daugherty. Then herself. "I guess I never thought about it like that before."

"I get a small taste of that world when I watch Kevin and Angie in action with each other and with the kids. The scraps are so good it makes my mouth water for the full banquet."

Noticing the time, Julia suggested they start walking back. As they turned toward the exit Troy hesitantly extended his arm. "May I escort you?" he asked with an air of gallantry.

An awkward second passed between them. Then she permitted herself a smile before self-consciously accepting his offer.

CHAPTER THIRTY-SIX

"Sorry to have kept you waiting." Kevin stood just outside Troy's open office door. "My one thirty call took longer than expected."

"Everything all right?" The question seemed to carry weight, as if Troy knew the call pertained to an ailing relative.

"Fine. Possible good news, in fact. I'll brief you later."

Troy looked at Julia like a dance partner reluctantly accepting another man's request to cut in. "Well then, the time has come for our parting. I thank you for the pleasure of your company."

Julia rose from a chair nestled between Troy's overflowing desk and the windowless wall. She extended her hand toward Kevin's. "Thank you for granting me an interview."

"How could I refuse?" he said while navigating Julia out Troy's door and through his own three feet away. "You were holding my kids hostage at the time of the request."

"I figured that might do the trick," she said, laughing.

"I did want to say thank you, again, for giving Angie and me a much-needed evening alone. It's been a bit stressful lately."

She wondered whether that stress was somehow linked to the

potential good news from Kevin's phone call, a concern neither he nor Angie had invited her to share.

"They're great kids. You must be proud." She hoped the compliment sounded sincere.

"And busy! For some reason kids don't stop demanding attention just because Dad gets elected to Congress. Pretty selfish of them."

Julia smiled politely as she took the seat Kevin offered. It was still a tight squeeze, though his office offered a bit more breathing room than Troy's, including the miniature sitting area essential for the many occasions when a congressman receives visiting guests and colleagues. To describe the office in print Julia would choose the word *functional*. A room more suited to getting things done than to making a good impression.

She reached into a bag for her tablet, then glanced at the display screen listing three recent files: the interviews with Jeremy Santos, Hannah Walker, and Nicole Florea. She hit RECORD before remembering her manners.

"Sorry. Do you mind if I record our conversation?"

"I do."

The answer caught Julia by surprise. She couldn't recall anyone's refusing the request. A bit flustered, she quickly tapped STOP.

"I'd like to keep our conversation off the record for now," he explained.

A hint of outrage rose in Julia. *Off the record?* She wanted to object, to remind Kevin that smart politicians craved the kind of exposure a RAP feature might give, or at least feared the kind of damage it could do. Either way, they never risked spurning a journalist. But she thought again. *I'll make more progress as a friend seeking a favor than as a reporter cornering a victim.*

"I'm involved in some highly confidential work right now and I can't take a chance that I might inadvertently leak anything. I'm sure you understand."

"Of course," Julia forced herself to say. She switched to Plan B. "Then can I ask for first break?"

"What's that?"

"You would give me a twenty-four-hour window ahead of other journalists to report on what we've discussed."

Kevin appeared to be examining the request in his mind to check for scratches and dings before deciding to buy.

"Listen, Kevin." Julia appealed to sympathy to close the deal. "It would really help me out. To be honest, I've been in a bit of a dry spell lately. I thought a feature on a young congressman's efforts to tackle tough economic issues might play well."

As she'd hoped, Kevin seemed flattered by the suggestion. "Sounds reasonable," he said. "I'll think it over and let you know by the end of the day." Still cautious.

"That'd be great." Getting her story was going to be more difficult than Julia had hoped.

"Am I correct in assuming you asked for an interview because you know about my role on Franklin's austerity team?"

The question made her feel as if the teacher had caught her peeking at another student's paper. She decided to come clean. "Well, I confess that had something to do with it."

"Tell me what you know."

"Not much. Just that Franklin invited you to be part of a confidential austerity team and that you chair a subcommittee exploring something about bright spots."

"Any idea why the austerity team was formed?"

"I assume a new phase of Franklin's SLASH project," Julia replied. "I read the other day that epi-genomic research would be his next target, after the project received a thumbs-down from his constituents."

"And who told you about the Bright Spots proposal?"

Julia feared losing control of the conversation, if she'd ever had it. "I'm afraid I can't name sources. But I do have a list of questions I'd like to ask."

"Off the record?"

"Right." *For now*, she thought.

Julia scrolled through her tablet to find her prepared list.

"First, is there more to the austerity coalition than meets the eye?"

"That depends. What meets your eye?"

"To be honest, a group of heartless fiscal conservatives slashing vital governmental services."

"In that case, yes, there is more going on than meets the eye," he said. "Our economy faces dire problems, more than you probably realize. We hope to propose solutions before things get out of hand."

"How out of hand?"

"I prefer not to comment on that at the moment."

"Is something going on our readers should know about?" She sounded a bit more like the hard-hitting journalist she aspired to be. "I'd hate to think the government is withholding information from the public."

"Nothing has been hidden. All of the information we are discussing is currently accessible to anyone who cares to look."

Julia ran through a mental list of usual suspects.

The quarterly report on housing vacancies?

The mushrooming cloud of national and personal debt?

Another stock market decline?

There were so many possibilities, since nearly every economic trend had been moving in the wrong direction for years. Which would prompt a sudden call for draconian budget cuts?

"Look where?" she asked.

"Again, I'd rather not comment. Except to say I'm surprised how little attention the news syndicates have given to falling fertility."

The topic hadn't crossed her mind, but the comment stepped on her toes. "Not true. Just last week I did a column on the topic. And we did that big hoopla last August over the population tipping point."

"I stand corrected," he conceded.

"But I don't understand what fertility has to do with austerity measures."

"You'll need to figure that out on your own. Next question," he said.

Dissatisfied, she reluctantly looked at her list. "What are bright spots?"

"A reference to the process of finding isolated pockets of success or health in the midst of an otherwise dismal situation," he explained. "You know, like finding the silver lining, only applied to economics. When we identify micro–bright spots we can learn a lot about potential solutions on a macro level, or at least what behaviors to encourage rather than dissuade. The specific subcommittee I chair has been looking hard at pockets of economic strength. I think we've identified strategies that will give the ailing patient a health spa membership instead of admitting him to an intensive care unit."

"That sounds like a speech applause line," she chided.

"A pretty good one too, don't you think?"

"Maybe for a speech. But it sounds naïve for national policy. You can't just tell a sickly patient to suck it up and run the Boston marathon."

"I'll grant you that," he acknowledged. "No one thinks any single idea will turn things around. My proposal will become part of a much larger package."

She remembered Paul's concern that the Bright Spots proposal would likely advance a radical breeder agenda. Nicole Florea had said the same. Julia decided to go out on a limb.

"I understand you plan to propose reintroducing child tax credits."

The statement seemed to jolt Kevin. "Who told you that?"

"I can't reveal sources," she said, sustaining the ruse. "But you could confirm or deny that part of my story. Assuming, of course, you'll go on the record." She held her breath as he formulated a reply.

"Nice try, Julia," he said. "But I refuse to say anything about specific proposals. And I won't confirm speculations one way or the other. Next question."

The conversation went on in a similar fashion for fifteen minutes, Julia fishing for details while Kevin remained vexingly evasive. After nearly half an hour she had managed to extract few details, none of which could be used since everything remained off the record. Paul would be displeased.

She threw in the towel, abandoning her prepared list of questions. "Come on, Kevin. Can't you give me anything?"

He leaned back in his chair like a high school teacher hoping to nurture a student's curiosity rather than give the answers. "What was your reaction to the most recent census?"

"I don't know. Why do you ask?"

"Like I said earlier, all of the information is available to anyone who cares to look."

Julia sensed Kevin was changing the game. "Well, like everyone else I'm a bit concerned about how we'll deal with so many senior citizens. But on the whole I'm optimistic. Birth rates continue to drop. That should reduce the drain on scarce resources."

"What kind of resources?"

"Fuel. Trees. Food. Everything."

"So you think food is a scarce resource?"

"Come on, Kevin. You know as well as I do that millions are starving."

"Really? Where?" he pressed.

"I don't know. Africa."

"What part of Africa?"

"Do you want the ZIP codes?" she objected. "I don't know what parts. What are you getting at?"

"Did you take Economics one-oh-one?" he asked.

"I did."

"Then you know about the law of supply and demand."

"Of course."

"Are you aware of the fact that it costs less to buy a calorie of food today than ever before in history?"

No, she wasn't.

"So why do we continue to consider food a scarce resource? I agree there are starving people in the world. But when you get specific about where they starve, you find it invariably the result of war or corrupt leadership."

"Is there a reason we're heading down this rabbit trail?" Julia asked.

"Just to say that we don't have a global food shortage, especially in this nation where more people become obese than go hungry. So, when you say scarce resources, don't you really mean money?"

"Well, you wouldn't be trying to find cuts in federal spending if we were rolling in cash. Would you?"

"There. Now we're back on the main trail," Kevin confirmed. "In this country we face a financial crisis, not a resource crisis. Just to be clear."

"Okay. You win. Scarce financial resources then."

"And you think children cost a lot of money?" he continued. "Money that could be spent on...?" His voice lingered, inviting Julia to complete the sentence.

"Taking care of seniors, for one."

"So we need more money to take care of our elderly citizens. Is that what you're saying?"

"I feel like I'm talking to Socrates!" she mocked. "Yes, we need more money for things like health care. Isn't that obvious?"

"And where does the money required for those expenses come from?"

Julia thought the answer too obvious. "From taxes."

"Paid by...?" Another fill-in-the-blank.

"Taxpayers, of course."

"Wrong," Kevin said, as if he were swatting a fly with a magazine. "The money comes from human beings. And the fewer human beings involved in the economy there are, the scarcer that all-important resource called money becomes. In each of the past ten decades this country has followed the rest of the developed world down a path toward depopulation. The same reality squeezing the federal budget is also creating a housing glut, a manufacturing slump, and an overburdened health-care system. Our scarcest resource is not food, trees, or fuel. Our scarcest resource is people."

The idea struck Julia as sacrilege offending an orthodoxy to which she and her readers unquestioningly subscribed. She started to search for a hole in Kevin's rationale but stopped when she suddenly grasped his likely motive.

"Wait a minute," she said. "You *are* considering tax credits for having kids, aren't you?" She felt herself becoming upset by the possibility. "You want to go back to the days when the federal government stuck its nose in America's bedrooms. I thought we outgrew that kind of nonsense decades ago. I assume you've heard that we had a sexual liberation movement on this planet. Kids are a choice, not an obligation. Women are good for more than becoming baby factories!"

Mid-diatribe Julia remembered Angie. She regretted her statement immediately, the look on Kevin's face confirming an offense. "I'm sorry. I didn't mean to imply..."

"No need to explain yourself, Julia. I understand your position. You think women like Angie are squandering their potential."

Julia sat silent, owning the accusation.

"Well, I respectfully disagree," Kevin continued. "A lot of people consider bearing and rearing children a noble and highly meaningful calling. But we can set that aside for the moment. More to the point, both short- and long-term economic trends make it an important national priority."

She felt the need to pull back, softening the edge of her heat-of-the-moment speech. "You know I think the world of Angie. I don't mean to minimize what she's done or any other woman who chooses motherhood. My own sister decided to keep a baby. We share the load raising my nephew. But you don't really think you can coerce women to have more babies in this day and age, do you?"

"No, I don't," he answered. "But I do think we can stop making it so difficult to do so. We can stop penalizing those willing to have children to reward those who don't. Take a look at the numbers, Julia. Our tax code makes doing what's difficult harder and doing what's selfish easy."

"So people like me are selfish?"

Now Kevin appeared to regret his words. "I didn't mean it like that. There are plenty of valid reasons people avoid marriage and parenthood. But far more choose childlessness than ever before in human history. The trend lines are clear, Julia. If we don't see a pretty dramatic fertility jump soon we will look a whole lot like Japan, Russia, and China in a few short years."

He stood and turned toward the window to gaze like a protective father spotting an approaching storm. "Based on the latest census, I fear we may have already gone too far to turn back."

Julia rose to her feet to join him, noticing the tip of the Capitol Building Rotunda just above a line of trees a thousand yards beyond.

"You may find this hard to believe. But people like me love our country too."

"I know," he said.

They continued staring out the window for several seconds, two doctors conflicted over how to best treat the same ailing patient.

Julia spoke first. "Listen, Kevin. RAP Syndicate is going to run a story on Franklin's austerity committee, including something about the Bright Spots proposal."

He looked in her direction. "With or without the facts?"

"With or without your perspective," she replied. "A perspective I would much rather include if possible."

He turned back toward the window.

"I have an idea," she said. "If you agree to give me access to the substance of the discussions before anyone else I'll guarantee space in my feature to let you make your case in your own words. Nine million readers."

"All of them ready to throw stones."

"Probably. But at least they will have a chance to hear your side of the debate. That won't happen with any other syndicate. You never know, you might just woo some of them to your side. That is your specialty, is it not?"

A deep breath lifted his sagging shoulders. "Deal."

"Really?"

"Why not? I'll be fighting an uphill battle anyway. I might as well do it on my own turf."

"So, can we go on the record?"

"Not yet," he said. "But if you plan to stay in DC through tomorrow I might just be able to give you the kind of access other journalists would kill for."

Julia's face lit up. "Such as?"

"How would you like to sit in on my proposal presentation in the morning?"

Five minutes later Julia stood outside, her hair blowing in the chilly wind as she tapped out a time-buying message to Paul Daugherty.

GOOD NEWS. JOINING MEETING WITH FRANKLIN'S TEAM IN THE MORNING!

CHAPTER THIRTY-SEVEN

It was nearly ten o'clock before Matthew arrived at work, two hours later than he'd intended. Dozens of crumpled napkins scattered beside half-empty mugs of lukewarm coffee told him there had been a morning rush. Had he arrived earlier Sarah would have asked him to clock in before his scheduled shift. Disappointed, he reminded himself it had been a rough few nights and that he'd had good reason to ignore the alarm clock. He'd needed the extra sleep more than he needed the extra money.

Matthew had spent much of the prior two days battling his mother's unsettled nerves. It had started Sunday. He'd known it was risky leaving her alone for the time it took him to meet with Father Tomberlin. Something must have disoriented her, causing her to forget his predeparture instructions.

"Donny won't be here to stay with you, Mom," he had explained. "I promise I won't be gone long. I'm going to visit Father Tomberlin."

Her face lit up at the mention.

"You remember Father Tomberlin, don't you?"

A nod told him that she did.

"What time is Mass?" she asked.

Matthew didn't bother reminding her of Father's retirement or that he no longer led Mass at St. Joseph's. Nor did he see any point explaining the real purpose of his visit.

"I'm not attending Mass," he replied. "I'm just going to talk to Father Tomberlin. I should be home before two o'clock." He showed her a small clock as his finger mimicked the hour hand moving from the eleven to the two. "I left you a sandwich on the kitchen table. Just remove the cellophane wrap when you get hungry. OK?"

The sandwich remained untouched when Matthew arrived home, the first of two instructions forgotten.

"If you need anything or feel scared just say, 'Call Matthew' and the phone will ring me. If you forget that, just press my image on this screen," he had said, pointing to a large digital tablet sitting beside her chair. "One tap and I'll be on the line with you in five seconds."

Also forgotten, evidenced by the puffy eyes that greeted him when he found her whimpering in the corner of her bedroom. She had apparently searched every inch of their tiny home dozens of times over the prior two and a half hours, eventually giving up at the mistaken realization that her son had gotten lost, or had left her, or had died.

Matthew spent the rest of Sunday holding his mother's hand in a tangible guarantee of his promise never to leave her alone again. It didn't work. She spent much of the night crawling in and out of bed, reliving her frantic search for a son who might vanish at any moment. It wasn't until Monday evening that she seemed back to her normal, semi-befuddled self. That's when he made an even bigger blunder.

He raised the subject while sitting beside her as she watched television, a hesitant child broaching a difficult topic. Unable to look her in the eyes, he muted the television during commercial breaks to toss fragments from what he had intended to be a carefully crafted, coherent script.

"I took a big step today, Mom," he began, eyes fixed on the screen. "I submitted my application to the University of Colorado."

She looked toward Matthew, pleased at the reminder of her dream for him.

"I've always said you should be a professor." She sounded like her old self, a proud mother flattering her faultless son.

"I know," he continued. "You convinced me it was a good idea to see if they will admit me on probation. I got pretty solid grades at Front Range Community College."

"I remember. They'll accept you. And you'll do great."

"Anyway, if I get accepted we'll have some pretty important decisions to make."

She said nothing. The corner of his eye perceived a head nodding in oblivious agreement.

The commercial ended, triggering Matthew to un-mute the sound. He would use the ten minutes of onscreen drama to decide how he would word the second of four points.

"Did I ever tell you how much tuition costs?" he asked, muting the next commercial. They both watched gorgeous mimes promote a new perfume or luxury automobile.

"What's that?"

"Tuition. I was looking into how much it will run for tuition, tech access, on-campus housing." He sensed her head turn toward him. "All of the expenses of going to college full time."

"On-campus housing?" A slight panic rose in her voice.

He pretended not to hear. "So the total, near as I can figure, will run about sixty thousand per year. A quarter million for the full degree. Then graduate school."

"Why would you need on-campus housing?" she asked. "Can't you live at home?"

"Sure I could," he backpedaled. "I'm just checking into all the options. You know, in case."

Her breathing slowed back to normal. "I see."

He raised the volume in the middle of a second commercial, pretending interest in the ad because he wasn't quite ready to raise point three.

"I got an auto-reply message from the college financial aid office that included tips on how to pay for school," he continued ten minutes later, the dancing light of silent images bouncing across his tentative face. "My job might cover about ten percent of the cost if we can wean you off of some of the more expensive medications."

She didn't react. It had been some time since she'd known which daily pill treated which ailment. Matthew would know what was best in that arena anyway.

"They don't really offer many four-year student loans anymore," he continued. "The whole austerity budget thing pretty much eliminated that option. And we can't expect any kind of academic scholarship since I'll be lucky to get accepted on probation as it is."

As he'd hoped, she seemed to recall an offer made years earlier. "What about the money your grandfather left us? Can't we use some of that?"

"That's a possibility," he responded. "But we currently use that money to live."

The program returned on cue. In ten minutes Matthew would ask his mother the hardest question of his thirty-three years. He used the time to mentally rehearse his rationalization.

SPIRIT GOOD. BODY BAD.

"*Jesus…was a death-embracing mystic,*" Dr. Vincent had said. "*The Manichaeans taught that the physical body is evil, a prison cell keeping us from our true nature…We decay.*"

GIVE THOSE BURDENED THE FREEDOM TO THRIVE.

A commercial break and tap of the mute icon shoved Matthew into the deep water of his fourth and final point.

"The material I received said a lot of college students receive funding through the generosity of transitioning loved ones." He said no more, instead waiting for any clue of reaction one way or the other. A gasp or a sob suggesting he had cut her heart with a knife. Or perhaps prolonged silence as she contemplated an idea she might have already considered, no matter how remotely.

They sat together quietly staring at the screen. Matthew felt a sense of relief, glad to have completed his mission. He had not suggested that his mother transition. He had merely mentioned what others had done in similar circumstances. The choice, as the law required, must be entirely her own.

"Hi, Matt!" The sound of Sarah's upbeat voice yanked him back to the present moment and reminded him of his duty to several dozen abandoned mugs and napkins. "Boy! We sure could have used you earlier this morning. Pandemonium city!"

"Sorry. Late night." It felt good to hear Sarah acknowledge his missed usefulness. "I'll grab these tables over here."

He noticed the only remaining customer, a well-built athlete admiring the same red blouse and tight-fitting jeans that captivated Matthew every time they cycled into Sarah's wardrobe rotation. It bothered him to see another man looking at her the way he had on countless occasions. It bothered him even more to overhear the younger, stronger, scholarship-receiving hunk smooth-talking her into dinner and a movie and, Matthew presumed, the rest. The moment reminded Matthew of his place at the bottom of the masculine hierarchy, where he would likely remain in light of his mother's reaction to the transition option.

She'd wept as he had never seen her weep before. It took him hours to calm her down, promising he did not mean she should transition, agreeing that suicide was a mortal sin, convincing her to take something that would help her sleep.

How can she forget to take her medicine but remember the definition of a mortal sin? he wondered, freshly stoking the anger he had fueled much of the night.

The door opened as a second customer walked into the café. Matthew noticed Sarah run the back of her hand along the hunk's broad shoulders as she moved toward the counter where two other employees were trying to restore pre-rush sanity to the place.

"Hello, Mr. Adams." It was the voice of Dr. Thomas Vincent. "Doing well today?"

Matthew smiled at the good fortune of seeing the professor again on a day he very much needed a confidant. "Hello, Dr. Vincent. Doing fine. You?"

"Can't complain. And even if I did no one would pay attention!" He chuckled at his own comment.

"Are you in a hurry this morning or do you have a minute?" Matthew asked.

Thomas Vincent glanced at the clock. "I have twenty-two minutes until my next lecture. I'll split it with you. Let me order my drink and I'll be right with you."

Matthew looked toward Sarah, who was already nodding approval for the delayed start, a favor both knew she owed him after reducing his last three shifts.

He wasted the first few minutes on useless chatter about weather and the weekend game UC had barely lost, trying to appear at ease with the professor. Thomas quickly detected the con.

"What's troubling you, Matthew?"

"Is it that obvious?"

"Afraid so."

He decided against mentioning his mother to avoid contaminating a question better left in the sterile world of the abstract.

"I know you no longer subscribe to the teachings of the

church," he began, "but I was wondering, what are your thoughts about mortal sin?"

Thomas's eyes fixed on Matthew over the top of his disposable cup. He gently blew the steaming surface before taking a trial sip.

"Which mortal sin?"

"I don't know. Let's say suicide." Fearing the implication, Matthew quickly added another. "Or sexual promiscuity."

"Twenty years ago I would have said I'm against both, but I've become a bit partial to the second." He laughed silently. "Besides, I'm pretty sure promiscuity falls under venial sins, not mortal sins. A mortal sin…" He paused and closed his eyes as if reaching for a distant memory. "Let me get this right, 'A mortal sin breaks the link between the individual and God's saving grace.' Suicide definitely qualifies."

"Do you consider it suicide if someone volunteers to transition?" Matthew asked. "I mean, would the church call that a mortal sin?"

"Probably would," Thomas confirmed. "Another reason I could no longer affirm Catholic teachings."

"So you consider transitions a good thing?"

Dr. Vincent appeared to experience a sudden awakening. "We aren't having a hypothetical conversation, are we, Matthew?"

Matthew hesitated. "No, sir. I had two conversations over the weekend that have put me in a difficult position."

"With whom?"

"My mother." He looked toward the window to hide false eyes. "I'm…I mean she's considering a possible transition. Wants me to use her assets to pay for college."

"Really? She wants to fund your dream?"

"And hers. She always wanted me to become a professor."

"But?" Thomas poked.

"But I'm wrestling with the idea. She was always pretty religious. Still prays the rosary on her good days."

"And you wonder whether volunteering to transition is the same as committing suicide?"

"Her former priest, Father Tomberlin, says the human body is sacred. I disagree, of course, but worry the church will reject her if she decides to go through with it. Renege on her baptism or something like that."

Thomas noticed the time. "Listen, Matthew, I need to head to class and I don't want to rush this conversation. Let's make an appointment for when we have more time. I fly out of town this afternoon for a lecture series in Chicago but I have office hours available next week."

Matthew nodded absentmindedly while trying to evade self-doubt.

If he convinced his mother to transition, would she be committing the mortal sin of suicide?

If he convinced her on a day when dementia impeded a sound mind, would *he* be committing the mortal sin of murder?

Dr. Vincent stood and moved toward the door while throwing a slight wink in the direction of Sarah's red blouse. Desperate for guidance, Matthew spoke up to avoid losing the professor's attention.

"Just answer me this. Would you help your own mother transition, you know, if she asked you to?"

Thomas stopped and turned back toward Matthew. He said nothing for a moment, slowing zipping his leather jacket as if inching an answer upward from the center of his being.

"My mother transitioned back in '39 shortly after my dad died. That was before they recommended input from loved ones, so she never discussed it with my brother or with me."

He said it in such a manner that Matthew assumed it was not something Dr. Vincent liked to discuss. But he needed to know, so he gingerly asked one last question.

"Would you have helped her if she had?"

Thomas began rubbing his chin the way Matthew had noticed him doing in class. Fifteen seconds later, the answer came.

"Yes. Remember what we discussed before, Matthew. We all decay. Why would I prevent my mother from sidestepping such an unpleasant process? Yes, I believe I would have helped her."

He turned to leave. The door had barely closed behind him when it opened again. Dr. Vincent threw his would-be protégé one final thought.

"Remember, Mr. Adams. There's no such thing as a mortal sin. Just hard choices."

Matthew resumed cleaning tables. Dr. Vincent's advice was just what he'd needed to hear. So why, he wondered, did he feel worse instead of better?

CHAPTER THIRTY-EIGHT

A chilly breeze blew off the Potomac, quickening Julia's pace and making what she had intended to be a thirty-minute power walk into a vigorous sprint between wind-shielding monuments. She had planned to wake early and begin shaping notes and interview recordings into the beginnings of a feature story. But another exhausting dream and a two-hour time zone difference had conspired against her best intentions. Several fruitless attempts to compose an opening paragraph had digressed into a halfhearted effort to craft an outline. After nearly an hour, Julia threw in the towel. She decided to catch a transport from her hotel to the National Mall, where she hoped to sort through the clutter in her mind.

She began her walk at the Jefferson Memorial with an eye toward the massive granite bust of Dr. Martin Luther King Jr. The fifteen-minute route fell to six as Julia rushed for protection from the cold offered by the form of the slain civil rights leader. His eyes seemed to look across the Tidal Basin toward founding father Thomas Jefferson. She considered the irony of slaves working Jefferson's plantation while he penned the famous words of the Declaration of Independence that later seeded Dr. King's dream.

As she blew warming breath into her cupped hands Julia admired how far her nation had come in the nearly thirty years since the King memorial had been built and dedicated to the memory of a man who embodied consummation of the founder's vision.

All men are created equal. Despite the annoyance of a masculine pronoun she admired the progress the idea empowered.

And they are endowed by their Creator with certain unalienable rights. She wondered why Jefferson had rooted his big idea in a creator's intent. Wouldn't personal autonomy have been equally self-evident? Didn't one's unalienable rights include controlling one's own body, choosing one's own offspring, and ending one's own existence?

Julia found it odd that the man credited with separating church and state had included a religious argument in his most important founding document and that the memorial celebrating civil rights used the form of a former pastor. Everyone knew that innovative solutions such as the Youth Initiative would have been impossible in either Jefferson's or Dr. King's generation. Hers, by contrast, enjoyed the benefits of activist courts and pragmatic politicians who had managed to untether national policy from religious ideals.

The wind died down a bit, offering Julia motivation to continue her run. Assuming she could make the Lincoln Memorial in about seven minutes, she slid her numbing hands inside the thin protection of her jogging suit pockets. She began running at a slow pace to give her mind room to think through the conversations of the previous day.

Nicole Florea had characterized Kevin Tolbert as a radical who wanted to undermine the Youth Initiative by proposing crazy, unworkable ideas.

Despite sounding reasonable and articulate, Kevin had indeed appeared eager to advance ideas that Julia considered naïve. Even if it was true that the primary resource shortage was young people and even if one could entice women to have more kids, it would be decades before those children would make any serious contribution to the economy. The Youth Initiative had generated immediate fiscal savings by going with the grain of public sentiment. Breeder values, by contrast, ran opposite to common assumptions and against the new American dream.

And then there was Trisha Sayers. Julia had enjoyed the tour of the Her Look Inc. corporate office complex. The entry and every hallway displayed life-size photographs of glamorous models strutting the world's most trendy runways, a stroll down memory lane of the gradual shift in women's power fashions over the prior decade. After giving Julia the grand tour the superstar-turned-fashion-mogul invited her to dinner at one of the finest restaurants overlooking the Potomac. It was there that Julia recorded Trisha's criticism of the bright spots perspective.

"I couldn't believe when Anderson approved further exploration after Tolbert's pitch," she explained while sipping wine with an elegant grace Julia found striking. "I mean, does he really think we can sell such an outrageous idea?"

"How outrageous?" Julia had asked.

"He wants to bring women like us back to the Middle Ages. He didn't even seem embarrassed when he said we should penalize those who choose childlessness. As if the government has any business forcing us to lose our figures to wipe snotty noses!"

Julia remembered the nonstop action of her evening with Tommy, Joy, and Leah and the relief she had felt driving away from the Tolbert home Sunday afternoon knowing she would spend that night in a quiet hotel room. She also remembered the look on Angie's face when Joy leaped into her mommy's arms during their Sunday-morning reunion. Angie had clearly enjoyed the break, but also missed the source of her exhaustion.

"By the way, your figure's adorable! Ever model?"

"Thank you. No, I never modeled." Julia blushed slightly before pressing on. "Did Kevin Tolbert actually say we should penalize childless individuals?"

"Almost. He said we should make it easier for those who choose parenthood."

"Because?"

"He claims we should consider the time and money they put into raising kids an investment in our long-term economic stability. He actually wants us to subsidize parenthood!"

Julia remembered thinking Trisha's derisive laugh tarnished her lovely face.

"That's why I called Paul."

Trisha called Paul? I thought it was the other way around.

"I knew RAP would spin the story well. But I never imagined he would assign a powerhouse like the famous Julia Davidson! I'm a big fan of your column."

Julia savored the memory of the compliment while ascending the steps toward a massive Abraham Lincoln sitting in stoic contemplation. She was not breathing as heavily as she'd expected, which reminded her of the one-mile altitude drop from Denver to DC. She approached the sixteenth president's feet, jogging in place to keep her heartbeat steady. Turning to the left she noticed the text of his most famous speech inscribed on the south wall. She moved closer to read the familiar 271 words.

FOUR SCORE AND SEVEN YEARS AGO OUR FATHERS BROUGHT FORTH ON THIS CONTINENT A NEW NATION, CONCEIVED IN LIBERTY, AND DEDICATED TO THE PROPOSITION THAT ALL MEN ARE CREATED EQUAL…

Before she reached Lincoln's references to the bloody Gettysburg battleground a familiar ping interrupted Julia's reading. She tapped the headset in her ear. A voice message from Paul Daugherty.

"Hi, Jewel. We've got trouble. But don't worry. I have an idea. Listen to the attached, then call me right away."

Julia opened the pocket zipper to remove a tiny control center device and tapped the PLAY ATTACHEMENT option. She didn't recognize the voice, probably that of a no-name research assistant or one of countless freelance academics paid on retainer by the RAP Syndicate.

"Hi, Paul. I looked into the breeder question you floated and found something you might find useful. It appears that somebody on the Hill named Simmons requested numbers in anticipation of an upcoming task force presentation."

Troy Simmons? Julia wondered.

"This Simmons guy asked the research team to either substantiate or repudiate something labeled…let me see…here it is…something he called 'bright spots trend lines.' Unfortunately, I only managed to access one side of the conversation. I don't have the questions, just the answers. Get this. The summary shows economic growth pockets that run polar opposite to general trends. From what I can piece together the data seem to correlate high fertility and low transitions with economic strength. It looks solid at first glance, but I can't imagine. There must be a flaw in the analysis somewhere. I'll keep you posted as we dive deeper but I wanted to get you what I had. You know where to send questions."

The message ended, prompting Julia to tap Paul's image to return his call.

"Hi, Jewel. You got my message?"

"I did. Did I hear correctly? The Bright Spots proposal has merit?"

"Whoa…slow down, Nelly!" Paul said. "Let's not jump to conclusions. All we know at the moment is that some analyst somewhere gave data to an anonymous congressional aide that supports a proposal we haven't seen."

"Troy Simmons."

"Who?"

"It's not an anonymous congressional aide. I've met him. His name is Troy Simmons, Kevin Tolbert's chief of staff. He and I spent an hour together yesterday afternoon."

"Wow. You really did get inside!" Paul sounded genuinely impressed. "What did you learn?"

"Not much. Sharp guy. Seems genuine."

"A breeder?" Paul asked.

"No. Well, not the way you mean it, anyway. But I think it's safe to assume he falls in the anti–Youth Initiative camp."

"What about Tolbert?"

Julia hesitated. Could she trust Paul with details of an off-the-record conversation?

"Nothing official yet."

"Anything unofficial?"

"Not really. Like I said in my text, he invited me to attend the austerity coalition meeting this afternoon. I hope to learn something useful then."

"Look, Jewel. The editorial board is breathing down my neck here. They expect a proactive piece ready for review soon. I've told them I've got my best people on the story and that we'll deliver with our usual excellence."

"Best people? Who else?" Julia heard herself ask.

"Best person, then. But I have to tell you I'm getting sweaty palms here. I stuck my neck out to get you this gig, Julia. Please tell me you'll deliver."

Julia could not recall a time when Paul had seemed so anxious for a story. "Of course I'll deliver, Paul! But why the panic? Is there something I need to know?"

"No!" he snapped. "There's something I need to know. Can you deliver a feature story that links this Bright Spots proposal to the source?"

"Source?"

"You know, guilt by association."

"I'm not sure I follow you," she confessed.

Paul assumed the vocal posture of a mentor tutoring his young apprentice, causing Julia to chafe while listening. "People care a whole lot more about being with it than they do about being right. All you need to do, Jewel darling, is craft a story that will make it easy to frame details about economic growth pockets and demographic trends with the more important reality of the situation."

"Which is?"

"Which is that the people proposing these changes are hopelessly behind the times. Come on! Increased fertility? Reduced transitions? What kind of nonsense is that in this day and age?"

The idea had merit. It would be easy to associate the Bright Spots proposal with her assigned title, *Breeders*. She would fulfill her promise to let Kevin make his case in his own words, and she was confident she could also link the ideas to a religiously extreme mind-set.

"Don't worry, Paul," she said. "I promise you the editorial board will be pleased."

"That's good," he replied. "Because all eyes are on this one, love."

The call ended.

Julia thought of four million transition volunteers as her eyes fell on the words President Lincoln once spoke about previous national heroes.

FROM THESE HONORED DEAD WE TAKE INCREASED DEVOTION TO THAT CAUSE FOR WHICH THEY GAVE THE LAST FULL MEASURE OF DEVOTION—THAT WE HERE HIGHLY RESOLVE THAT THESE DEAD SHALL NOT HAVE DIED IN VAIN.

CHAPTER THIRTY-NINE

Julia entered Kevin's office ten minutes before the two o'clock start of the austerity committee session. A small team of interns rushed about handling Troy's final-detail commands.

"You replaced yesterday's trend graph with the one I sent this morning?" he asked the back of a head that was facing a computer screen.

"Yes, sir." The young man swiped his display. "Here it is."

Troy moved closer, confirmed the change, and gave an affirming nod. "Thank you, Shaun." He placed his hand on the intern's shoulder. "I guess we're ready to send it."

"Good thing, seeing as how the meeting starts in eight minutes!" Shaun said as he moved his finger toward a SEND icon at the top right corner of the screen. He froze his extended hand. "Speak now or forever…"

"We're out of time," Troy said. "Do it." A field commander reluctantly advancing his outnumbered troops.

The intern tapped the screen, placing the confidential document onto thirteen digital tablets soon to assemble in a nearby conference room.

Julia watched Troy for a moment, a man standing at the intersection of elation and unease. "Hello, Troy."

He turned toward her voice and offered a welcoming grin. "Hello, Ms. Davidson." He sounded like a man eager to escort a lovely debutante to the ball.

"Nerve-racking, isn't it?" she asked.

"You could say that."

"I get the same feeling every time I send a column. I just know it could be a little better if only I had a few more minutes to change a word here and there."

He smiled. "It's only the most important presentation Kevin may ever give. I should have an endless window for tweaks, don't you think?"

"I'm sure it's great."

He took one last look around the room, apparently running through a mental checklist. The final item confirmed, Troy darted into his office to retrieve a suit jacket hanging over his chair. "Shall we go?" he asked while reaching back awkwardly for the second armhole.

"Aren't we forgetting your boss?"

"He went over fifteen minutes ago. Wanted to confirm your attendance with Anderson."

"Anderson?"

"Brent Anderson. He runs the austerity coalition for Franklin."

"Is he the one they call Franklin's Scalpel?"

"One and the same. But I like him. He's managed to keep soapboxing and grandstanding to a minimum so the committee could move quickly."

"He approved my attendance?" Julia asked.

"His office sent the OK last night in reply to Kevin's message explaining your deal. You attend as our guest with the assurance everything you hear in the meeting will remain off the record until Congressman Tolbert approves going public."

The description made Julia claustrophobic as the walls of journalistic freedom closed in. She tried to remain optimistic by telling herself the gamble would pay off.

"Right. Any concerns?"

"No. Kevin just wanted to confirm it with Anderson in person to avoid misunderstandings. He's got good instincts about that sort of thing." Troy moved in front of Julia to open the door. "After you."

She walked through as Troy quickly thanked the team of exhausted well-wishers staying behind in the office.

A flight of stairs and a few hundred feet later they entered a room where twenty chairs surrounded a long conference table. Smaller seats lined the walls on either side. Julia immediately noticed Kevin Tolbert leaning into a man sitting at the head of the table, presumably Brent Anderson. She also recognized the woman seated in the middle who, seeing Julia enter the room, motioned toward her.

"Excuse me, Troy," Julia said. "I need to say hello."

Troy appeared concerned. "You know Trisha Sayers?"

"We've met once before," she said casually. "I'll be right back."

Julia continued scanning the room while Trisha gushed flattery over her blouse and shoes. A few other faces seemed vaguely familiar, quick images flashed on the television whenever Congress sat listening to the president's State of the Union address. Gradually the wheat began to distinguish itself from the chaff as other official coalition members joined Tolbert, Anderson, and Sayers sitting at the conference table. The other two dozen attendees found chairs against the wall. Like Troy, most of them placed an open tablet on their laps from which they could deliver on-cue talking points to a boss's screen four feet away.

The room quieted from informal chatter toward a gradual hush as each member noticed the time. Trisha patted Julia's hand, a new-best-friend gesture doubling as a condescending dismissal. She moved quietly to the open seat beside Troy, who held his head at a slight bow.

"Sorry. Everything good?" she asked.

"This is it," he whispered anxiously.

In contrast to her host, Julia felt a sudden wave of confidence. The only journalist in the room, she had managed to gain exclusive access to a presentation likely to stir tremendous controversy. Over the next hour she would receive the intelligence needed to craft the most important feature story of her career, one that might very well put her back on top of the RAP journalistic empire. This was going to be a good day.

"Thank you all for arriving on schedule," Brent Anderson began. "You all know it goes against every fiber of my being to say it, but I need to delay our start a few minutes."

Troy raised his head and looked directly toward Kevin. Both seemed troubled by the departure from protocol.

The doors opened. Senator Franklin walked in with an entourage of five or six others.

"It appears that delay will be unnecessary," Anderson said. "I guess even my boss fears arriving late to one of my meetings," he added with a slight chuckle.

"My apologies, everyone," Franklin said. "Please, carry on."

"They didn't tell us Franklin was coming," Troy whispered to Julia.

All eyes watched Josh Franklin as he took a seat beside Trisha Sayers, to her obvious delight, while the other newcomers slid into remaining open spots along the wall.

"Before today's presentation I'd like to wrap up one matter from our last meeting." Anderson glanced at his tablet. "The coalition voted ten to three in favor of the neutral consent confirmation proposal presented by Representative McGurn. But in hopes of reaching unanimous consensus we asked the congressman to recommend alternative language that would accommodate concerns raised by the minority. I'll let Mr. McGurn explain."

"You'll find the revised wording on your tablet now," McGurn began. "Please open the document titled *Neutral Consent Draft Two* and follow along."

He read the document aloud. Despite lawyer language, Julia caught the gist. The fiscal austerity coalition would recommend making it harder for transition volunteers to sidestep co-approval. Mere digital signatures would no longer suffice. Clinics would be required to obtain fingerprint confirmation by a neutral party. "I believe adding the fingerprint requirement will satisfy Dr. Richert's concerns over potential abuses in the system."

"Doctor?" Anderson asked.

No comment. The doctor gave a solitary nod, as if reluctantly coerced to accept minor edits to a useless proposal.

"All in favor of the amended language?" Anderson hurried on.

A dozen hands went in the air. Anderson's followed, making the recommendation unanimous.

"Done." He handed the meeting to Kevin. "Representative Tolbert."

Julia glanced at the nameplate sitting on the conference table in front of the intense-looking gentleman who had prompted the fingerprinting proposal. She typed DR. BRYCE RICHERT into her search field to learn more about the mysterious yet obviously influential man. Details immediately populated her screen: head of obstetrics and gynecology for a network of regional hospitals who had five grown children and a dozen grandkids.

Julia jotted herself a note: *Research Dr. Richert.*

She turned back to see Kevin standing. He scanned the delegates like a rookie skier mentally preparing for his first downhill run.

"You should have received an executive summary of my presentation on your tablets just before this meeting began."

He looked toward Troy, who winked confirmation of delivery.

"Please open the document labeled *Bright Spots Proposal* if you wish to follow along."

Julia circled the table with her eyes, trying to pick up body language clues. Not surprisingly, Trisha's posture evoked images of a stubborn child holding her breath to protest the dab of spinach on her plate. Senator Franklin, by contrast, appeared eager to learn more about the young congressman's innovative idea.

It was then that she lost her ability to focus. Just over Franklin's shoulder she noticed the smug face of one of the senator's tardy guests. It was Monica Garcia, apparently pleased to finally catch Julia's eye.

How on earth did she get in here? Julia fumed. She quickly reached the only available conclusion. Paul had thrown Julia the scraps by connecting her to Nicole Florea and Trisha Sayers. As usual, he had reserved the prime cut for Monica.

Anger quickly morphed into alarm. Inside access to a presidential hopeful would trump anything Julia might write from the perspective of a mere first-term congressman. She wondered whether Paul even intended to publish Julia's story. Was the whole assignment a charade?

Don't be ridiculous! she scolded herself. *Why would he waste my time and his? Why bother badgering me for progress? Why suggest a story angle and title so perfectly suited to my reputation?*

Julia willed herself past a budding paranoia by reminding herself of the facts. Monica might have had what it took to earn a senator's favors, but she didn't have the journalistic instincts necessary to craft a convincing exposé on an entire subculture like the breeders. Julia might have been forced to remain in the bullpen the past few seasons, she told herself, but she remained the most experienced, strongest pitcher on the RAP team. And Paul Daugherty knew it.

Shifting her eyes back toward Kevin as he began the most important presentation of his political life, Julia recognized the time had come to write the most compelling story of her fading career.

PART THREE

CHAPTER FORTY

Kevin paused at his own front door, watching the vapor of his breath dissipate in the chilly midnight air. He would have preferred walking through its threshold five hours earlier, the excited squeals of children greeting their daddy to put the icing on the cake of an already amazing day. He imagined his darling wife waiting up for him, eager to hear about the big presentation. He would have given her a long kiss in self-congratulation on a job well done mixed with gratitude for a better-than-expected outcome.

He knew, of course, that Angie and the kids would be sound asleep. So he stood beneath the dim glow of a single bulb, exhaling long streams of misty joy into its light, a contented boy rewarding himself with small marvels.

Thank you, he prayed in silence, smiling upward before reaching to unlock the door.

As expected, he entered a dark house. Placing his tablet on the entry table he moved toward the kitchen, hoping to find a snack worthy of the moment. He opened the refrigerator to find the usual assortment of condiments, dairy products, and fruit. Nothing exciting like leftover cake. Retrieving the half-empty carton of milk he opened the pantry to seek a perfect accomplice. A box of Tommy's favorite sugar cereal sat seductively at eye level. It was normally off-limits to Dad, but Kevin decided tonight was different. This day deserved the simple reward of crispy flavor doused in fresh milk.

While relishing his third mouthful Kevin noticed the lovely form of his wife glowering in his direction. Her arms were crossed sternly like those of a cop catching a burglar in the act. A guilty smile forced a drop of milk from the side of his mouth. She laughed quietly and approached.

"What am I going to do with you?"

His eyes moved up and down to admire her thin nightgown. "I bet I can think of something."

A tiny dimple showed beneath a slight blush. Angie slid behind Kevin and wrapped her arms around his back. "It went well today?" she asked.

"Very well." He moved the bowl aside and turned around on his bar stool to face her, slipping his hands around her waist and pulling her body close. "So well I wanted to celebrate. I figured you were asleep so I settled for this bowl of contraband. But you look much more appetizing!"

"Behave," she pretended to protest. "First tell me what happened."

He patted the stool beside him, inviting his wife to sit.

"I was given fifteen minutes to make my case and fifteen for questions," he began. "But the questions and discussion stretched into two hours!"

"Is that good?"

"I didn't think so at first. There were lots of objections that became arguments. By the time I reached my allotted time I figured the whole proposal was going down in flames. But rather than cut off the discussion to call for a vote, Anderson kept extending our time. He would look toward Franklin—"

"Senator Franklin was there?" Angie interrupted.

"He was."

"Did that make you nervous?" She reached over to rub Kevin's arm.

"At first. I wanted to work through any committee objections before he saw it. But then I noticed Anderson making eye contact with Franklin moments before each time extension. A slight nod cued Anderson to keep the conversation alive."

"For two hours? I thought you said Anderson was a schedule stickler."

"Exactly! I figured there was only one possible reason Anderson kept the conversation going. A quick vote would have killed my idea. Franklin must have wanted me to overcome each objection."

"Did you?"

"Enough of them to win the day." His voice had a mock braggadocio's tone. "You're looking at a boy who spent his day defeating giants!"

"Like Trisha Delisha?"

"She was the most vocal. No matter what I said she shot back a hostile, usually harebrained complaint."

"I still don't understand why that woman is in the coalition."

"I'll tell you why. She will become important when the time comes to go public with the austerity proposals. Franklin is no dummy. He knows the medicine will go down much easier if presented by a spoonful of sugar like Trisha Sayers."

An icy glare told Kevin Angie didn't appreciate the analogy.

"Anyway, we got nine votes. That's two more than we needed to include the bright spots concept in the final bundle of proposals."

"Bundle?"

"I expect Franklin will want to present three or four big ideas to address the crisis, each targeting a different economic segment. That's how he'll garner a broad base of support."

Both sat quietly for a moment, Angie's fingers squeezing Kevin's in a show of pride in her husband's accomplishment.

"What about the transition idea?" she asked.

"They cut me off at the knees on that one weeks ago. Trying to reduce transitions was a bridge too far."

"I thought the whole idea was to replicate what happens in bright spot regions." Her words seemed pregnant with concern.

"Politics is about getting what you can," he said. "I got half of what I wanted. Franklin will propose a package that includes tax credits for new parents. That's a pretty big win that should make it easier to choose parenthood."

A slight delay. "I'm sure it will. And you should be proud."

"But?" he prodded.

"Well. I just wonder whether one bright spot trait will have much impact without the other. Are you sure increased fertility alone will help? I mean, it took both of us to make a baby. Neither of us could have created a child alone."

Kevin looked into Angie's eyes, trying to decipher whether she was seducing him or instructing him.

"Isn't it the combination of the two trends that creates economic strength? One without the other seems, I don't know, like a single spouse trying to create half a baby."

The comment sobered Kevin's celebration.

How could I have made such an obvious mistake?

It was a serious leap in logic to assume high fertility accounted for 50 percent of bright spots' economic growth. It had never occurred to him or to Troy, who usually thought of such things, that both were crucial parts of a single whole. One without the other might be useless.

"I hadn't thought of that," he confessed dolefully.

Angie patted Kevin's shoulder. "Well, let's not worry about that now. Just because you have another battle to fight tomorrow doesn't mean we can't celebrate today's victory."

She moved him sideways on the stool and climbed onto his lap to wrap her body tightly around his torso while touching the tips of their noses together.

Their eyes met, hers sparkling with invitation, his submerged by apprehension.

"I should probably call Troy," he said.

She took his hand and placed it on her thigh. "I think that can wait."

He kissed her mildly.

"Kevin Tolbert," Angie said while leaning away. "That's not what I had in mind."

She pressed her lips severely to her husband's while guiding his hand higher.

CHAPTER FORTY-ONE

Julia traded her empty glass for a tiny pillow and neatly folded blanket. She had never been more grateful for an upgrade in her life, which must have shown in her eyes as she thanked the flight attendant.

"Rough day?" he asked.

"Long day," she responded. "Actually, long week."

He smiled politely and offered a refill. She declined, hoping to use the three-hour flight home to drift into blissful unconsciousness. As soon as Julia had found and occupied her first-class seat she felt the physical and emotional toll of the past few days. Much of the adrenaline masking her tension ebbed, her body finally granting itself permission to enjoy a brief reprieve from the stress of tiptoeing around a strained friendship, fighting desire for a charming gentleman, and maneuvering into a confidential meeting of Washington insiders. A nap was just the thing she needed before tackling her next high-adrenaline task: beating Monica Garcia to the editorial punch.

She recalled the sting of her rival's presence at the austerity coalition meeting, wondering whether Monica had made the same deal with Senator Franklin that Julia had made with Kevin, preemptive access in exchange for fair representation. Or had Monica simply seduced her way into the good graces of a Franklin staffer, posing as an eager intern who would make a nice addition to the growing harem? Either way, the game had changed.

As the alcohol began inviting her body to relax, Julia reminded herself of her opponent's limited journalistic experience. Monica could report the basic facts of a story well enough. But Paul wanted an article carefully nuanced yet unflinchingly damning. Pulling that off would require more than naked ambition. It would take a Pulitzer-winning intellect.

She wanted to compile a mental list of story elements but her brain refused to help. Julia found the audio symphony channel on the screen embedded in the seat in front of hers and closed her eyes while the London Philharmonic washed gentle waves of beauty over her restless mind.

Five minutes or an hour later Julia felt herself gasp desperately for air, her limbs flailing frantically to counter the pull of a waterless undercurrent. As before, it drew her downward. As before, the shadowy figure of a man stood unable or unwilling to rescue her from a vortex she didn't understand but knew to be evil.

Joyless laughter invaded her sleeping ears. At first she assumed it came from the figure fading in the distance, the man toward whom she pleaded. But then she realized the sound rose from beneath. It was a vile and indulgent laughter, the kind that might accompany the foul breath of a gluttonous man raping an innocent child or devouring a cannibal's feast.

"Don't leave," she screamed toward the barely visible man in the distance, her heart pounding in her throat. "Please help me!"

He made no move beyond extending a hand she could not possibly reach.

The texture of leather chafing the fingertips of her right hand woke Julia from the nightmare. Opening her eyes, she saw her arm reaching toward Seat 2B eighteen inches ahead, the face of its occupant swiveled toward her in apparent irritation over her disruptive thrashing.

"I'm sorry," Julia said dimly while locating herself. "A bad dream."

She turned left, grateful to see a vacant seat. Turning right, she spotted a blinking wing light cutting through an oppressive external darkness. She found and tapped a faint blue icon on her armrest to kindle the overhead lamp. It took a moment to notice Mozart's Serenade No. 12 rising in her ears, the Chamber Orchestra of Europe attempting to calm Julia's palpitating heart.

She picked up the tablet resting beside her and quickly retrieved the document she had begun after visiting Maria's therapist.

DREAMS: MAN, SHADOW, FEAR, ANGER, ABANDONED
DR. MORELAND: "I think your subconscious may be urging you toward something important...something to do with your dad...Talk to someone who can help fill in your father's face."

She had captured and ignored the notes like an unpromising lead on a story she didn't want to write.

The dreams reflect self-doubt and a declining career, she told herself. *They have nothing to do with deeper conflicts or mysterious messages from my subconscious psyche.*

Or did they?

Julia added three words.

DESCENDING INTO HELL

While she stared at the phrase a slight shiver provoked her to squeeze the pillow tightly. Tapping a TO DO icon on the screen Julia reluctantly added "See Dr. Moreland again" to her list, a small action that gave her the sensation of retaking control.

Julia searched for something to occupy her mind for the remaining ninety minutes of the flight home. Three taps later she weighed two options, the final journal entries of Sylvia Santos or the first of her son. She chose the file titled ANTONIO'S MUSINGS.

August 14, 2035: Today I begin my journal titled Antonio's Musings. Yesterday was my twelfth birthday. Mom and Jeremy got me this really cool tablet that connects to my chair. It lets me type using only my good finger. I'm slow, but I'll get faster. What else do I have to do? I have a zillion thoughts cooped up inside my head. I can hardly wait to start writing them down. Thank you for reading this, whoever you are. Brace yourself for the most amazing story ever. Mine!

August 15, 2035: You probably want to know about my early life. It began pretty normal. Mom said I was a perfect gentleman as a baby. I hardly ever cried. That's good since she needed to rest up for the hard days to come. I still don't cry much. Mom handles that for the both of us. She tries not to let me see, but I know more than she thinks. I know Dad left because of me. I know she can't work overtime because of me. And I know she never remarried because of me. But she likes me anyway. I know that because I see it in her eyes, not because she tells me. She would tell me either way.

For as long as I can remember we've enjoyed a word game Mom invented. She tries to stump me by reading a dictionary definition. I get a point when I guess correctly and she gets a point when I'm wrong. I was winning 1236 to 843 before I lost the ability to speak ten months back. We restarted the game yesterday to test-drive a voice replacement software Jeremy downloaded to my tablet. She read "No longer in use or out of date." I knew even before asking which half of the dictionary she was in. I tapped out OBSOLETE and a computer voice spoke the word. Mom cried, I guess because she missed our game. I just glared at Jeremy who was laughing hysterically because he chose a little girl's voice. Mom made him fix it. Now I sound like a British intellectual. Much better.

You may already know that I have a rare disease. Did you know several famous people had a similar condition in the past? Look up a guy named Stephen Hawking. He won the Albert Einstein Award for physics about fifty years before I was born. Hardly anyone has the disease now. Parents deselect kids like me while still zygotes or embryos. I've often wondered what kind of child Mom might have had if she had prescreened. Would Jeremy have a cute sister rather than an invalid brother? Would Dad have stuck around? Would they live in a big house instead of this cramped apartment? One thing is sure. Mom probably wouldn't have invented our word game.

Antonio wrote two dozen entries that first month, some longer than others. Each provided a brief window into the mind of an adolescent boy trapped in a mostly inept body. Julia learned that he loved an outdated robotics program he had received from his mom's friend, which sat idle after he lost his ability to steer a mouse. There were several comments she found surprising but would have considered typical for any other adolescent boy. Inappropriate sexual daydreams about the few girls his brother brought by the house. He shared how it felt when they recoiled at his appearance, politely shaking his twisted hand while looking away to avoid eye contact. A few entries described life's small pleasures, such as the taste of a banana-fudge milk shake and the thrill of launching into the next book in his favorite fantasy series. His vocabulary and breadth of knowledge suggested a keen intellect, perhaps someone who would have been a terrific copy editor or research assistant. They were abilities, she discovered, he would put to use in short order.

<u>May 10, 2036</u>: This morning Mom brought me with her to a meeting at the headquarters of Lance Lowman's presidential campaign. It was so cool! An important-looking woman explained different opportunities for volunteer participation. Get this—I'm now an official online campaign specialist for the man we hope will become the next president of the United States. I send messages from my tablet to a list of prospective donors. I ask them to make a $100 gift toward a major media effort the campaign hopes to launch just before the election. I managed to send out ten this afternoon and then checked the system. Two of the ten already gave! I'm going to try sending out a hundred messages per day over the next few months. I bet I can generate a hundred thousand dollars all by myself! Mom says we need a person like Lowman in the White House to expand the boom and keep her in a decent job. I asked Jeremy to help me get to bed early tonight. I can't wait to get started tomorrow!

Julia remembered the national excitement over Lance Lowman's campaign. He had managed to corral the enthusiasm of a nation giddy over what turned out to be a short-lived economic boom. Even those living near the poverty line joined his bandwagon, eager to accelerate the upward momentum. Lowman promised a decade of growth if his party took power. He would remove cumbersome regulations to help the market capitalize on burgeoning gen-tech innovations, which, in turn, would lift all boats by raising the water level of every segment of the economy. He also promised to reduce taxes that had mushroomed thanks to rapidly expanding entitlement spending. Clearly, the Santos family believed every word.

Julia scanned several pages reflecting Antonio's weekly tally of messages sent and donations generated. Then she camped on an entry the now thirteen-year-old considered the most important of that year.

> November 8, 2036: We stayed up most of the night watching election results. Governor Lowman is now the forty-ninth president of the United States. We celebrated by eating Mom's famous chocolate chip pancakes before she went to work and Jeremy went to school. Nancy (my day nurse) must have stayed up late too. She looks as groggy as the rest of us. But it feels great knowing I helped make history.

That post-election euphoria set up the downward tipping point of Antonio's short life. Within twelve months circumstances began to undermine whatever sense of significance he had gleaned from Lowman's victory. The gen-tech market crashed, throwing his mom out of work and forcing the family to live with his aunt and uncle for six months. Jeremy hated the place. Got into fights at school. Resented any input or guidance from Uncle Marcos who was "Not my father!" Antonio wished he could talk to his brother about what both of them were feeling. But one sentence in an English accent every two minutes could not keep up with Jeremy's rapid-fire venom that was poisoning the household and breaking their mother's heart.

Julia found only four quick journal entries from 2038, each suggesting Antonio had become increasingly pessimistic about life.

> March: I'm starting to doubt Mom will ever get another decent job.

June: Mom said she had to take another pay cut. We'll need to move.

July: The new apartment has a funky smell.

September: Poor Jeremy. He hates his new school even more than his last.

Julia filled in details with recollections from Sylvia's journal. The family had moved into a low-rent apartment in a rough school district where Jeremy continued to be mired in resentment. Things improved slightly when Sylvia began dating a man from church who helped out financially from time to time. But the relationship went nowhere after the man spent time at their apartment observing life with a severely disabled boy and an older brother angry with God and the rest of the world.

"Who could blame him?" Antonio wrote with resignation in November.

Antonio seemed to rediscover his Musings journal along with a new fixation in the early part of 2039.

February 7, 2039: The president's plan to save the economy seems to be gaining traction. He's getting surprisingly little resistance in Congress despite condemnation by the Vatican and a few Southern preachers. Mom says his proposal will never fly. But she's been critical out of spite ever since losing her gen-tech job. I read the details online last night. That took me about an hour. I think I like it, a commonsense strategy for tackling the deficit and spurring new economic investment while allowing those brave enough to do so to become part of the solution rather than part of the problem.

She continued reading, several entries providing progress reports on what would come to be called the Youth Initiative.

<u>March 2, 2039</u>: The president's plan passed an important subcommittee vote in the House of Representatives yesterday. It will go to the full House in a few weeks.

<u>April 10, 2039</u>: A senator from Texas proposed an amendment to the president's plan, suggesting they should add two restrictions. Adults must state they have volunteered free of coercion. Minors can only volunteer with the approval of all living parents. Both were accepted as reasonable changes.

<u>May 17, 2039</u>: Someone labeled the Senate version of the president's plan the *Youth Initiative* because, in theory, it should lower the average age of the US population. The media keeps using the label, so I think it will stick.

<u>June 21, 2039</u>: A historic week. The Youth Initiative passed both houses of Congress by a two-thirds majority. Economists are already projecting significant savings and growth.

<u>August 30, 2039</u>: The first month of the Youth Initiative brought an unprecedented transfer of wealth. A high percentage of recipients say they plan to use the money to pay off debt. But some recipients are entrepreneurs who, it's assumed, will invest in new businesses to grow the economy.

<u>September 30, 2039</u>: NEXT Inc. announced that it plans to purchase and renovate vacant office buildings in major markets over the coming months in order to open clinics specifically designed to serve the growing demand for transition services. The program has proven more popular than expected and the supply of doctors willing to facilitate the process simply can't keep up. NEXT said they plan to hire attending physicians supported by a team of transition specialists rather than continue directing people into existing doctors' offices and hospitals.

Antonio went on to trace the growth of the NEXT infrastructure from the first few clinics in New York, Los Angeles, and

Phoenix into progressively smaller communities. The company achieved its stated goal of opening three hundred clinics within twelve months. Thousands of high-paying jobs were created as contractors bid for renovation projects and elder-care workers moved up the food chain to become transition specialists. And all of it was funded by a deluge of cash previously trickling from retirement and medical savings accounts.

A faint ping interrupted Julia's reading. The cabin lights gradually rose and the other first-class passengers woke to the captain's voice inviting the flight attendants to prepare for landing. Julia glanced at the clock on her tablet. An early arrival.

Anticipating the next voice on the intercom, Julia closed the MUSINGS file to store the tablet in the carry-on bag lying at her feet. With the touch of a button her seat gently eased itself toward an upright position as she pondered Antonio's final years. He seemed genuinely excited each time the Youth Initiative cleared another hurdle toward passage. He tracked the progress of the transition industry like a teenager anticipating opening day of a summer action flick. What would he have thought of Jeremy's lawsuit? What would he have said to men like Kevin Tolbert who, Julia assumed, would have restricted his right to volunteer?

She closed her eyes as the wheels met the awaiting runway. An image flashed, echoing her dream of hellish descent. Forcing her eyes open again, she thought of a teenage boy eager for death and wondered what kind of images had greeted the closing eyes of Antonio Santos.

CHAPTER FORTY-TWO

It was nearly ten o'clock in the morning before Julia forced herself out of bed and into the shower. Arriving home somewhere between midnight and morning, she had instinctively turned off her alarm clock before falling into a welcome slumber. She had hoped to get an early start writing, possibly completing a first draft before dinner. That wasn't going to happen. A late start teamed up with writer's block. By four o'clock Julia was staring lethargically at a paragraph containing forced, clunky prose.

I bet words are flying effortlessly onto Monica's page.

She heard a rap on her closed door followed by Maria's perky voice. "Hey, Sis. Are you about ready?"

Ready?

"They'll be here in half an hour," Maria continued.

"Who?"

"What do you mean who?" Maria opened the door, her face forming into a reprimand after noticing Julia's jeans and baggy sweatshirt. "You aren't even close to ready. Didn't you read my note?"

Note?

Maria crossed her arms. "I knew you got in late so I didn't want to wake you before I left for work. I put a note right next to your toothbrush so you would be sure to see it."

Julia ran her tongue across her teeth and blushed at the exhaustion-induced oversight.

"Sorry, Sis. What's in the note?"

That's when she noticed Maria's outfit, an obvious clue to the mystery.

"Fin has a really cute roommate named Craig Gilman. They want to go dancing at the club tonight."

Julia rolled her eyes in disbelief. "And you said I'd go?"

"Of course! All work and no play makes you a boring writer. You need to get out."

"Maria!"

"Did I mention he's really cute?" she said while moving toward Julia's closet. "Bodybuilder type. You'll like him."

"I'm really in no shape for—"

"Wear these," Maria interrupted. "And he'll love your shape. Trust me!"

Julia looked at the skirt and blouse, gifts from her mischievous sister hoping to help her join life's party. She had only ever worn them in front of the mirror. They were tame by Maria's standards, but Julia had never been comfortable showing so much skin.

"Come on, Sis!" Maria pushed. "You know what they say. If you've got it, flaunt it!"

Julia glanced at the page onto which she'd only typed one paragraph in the past hour. She looked back toward her sister, imagining herself on the dance floor.

"I thought you had ended it with Fin," she said, easing her way toward a yes.

"Not yet," Maria replied. "Jared is staying over with a friend tonight, so he won't know. Come on. I said you'd love to go. Don't make me a liar."

"You *are* a liar," Julia huffed while wagging her head and accepting the clothes.

"I'll get you my black heels!" Maria said excitedly as she ran out of the room.

Twenty-five minutes later Julia heard the doorbell while standing in front of her full-length mirror. A rush of excitement met apprehension as she turned from side to side, inspecting every angle. The outfit gave her a mysterious sense of power, as if her femininity were a key that could unlock endless possibilities. She heard Maria greet their guests at the door. The sound of masculine voices deepened both her qualms and her confidence.

The sensation brought to mind the excitement that had been on Angie's face while she was purchasing Kevin's lacy surprise. She imagined the admiring look in Kevin's eyes, a man weakened and emboldened by his bride's alluring form. Had Angie felt the same sense of power and possibility?

The beauty of Angie's face quickly faded into the form of another. Julia thought of Monica Garcia, a woman who leveraged feminine power to unlock a different range of possibilities, probably seducing her way into Senator Franklin's inner circle and teasing her way toward prime assignments with RAP Syndicate.

Julia felt conflicted as she viewed her reflection. But it was too late to change.

"There she is," Maria sang as Julia approached the quartet of admiring male eyes. "Doesn't she look adorable!"

"Hello, Julia," Fin began. "I'd like you to meet my roommate, Gil."

"Gil?" Julia heard herself say. "Fin and Gil?"

"Fin's idea," Craig Gilman explained as Fin flashed a big grin. "But you can call me Craig if you prefer."

"No. Gil is fine," Julia answered as she slowly turned toward Maria's wink. "Nice to meet you."

"Shall we go?" Maria said, handing Julia her coat.

Julia relaxed a bit once the coat cloaked her bare shoulders and thighs, freeing Gil to finally notice her face.

"You look great," he said too eagerly as they walked out the door.

The evening was a catastrophe. Craig Gilman turned out to be the polar opposite of Jonathan Sowell.

Jonathan read the right books and drank the right wine. Craig spent the evening bragging about his latest virtual game conquest.

Jonathan had declined an offer to come back to Julia's room. Craig invited Julia to his place before they finished their first dance.

Jonathan had shown more interest in Maria than in Julia. Craig would have gladly taken either of them, or the girl behind the bar, or just about any willing female.

"It seems to be going great!" Maria whispered in Julia's ear as the four stood at the bar awaiting refills. "I told you he was hot!"

Julia said nothing, too embarrassed by her own stupidity to blame Maria or Fin or even Gil. Of course he anticipated a good time later that night. Why else would she have worn such an alluring outfit? Why else would she have responded to his touch while dancing? Why else would she laugh at his idiotic jokes?

"I knew you'd like him." Maria's last words before heading back onto the dance floor, where she relished the attention of Jared's teacher. Julia remembered the hurt on Jared's face from the taunting of his friends. She recalled Maria's decision to end the relationship out of respect for her son's feelings. Julia knew that wouldn't happen anytime soon.

"What do you say we get outta here?" Gil's breath reeked of alcohol as he placed his hand on her backside.

"That's a good idea." She shifted her body away from his paw. "I need to get an early start in the morning. I better get home."

A stunned look came over Gil's face as the rejection sunk in.

"Home?" he blurted indignantly.

"Thank you for a fun evening," she added quickly. "But I better call it a night."

Neither Gil nor Maria spoke the entire drive home. Fin tried easing the tension with an occasional inane question, but they didn't respond. Both were irked by the abrupt end to their party. Julia walked alone to her front door as the trio drove away toward Fin's place, where he and Maria could finish what they had started on the dance floor and where, she assumed, Gil would take a cold shower.

Closing the door behind her, Julia inhaled a deep breath of peaceful silence, a tonic for the noisy pretending she had endured the past few hours. She had learned that she, like her sister, could dominate the sandbox of Guyland, where women easily controlled the masculine sex. Wearing the right clothing was all that was necessary to obtain no-strings-attached delights. But she wanted more than a panting boy looking for a female in heat. She sensed her femininity held purpose beyond an erotic thrill with an overgrown adolescent gamer.

Changing into her favorite baggy T-shirt, Julia grabbed her tablet and slipped into bed. Having spent the entire day ignoring messages, she now wanted to clear the docket in order to start fresh in the morning. She deleted three automatic news alerts before opening message number four.

FROM TROY SIMMONS: *I enjoyed our conversation Monday. I'd love to see you again on your next visit to DC.*

Julia felt a smile form on her lips.

CHAPTER FORTY-THREE

Julia kept herself under the blanket like a girl holding her head under water. It didn't work. She remained wide awake despite nearly thirty minutes trying to force herself into a deep sleep. She vacillated back and forth between opposing sensations, her body echoing the rhythmic teasing with Gil on the dance floor while her heart recalled the admiring eyes of Troy Simmons during their Botanic Garden stroll. Against her wishes Julia's subconscious seemed to fuse the two very different experiences into a single romantic fantasy. It craved the thrill of uninhibited sexual fulfillment. But it also dreamed of pure, even noble love.

She pulled back the covers to resurface and to catch her breath. That's when she heard the familiar ping of a newly arriving message.

FROM PAUL DAUGHERTY: *Hey, Jewel. I need an update on your trip. Give me something I can use to buy you a little more time.*

"Buy me a little more time?" she barked at the tablet, abandoning her plan for an early-morning start. It would instead be a very late night.

Julia reached for her phone and pressed Paul's image.

"You're awake. Great!" His tone didn't match the words. He sounded jumpy, like a man with two left feet forced to perform a tap dance.

"What time is it?" she asked.

"Don't know. Midnight-ish?"

"Why do I get the feeling you're in panic mode?" she asked.

A short pause.

"Paul?"

"I'm still here. Just thinking."

"Thinking about what?" She braced herself.

"About how much to say."

"How much to say about what?" She swallowed back the irritation and anxiety surfacing in her voice.

Another pause.

"OK. I'm going to trust you with something, Jewel."

"I'm honored!" she said with biting sarcasm.

"Behave yourself and listen."

"Sorry. Go ahead."

"Complete confidentiality," he insisted.

"I understand."

"RAP has been sold."

"What? Why?" she asked.

"Who knows? Too much debt. Fewer subscribers. A drop in ad buys. Probably all three."

"What does that mean for us?" *For me?*

"Hard to say. I'll probably be replaced."

"Why?"

"New owner means new editorial direction." He sounded embarrassed. "I'm the old direction."

"Conservative buyers?"

"Not at all. Way left of me."

"There is nothing to the left of Paul Daugherty."

They shared a nervous laugh.

"Apparently times are changing."

Julia let a few seconds pass to avoid appearing eager to know her own fate.

"You have always been a great writer, Jewel."

Here it comes, she thought.

"Heck. I owe much of my success to your work in the early days."

It was the first time she had ever heard Paul acknowledge Julia's part in his rise up the RAP ladder.

"But memories are short in this industry."

He stopped, as if enough had been said.

"And?" she fished.

No bites.

"Paul? There's more, isn't there?"

"That's all I can say, Jewel," he mumbled.

"Please, Paul. Just say it."

"I think this would be a good time for your byline to appear on a big feature. That's why I've been pushing so hard on the bright spots thing. Like I said, memories are short."

Her stomach tensed as she heard what he had avoided saying.

"It's my column, isn't it?" she asked.

"I didn't say anything about your column," Paul replied.

"I'm losing it?"

Another silence.

"When?"

"I don't know."

"When?" Louder this time.

"I could get into real trouble if—"

"And I could be losing my job, Paul! Please, just tell me what they said."

He cursed. "OK. But you didn't hear any of this from me."

She spent the next few minutes trying to believe her ears. In a few weeks the new owners of RAP Syndicate would be canceling her contract for the weekly column. Apparently "respectable" numbers weren't good enough. They wanted to make room for a new, rising star of the political left.

"Who?" she asked.

Paul didn't know.

"Monica?" she assumed.

"Not a chance."

To his credit, Paul seemed uncharacteristically eager to use what little leverage he had left to put Julia in the best possible light with the new owners. They wouldn't care about her Pulitzer Prize–winning feature of days gone by. But they would have a hard time ignoring an unflattering scoop on Franklin's austerity measures in advance of his expected announcement to run for president.

"Time's short, Jewel," Paul explained. "I need something really good really soon. Any day now I might move from editorial director to copy editor. I won't have much say in things when that happens."

Swallowing hard, Julia thanked Paul for whatever he had done and would do to position her well. Then she ended the call.

CHAPTER FORTY-FOUR

A renewed sense of urgency compelled Julia to relocate to the kitchen to boil a pot of water. She made a single mug of caffeinated tea with milk and carried it to the sofa in the adjoining living room. Sleep no longer an option, she sat down to read and reread the outline of a story that had stalled inadequately twelve hours earlier.

THE BREEDERS
(OUTLINE DRAFT 3)
PART ONE = HISTORY OF THE FISCAL CRISIS: Two productive workers for every debit senior. An unsustainable ratio.
PART TWO = IMPACT OF THE YOUTH INITIATIVE: Four million transitions have helped balance the scale. Lower senior-care expenses and more capital in the hands of younger workers and entrepreneurs.
PART THREE = FRANKLIN AUSTERITY TEAM: Closed-door meetings with political and business leaders seeking solutions.

PART FOUR = BRIGHT SPOTS CONTROVERSY: Radical breeder agenda receiving unexpected attention. Claims raising national fertility levels better than increasing transitions. (Note: Quote Kevin Tolbert to keep bargain.)

PART FIVE = CRITICS SKEPTICAL: Breeder proposal faces opposition as influential Washington insiders and business leaders criticize it as unworkable and naïve. (Note: Quote Trisha Sayers and Nicole Florea.)

Julia closed the outline and opened the first draft she had been working on before the disastrous fishing expedition with Gil. As expected, the words were a disappointment. The story felt like a skeleton without flesh, accurately structured but lacking life. She recalled Paul's advice. "People care a whole lot more about being with it than they do about being right." She had to find a way to portray the people supporting the proposal as hopelessly behind the times.

She took a sip of tea while considering next steps. She had promised to include Kevin's perspective in his own words in exchange for preemptive access. But Kevin was too sharp to come off as either naïve or behind the times. She needed something else.

Scanning her outline one more time triggered an idea. She placed her mug on the side table to free her fingers for typing.

PART SIX = GUILT BY ASSOCIATION: Include an extreme example of the breeder culture to show the agenda they hope to force onto others.

She recalled the peculiar-looking gentleman sitting to her left during Kevin's Tuesday presentation. She remembered his seeming the most supportive of all attendees, and that she had jotted down his name and a reminder to research his background.

Dr. Bryce Richert was a successful ob-gyn. Several data points suggested the embodiment of a radical breeder agenda. He made a nice living delivering babies. He had five grown kids of his own who had spawned a slew of grandkids. And he seemed displeased with a minor amendment to some transition-approval policy, as if reluctantly accepting improvement on a program he would rather end.

Julia searched and found the right contact information to send a quick note.

DEAR DR. RICHERT: *I'm a friend of Kevin Tolbert writing a RAP Syndicate feature on the Bright Spots proposal that will include extensive quotations from the congressman. I would love to add your perspective if you are available for a brief conversation in the next day or two. You pick the time. Thank you, in advance, for considering my request. Julia Davidson*

She then sent another short message.

PAUL: *I'm very close. Two more short interviews to add that will add color. Please buy me a little more time. Thanks much!*

Creative juices flowing again, Julia began reworking her story. The summary of economic trends could be moved to the middle. The opening needed to grab the reader's attention and create a quasi-conspiratorial urgency. The words came quickly.

THE BREEDERS
By Julia Davidson (RAP Syndicate)

A coalition of influential conservatives has been meeting behind closed doors with presidential hopeful Senator Joshua Franklin to explore economic incentives that will increase fertility among women of childbearing age. Critics are crying foul, accusing the group of advancing a radical agenda masked as attempts to stabilize our faltering economy. What kind of agenda? America, meet the breeders.

She sat back and took another sip of tea while admiring the perfect opening hook. An hour later she had completed the entire first draft. Only two missing sections: on-the-record comments from Kevin Tolbert and a carefully nuanced portrait of a hopelessly-behind-the-times breeder named Dr. Bryce Richert.

CHAPTER FORTY-FIVE

Angie couldn't remember a time she had felt this angry.

It must be some kind of mistake, she told herself. *Kevin would never do something like this without speaking to me first.*

But he had. The official notice said so in digital black and white.

To the parents of Leah Angelica Tolbert:

We are pleased to inform you that Leah has received preliminary approval to participate in an Alpha Group to receive four infusions of GE633, a DNA booster in development at Genhance Laboratories. This treatment has been cleared for testing on human subjects after successful results in three closely related species. Treatments will proceed once both parents submit digital signatures acknowledging their understanding that this particular genetic enhancement therapy is currently classified as experimental. Please read the attached detailed description of the treatment history, process, and risks. Feel free to schedule an appointment should you wish to better un-

derstand the potential benefits of GE633 in improving Leah's condition.

Kimberly Johnson, Office Assistant to Dr. Wayne Galliger

"Can you believe this?" Angie spewed toward two-year-old Joy, who was peering at Mommy over a bowl of Fruity Pebbles. "An office assistant knew about a risky treatment for Leah before her own mother knew!"

Joy's brow furrowed in a sympathetic echo of her mommy's disgust.

Angie tapped Kevin's speed-dial image to deluge him with questions. When had he spoken to Dr. Galliger about Leah? Hadn't they agreed it wasn't their job to "fix" their baby? And most importantly, how could he go behind her back on something this important?

"Hi, beautiful." His unique greeting for Angie's calls. "Sorry, I'm tied up. Can't wait to talk to you." A brief ping invited her to leave a message. She hung up, refusing to raise the subject on a thirty-second recording.

Angie looked back at the message on her tablet screen. The name Dr. Wayne Galliger seemed vaguely familiar, but she couldn't place it. She decided to open the attachment to learn about the supposed benefits of GE633 and the risks she had no intention of taking.

Genhance Laboratories described itself as the leading epigenetic research company in the world, with a litany of drugs and therapies improving the lives of patients who suffered from genetic abnormalities or mental deficiencies. More recent research had focused on curtailing and potentially reversing age-related dementia. Testing GE633 on brain-damaged primates had proved to dramatically increase recall and, to the researchers' surprise, expand several higher-end functions in the animals' brains. Mentally impaired apes caught up with and in some instances surpassed their peers after only a few infusions of the formula. That's when researchers nicknamed the treatment "brain-boosters." The FDA had recently cleared Genhance to expand testing to human patients with age-related dementia and genetically rooted mental retardation. While early results had proven promising, most participants had been elderly patients with little to lose if the treatments failed.

Leah was not an elderly patient. And she had an entire lifetime to lose.

Kevin's voice interrupted Angie's growing discomfort. "Hi, beautiful. Have I told you lately how much I—" She answered before the custom ringtone could finish its thought.

"Hi, babe. I see you tried to call."

"Hello, Kevin." Not *sweetheart*. Not *babe*. Just *Kevin*.

"What's wrong?"

She hated that question. Fortunately for him he was already in trouble.

"Tell me about Genhance Laboratories."

A brief silence.

"I already tried."

"No you didn't," she said with more certainty than she felt.

"What's going on?"

"Have you checked your messages recently?"

"Not since last night," he confessed. "It's been crazy today. The speaker said he wants to call a floor vote on another stopgap budget and—"

"Kevin Tolbert." She didn't care about the details of his day. "You have some explaining to do. Check your messages this second!"

She smashed her thumb over the icon of his smiling face. It was the first time she had hung up on him since they were in college and he forgot the third anniversary of their first date. Now, as then, she felt vindicated and slightly nauseated. At least this time she knew for certain he would call her back.

"Hi, beaut—" She pressed the incoming-call icon immediately.

"You couldn't check your messages in ten seconds."

"Angie!" She recognized the tone from when Kevin suppressed his anger at the kids. "I'm not in a place where I can check messages. Just tell me what's wrong."

"'To the parents of Leah Angelica Tolbert…'" She reluctantly read him the opening sentence, paused, and continued until she finished the entire letter.

"Oh." His voice softened. "Listen, babe, I know what you're thinking."

"I'm thinking you seem willing to put our baby at risk on the outside chance you can fix her. We already discussed this, Kevin. She isn't—"

"Correction," he interrupted. "We tried to discuss this. But you didn't listen. You cut me off with something about how normal isn't always good."

Angie suddenly remembered why the name Dr. Wayne Galliger sounded familiar. It was Kevin who had mentioned him during their dinner date. She had been too upset by the suggestion to hear him out.

"I tried telling you about the application process but you were in no mood to hear it."

"Application process?" She decided to listen this time.

"Dr. Galliger is head of epigenetic research at Genhance. Troy knows him and suggested we connect. I wasn't interested at first, but Troy said he has a stellar reputation."

"With aging dementia patients. Not with babies."

"With reduced mental capacity, which is exactly what we're dealing with in Leah. He told me—"

"You met with him?" Another surge of indignation.

"We spoke by phone. He gave me thirty minutes he didn't have because he believes kids like Leah may reap even greater benefits from the treatments because young brains have more elasticity."

"Greater benefits than whom? The apes?" she scoffed.

"Better than dementia patients."

"Did he also explain the risks?"

A pause. "Yes, he did."

"And?"

"And I said I would submit Leah's application to protect a slot, but that I would not even consider moving forward until you and I could learn more together."

She sighed at the arrival of the Kevin she'd married.

Neither spoke for several moments, allowing the distance between them to close.

"I'm really sorry, Angie," Kevin said. "I had no idea they would reply to the application so soon. I thought I'd have plenty of time to discuss it with you."

She took a deep breath and winked at Joy, who was trying to slurp milk at the bottom of her bowl while fixed on Mommy's vacillating facial expressions.

"Promise me you'll at least think it over," Kevin continued.

It was a promise she didn't want to make. But she knew her husband well. He needed to explore every possibility.

"Make me a promise?"

"You bet."

"We'll meet together with Pastor Mubar before making any decisions."

"I like that idea," he replied. "Make an appointment."

CHAPTER FORTY-SIX

Matthew felt his mother's chilly fingers squeeze his arm doubtfully just as they had while the two of them negotiated their snowy driveway toward the car. But there was no risk of slipping on ice here, sitting safely inside a beautiful lobby ten minutes before their scheduled consultation. Still, he sensed her vague anxiety.

He moved his hand over hers and gave a gentle pat. "Relax, Mom," he said reassuringly. "It's just an exploratory meeting. We won't make any decisions today."

Matthew wondered how much his mother understood about what was happening. Three years earlier they had visited several senior-care facilities in the area to explore options. She had pleaded with him not to put her in what she called "an old folks' home." He had promised that wouldn't happen. Of course, he could not have anticipated the pace of her deterioration then. He looked around, pleased to be sitting in a lobby that felt more like a stylish living room than a sterile hospital wing.

He reached toward the coffee table in front of them to sort through a meticulously arranged selection of periodicals, careful to put each back in its place after scanning the cover. He found one promising title.

"Here you go, Mom," he said as he eased her clamped fingers from his constricted forearm. "Why don't you look through this while I ask how much longer it'll be."

Matthew rose from the sofa and walked toward the dark oak reception desk. A woman sat with legs crossed at the ankles. Sensing his approach, she looked up from her screen.

"I apologize, Mr. Adams," she said caringly. "It should only be a few more minutes."

"No problem," he said, feeling bad about the intrusion. "I just needed an excuse to stretch my legs."

She seemed to sense his discomfort.

"Your mother feeling a bit anxious?"

He nodded.

"That's normal. Don't worry. I'm sure Mr. Kohl will put her at ease. One of the kindest gentlemen you'll ever meet. And he has more experience than any of our other advisors. You'll both like him."

Matthew slid both hands into his pockets and smiled at the promise of a cohort.

"Here," she said. "Why don't you take advantage of the time to review some of our packages?"

The brochure felt elegant like a wedding invitation, pearl-embossed paper with silver trim.

Matthew returned to the waiting area and sat beside his mother. She hadn't yet flipped open her magazine. He angled his shoulders slightly to block the brochure from her gaze. A silly gesture, he realized, since it had been years since her last laser eye adjustment. She would not be able to read such tiny print.

The prices were much higher than Matthew had anticipated, especially with the two or three bonus services he would insist she receive. He wanted the absolute best for his mother. That's why he had chosen Aspen House.

A man approached who, at first glance, seemed out of place. Matthew had expected their consultant to look like an impeccably groomed banker rather than a retired piano tuner or plumber. He walked with a slight limp and wore a warm smile. He extended his hand. Not toward Matthew, but toward his anxious mom.

"Hello, Ms. Adams." He engulfed her slight hands in his large mitts. "I've been so looking forward to meeting you."

Looking forward since when? Matthew wondered while glancing at the only name on his tag, CHARLES. He looked more like a Chuck.

"Matthew here has told us so much about you." Matthew remembered the online questionnaire. Chuck would know a great deal about his mother.

He raised a hand to place it on Matthew's shoulder. "We can tell your son loves you a great deal." The voice reminded Matthew of everyone's favorite uncle.

Ms. Adams looked into her son's eyes. She received an affirming wink.

The tension began easing out of her body.

Chuck was going to make a terrific coach through a difficult decision-making process.

"Can I offer either of you a cup of coffee or tea? Perhaps a glass of water?"

"I'm fine. Mom?" Matthew asked.

She gave a timid nod. A good sign.

"She likes tea with milk," Matthew said on her behalf.

Moments later they sat in a small consultation room, where Chuck poured fresh milk into the china teacup he had placed before his guest.

"I like a good cup of tea myself," he began. "Soothes the anxious soul."

"Like Beethoven," she replied.

Matthew turned toward his mother in surprised delight. He couldn't remember the last time he had seen her sip hot tea while bathing in classical music. It had been her favorite way to rejuvenate after arriving home from work. A pleasant memory he'd assumed she had lost.

"Or the Beatles!" Chuck baited, prompting her to flash a playful smile.

He's very good, Matthew marveled.

Chuck strained slightly to cross his legs as he looked down at a digital screen embedded in the table. "If it's OK with you, Ms. Adams, I'd like to begin by asking you to fill in a few missing details on the application form."

"Missing details?" Matthew asked. "I don't think I skipped any of the questions."

"You didn't. I apologize for the inconvenience. Our company just added a few minor policy compliance questions. The usual legal mumbo jumbo." He rolled his eyes in mock exasperation.

"I see," Matthew said hesitantly.

"OK. First, I'm going to need some proof that you are indeed over the age of eighteen, young lady."

A momentary silence was followed by a unified laugh.

"That won't be a problem," Matthew said, reaching for his mother's purse. "I'll scan her identification card while you go to the next question."

"Great," Chuck continued. "As awkward as it sounds, I do need to confirm that you've made this decision while of sound mind."

Hearing the word *decision* prompted Mom to look toward her son.

"Um, we haven't exactly made a decision yet," Matthew explained. "We wanted to wait until after this consultation."

"Oh, I'm sorry." Chuck took the cue. "My mistake. I should

have said I need to confirm you are capable of making a decision while of sound mind."

She placed the teacup back on the table while shifting silently in her chair.

"Of course, anyone who loves both Beethoven and the Beatles can't be nuts," the consultant teased. "So I feel quite comfortable attesting to your sanity."

She offered a slight nod of confirmation.

"And finally, I need to know that any decision you make to use Aspen House services will be one hundred percent non-compulsory."

A look of confusion came over her face.

"He means nobody will make you do anything you don't want to do," Matthew explained. "This will be your decision, Mom. It can't be mine or anyone else's. Do you understand?"

She moved her head slowly up and down without conviction.

"Good," Chuck said in a sprightly tone. "I'll just need a thumbprint from each of you." He turned the screen toward Matthew, who pressed firmly between the lines.

He offered Ms. Adams the same opportunity. She hesitated.

"Is something wrong?" he asked.

"Mom?" Matthew prodded.

She rose from her chair and walked slowly toward the door.

"Where are you going?" Matthew asked.

"I would like to see the room before making a decision."

Why would she want to see the room? Matthew wondered.

"I really do want my son to finish his college education," she explained. "I know he'll be an excellent professor. And he can't do that if he has to take care of me."

It seemed she understood what was happening after all, despite the look of confusion on her face each time Matthew had tried to explain. She had indeed connected the dots between this decision and his ability to pursue his dream.

"I like this place," she continued. "And I like you, Mr. Charles."

The consultant grinned at what he apparently assumed to be a closed sale.

"But I would like to see where I'll be living first."

Living? Matthew thought. *Oh no!*

"I'm sorry, Ms. Adams." Chuck seemed eager to correct any misunderstanding. "But you do understand, don't you, that you would not live here."

She looked back from the half-opened door, confused by the comment. "What do you mean?"

"Aspen House is no longer a nursing facility. We're a transition clinic."

The words didn't sink in.

"We discussed this already, Mom," Matthew interjected. "I told you that the only way the money can go toward my education is if you transition. We can't afford nursing care and tuition."

He saw the mind that loved music by Beethoven and enjoyed Chuck's playful banter sink back into a fog of confusion.

"Transition?"

"Yes, Mom!" The volume of Matthew's voice swelled. "Millions of people your age decide to transition instead of suffer. Freeing yourself from a decaying body in order to help others is heroic. You want to be heroic, don't you?"

His voice changed from that of a son honoring his mother to that of a parent tutoring his child.

"But life is a gift."

"So is transitioning." He recalled the conversation with Professor Vincent. "I already spoke to a priest about it. He said it's not a sin. It's self-sacrifice."

"Father Tomberlin said that?"

Matthew said nothing.

"He said it's not a sin?"

More silence.

She looked into her son's eyes.

He willed them to look back into hers.

She turned toward Chuck, who was hastily typing something onto the screen, then back toward Matthew.

"Do you want me to do this?" The question he'd hoped she would never ask him.

"I told you, Mom. This is your decision. I can't make it for you."

"And you discussed it with Father Tomberlin?"

"I did."

"It's not a mortal sin?"

Matthew looked away. "No, Mom. It's not a sin."

"Look at me, Matthew."

He turned back.

"You've always wanted to become a teacher, haven't you?"

A single nod.

Her shoulders lowered ever so slightly. She removed her hand from the door handle, then walked back toward her chair. Chuck lifted himself slightly from his seat in courtly deference.

Neither man breathed for several seconds.

"Mom?"

She lowered her head and extended her thumb in resigned approval.

CHAPTER FORTY-SEVEN

Talia Mubar noticed a small spot on her husband's sport coat and moved in for a closer look. Mustard, as she had suspected.

"Seth Mubar!" she scolded. "When on earth did you manage to get mustard on this jacket? I just had it cleaned last week to get out the barbeque sauce stain."

Reverend Mubar paid no attention as she dabbed her napkin in a glass of water sitting beside her menu or when she began rubbing the spot, his eyes fixed instead on the restaurant doors as if he was expecting someone.

"Don't worry about the mustard," he said. "I need to tell you something."

"So speak," Talia replied as she continued scrubbing. "My ears and my hands can work at the same time. I won't have you looking like a muddled vagrant. At least not when we're together!"

He pretended to resent the affectionate jab.

"You remember our meeting with Angie Tolbert?"

"Of course. Sweet girl."

"She phoned yesterday to ask for another meeting, this time with her husband."

"I'm glad. Do they want to discuss the baby again?" Talia guessed.

"Yes," he said, appearing slightly uncomfortable. "They have an important decision to make and want our input."

She sat back from her cleaning to inspect her work.

"Hopeless!" she concluded. "Take it off."

"What?"

"You aren't wearing that jacket while on a date with me. I expect my man to be presentable in public."

Hearing *date* seemed to make him even more uneasy. But he obeyed, wrestling his way out of his favorite sport coat, which doubled as a bib.

"About date night..." he began. "I have a confession."

"Seth Mubar!" She didn't need to hear another word. "You invited them to meet us for dinner, didn't you?"

A sheepish nod.

She looked toward the entrance. "Is that why you've been watching those doors like a watchman on a wall?"

A stupid grin.

"I've been better," he said defensively. "Haven't I?"

"We've spent exactly two of our last eight date nights alone. You scheduled a counseling session during one. We ran into parishioners during two and you invited them to join us. And you spent most of the other three responding to crisis calls." She paused.

"I know."

"Which is it this time?"

"The first, I guess," he admitted.

He spotted Angie walking through the door. Noticing his face, Talia turned in time to see Kevin trailing his wife.

"Looks like we're on," Seth said contritely.

"Looks like you're in the doghouse, Mr. Mubar!" Talia teased while grinning and waving to the darling couple.

Seth knew that his wife didn't mind nearly as much as she pretended. Both knew that such interruptions came with a pastor's role.

"I'll make it up to you," he said while they rose to greet their approaching guests.

"Yes you will," she threatened.

"Hello Representative Tolbert." Seth extended his hand toward Kevin's. "I'm so pleased this worked out."

Kevin appeared embarrassed while Angie accepted a hug from Talia. "Please, Pastor, call me Kevin."

"Only if you call me Seth."

"Deal."

Both gave their prolonged handshake an extra squeeze to seal the pact.

They took their seats around the table as an attentive waiter rushed over to fill two more water glasses. Conversation bounced between insignificant topics to fill time until they could place their orders. Talia and Angie gave a glowing update on each of their respective children while Seth and Kevin found more shared interests than either had expected. No one watching would have assumed the scene a counseling session between pastor and parishioners, but rather a meeting of distant acquaintances quickly becoming dear friends.

Salads served, Kevin seized the opportunity to fulfill his promise to Angie.

"We asked to meet because Angie and I are facing an important decision." He placed his hand on Angie's. "And we trust your wisdom on such matters."

"What kind of matter?" Seth prodded.

Kevin reached into his breast pocket to retrieve the notice from Genhance. He read it aloud.

"I see." Seth's eyes momentarily met his wife's, hoping they would offer her usual unspoken advice. She seemed equally at a loss. He turned back toward Kevin. "I surmise the two of you disagree."

"I wouldn't say we disagree," Kevin said instinctively.

"We strongly disagree," Angie said, looking directly into Seth's face.

Kevin blushed slightly. "Yes, we do."

Seth looked again toward Talia, who appeared uncharacteristically neutral. Then he turned to Angie. "Tell me why you're considering the treatments."

She looked at Kevin, who accepted the handoff.

"She isn't," he began. "I did some research to see whether there is anything that might give Leah a shot at a normal life."

"What do you mean, normal?"

"You know. School. A job. Maybe marriage and a family," Kevin replied.

"Why do you want her to have those things?" Seth asked.

The question drew a reaction from Angie. "We both want those things for Leah. But I'm not willing to take the risks. This is an experimental treatment."

"What are the risks?" Talia interjected.

Angie looked back toward Kevin.

"Galliger told me most participants to date have experienced a gradual, long-term improvement in mental acuity."

"Galliger?" Seth asked.

"Sorry. Dr. Wayne Galliger heads up Epigenetic Research for Genhance Laboratories. He's considered one of the world's foremost authorities on cognitive disabilities. He directed the development phase for GE six-thirty-three and is personally overseeing the tests."

Seth gave a slight nod, prompting Kevin to continue.

"Anyway, he told me that a small number of the test patients experienced dramatic changes, including healing of patches of brain tissue that had been assumed dead or too damaged for repair."

"Those sound more like potential benefits than risks."

Kevin accepted the redirection back to Talia's original question.

"He said about twenty percent of patients experience dramatic, short-term gains followed by a sharp turn for the worse. A few have even ended up comatose."

Talia and Seth sighed in unison.

"A difficult decision," Seth admitted. "You love your baby girl and want what's best for her. You find a program that looks promising only to discover serious risks."

"The same decision people face every day when deciding whether to accept the risk of surgery to remove a deadly tumor."

Kevin's comparison clearly bothered Angie. "But Leah doesn't have a deadly tumor. This isn't a life-or-death decision. It's a try-fixing-her-or-not decision."

Kevin visibly reacted to Angie's indirect accusation. They seemed to have had this argument before.

"I'm not trying to fix her!" he told Seth with slightly raised volume. "I just want what's best for her."

Seth took a bite of salad. Kevin and Talia followed his lead, creating a perfect distraction from the rising tension. Angie refused to join the feast.

"Tell them the rest," Angie insisted.

Kevin's fork halted en route to his mouth. He slowly lowered it to the plate.

"We checked our insurance to learn about coverage for experimental treatments," he began. "In light of the risk of coma they require parental preapproval for the child to transition if necessary. They want to avoid an indefinite period of costly life-support services."

Talia gasped. "They transition the kids?"

"There haven't been any kids treated yet," Kevin explained.

"But they have found it necessary to transition about ten percent of elderly test participants."

"I won't sign a paper saying they can kill my daughter if the treatment goes bad."

Talia nodded in maternal solidarity while looking toward her husband, who appeared alarmingly undecided. "We agree," she said preemptively.

Seth's hand formed into a not-so-fast gesture as he leaned toward Angie.

"Do you remember what we discussed in my office?" he asked. "About the burden Leah will be on your family?"

The question appeared to bother Angie until she noticed Seth's knowing wink.

"I think so," she replied. "You asked me whether I resented Leah."

Kevin's head jerked toward Angie and then toward Seth, clearly offended for his baby girl. "Resent Leah?"

"Then you asked me whether I was upset with God for failing to protect her from fragile X syndrome."

Kevin leaned back in his chair, appearing less upset but still alarmed.

"You said Leah would be a whole lot of work and very expensive to raise," Angie continued.

Talia, finally understanding the direction of the conversation, decided to join the ambush. "Do you remember what I said?"

Angie paused, then nodded. "I do."

"Leah may cause you embarrassment in public, especially as she gets older. She could even become a source of tension in your marriage."

"Wait a minute." Kevin couldn't listen any longer. "Why would you say those things?"

"Because they're true," Seth replied firmly. "Because they are the reality when raising a debit child."

"What did you say?" Kevin asked, visibly angry over Seth's use of such an insulting term to describe his precious little girl.

Seth flashed his bright white teeth toward Angie and Talia. They grinned and nodded in quiet satisfaction at having so easily sprung the trap.

"That bothers you, doesn't it, my friend?" Seth said while placing a pastoral hand on Kevin's shoulder.

He nodded, the seething subsiding in apparent recognition of the ploy. "Of course it bothers me."

"Good," Seth replied. "Then I think we can change the subject now."

"Change the subject?" Angie protested. "But we have so many questions. We're supposed to make a decision on the test by next week."

Talia reached across the table to pat Angie's hand. "Sweetheart, the decision is already made."

Angie looked at Kevin, his eyes fighting a losing battle against invading moisture.

"I have a hunch your husband will be entering Leah's room when you get home and holding her extra close tonight," Talia predicted.

A lone tear escaped Kevin's defenses, a white flag surrendering to friendly conquest.

Seth paraphrased the admonition he had given Angie in his office. "Children are a gift from the Lord, each one of them a unique reflection of the One Whose image they bear. You wanted to slug me when I called her a debit. That tells me everything in you knows Leah possesses infinite worth and dignity. You know that her value isn't based upon her capacity to go to school, get a job, or even have what you called a normal family life. She's beautiful, not because she will make the dean's academic list or become a cheerleader or win a beauty pageant, but because she's a unique icon of God himself."

Kevin snorted to regain an at-risk composure while avoiding eye contact with Angie. "You're right."

"I'm a father too, Kevin. I know how it feels to want to fix what's broken in your child's life. We have that feeling because we are made in the image of another dad, one who would do anything to restore his wayward and damaged kids."

Both Angie and Talia reached for their napkins rather than fight back tears.

"Little Leah is part of a sacred portrait God is painting called the Tolbert family. He plans to hang that picture on some gallery wall to reveal part of himself," Seth continued. "Leah doesn't need to be fixed. She needs to be put on display!"

The sound of sniffles continued as the waiter replaced partially empty salad plates with entrées. It was then that Talia noticed a small dab of salad dressing easing its way down the front of her husband's shirt.

CHAPTER FORTY-EIGHT

Angie's eyes opened to streams of bright morning sunlight sneaking around the edges of her closed window blinds. Her dilated pupils adjusted gradually until she could see the angled numbers on a digital display sixteen inches from her nose. She started to move toward the clock to confirm the time, only to notice the pleasant warmth of Kevin's right arm swathing her torso and his right leg resting across her upper thigh. She abandoned her routine, choosing instead to nestle herself closer into Kevin's spooning embrace and entwine her fingers with his to pull them slowly to her lips. She smiled, remembering their agreement the night before.

"Let's turn off the alarm and sleep until we wake," she had suggested.

She couldn't believe his immediate agreement. No meetings until lunch. Time to enjoy breakfast with the family as he had every Wednesday when they lived in Colorado. "Troy can handle whatever comes up," he had said. "I need to be home in the morning."

She kissed Kevin's knuckles gently and listened for the sounds of stirring children. Hearing nothing, she knew Joy's internal clock had not yet reached seven thirty. Angie reclosed her eyes to accept another moment of slumbering bliss.

The next sound she heard was Tommy's hushed voice coaching his perplexed little sister, who, it seemed, had not expected to see her mommy and daddy asleep in their bed.

"Shh," he said. "They'we sweeping."

The noise startled Kevin awake.

"Hey, buddy," he groaned at Tommy. "How's my champ doing this morning?"

"Shh." He raised the volume several decibels. "Mommy's asweep!"

Angie opened her eyes to end the big-brother-enforced stillness. A giant smile formed across Joy's face as she pressed her nose to her mommy's.

"Good morning, beautiful," Angie whispered to her new source of sunshine. "Did you wake up?"

Joy's vigorous nod launched the day. Kevin kissed Angie on the cheek before rolling out of bed with a yawning stretch. Angie slipped into her robe before taking Joy's hand and heading toward Leah's door to listen for motion. Tommy took his usual seat on the master bathroom floor to watch Daddy shave.

Fifteen minutes later the Tolbert family sat around the kitchen table listening to Joy parrot the sounds of words Tommy spoke with hands folded and head bowed over a bowl of instant oatmeal.

"Thank you for the food."

"Tankoo da ood," Joy repeated.

"Thank you for baby Weah."

"Tankoo aby eah."

"Amen."

"Men."

Angie nursed Leah while watching Kevin pour the apple juice.

She sent a wink of reassurance in his direction, indicating the moment of truth had arrived. They had agreed to tell Tommy during breakfast but hadn't determined who would speak first. He winked back to accept the assignment.

"Tommy, your mommy and I need to talk to you about something very important."

Even a five-year-old could sense Kevin's uncertainty.

Angie recalled their questions to Pastor Seth during dessert. Was the news too much to lay on the shoulders of such a young child? Should they wait until Tommy was old enough to understand more fully?

No. They should tell him right away.

Tommy swallowed a mouthful of mushy oats to clear the way for what seemed an important conversation.

"What is it, Daddy?"

"I want to tell you something about baby Leah," Kevin began.

Tommy placed his spoon on the table, then reached for his juice cup. He emptied it like a shot glass of whiskey in anticipation of bad news, then turned squarely toward his father to give his undivided attention.

"Several weeks ago we found out that Leah has something called fragile X syndrome." He paused. No question came. "It's a genetic disorder…"

Angie cleared her throat, reminding Kevin to keep the language simple.

"I mean, it's something that makes Leah different from other babies."

Tommy didn't move, hanging on every word.

"Have you noticed anything different about Leah?"

He squeezed his eyes in concentration. Nothing came, so he shook his head slowly back and forth.

"What your daddy is trying to say, Tommy," Angie added, "is that Leah may not be able to do all of the things Joy can do when she's two or the things you can do now when she turns five."

Tommy turned to look at Joy, then Leah. "Like wee-wee in the toiwet and wide a bike?"

"Sort of," Kevin continued. "We don't actually know what she will and won't be able to do. We just know it will be more diffi-cult...I mean...it may not be as easy for Leah to do those kinds of things as it is for you and for Joy."

Tommy nodded in agreement but didn't seem to understand. Kevin looked toward Angie for more help.

"Do you remember when Joy started to walk?" Angie asked.

He nodded again while lifting his hand. "I was this many."

"That's right. You turned four a week before Joy took her first steps." Angie smiled broadly, recalling the excitement on Tommy's face watching his little sister judder her way toward Mommy's open arms thirteen months earlier. "Leah will proba-bly be much older than Joy was when she takes her first steps."

"Oh." Tommy's concern seemed to grow rather than lessen.

"Do you remember when you learned your ABC's?" Kevin asked, picking up on Angie's successful strategy.

Tommy nodded slowly.

"That will take longer for Leah also."

Sensing Leah's waning suckle, Angie moved the baby and be-gan patting her gently on the back. She tried to recall what she had read about the intellectual capacity of fragile X children. Would she learn her alphabet? Would she ever know the joy of reading a favorite book, writing a simple story, or coloring between the lines? She paused the patting to squeeze Leah close, grieving over a disheartening list of limitations her daugh-ter might know.

Shifting his attention from Kevin's third or fourth example of how Leah might be different, Tommy noticed Angie's face.

"Don't cwy, Mommy," he said.

The slight sound of Leah's burp lightened the moment.

"There you go!" Angie celebrated while sniffling back emotion. "I bet that feels better."

Tommy got up from his chair and moved toward Angie and the baby. Then he turned back toward Kevin with a tortured look of worry under an apple juice mustache.

"Do you understand what we've been trying to say, Tommy?" Kevin asked.

A slight, anxious nod.

"Do you have any questions?"

His hand reached toward Leah's, then pulled back. He seemed nervous about touching her, as if she had suddenly become more fragile than he could fathom.

"Tommy?" Kevin prodded. "What are you thinking, buddy?"

A fretful quaver filled his voice. "Does this mean...?" He paused.

"Does it mean what, sweetheart?" Angie asked while reaching over to rub his little back.

He swallowed hard, seeming to force himself to ask a question he hoped they wouldn't answer.

"Will I still be able to hug her and kiss her every day?"

CHAPTER FORTY-NINE

"That'll be Troy," Kevin guessed before the audio butler could announce the caller's name.

"Why would he call the home number instead of your phone?" Angie was still enjoying the "gwoup hug" launched at Tommy's decree. Leah sat on her lap, enduring Joy and Tommy's combined embrace, clearly less fragile than her big brother had feared.

"I turned off my phone," Kevin confessed.

Angie smiled like a mother proud of her child for tying his own shoes.

"But I better get this," he continued. "Troy wouldn't use our home number unless it was important."

Kevin brushed aside Troy's unnecessary apology for calling so early. "Is everything OK?"

"I think so," Troy began. "I just hung up with Dr. Richert."

"Bryce Richert?"

"He seemed pretty upset."

Kevin waited for Troy's usual specificity. Silence.

"That's it? No details? He's just upset?"

"I tried but he insisted on speaking to you directly. He wouldn't even let me set an appointment. He wants you to call this morning."

Kevin glanced toward Angie, her face balancing curiosity about her husband and delight in her kids. He shrugged with a grin, releasing her to ignore his telephone crisis.

"Put me through to his office," Kevin ordered as he moved from the table toward his desk.

"In a second," Troy answered. "There's more."

"More?"

"Senator Franklin's office asked if you could meet privately for lunch."

"Today?" Kevin asked.

"Noon. At McGuffey's."

Kevin recognized the restaurant's name immediately. McGuffey's had become both famous and infamous in DC lore. Famous as the place presidents-elect chose to meet with potential cabinet appointees, major donors, and celebrity backers. Infamous as the place in which President Lowman had requested the resignation of his former press secretary. Everyone knew that dessert at McGuffey's usually included some sort of press release.

Allowing a moment for Kevin to absorb the news, Troy went on to explain that he had already moved Kevin's planned lunch with the Bright Spots subcommittee. Tweaking the proposal language would have to wait until late afternoon.

"Make us proud, Congressman," Troy added.

Kevin looked back toward Angie, who had begun directing the cleanup process, Tommy insisting he could carry the half-full carton of milk while Joy placed her empty sippy cup on the kitchen counter. He decided not to tell her about the lunch meeting. Whether good news or bad, he would rather explain specifics than speculate over possibilities.

He waited in silence while Troy transferred the call to Dr. Bryce Richert's office.

"Congressman Tolbert?"

"Please, call me Kevin." His customary request. "I understand you needed to speak to me about an urgent matter."

"Yes, I do. It's about the RAP interview."

Kevin searched his memory for a connection. Nothing. "RAP interview?"

"The story about the Bright Spots proposal," Dr. Richert said, causing Kevin's stomach to tighten.

"How do you know about that?" he asked. "I've only had a preliminary discussion with a journalist. No details."

"Julia Davidson?"

"That's right. We had an off-the-record conversation."

"You also invited her to attend Tuesday's presentation," Richert added with irritation.

"With Anderson's approval and an agreement she could not release anything without my express permission. Why? What's happened?"

"I spent about three hours with Ms. Davidson yesterday. I was led to believe you encouraged her to interview me."

Kevin mentally studied his conversations with Julia. "No, sir. I never mentioned you or any other member of the subcommittee."

A brief silence told Kevin that Dr. Richert was redirecting his anger.

"I guess she never actually said you proposed the interview."

"What *did* she actually say?" Kevin felt his own dander rising.

"She said she was writing a story on the Bright Spots proposal that would include substantial comments from Congressman Tolbert. She told me you had invited her to attend the austerity coalition presentation. I vaguely remembered her face as soon as we met at the ranch."

"The ranch? You invited her to your home?"

"For lunch. She said she wanted to include my wife in the interview, see photos of the kids and grandkids, that sort of thing. I figured it was a good idea since we were talking about encouraging parenthood."

Kevin said nothing while assessing whether the interview was good news or bad, whether Julia had kept or broken her word.

"She took quite a few pictures at both the house and the office."

"You took her to your office too?" Kevin grew more uncertain.

"She said it would help to show me in my professional context. What better showcase for a fertility proposal than an ob-gyn who has delivered as many babies as me?"

Kevin had to agree. But then he remembered that Dr. Richert had phoned because he was upset about something. "How'd you feel about the interview?"

"Not good." The anger returned to the doctor's voice. "Not good at all. That's why I called your office so early this morning."

"Go on."

"I very much doubt Ms. Davidson or RAP Syndicate plans to present your proposal in a positive light."

No surprise.

"Tell me what happened," Kevin said.

"Everything began just fine. Ms. Davidson seemed genuinely interested in Carol's and my decision to have such a large family. Asked about the good and the bad, our food budget, that sort of thing." He paused. "But the more questions she asked the less comfortable I became about her agenda."

"Like what?" Kevin wondered.

"The usual nonsense. How do we justify bringing so many children into a world with scarce resources? Do I ever feel bad that Carol curtailed her career to raise children? Does our religion oppose birth control? You know the litany."

He did.

"Anyway, by the time we had toured my office and she had taken a picture of our wall of babies I sensed the tone of her questions shift from mildly antagonistic to overtly hostile."

"Wall of babies?" Kevin asked.

"Since my first delivery I've taken a picture of every baby. We've been adding those pictures to a montage on the hallway between the waiting area and my examination room. Must be nearly two thousand by now."

"She took a picture of your pictures?"

"Yep. You should see it. Pretty impressive. I didn't think anything of it at the time."

"And now?"

"Now I worry. It felt like that wall turned her from Jekyll to Hyde. It also seemed to put an idea in her head."

"What kind of idea?"

"Not sure. But I don't think she wanted the picture to show how much I've contributed to the world. It was more like she thinks I've been cluttering it."

Kevin's gut tightened further.

"I'd bet my last dollar Ms. Davidson wants to portray your proposal as something that would clutter rather than help the financial crisis."

He let the comment settle, then continued.

"Be careful, Kevin. I've seen this before, back in '38 and '39. They won't play fair."

Kevin recalled Dr. Richert's early efforts to oppose the Youth Initiative. He had been part of a small but vocal cohort of medical professionals condemning subsidized transitions as a violation of medical ethics. Few listened. Any press that did cover them took cheap shots by labeling them moralizing crusaders more interested in a steady stream of private-pay patients than the overall health of public coffers.

"I apologize, Dr. Richert." He meant it, both for the present situation and for his silence back then.

"Call me Bryce." The angry colleague had become a close ally.

"I was trying to be proactive, Bryce. They plan to do a story with or without my input. I cut a deal. I gave Julia preemptive access in exchange for a guarantee."

"What kind of guarantee?"

"Whatever else she includes in the story, she must allow me to make the case for our proposal in my own words."

"And you expect RAP to play fair?"

"I expect Julia Davidson to play fair."

"Have you read any of her previous columns? I hardly think she will suddenly become neutral after a successful career undermining everything people like us believe."

"I don't expect her to change her bias. But I think she'll do her best to be evenhanded."

"Why?"

Kevin hesitated to explain, but decided Bryce deserved to know.

"She and my wife were best friends during high school. I don't expect journalistic integrity to win the day. But I think the lingering affections of a childhood friendship might motivate her to cut us some slack."

"Humph. Don't forget. Brothers shot each other during the Civil War. You don't really think friendship trumps headlines, do you?"

It was a question Kevin couldn't answer. Yet.

CHAPTER FIFTY

Kevin apologized self-consciously while grinning at the valet after searching his wallet for an appropriate tip. He had forgotten to get cash before rushing to the restaurant.

"Catch you on the way out?"

The boy offered a deferential nod but appeared doubtful after noticing the ice-cream-stained stuffed animal and three child car seats in the rear of the vehicle. Hardly the wheels of the typical power broker who would slide him the usual fifty.

"Don't worry about it, sir." Kevin couldn't quite decipher whether the tone was one of disgust or pity. "A pleasure to serve."

Pity.

Turning toward the door, Kevin paused to relish a few moments before entering McGuffey's Restaurant. Inside he would enthusiastically greet the leading contender for the nomination to the presidency. Senator Joshua Franklin had requested a private meeting, meaning he had some important agenda. At this very moment the senator could be holding a first-draft statement for the press announcing who knew what but requiring one last detail to be handled during a lunch conversation with the rising political star from the great state of Colorado.

Kevin had cautioned himself. *Keep your expectations low.* Advice he was struggling to heed.

"Good afternoon, Congressman Tolbert." The hostess stood behind a carved oak pedestal wearing a black cocktail dress and heels. It had taken less than a second for the face recognition system to find his image on her list of reservations. "Senator Franklin is waiting. May I take your coat?"

Kevin laughed to himself while the woman handed his coat off to another hostess. He was a long way from the hot dog cart where he and Troy held their daily campaign strategy meetings.

"Please follow me," she said, rounding the station.

He followed the woman through a labyrinth of tables occupied by various Washington elite: secretary of this, chairwoman of that, legal council for such-and-such political action committee, each immersed in a conversation that traded the landscape of one constituency in favor of another. The fate of someone's health insurance program, school lunch funding, tax bill, business regulations, research grant, or any one of countless other real-world priorities depended upon how well those enjoying the McGuffey's daily special played the power lunch game.

The hostess approached Senator Franklin's table, where he was seated with two other guests rather than alone as Kevin had expected. Apparently "private lunch" had more than one possible meaning.

"Kevin!" the senator said, offering his campaign-trail handshake. "So glad you could join me on such short notice."

"Of course." He looked at the third and fourth wheels, recognizing both.

"I believe you've met Kari."

Kevin smiled nervously at the attractive aide he'd last seen walking away from his front porch after an unannounced visit to his home.

"We met briefly," he acknowledged.

"I'd also like to introduce you to a very good friend to our party, Evan Dimitri."

The man sat motionless, every bit as unimpressed with Senator Franklin as he had been with Kevin Tolbert or, presumably, any of the other politicians receiving his generous support.

"We've met," Dimitri said, annoyed by the social formalities. "Stop wasting time."

The senator took his seat like a scolded schoolboy, leaving only one opening. Kevin took his place beside Kari Samson. As soon as he was seated she leaned slightly closer and placed her hand on his forearm.

"Good to see you again, Mr. Congressman."

Kevin reached for the menu sitting on the table in an attempt to create a bit more distance between himself and her alluring gaze.

"I hope you don't mind that I invited Kari and Evan to join us," Franklin began. "But I want to move quickly on something and I thought it would be best for you to hear directly from the horse's mouth. The horse being Evan, of course, not the lovely lady."

Franklin laughed while placing his hand playfully on Kari's bare shoulder.

"Horse's mouth?" Kevin asked, turning toward Dimitri's stern face.

"Tell him, Evan."

"Ever hear of the Saratoga Foundation?"

"I don't think so," Kevin confessed.

"Good. We like to stay below the radar."

"It's one of the most generous funding machines behind key races for national office," Franklin interjected.

"Are you explaining this or am I?" Dimitri looked perturbed. Franklin turned sheepish. "Anyway. I chair the foundation. Our most important fund-raising event takes place in a few months. We're going to charter a cruise ship for about seventy of the wealthiest political action donors. We've planned two days for them to interact with guys like Josh and yourself."

Did he just place me in the same category as Joshua Franklin? Kevin thought.

"The best way to get donors excited about your campaign is to let them speak into your agenda," Dimitri continued.

"Speak into it?"

Dimitri rolled his eyes as if talking to a naïve child. "Small gifts come from small people willing to cheer at your rallies and vote for your reelection," he explained. "But the big money, the kind that wins national elections, comes from people like me."

Kevin believed it, especially in light of Dimitri's earlier gift.

"Serious donors want some say in how those in office leverage our financial backing."

He remembered the earlier lunch when Dimitri had "requested" that Kevin keep his mind open to a range of economic solutions. He had hinted the bright spots concept would "round out" a bundle of ideas like the garnish on a main course.

"I need to know if you're interested," Dimitri added unnecessarily.

"Of course he's interested," Franklin said tepidly, looking toward Dimitri to make sure it was OK to continue. "Congressman Tolbert is a smart lad. He'll make a great contribution to the event. Just the kind of rising star donors like. Young. Bright. Persuasive."

Kevin said nothing while observing an exchange of knowing glances between Franklin and Dimitri.

"I think he'd be a great addition to something else," Kari suggested.

"Let's not get ahead of ourselves, young lady," the senator said with a photo-op grin. "I haven't even received the nomination yet. It's way too early to think about cabinet posts or running mates!"

Running mates? Kevin's head began to spin.

"I want you to unpack the Bright Spots proposal," Dimitri ordered. "Explain the research, the long-term benefits, specific policy changes, the whole thing."

The words finally came. "I'd be honored."

"I plan to make it a big part of the austerity plan," Franklin added. "And I want our donors to get excited about the concept. But I also want them to get excited about you, Kevin. Even if we can't sell your idea I'm confident we can sell you."

"Can't sell my idea?" Kevin felt a sudden surge of caution. "But I thought you said—"

Dimitri cut to the chase. "Listen, Tolbert. People want to feel good about our future. They like optimism about a brighter tomorrow and all that."

He paused as he noticed a passing waiter. "Four daily specials," he shouted, flashing four fingers.

"A half portion for me, please," Kari inserted, patting her firm tummy as if to suggest she needed to shed a few pounds.

"Where was I?" Dimitri asked. "Oh yeah. Your Bright Spots proposal sends all the right messages. Celebrate the young. Invest in the future. Play with your grandkids. Who wouldn't donate to that vision?"

"And it will balance out the tougher aspects of my plan," Franklin added. "We need the financial impact of transitions, but nearly forty percent of our base say they wish there were a better solution."

"There is!" Kevin said, encouraged by a sentiment he had not heard Franklin acknowledge before. "In fact, my first draft of the Bright Spots proposal included two halves of a whole. The strongest economic pockets show both high fertility and low transitions. They combine for impact. You know, one plus one makes three."

Dimitri looked disapprovingly toward Franklin. "What's this about?" he asked, like a man spotting a dead fly in his soup.

"The senator missed my first-draft proposal," Kevin said before Franklin could respond. "He didn't get to hear all of the research because Anderson tabled half of what I presented. In short, the brightest economic spots include two key trends, more children and fewer transitions."

Franklin lowered his hand from Kari's shoulder and leaned inward. "I saw the research, Kevin," he began. "But we can't risk losing the guaranteed savings and growth capital transitions create. If anything, we'll need more transitions, not fewer."

Kevin's heart sank as Evan Dimitri retook the lead.

"Have you heard about a recent wrongful death claim against NEXT Inc. Transition Services?"

"Sure. A minor and his mother."

"That case has many of our donors nervous."

"Nervous?"

"Yes, Mr. Tolbert. Nervous. Do you have any idea of the potential legal ramifications of that case? Not to mention the political fallout that could ensue."

"I'm afraid I don't follow," Kevin confessed.

"There's talk among some in our base that we should revisit the ethics of transitions."

Kevin held his tongue, resisting the urge to show agreement.

"It's a dangerous time to let research like yours throw gas on that sputtering flame," Franklin added. "Especially when our austerity package projects dramatic growth rather than decline in the practice over the coming decade."

"What?" The shock outran Kevin's composure. "You want to increase transitions?"

"Of course," Franklin replied. "You've seen the census numbers. How else could we possibly avert another economic free fall?"

Kevin's brain scrambled for a quick, obvious rebuttal. None existed.

A light seemed to go on inside Dimitri's head. "I see," he said knowingly.

"See what?" Franklin asked.

"I'm surprised at you, Congressman," Dimitri said to Kevin, prompting a quizzical expression. "I would have thought your team had researched my company before you cashed my donation check."

"They did. Based upon your pattern of giving to fiscal conservatives we saw no reason to dig further."

"So you have no idea why I would be troubled by the notion of curtailing transitions?"

Kevin stared blankly as Franklin shifted in his seat, apparently embarrassed by an unspoken oversight.

"Mr. Dimitri's company owns the patent on PotassiPass."

Kevin didn't recognize the name, prompting Franklin's further explanation.

"It's the lethal injection serum used by NEXT transition clinics."

CHAPTER FIFTY-ONE

Julia scheduled nothing on Thursday so that she could remain in her hotel room. She planned to use the whole day writing up her Wednesday interview. She had always done her best work when creating and reaching mental milestones. Today she would finalize all but one section of *The Breeders*. Friday she would cross the finish line by recording and inserting an on-the-record conversation with Kevin Tolbert.

At two o'clock in the afternoon Julia caught herself rereading the same perfectly crafted paragraph she had read the hour before. Any additional tweaks, she realized, would add nothing. She had even found time to select the ideal pictures to include with each section. It had been an unusually productive morning thanks to the unbelievably useful notes captured the prior day. She congratulated herself on the decision to get back to DC early to speak with Dr. Bryce Richert.

She closed the document and opened another, falling into her instinctive pattern of using the momentum of one productive milestone to propel her toward another. Scanning the list to find the most promising topic for her next column, Julia recalled the pending sale of RAP. She imagined handing all nine million of her loyal readers over to the next flavor-of-the-month writer. Creative motivation died, replaced by a perplexed gaze.

Why would RAP cut my column when so many readers love my stuff? Or did they?

No other columnist will attract as many subscribers as me. Or would they?

I'm sure I'll land an even better opportunity elsewhere. Or could she?

The snowball grew throughout Julia's treadmill jog and followed her into the shower where she had hoped to melt anxiety in the warm water of relaxation and stubborn heat of self-confidence. No change.

She heard a ping while brushing through freshly washed hair and gazing searchingly at the woman in the mirror. Securing the sash around her waist she found her phone buried at the bottom of her purse.

Two messages had arrived during her forty-minute retreat.

"Paul?" she said after tapping the RETURN CALL option.

"Jewel!" He seemed agitated. "Where have you been?"

"You mean for the past twenty minutes?"

"Thirty-one!" he corrected. She glanced at the time marker on his message to confirm.

"Thirty-one, then. I was in the shower, if it matters."

"It's one o'clock in the afternoon for Pete's sake!"

"Three o'clock in DC," she explained. "I'm in a hotel room where I've nearly finished the breeder story."

"Good." Air seemed to seep from his uptight balloon, his voice gradually lowering as he spoke. "That's why I called. Things are moving fast around here."

"Fast how?" She braced herself for devastating news.

"They announced the sale to the editorial board this morning."

She said nothing.

"No news yet on the fallout, but I'm worried."

"About?" she asked.

"About my job. Your column. Everything."

"What do you need?" Julia asked, one drowning person hoping to rescue another.

"I need a very strong piece from you. And I need it fast."

Julia placed her hand on top of her closed tablet. It contained 90 percent of what Paul wanted. But the missing 10 percent represented a promise she had made to Kevin Tolbert, his proposal in his own words.

"The story's written, Paul," she said to shore up his wavering confidence. "I only need one more day to add the final bit."

"Thank God!" he exhaled. "Send it."

She hesitated. "I can't."

"What do you mean you can't?"

"I don't yet have clearance to use the most important parts."

"What do you mean clearance?" he asked warily.

"I cut a deal, Paul. Kevin Tolbert gave me first option. We'll have twenty-four hours to scoop."

"Twenty-four hours before what?"

"Before Franklin's austerity proposals go public," she explained. "Trust me. It'll be worth waiting another day."

"One day?"

"One day," she said hopefully. "I have an on-the-record interview with Tolbert in the morning. I should have it written up by end of day tomorrow."

She heard muffled mumbling on the other end of the line, probably Paul counting backward from his final copy deadline.

"I need it by five o'clock mountain standard time."

"You'll have it." She sensed the net being removed beneath her.

"Good. I secured prime placement for this piece," he said. "Lead story in the weekend culture watch section."

Lead story? Julia thought with delight.

"The editorial board started salivating when I told them what was coming."

"Wait." What Paul was saying suddenly sank in. "You had no idea when I'd be finished with the story."

"I would have if you had answered your phone!" he said defensively. "I had to act fast or we'd have lost our window. Maybe the only window we'll get."

Julia felt a slight wobble in her high wire.

"I need a preview, Jewel. If you can't send it, then read it to me."

"Read it?"

"Yeah, read it. I want to hear what you've got."

Julia hated reading her own writing aloud. Her voice never carried the force of her words as powerfully as black text on a white screen. But she reluctantly began, gaining confidence with each paragraph as she heard Paul's audible grins grow more pronounced. She paused midway to get reactions from her audience of one.

"Good opening hook," he said reassuringly. "And I love the way you've portrayed Franklin. What an arrogant conniver!"

She continued, finally reaching the portion where she described Dr. Richert's mantel filled with photos of grown kids and their broods of grandchildren.

"Very nice," Paul reacted. "The embodiment of Breederville!"

She continued reading, placing special emphasis on the demonizing descriptions of Dr. Bryce and Carol Richert, complete with subtle mockery of their inane justification for overpopulating an overcrowded planet.

"'Every baby born brings one mouth to feed but two hands to work.' He actually said that?"

"Every word. Not a second of hesitation. He really believes it."

"Scary! Perfect!" Paul exclaimed.

"Wait till you see the picture I took in his office. Here it is."

Three taps on her tablet sent the image to Paul's in-box.

"Brilliant!" he reacted four seconds later. "Is this for real?"

"He estimated two thousand newborn pictures, every one of them hanging side by side in his office hallway."

"This is it!" Paul exclaimed.

"This is what?"

"This is what we need for the title screen! Just think, Jewel, a clean headline: *THE BREEDERS* in all caps overlaying this image. Talk about evoking nightmares in your single and carefree fans!"

Julia imagined and liked the idea.

"The only thing that would make it better is a picture of a younger, haggard Mrs. Richert with a crib-lizard hanging on her breast!" He laughed irreverently. "You didn't get anything like that, did you?"

"Don't be ridiculous!" she retorted good-naturedly.

"No matter. This image alone says it all. Readers will hate Franklin's plan before they've even heard what's in it! The editorial board is gonna love this. Well done, love!"

Back on top, she thought.

Paul took a long, deep breath in satisfaction and relief. He said nothing for several moments.

"What?" she prompted.

"I owe you an apology, Jewel." The words didn't come easily.

"For what?"

A long silence. She waited, certain Paul was seeking words to fess up about Monica Garcia.

"I don't know. I guess I forgot just how good you could be."

"Thanks, Paul. But you don't owe me an apology. I owe you my thanks. I know you took a risk assigning me this piece. I just hope it pays off."

Another gap in the conversation.

"One last thing," Paul said. "I think we need an insurance policy just in case."

"Insurance? What do you mean?"

A slight hesitation, the kind liars use to turn corners in their tall tales.

"I think we need to go a step beyond demonizing the Bright Spots proposal and mocking the breeder culture," he mused. "After all, Franklin's austerity plan will be his opening salvo in pursuit of the presidency."

"I'm listening," Julia said.

"There are rumors Franklin asked Congressman Tolbert to draft and present his full plan."

"Really?" Julia understood why. Kevin Tolbert was an impressive and articulate young leader, the kind of person Franklin would like to have at his side when conducting press conferences and explaining big ideas. All Kevin lacked was a national platform, a proving ground for more influence. Something Franklin was in a position to give.

"Every visionary leader needs an expendable team member," Paul added.

"What do you mean by *expendable*?"

"You know. If the austerity plan is well received Franklin looks brilliant and Tolbert moves up a notch. But if the plan falls flat Franklin can distance himself from any unpopular elements."

"The Bright Spots proposal?" she realized. "He wants it in the package but wonders how it will be received."

"That's my guess. Anyway, we need to cover our bases regardless of whether Tolbert is a hit or a flop."

Julia tensed. "Cover our bases?"

"What you've written so far will leave a very bad taste in the mouths of readers. But guilt by association is one thing. Actual guilt is another."

She didn't follow.

"This story needs to do more than leave a bad taste. It needs to trash the reputation of the leading voice for breeder ideals."

"Wait a minute, Paul. You know I've never played that game. I'm as willing as anyone to portray stupidity as stupid. But I won't manufacture—"

"You won't need to manufacture anything, Jewel," Paul interrupted. "I've received dirt on Kevin Tolbert that will significantly sharpen the teeth of your story."

Four faces flooded Julia's mind. First Angie's, then Tommy's, Joy's, and Leah's.

"What kind of dirt?" she asked.

"It'll be in your message box no later than tomorrow morning."

CHAPTER FIFTY-TWO

"Where have you been?"

Kevin sensed a level of frustration in Troy's voice that would have prompted his friend to rub a bald spot onto Kevin's head if they had been in the same room. He glanced at the display on his phone, the same phone that had been sitting in his car for the past hour. Six new messages. Five of them from Troy.

"I'm sorry, buddy," he said. "I took a walk after lunch. I needed to think."

"I figured your lunch would have ended hours ago."

Kevin looked at the time. "I guess it did. Sorry."

"You already said that." A brief silence turned fury into alarm. "Is something wrong? What happened?"

It was the question Kevin had spent the past few hours trying to answer for himself. What *had* happened during his lunch with Franklin and Dimitri? Had they courted him or cornered him? Was he being invited into the corridors of power or ousted from the think tank of solutions? And more importantly, should he accept Franklin's offer?

"Well, he started by asking me to present the bright spots concept to a gathering of big donors, some event sponsored by a group called…" He tried to remember the precise name. "Something like the Saratone Fund."

"The Saratoga Foundation?" Troy asked.

"That's it. You've heard of it?"

"Heard of it? Yes, I've heard of it. The Fort Knox of campaign funding. Every fiscal conservative in the Senate owes his or her election to the Saratoga Foundation. He asked you to speak at their fund-raising event?"

"That's what they said," Kevin replied.

"They?"

"Evan Dimitri was with him."

"Aha!" Troy said, as if finding a missing puzzle piece on the floor.

"What?"

"That explains the sudden generosity of our mysterious donor." Kevin couldn't remember a time when Troy had sounded so excited. "Well done, Mr. Congressman!"

An unsettled feeling prevented Kevin from joining the celebration.

"That's not all," he continued.

"I bet. Tell me everything!"

"Franklin asked me to oversee the draft process for the full austerity coalition plan."

"No way!"

"He also wants me to present it during his press conference next week."

"Holy…" Troy took a deep breath. "Kevin, do you have any idea what this means?"

"Don't jump to conclusions, Troy," Kevin cautioned. "I see red flags all over this one."

"Red flags? You must be kidding. The cutest girl in school just winked at you and you're reluctant to wink back?"

The analogy prompted a laugh that released part of the tension that had been building in Kevin for hours. But the conversation with Dr. Richert about Julia reminded him that Washington, DC, attracted Machiavelli disciples and Dorian Gray clones. Things were rarely as they appeared. Especially when they involved mysterious donors and flattering invitations.

"What happened to the Troy Simmons who never trusts anyone and who remains skeptical to the end?" Kevin asked.

"You're right, of course," Troy acknowledged. "But I've spent nearly four hours imagining the worst, then the best, then the worst again. So you'll forgive a little enthusiasm in light of what seems pretty good news."

"We'll see."

"We'll see? Tell me you said yes."

"Franklin said it for me."

"You honestly considered saying no?"

"I don't know, Troy. Something just doesn't feel right."

Troy curbed his enthusiasm to offer Kevin breathing room, slipping comfortably into his position as chief confidant. "I'm all ears."

"Evan Dimitri makes me nervous, for starters. He comes off like a guy accustomed to pulling strings."

"Money is a pretty effective puppeteer," Troy confirmed. "But you know how to navigate power players. Why the concern about Dimitri?"

"His vested interest in growing the transition industry, to start."

"What?"

"His company owns the patent for the main serum used by NEXT."

"You mean…?" Troy prompted.

"The check we deposited came to us compliments of the very

transitions we came here to end." The admission sent a mild nausea into Kevin's stomach, a sensation Troy seemed to share during a long silence.

"I'm sorry, Kevin."

"For what?"

"We should have researched Dimitri more closely. I hate that you were caught by surprise."

"It's not your fault. If I recall correctly, you were the cautious one. I guess I was too eager to believe my own optimism."

"So what'd you say when you found out?"

"I held my tongue. I wanted to hear them out."

"And?"

"And Franklin made a point of emphasizing how important it was for his plan to incorporate a wide range of ideas. They like the bright spots concept because it will round out the package with something upbeat and positive to offset proposed expansion of the transition industry."

Another long silence.

"That's when Franklin said he wants me to write and present the full plan. Put his arm around me like his best friend and potential running mate."

"Did he mention running mate?"

"Kari mentioned it. But he didn't dismiss it."

"Kari?"

"Kari Samson, Franklin's favorite aide. She joined the lunch." He paused. "Don't ask."

"You did need to take a walk!"

"I honestly don't know what to do, Troy. Franklin seems to be handing me the keys to the kingdom, opening doors of influence I can't imagine opening any other way."

"Do you think God might be working in one of his trademark mysterious ways?"

"Maybe. How could anyone be sure?" Kevin wondered aloud.

"But what I do know is that I can't sell policies that will grow an industry I consider evil."

"Did you tell him that?"

"Not directly. But he said he had read my original proposal, including the part about restricting transition wealth transfers to charity."

"So he knows how you feel about the Youth Initiative?"

"He knows."

"Then there's only one explanation," Troy suggested. "He's testing your loyalty."

"I considered that, which puts me in a difficult spot. If I hold my nose to support Franklin's full plan it could open doors for greater influence. Doors, as you suggested, God himself may be opening for reasons I don't yet understand."

Kevin recognized a series of faint taps on the other end of the line, indicating Troy's habit of drumming with a pencil when untangling a thorny issue.

"Listen, Kevin. Someone has to write Franklin's plan, right?"

"Yes, Troy. Someone has to write the plan. What's your point?"

"You, unlike anyone else I can think of, would craft language that could shift the debate slightly in our direction."

"If I accept the assignment, I suppose I could try."

"And someone has to present Franklin's plan, right?"

"Or Franklin could present it himself."

"If it's you the Bright Spots proposal would get the emphasis it deserves. I don't know for sure, Kevin, but I think saying yes to this offer could be the lesser evil. It might be a detour that lets you do more good than would be possible on the main path."

"Or it could lead to places I don't want to go," Kevin said hesitantly.

Troy waited, sensing there was more.

"After Dimitri excused himself from the lunch Franklin asked me to stay for a few more minutes. I figured he sensed my hesitation and wanted to close the deal."

"What did he say?"

"He said he had given serious thought to my original proposal and understood that I might be uncomfortable advocating certain elements of his plan. So he asked me to think through language that would appear to restrict practices like the one that led to the NEXT lawsuit."

"That could be good," Troy interjected.

"I thought so too, until he explained the idea. He suggested requiring something called neutral consent confirmation for every transition volunteer in lieu of my proposal that all moneys go to charity."

"Meaning?"

"In his words, we would protect potentially vulnerable volunteers from undue pressure from greedy family members trying to preserve an inheritance."

"I like the sound of that," Troy said.

"So did I, at first. Current policy asks clinics to recommend discussing the decision with a loved one. The revised policy would require every transition volunteer to find a neutral party willing to confirm that the person has made the decision while of sound mind and with no undue pressure."

"What's wrong with that?"

"The definition of neutral party, for starters. Anyone with a relational attachment or religious bias would be considered partial so wouldn't qualify."

Kevin heard a low groan coming from Troy.

"So a wife who disagrees with her husband's decision wouldn't qualify as neutral?"

"As I understand it."

"An adult child with a deep emotional bond or a sibling who considers suicide against their religion?"

"Both biased. Neither neutral enough for consent or opposition."

"Oh."

"I guess NEXT has already started implementing a similar policy. Franklin envisions a network of detached professionals willing to review case after case like a bunch of auditors proofing spreadsheets. He sees the requirement creating additional jobs."

Troy considered the implications. "All that would do is protect a few sloppy transition clinics from costly lawsuits. 'Don't blame us! We have signed neutral consent forms right here!'"

"Exactly," Kevin confirmed. "I have a feeling that's what Franklin wants. Or should I say what Evan Dimitri expects."

A long silence as both men considered options.

"So what are you gonna do?"

"I'm still not sure. We need to pray for wisdom."

"Have been."

"I think I'm going to head home. I'll see you at the office in the morning."

"See you then," Troy replied. "Oh, and don't forget, Julia Davidson is scheduled to interview you at nine thirty."

The reminder prompted a moan. He had completely forgotten about his obligation to walk the plank.

"Do you want me to reschedule her?"

Kevin remembered his agreement. Julia had promised to let him present his concept to nine million readers in his own words.

"No." His voice lifted, an idea forming in his mind. "I'll do it."

As soon as he ended the call with Troy, Kevin dialed the number of Dr. Bryce Richert.

CHAPTER FIFTY-THREE

Before Julia could reach for the passenger-side handle Troy bounced around her petite frame to do the honors. "Allow me."

She didn't chafe at the offer, to her own surprise. Julia had always resented men who treated women as helpless creatures, whether offering to stow her baggage on a plane or hold the door for her when entering a building. Rather than fragile, however, Troy's offer made her feel treasured.

An involuntary smile lifted her voice. "Why thank you, kind sir."

Troy eased the door closed after watching her legs safely clear. Julia rolled her eyes at herself. *Thank you, kind sir? Good grief*!

Pretending to check her makeup in the visor mirror, Julia watched Troy walk around the back of the automobile. He seemed to move slowly, as if using the few moments to shore up his wavering confidence. She did the same, wondering why she had changed her mind and accepted Troy's invitation to breakfast.

I had another nightmare about descending into hell. A truth she didn't want to share.

My flight got in very late last night. A lie too easily exposed.

I should prepare for my interview with Kevin.

I need the time for research.

Each a legitimate-sounding excuse, none of which she had used.

"I'd like that." The words had escaped before she could stop them.

Troy closed his own door almost as cautiously as he had Julia's.

"You look lovely." It sounded more like a question than flattery, as if he had run out of time while debating what to say next. A good choice, the compliment confirming that it had been a good idea to wear her hair down. Up would have given her more authority during the interview. Down matched the look Troy had seemed to admire the day they met at Angie's church. "I like your hair like that."

She was glad he couldn't see her smile, his eyes fixed on the driver-side mirror, watching for an opening in traffic that would let them pull away from the hotel curb.

Julia noticed that Troy was wearing the same dark suit, white dress shirt, and tie she recalled from the day they had strolled through the Botanic Garden. On second glance, the stripes on his tie might have been a different shade of blue. But the effect remained the same, that of a plain-vanilla congressional staffer too focused on an endless list of tasks to worry about wardrobe variety. A simple haircut, clean-shaven chin, and non-sporty car rounded out the package. Troy Simmons was a man every bit as loyal to his rut as he was to his best-friend-turned-boss.

She thought of the contrast between Troy and the string of dates Maria had arranged for her. Like the mythic Narcissus, they loved their own reflections. They worked hard shunning the stabilizing habits and settled patterns that define mature masculinity. They insisted on wearing the latest styles to impress the latest lady willing to accommodate the hollow policies of a town she had labeled Guyland: no demands on their time, no limitations in the bedroom, and definitely no babies in the future. Boys eluding the very burdens of fidelity Troy seemed eager to assume.

"Have you seen Angie?" he asked while nosing the car into westbound traffic.

The question caught Julia off guard. "Not this trip." She hadn't even bothered to tell Angie she was in town. How could she forget that Kevin would mention it? "I wanted to have lunch with her but need to rush to the airport after the interview."

"I guess she's sick."

"Sick? Anything serious?" She felt even more guilty.

"Nah. Kevin called me a few minutes ago. Said she was feeling a bit nauseated so he needed to get Leah settled before heading to the office. He didn't sound concerned."

"Will that delay our interview?" She looked toward the clock on the dash and counted backward from her scheduled departure time.

"Nope. He'll be in at nine thirty sharp."

A bullet dodged, Julia told herself to relax and try enjoying Troy's company. As long as she got a few on-the-record comments from Kevin before her flight she could meet the commitment to send her finished story to Paul by the end of the day.

"Angie's a trooper," he continued. "Tough as nails yet soft as a feather."

The esteem in Troy's voice sounded like that of a schoolboy with a crush on a first-grade teacher, a platonic infatuation with the woman who could gently entice boys away from childish frivolity toward classroom industry. Julia felt a tinge of wholesome envy, jealous of Angie's influence rather than Troy's admiration.

"I know what you mean," she admitted.

A slight drizzle peppered the windshield as they approached the fuzzy glow of countless taillights ahead.

"This doesn't look good," Troy complained as he glanced at the clock. "We might need to abandon Plan A."

"Plan A?" she wondered aloud.

"I wanted to take you to this historic bakery across town called Heller's. Ever been there?"

She hadn't.

"Best doughnuts east of anywhere!"

Dull wardrobe, simple haircut, boring car, and a doughnut shop to impress his date, Julia thought with a grin.

"Doughnuts?"

"Not just any doughnuts!" he countered. "Heller's doughnuts. Great bakery with a great ambiance. The place was established back in 1922 when Roosevelt was president."

"Warren Harding was president in 1922." Her smile brightened further, which seemed to have a settling effect on Troy.

"Harding? Are you sure?"

"Fairly."

"No matter. I'm sticking with FDR. Gives the doughnuts a more significant flavor."

They laughed as he flipped on his right-turn blinker.

"So what's Plan B?"

"A coffeehouse around the corner," he said in defeated resignation. "I promised you I'd get you to the interview on time, so I'm abandoning what might have been for what needs to be."

He turned toward her with a warm smile.

"OK," she said. "But I expect a Heller's doughnut rain check."

I can't believe you just said that!

"Deal!" A look of ecstatic surprise. "We'll go all out. Might even order you a jelly-filled!"

After a five-minute navigation through DC side streets and a hasty trot through the misty rain Julia found herself sitting at a table alone while Troy shrugged apologetically in her direction. He stood at the tail end of a serpentine line of customers waiting to order their morning verve. Troy had insisted she relax by the artificial fireplace while he braved the hazards of the morning rush at Capitol Java Café. It would be several minutes before her valiant prince would arrive with her tea and raspberry scone.

She tapped her phone to check messages, finding two.

FROM MARIA DAVIDSON: *Hi, Sis! I'm done being mad at you in case you wondered. I need your help. Jared knows about the date with Fin. Don't know how. He's gone quiet on me again. Can you give him a call? He might talk to you. Hugs!*

Julia sighed at her sister's folly, then tapped a quick reply.

I'll try calling him from the airport in about four hours if you promise to end it with Fin.

She hit SEND as she looked back at Troy, whom she caught staring at her. He seemed momentarily embarrassed, leaping forward to close a two-person gap in the line that his inattention had created. Julia beamed at the comically pleasant mishap before returning to her message box.

CONFIDENTIAL FROM PAUL DAUGHERTY: *I'm forwarding the attached, the promised dirt on Kevin Tolbert.*

She scrolled to the bottom of the message. No attachment. Julia typed a quick note.

Got your message. You forgot to confirm the attachment before sending. Try again.

She paused, rereading the request she didn't want to make. Her story was strong and clean. Whatever dirt Paul did or didn't possess might sully her journalistic reputation, not to mention Troy's friend's career.

"Here we go," Troy said, placing two mugs and a plate on the table. He seemed impressed with his own balancing acumen.

She closed her eyes and hit SEND. Decision made, she willed her attention back to her handsome suitor.

Noticing the look on her face he asked, "Is everything OK?"

"Fine." She nodded more vigorously than required. "Just checking messages. Nothing important. This looks yummy!"

He took his seat while shooting a glance toward the stone-cold fireplace. "Well, it ain't Heller's," he chided. "But as a consolation prize I can guarantee we'll make it to the office on time for your interview."

The ping of a new message invaded the moment as they sipped their drinks.

Julia ignored the sound uneasily.

"Do you need to check that?"

"I'm sure it can wait," she said, forcing her eyes to remain on his.

"Go ahead." He motioned toward the device. "I understand. Trust me, I have my own digital leash to hear and obey!"

A knowing chuckle shifted her gaze downward.

FROM MARIA DAVIDSON: *Deal! No more Fin. Thanks, Sis!*

Pleased, Julia looked back toward an endearingly patient Troy, who was taking his first bite of a merely adequate doughnut.

"I've been meaning to tell you something," she said.

He lifted a curious eyebrow, mouth too full for a proper reply.

"I like the way you talk about Kevin and Angie. You really admire what they have, don't you?"

A sip of coffee helped him swallow his mouth clear.

"More like who they are," he explained. "I've been pretty

close to them for a long time, before the kids and the stuff and the accolades. It's easy to be impressed with either of them separately. But I'm in awe of the two of them together."

"I remember you saying that last time we spoke," she mused. "Tell me more."

"I don't mean to imply they're perfect. Trust me, I know. I'm the guy who kept a spare pillow and blanket around for the times Kevin was in the doghouse."

"He sleeps on your couch?"

"Not anymore. But he did back when they first got married. They had a few rough spells early on."

Julia had never considered what a fight between Angie and Kevin might entail. She had imagined five-minute spats with passionate reunions. Not knock-down drag-outs with overnight exiles.

"But things calmed down as he got less cocky and she became more confident."

"More confident?" she asked with surprise. "The Angie I remember always seemed to be pretty together."

"Maybe *confident* is the wrong word. How about *contented*? Yeah. That's what I mean. She seemed to become more secure in Kevin's love at the same time he became more assured of her support."

The word *support* triggered a slight surge of offense, but Julia dismissed it as she recalled what had attracted Troy to Christianity.

"Two people trying to out-serve one another. Isn't that what you said before?"

"Exactly. Two people helping one another become more like Jesus Christ, who…" He paused, closing his eyes as if searching for a mental script. "Let me see if I can remember the exact words."

"To what?"

"Something Saint Paul wrote," he said. "'Let the same mind

be in you that is in Christ Jesus, who, being in the form of God made himself nothing, taking the form of a servant.'" A slight pause. "Wait, let me think for a second."

She broke off a bit of scone as he assaulted his failing memory.

"I'm sorry, I can't recall the rest exactly. But it has something to do with Jesus humbling himself to the point of death on a cross."

Julia felt genuinely impressed, both with his recitation and with his seemingly genuine regard for a posture foreign to her world and thinking. "I thought you believed Jesus was God."

"I do."

"Then why the emphasis on humility? You wouldn't call God humble."

He looked puzzled by the comment. "Of course I would call God humble."

"Seriously? But he's the head honcho, king of the mountain and all that."

"Who made himself the lowest of the low."

"I don't understand," Julia confessed. "How do you reconcile those things?"

"I can't reconcile them," he admitted. "But I've seen it in action."

"Kevin and Angie?"

"At times. I feel like I've been watching someone paint them into a portrait of a mysterious beauty hanging on a gallery wall. They seem to portray a scene I've never witnessed firsthand but that I know has existed or will exist. Maybe both."

It was a lovely sentiment Julia wished she could grasp.

"How they've responded to the news about Leah is a great example." He stopped suddenly, as if he had said something wrong.

"Leah?" Julia prodded. "Is something wrong with Leah?"

Troy lowered his head in embarrassed regret. "I'm so sorry. I'm not supposed to say anything. I guess I assumed Angie had told you."

"Told me what?" Her mind went back to her first glance at Leah's picture on the hallway wall and the evening she had watched the children. Something had seemed odd, but she hadn't been able to put her finger on what it might be.

He hesitated, appearing to weigh the risks and rewards of spilling the beans. "You need to assure me of complete confidence. Not just off the record for the press. You can't let on to Kevin or Angie that you know anything."

"I promise," she replied, eager to know what her former best friend couldn't trust her enough to share.

"Leah has a genetic disorder that affects mental acuity," Troy explained. "They found out a few weeks ago when they got her genetic profile."

Julia felt her breath quicken into a sense of vague regret. Had she said anything about debits to Angie or Kevin? Had she written a column they might have read berating parents who refused genetic prescreening? Had she kept the baby at a distance after sensing something unusual or unattractive? Had she done all three?

"I'm sorry to hear that," she finally said. "How are they taking the news?"

"That's what I mean. I helped Kevin research options and found an experimental treatment that might improve Leah's brain capacity. But they've decided against taking that path."

"Why?"

"It carries pretty serious risks," he explained. "They spoke to Pastor Mubar. You remember him?"

She did.

"After that they decided God gave them Leah as a gift to cherish and a masterpiece to display rather than a problem to fix."

Julia sipped her drink as the exquisitely mysterious words settled themselves in her mind.

Troy's phone rang. He glanced at the screen. "It's Kevin. I better take this. Excuse me a second."

Julia used the interruption to absorb all Troy had said.

The decision that created Leah's problem: *How could they skip the screening process?*

The heartache Angie must be enduring. *Why couldn't she tell me?*

The motivation behind Kevin's Bright Spots proposal. *This isn't mere theory for him. It's personal.*

She heard the familiar ping of her message box.

FROM PAUL DAUGHERTY: *Sorry, Jewel. Images attached.*

Julia tapped the first, dated April twenty-fourth. She remembered flying to DC on the same day for the girl's-night-out reunion with Angie. The picture showed Kevin on his own front porch placing a jacket over the shoulders of an attractive young woman wearing a short dress and heels. His face appeared nervous. Hers triumphant.

She quickly opened the second image. It had been taken on Thursday, less than twenty-four hours earlier. The same attractive woman wearing a sleeveless top sitting beside Kevin. They appeared to be dining together at a five-star restaurant, her hand resting affectionately on his forearm as she eyed him wistfully.

She opened a third attachment, a text document presumably providing details of Tolbert's indiscretions.

"Good news!"

Troy's voice interrupted Julia's stunned appraisal. She hastily blackened the screen.

"Kevin said he's ready and will meet us at his office in a few minutes. Shall we go?"

CHAPTER FIFTY-FOUR

As they entered the congressional office building Troy stopped and shook moisture off of the suit jacket he had held over Julia's head as they ran from the coffee shop to his car.

"I'm sorry," Julia said. "It's soaked!"

"Not a problem," he replied. "A small price to pay to protect your lovely hair."

She would have relished the compliment if not for thoughts of Kevin with another woman lingering in her mind. *Poor Angie.*

"Right this way," he said.

Julia entered Kevin's empty office while Troy draped his soggy coat across a chair.

"Make yourself at home," he offered. "I'm sure Kevin will be here any minute. He never could drive in the rain."

She moved toward the window to look at nothing in particular while gathering her thoughts.

Think, girl. Think!

She needed to assess the situation with detached objectivity, to force whatever concern she felt for Angie and the kids out of her mind.

Put on your journalist hat!

Kevin Tolbert was a politician vital to her story. A man who had granted preemptive access in exchange for on-the-record quotations she would get during the next several minutes. The fact that he might be an unfaithful pig was irrelevant to her agenda. Possibly even advantageous.

She turned away from the window, her eyes meandering through Kevin's office with no specific target in mind. They landed on a picture of Angie and the kids sitting behind a large file on top of his desk. Her aversion to snooping caved to curiosity, drawing her toward the folder filled with what appeared to be a disheveled collection of pages. Their placement on top of other important-looking documents suggested Kevin had reviewed them recently, possibly while working through details of his Bright Spots proposal.

She flipped open the file. A pile of papers of various shapes, sizes, and colors. Glancing toward the door to make sure the coast was clear, Julia reached for a sheet of yellow construction paper sitting on the very top.

Crayola lettering without symmetry spelled out the phrase *WE LOVE YOU DADDY*. On the bottom right appeared a series of names in the unmistakable handwriting of Master Tommy Tolbert: *MOMMY, TOMMY, JOY, AND BABY LEAH*. Each name was accompanied by a stick-figure rendering. The first was tall with long pencil-colored hair, then a short boy with messy bangs next to an even shorter girl with golden curls. The final figure above Leah's scrunched name appeared with a disproportionate pacifier in an enormous hand.

She sorted through several more of the carefully preserved pages, each prompting a larger smile than the last, followed by an immediate fury at a man who would hurt her friend Angie and her precious kids. His precious kids!

Something doesn't fit, she thought. Julia couldn't imagine Kevin betraying Angie on a whim. Maybe the insecurities she had sensed in Angie reflected unspoken tension in the marriage. What if the stress of Leah's situation had pushed Kevin over some edge, made him yearn for the kind of carefree fling other guys enjoyed without remorse. Regardless, she felt something had to be done.

She heard the outer door open. Quickly replacing Tommy's treasure and closing the folder, she moved casually toward the sitting area.

I can't ignore this.

She considered telling Kevin about the photos. She would ask for, no, *demand* an explanation. She might even promise to keep the evidence confidential if he agreed to make things right by restoring the fidelity Angie took for granted and Troy admired. Julia hated the idea of including the scandal in her feature. She'd bury it if he just came clean.

Then she remembered how much she needed Kevin's co-operation to finish her story. She couldn't risk driving him to self-protective silence.

Troy's voice interrupted Julia's debate. "Here we are. I believe everyone has met."

She looked toward the door. Kevin entered the room. He wasn't alone.

"Oh," Julia said. "I didn't realize you would be attending the interview, Dr. Richert."

"Good to see you again, Ms. Davidson," he responded coldly.

"I thought it would be a good idea for Bryce to join us in light of your earlier conversation," Kevin explained. "As you know, he's been a key member of the austerity team. I hope you don't mind if he sits in."

Kevin was better at the game than Julia had assumed.

"Of course not," she lied. "The more the merrier."

"I'll leave you to it then." Troy excused himself from the room.

All three took a seat.

Julia reached into her bag, then paused to look toward her host. "May I record our conversation?"

"By all means," Kevin replied. "You'll need that to capture my comments word-for-word."

Julia restrained a reaction. "We rarely include comments word-for-word, but I definitely plan to summarize you accurately."

"Our agreement, Julia, was that I would grant you preemptive access in exchange for the opportunity to make my case in my own words."

"Yes. But—"

"Word-for-word," he insisted.

A long game of silent chicken ensued. Julia spoke first, handing victory to Kevin. "All right. Word-for-word."

"Good." He smiled. "I gave Troy my official statement to send. It should arrive in your in-box shortly, along with my instructions."

"Instructions?"

"In short, you can publish information obtained during the austerity coalition meeting if you include my comments in your story. Otherwise RAP Syndicate will hear from my lawyers. Maybe Franklin's too."

Julia considered the threat. The last thing she needed was for a lawsuit notice to create first impressions of her in the minds of the new owners at RAP. She was tempted to counter-threaten by referencing the photos but decided she might need that ace up her sleeve.

"I understand. I'll include your statement as given."

"Good," he said smugly.

"Well. Since we have the time, would you mind if I go ahead and ask a few supplemental questions?"

No objection.

"Is it true that you've been asked to draft and present the full Franklin plan?"

His eyes darted toward Dr. Richert, who appeared pleasantly surprised by the possibility.

"Yes it is," he confirmed. "I don't suppose you can tell me how you knew that."

She ignored the question. "Do you think that assignment will position you well for his cabinet?"

"He's a senator, not the president."

"Yet," she added.

They sat without speaking for several seconds.

"I have no idea what Senator Franklin intends," he said, breaking the silence. "I assume he wants someone to clearly articulate the urgency of our fiscal crisis and the need for bold solutions."

"So you said yes?"

"I said I'd help craft the plan."

"Does the plan include all of your suggestions?"

"Most," he confirmed.

"What about transitions? Will your opposition to the Youth Initiative be included in the plan?"

He exhaled deeply like a tutor annoyed by a child's wandering attentiveness. "I thought this story was about the Bright Spots proposal."

"It is," she agreed. "But it seems relevant that the man who advocates parenthood incentives also wants to end transitions."

"How would you connect the two?" Dr. Richert asked Julia, no longer able to conceal his annoyance.

She stared blankly. Were they connected? She had always assumed religious dogma motivated breeder antagonism. But she had never traced their pet issues to anything resembling a cohesive philosophy.

"Do you have any idea why and how the drop in fertility and the spread of transitions are linked?" Dr. Richert's question carried the tenor of a lecture.

"Bryce, I'm not sure this is the time or place to—" Kevin began.

"It's the perfect time and place!" Dr. Richert interrupted. "I'm sick and tired of the mindless drivel these reporters parrot with no idea of the meaning or importance of what's at stake."

Kevin made a motion as if to dissuade the doctor from his passionate speech.

"Please, Dr. Richert, continue," Julia suggested in hopes of capturing a useful misstep.

"Human life isn't a commodity to manage, Ms. Davidson," he continued. "It's a treasure to preserve."

"If you don't mind," Kevin intercepted, "I'd like to keep this conversation limited to the reasons for and benefits of my Bright Spots proposal."

Dr. Richert slid back from the edge of his chair in apologetic deference. "Of course. Forgive me."

Julia stifled any reaction, knowing she would put the doctor in his place very soon. He might speak his mind in Kevin's office, but she would have the last word in print.

As the tension dissipated, Kevin sat back in his chair like a Southern gentleman rocking on his porch while recollecting a story. "Did I ever tell you about Eric Shepherd?"

Julia looked away from Dr. Richert's fuming toward an oddly relaxed Kevin. "I don't think so."

"Eric Shepherd was the school bully at Kinyon Elementary. While he wasn't the biggest kid in the sixth grade, he was definitely the meanest."

Both Dr. Richert and Julia settled in for the tale.

"Eric ruled the Kinyon playground. He organized the daily touch football game at lunch. Boys only, of course. Actually, big boys only. Eric even chose the other team's captain before giving himself the first pick of players."

Dr. Richert smiled, recognizing an all-too-familiar reality of junior Guyland.

"One day a new kid came to the school who didn't seem to appreciate or acknowledge Eric's undisputed turf. Rather than ask if he could play on one of the football teams, this kid ignored the football clique and started recruiting boys and girls for a daily soccer tournament.

"Suddenly Eric had competition for playground dominance. And he didn't like it. Especially once some of the bigger kids left his fiefdom to join the scrawny kids playing an inferior sport. When that happened, he decided the time had come to remake his image."

"He stopped bullying?" Julia wondered aloud.

"Oh no. One day after school he waited behind some trees hoping to catch the new kid alone. He proceeded to beat him to a pulp. And it worked. Eric reestablished himself as someone to fear, drawing all of the bigger kids back to football."

"Was the boy hurt badly?" Dr. Richert asked.

"Enough for the other kids to fall in line."

"Did Eric get in trouble?" Julia asked.

"The kid explained what happened to the teacher, which led her to pull both Eric and the bruised soccer player into the school counselor's office for a joint seminar on getting along, complete with a lecture about the school's zero-tolerance fighting policy."

"Things got better for a week or so. But Eric wasn't satisfied with just intimidating the big kids back to his game. He also wanted the girls and small kids cheering on the sidelines rather than playing soccer."

"Did they?" asked Dr. Richert.

"Not until Eric beat up the new kid a second time."

"Please tell me the school counselor stepped in at that point."

"Sure did. She suspended the new kid for fighting."

"What?" Julia reacted. "Why?"

"To avoid conflict with Eric's mom."

"Eric's mom?"

"Yes. You see, the bully's mom was the teacher."

"You're kidding!" Julia snarled.

"I'm serious. Anyway, the cycle continued for the rest of the school year. It even followed them into junior high the following year."

Julia seethed. "I hate bullies!"

"But things got better in seventh grade," Kevin continued. "That's when I met Troy."

"I figured you were the new kid," Dr. Richert said proudly.

"Troy was much bigger than Eric. He also preferred soccer to football."

"Was Eric's mom or the school counselor ever exposed?" Julia asked.

"They weren't, which is the reason I shared the story." He paused, glaring directly at Julia. "Julia, there have always been people who use their size or position to abuse the little people just because they dislike the way a person looks, or talks, or thinks. Or maybe because they are debits. Or worse, breeders."

She felt the blow. "Now wait a second, Kevin—"

"Let me finish, Julia," he interrupted. "I'm not as naïve as you or RAP would like to believe. I know what you're doing here."

She said nothing.

"I accept your bias. That's fine. All I ask is that you accurately represent mine."

"I'm a respected journalist, Kevin!" She couldn't hold back.

"Yes, you are. And I'm sure you're a good one. But none of us is unbiased. Not you. Not me."

"Certainly not me!" Dr. Richert interjected with a laugh.

"Part of my bias is the belief government exists to make it harder for bullies to win. Our current policies, by contrast, give bullies free rein."

"What bullies are you talking about?"

"Those who have an irrational fear of children would be a good example. They advance tax policies that make it nearly impossible to afford the extra cost of raising kids."

Julia started to speak, but something in Kevin's face said not to.

"And then there are bullies who want to grow an industry that victimizes the poorest and most vulnerable members of society. Eighty percent of transition volunteers are poor, disabled, or both."

She thought momentarily of the Santoses' journals, but quickly pushed them out of her mind.

"We live in a world where the weak and scrawny have little choice but to play by rules set by the big and powerful. By those who rig the game against the dignity of human life."

"No one forces people to transition."

"And no one forced kids to quit playing soccer or cheer for Eric. They did it voluntarily, or else!"

Kevin took a deep breath to reclaim his formerly calm demeanor. It didn't work.

"I don't blame Eric or the kids who did what he wanted. But I do blame the adults who knew what was happening and did nothing to intervene. I get upset with leaders and policies that make it easy to bully the weak!"

"So I should say you oppose transitions on the grounds of a childhood trauma?" Julia asked.

He didn't appreciate the sarcasm.

"You'll say that the Youth Initiative makes doing what's wrong easy and doing what's right hard."

"The worst tyranny," Dr. Richert mumbled beneath his breath.

"What's that?" Kevin prodded.

"It's something Edmund Burke said. 'Bad laws are the worst sort of tyranny.'"

"Exactly! I want to see us amend, improve, replace, or oppose laws and programs that push our weakest, most vulnerable citizens to make choices they would never make otherwise."

"What kind of choices do you want them to make?" Julia tried to sound sympathetic.

"Natural, commonsense choices," he replied. "Like getting married and raising a family. Like protecting the dignity of aging citizens rather than making them feel guilty every time they take another breath. Like protecting our disabled rather than labeling them worthless debits."

Kevin cleared his throat to mask a breaking voice. An awkward silence ensued.

"So much for saying this isn't the time or place," Dr. Richert laughed. "That was a much better speech than I planned to give!"

"Sorry." Kevin seemed embarrassed by his emotion. "I didn't mean to preach."

"No need to apologize." Julia sensed Kevin's deep love for baby Leah. The thought forced her mind back to Angie. Back to the mysterious woman fawning all over Tommy's daddy. She felt a sudden desire to end the meeting.

"Listen, I think I have all I need. And you said Troy would send me your complete statement?"

"That's right."

"Then I want to thank you both for your time. Other than a possible clarification statement here or there I'm confident I'll be able to craft a story that's fair and balanced."

"I hope so," Kevin responded warmly.

"I doubt it," Dr. Richert spat.

Julia left the room more abruptly than she'd intended. Five minutes later she hailed a cab to drive her to the airport. As the taxi pulled away from the curb she typed a short message to her editor.

You'll have my story later tonight.

CHAPTER FIFTY-FIVE

The symptoms came suddenly and severely. For almost two hours, while waiting to get into Dr. Ryan's office, Angie's imagination created one panic-ridden scenario after another.

She recalled losing her aunt Cheri, who had died at age thirty-five, leaving Angie's then-three-year-old cousin Andrew without a mom. Liver cancer. By the time Cheri noticed any symptoms the disease had spread too far for surgery.

Her grandmother had fallen victim to breast cancer at the relatively young age of fifty-seven, prompting family doctors to recommend annual mammograms for her mother, her sister, and herself. "Early detection is still the best defense," they had said. But Angie had been so busy with Kevin's election and managing the kids that she had neglected that advice for each of the past two years. Despite a genetic predisposition to cancer, she had always felt fine and never worried.

Until now. Despite a full night's sleep Angie had woken to a debilitating exhaustion that would have kept her in bed had it not been for an intense nausea that forced her to cling to the master bath's toilet. She emptied her stomach on the third or fourth violent retching. That's when Kevin helped her back to bed.

"I think you have a fever," he had said while gently stroking her cheek.

A good sign? It seemed unlikely cancer would prompt a fever. But then it could weaken the immune system and make infection more likely. Either way, Kevin insisted she see a doctor. He made her an appointment and started to cancel his morning meeting. But Angie said not to do that. He reluctantly agreed, instead arranging for one of the office interns to sit with the kids and another to drive her to and from the doctor.

"Probably just the flu," he assumed.

Something more serious, she quietly feared.

Twenty minutes after providing a urine sample and enduring a slight finger prick, Angie sat waiting for the doctor. She felt a chill while rubbing her fingers along the ridge of her lower jaw to confirm a tender, swollen gland. She moved her hand lower, reaching inside her blouse for another self-examination of her tender breast.

Two quick raps on the door warned of the doctor's pending entry.

"Good morning, Angie," Dr. Ryan sang casually. "Feeling any better?"

She offered the sprightliest moan she could muster. "A bit. But—"

"Good, good," he interrupted while sliding a stool close. Scrolling through details displayed on his digital tablet, the doctor quickly absorbed the information. He looked up at Angie, then back down. She assumed he needed another moment to find the right words.

"Let's start with the good news," he began. "It's very early, so we have several noninvasive options."

Options? Options for what?

"Most women in your situation choose an oral prescription rather than vaginal removal."

Angie struggled to find her suffocating voice. "Please, Dr. Ryan," she managed to say. "Just tell me what's wrong. How serious is it?"

A puzzled glance.

"You don't know?" he asked.

"Know what?"

An embarrassed look.

"I'm sorry. I assumed the nurse had already told you."

Why would you expect the nurse to tell me I have a tumor?

"You're pregnant, Angie." His voice became grave. "But it's very early, two weeks, so you have several options."

Her mind vacillated between relief and anger, joy and dread.

"But I'm still nursing Leah."

"Leah?"

"My daughter."

"I see. An old wives' tale. You can get pregnant while nursing. I'm so sorry."

Sorry?

"But like I said, you have several great options."

"End the pregnancy?" A tone of indignation.

He stared blankly, as if never having been asked the question before. "Well, I just assumed—"

"Please don't assume, Doctor," she said sternly.

"Yes, ma'am. But…" He paused. "But you're well into your thirties now and already have two children."

"Three!" she corrected.

"Right. Three children." The reminder raised his brow.

Both sat silently for several moments as Angie digested the news.

Four children! She could already hear the jibes.

Hasn't anyone told you how babies are made?

You two need to get a television!

I guess Kevin Tolbert hopes to breed an entire soccer team.

The thought of Kevin made her smile. *Two weeks? This baby was conceived the night I wore Kevin's surprise. The night Julia put the kids to bed.*

Thinking of Julia made her queasy stomach tense.

"Another baby?" Julia would react condescendingly. "Really? On purpose?"

It hadn't been on purpose. They hadn't been trying to conceive, and were even nervous about the possibility in light of Leah's disorder. Angie had already begun considering birth-control options to use once the baby finished nursing. She had planned to discuss them with Kevin as soon as life settled down a bit.

Angie heard Dr. Ryan speaking. "May I at least explain the risks?"

She felt herself nod.

"The older a woman gets the more difficult it becomes to deliver a healthy child, unless of course she prescreens."

She clearly hadn't.

"In cases like yours I typically prescribe an oral stimulant that prevents the embryo from attachment."

The words sent a shiver down Angie's spine. "Prevent the embryo from attachment?"

"A fancy way of saying you would miscarry naturally."

It sounded anything but natural.

"Anyway," he continued. "I would advise against continuing this pregnancy. The potential child could have serious health problems."

The phrase *potential child* bothered Angie. It felt as if the doctor were describing a subhuman species rather than the blossoming seed of Kevin's and her love.

"Problems like fragile X syndrome?" Angie asked.

He appeared surprised by the question. "Well, yes, that's one possibility. Along with many others."

Angie looked away and thought of Kevin. She wished he had come with her but felt glad he hadn't. Her husband was under too much stress already. He didn't have time to deal with a flu-bug-turned-cancer-turned-fourth-child. *A fourth child*! But he would have to deal with it. They both would.

"No. Thank you."

"Excuse me?" Dr. Ryan asked.

"I have no interest in a prescription to end the pregnancy." She felt a rising distress.

He slid his stool back from his wayward patient. "I understand," he yielded. "But I think I should go ahead and order an in utero genetic profile so we can talk again in a few weeks."

She started to object but a series of internal questions kept her silent.

What good would come of knowing a baby's genetic weaknesses before delivery?

Would it have been better to know about Leah's problems before delivery?

Would it have tempted them to intervene or simply made them better prepared?

"Well," she finally said, then sighed. "I suppose there's no harm in knowing what to expect."

"We can discuss your options again once we have all the information."

She felt another hesitant nod.

CHAPTER FIFTY-SIX

Sarah had never looked lovelier as she walked in Matthew's direction. The long brunet hair she pulled back in a ponytail at work now fell on her shoulders, framing a face he thought a perfect blend of innocence and allure. But her deep blue eyes didn't notice him, fixed instead on the man holding her hand as they left the same coffee shop Matthew approached.

"Hi, Sarah," he said preemptively. "Shift over already?"

A moment for recognition passed. "Oh, hi, Matt. No. I don't work today. I was just meeting up with Ian. Have you met?"

The statuesque shape extended his free oversized hand. "Ian Fletcher." An indifferent statement in lieu of a friendly greeting.

"Matthew Adams," he volleyed back, wondering whether such a man was capable of feeling threatened by the competition, whether a girl like Sarah would ever consider Matthew an option.

"Heading to work?" Sarah asked.

"Actually no. Stopping by to celebrate." *I had hoped with you*, he thought.

"Celebrate what?" she asked while Ian tried resuming their walk. Her fingers tightened to rein in his advance.

"I just came from the admissions office."

Sarah smiled, anticipating the good news. "What'd they say?"

"The enrollment counselor looked over my records and said I could use all six of the community college classes as electives if I get accepted."

"And?" she enticed.

"It looks like they'll admit me on probationary status."

Sarah leaped forward with a congratulatory hug as Ian's eyes rolled.

Her body vanished before Matthew's arms could close to relish the embrace. It was not at all as he had imagined.

"Congrats, man," Ian offered while obliging Sarah's returning fingers.

And the moment passed. Matthew sensed no change in Sarah's demeanor toward him. Perhaps it was silly, but he had hoped the news might ease him up the ladder of possibilities. No longer Matt the coffee shop employee, but Matthew Adams, burgeoning professor.

He stood alone watching the pair walk away before turning toward the Campus Grinds entry. He didn't open the door, walking instead back toward the parking lot.

Thirty minutes later Matthew found himself sitting across from Donny at his kitchen table, opening a can of celebratory beer.

"Thanks for the brew, man!" Donny said while raising a silent toast.

"Thank you for watching Mom this morning," Matthew said. "What time did she lie down for her nap?"

"Right after lunch. She should be up any time now." Donny appeared to feel out of place, as if assuming Matthew would have preferred celebrating with his mother.

"Good," Matthew replied flatly.

The two sat in silence for several minutes, sipping from their cans.

"A big day," Donny said awkwardly. "College life, here you come!"

Matthew forced a grin.

"When do you start?"

"September. Well, there's a new student orientation in late August. But classes don't begin until September."

Donny seemed at a loss for another question to keep the conversation going. Having barely graduated from high school he had no sense of how to express his curiosity about the lofty realm of higher education.

"You'll need more help with your mom?"

Matthew said nothing.

"Any idea which days?"

Their eyes met pensively.

"Sorry. I don't mean to assume. You might want to hire someone else. It's just that, I don't know, I kind of sense she's starting to remember me. Or at least feel comfortable with me."

Matthew looked away.

"Like this morning. I sensed she was feeling down, maybe a bit depressed. I asked if something was wrong, like I've done before. Only this time, instead of slumping alone in her chair, she looked in my eyes. It felt like, I don't know, like she wanted to confide in me."

"Did she?" Matthew asked.

"Not exactly. But she came over to me. Stood real close. Then she squeezed my hands and said, 'Thank you.'"

"For what?"

"Dunno. But it felt like some sort of breakthrough. Like we became friends or something."

"She doesn't know you, Donny," Matthew said coldly.

Donny appeared momentarily hurt but it passed with his next swig. "You're probably right. Still, I can help out if you need it once you start college."

Matthew gave a grateful nod before joining his lone cohort in another drink.

"I should probably go," quickly bled into "See you next time."

As soon as Donny left, Matthew crept toward his mother's bedroom door. It was partially open, so he leaned in to listen for clues. Slow, shallow breaths would mean a deep slumber. Deep exhalations with long gaps would mean she'd wake soon.

"Hello, Son."

Already up.

"Hey, Mom. Did we wake you?"

"I never fell asleep," she confessed.

"But Donny said—"

"I needed time alone. Time to think."

She seemed uncommonly lucid, especially considering she'd missed her afternoon nap. One of her good days.

"About what?" he asked.

"About you. Your future."

He entered the room and sat on the edge of her bed to help her prop a pillow for a better angle to chat.

"So, what did they say?" she asked, gently patting his arm.

"I'm in, Mom! They said I would probably be accepted on probation for the fall. They're even going to look into taking my community college credits."

She smiled broadly, not at all surprised. Another pat on his arm told him she was very proud of her son.

He started to say more but stopped short.

"What else?" she asked.

"We can talk about the rest later. You need to rest."

"I'm not tired," she insisted.

"Donny said you seemed down. You feeling OK? Need anything?" He felt eager to serve the woman who was making his dreams come true.

"I'm fine," she said, reaching toward the nightstand. "But I need you to help me with this."

She handed him a letter.

"What is it?"

"It arrived while you were out. They asked for my fingerprint and left it with me. Said it was for my eyes only. But my eyes aren't as good as they used to be."

Matthew became angry. He had given Donny explicit instructions to intercept any mail or messages. "I don't want her messing with the bills or becoming confused by medical notices," he had said.

"They wanted your fingerprint?" he asked, unfolding the page. His eyes landed on the masthead. Large gold print read ASPEN HOUSE above much smaller lettering that said A SUBSIDIARY OF NEXT INC.

Dear Ms. Adams:

This letter has been sent by secure parcel in anticipation of your transition appointment scheduled for June 2, 2042. Due to changes in the legal climate we have adopted a new internal policy requiring secondary confirmation for all volunteers. We need to meet with you and someone you trust who is willing to accept legal responsibility in the unlikely event a wrongful death claim is made against Aspen House following your appointment. A close friend or relation is preferred. Whoever you select will be asked to attest that you have made the decision to transition without undue pressure and that you have done so while of sound mind. It is also essential that the person NOT be included among those inheriting any portion of your estate. Once you have named the person, please contact us online or by phone to schedule a joint appointment. We apologize for any inconvenience this additional requirement may create. I trust you understand that our goal is to prevent frivolous lawsuits from interrupting our valued clients' intentions.

Warm regards,
Dr. Paige Trenton
Attending physician

The color drained from Matthew's face. "Do you understand what this means, Mom?"

She nodded slowly.

Matthew cleared his throat nervously. "And?"

"I don't know. That's why I wanted time to think."

"Did you think of anyone?"

"Anyone to what?" she asked.

"Anyone to provide secondary confirmation."

Her eyes dropped, as if she had anticipated a different reaction from Matthew.

"I suppose you'll need to do it," she replied. "Who else do I have?"

"I can't do it, Mom," he said, the desperation rising in his voice. "It says right here that the person can't be a recipient of your inheritance."

"Inheritance?" She seemed confused.

"Your estate. The money you're giving me for college."

"Yes. I want you to go to college. You'll be a fine professor someday."

"Mom!" He was losing her window of coherence. "Listen to me. This letter means you need to ask someone besides me to approve your transition. Do you understand?"

Another slow nod gradually transitioned into a timid shake.

"I'm sorry, Son," she said. "I'm suddenly feeling very tired. Maybe I should lie back down."

"We need to figure this out now."

But he knew it was too late. The familiar ashen look on her face told him it was no use pushing any further.

"OK," he said, reaching for her pillow. "Let me help you with that."

He stood up, folded the letter, and placed it in his pocket before turning off the light.

"Matthew," she said as he began closing the door.

He turned back.

"I love you, Son."

"I know, Mom. I love you too."

Moments later Matthew dialed the number at the bottom of the letter while trying to recall the name of the gregarious gentleman his mom had seemed to like so much.

"Aspen House Transition Services. How may I direct your call?"

"I need to speak to Chuck," Matthew said feebly.

CHAPTER FIFTY-SEVEN

"Am I glad to see you!" Maria appeared distraught. "I've been on pins and needles. How'd it go?"

"I got what I needed," Julia replied flatly, wondering why the sudden, energetic interest in her work. "More than I wanted, actually."

"More than you wanted? Why, what'd he say? He won't speak to me at all."

Julia remembered her broken promise to call Jared from the airport.

"Oh, Sis." She sighed while placing her bag on the kitchen floor. "I'm so sorry. I completely forgot to call Jared. I had to rush right from the Tolbert interview to the airport and start writing up the—" She halted her explanation. Maria wouldn't care about deadlines or journalistic dilemmas. She cared about ending her son's silent treatment. "I'll go in and speak to him right after—"

"Please, Julia," Maria pleaded. "I can't take this another minute."

It was then that she noticed Maria's shoes glimmering beneath her ankle-length robe. "Don't tell me you have a date tonight."

Maria lowered her head, then slowly unwrapped the robe to reveal yet another new, alluring outfit. She flashed a self-conscious grin.

"Fin?"

"I need to break up properly," Maria explained. "I couldn't just cut him off over the phone. That would be tacky!"

"What's tacky," Julia reacted, "is expecting your son to forgive and forget on cue just so you can have one last date with his teacher without feeling guilty. If it is one last date."

"I told you. I'm ending it with Fin." A long pause. "But I want to do it in a way that'll keep our options open."

Julia pursed her lips as she reached for her travel bag.

"Where are you going?"

"I don't have time for this, Maria. Deal with Jared yourself for once. He's your son, not mine!"

Julia ignored her sister's pleading all the way to the bedroom, where she closed herself in to tackle her own, more pressing crisis. If Paul Daugherty didn't receive a feature-length story before ten o'clock she could kiss any future with RAP Syndicate goodbye. She looked at the clock. Two hours to go, and she still hadn't decided which draft to finalize and send.

Both versions of her feature contained select characterizations and pictures from the interview with Dr. Richert painting him as typical of a threateningly influential subculture of people who rejected common sense and, given the chance, would require others to do likewise. The cover photo alone, Dr. Richert standing before a wall full of breeder babies, would fan the flame of disdain against whatever his sort wanted. But she also quoted from highly respected fiscal conservatives like Nicole Florea and Trisha Sayers. They describe the economic burden breeders added to society when they skipped genetic prescreening at the start of life and discouraged transitions at the end.

Both versions of the story suggested the philosophy behind the Bright Spots proposal came from an extreme, religiously motivated bias and that it advanced environmentally irresponsible policies in the name of fiscal austerity. She even managed to protect her journalistic integrity by including extensive quotations from the author of the Bright Spots proposal, rising political star and key member of Franklin's team Congressman Kevin Tolbert.

Her dilemma, still unsettled, was whether to include the photos and information Paul had sent earlier in the day. If she used them to imply Tolbert lacked credibility with his own supporters due to recent accusations of infidelity, millions of readers, not to mention the new owners of RAP, would admire her "take-no-prisoners" approach. It would propel her career, placing her squarely back among the journalistic elite.

But it would also destroy Angie's happy home.

Julia decided to give herself the essential luxury of a post-flight shower, settling her nerves and clearing her mind for the task ahead. She heard and ignored three separate knocks on the door, the first while combing through her wet hair, another while tying the sash of her most comfortable robe, and a third while booting up her computer.

"Go away, Maria. I don't have time—"

"It's me, Aunt Julia," Jared said through the closed door. "Mom left. Can I come in?"

Julia looked at the beckoning glow of her computer screen. She needed more than a shower to resolve her daunting sense of urgency. She needed two solid hours at the keyboard.

Easing the door open she saw the smudge of recently wiped tears on Jared's cheeks. She raised her hand gently to his face. "Rough day?"

"I hate her!" He entered the room.

"You don't hate your mother, Jared."

He walked silently toward the bed and settled himself on the edge.

"Why couldn't you have been my mom?"

The question stunned Julia. She felt at once flattered and dismayed.

"Your mother is a beautiful person."

He sniffed back remnants of an earlier cry. "Exactly. That's the problem."

"I didn't mean it like that," she continued. "I mean your mother has a sweet spirit. She has a spark for life that makes other people like to be around her. I know I do."

A brief pause.

"I think you do, too."

Jared's eyes appeared to moisten. He closed them tightly to hold back tears.

"She's a beautiful person, but she's not a perfect person." Julia looked toward her computer to protect Jared's teetering male ego. "That same spark for life comes with a penchant for mischief."

"I'll say!" Jared added crossly. "And embarrassment."

Julia hesitated. How much to say? Was Jared old enough to know? Would it help or hurt his relationship with Maria?

"Listen, Jared," she began timidly. "How much has your mom told you about her childhood? Our childhood?"

A shrug.

"I'm not sure how much I should say. Or if you even want to know."

He gave a nod, his curiosity piqued.

"How old are you now?"

Jared rolled his eyes and grinned. "Fourteen months till I'm a teenager."

Julia glanced at the clock. Ninety minutes to deadline. *Another time perhaps? No.*

"Well, Mr. Almost Teenager, I could use a cup of hot chocolate. You?"

He nodded eagerly.

"You fix the drinks while I get dressed. Then we'll chat."

She took advantage of the ten minutes during which Jared boiled and stirred to rescan the second version of her story. The alleged dirt on Kevin Tolbert made her stomach heavy. Julia willed herself to push Angie's face out of her mind.

Detach, she ordered herself. *Review both versions through the eyes of your readers. Not Angie. Not Paul. Not the new RAP owners. Only your readers!*

"Hot chocolate's ready," Jared announced while handing Julia her favorite mug. Steam overpowered a mini-mountain of whipped cream, turning it into a sinking island of foam. Reclaiming his spot on the edge of the bed, he faced his aunt with open ears.

"I don't have long," Julia began, "but I think you need to know something that your mom will probably never tell you. Something that might help you understand. Maybe even forgive."

She started with the bits Jared already knew. That his grandfather had left them before Maria knew her dad. That his grandmother was a strong, independent woman who never remarried. Then she eased into the important part.

"After our daddy left us your grandmother spent time with a series of boyfriends."

"Like mom does?"

"Yes. But your grandma didn't have a sister living with her. She made mistakes."

What kind of mistakes? his eyes asked.

"Two of her boyfriends moved in with her. With us."

"Really?"

"Yeah. The first stayed for almost three years. He was pretty nice." She hesitated before continuing. "The second only stayed for a few weeks."

Was he old enough to hear the rest? Of course he was. Eleven years old is the same age Julia had been when she discovered what was happening.

"The second man did some bad things."

Too vague.

"He hurt your mom."

Jared stopped mid-sip, a confused fury rising in his eyes. "Hurt her how?"

Another delay. *What to say?*

"Hurt her in ways that can make a girl feel…" She couldn't say the rest.

"Angry?" he inserted.

She thought for a moment. "Yes, angry. And insecure. And, well, stained."

He didn't understand.

"Dirty. It made your mom feel dirty."

Realization overtook curiosity. Jared's face assumed a courageous air, young valor eager to punish an unknown but evil adversary.

"Did he hurt you too?"

Julia wanted to say no, to explain that she was the one who put a stop to the abuse by threatening to call the police.

"He tried," she confessed. "He exposed himself to me one night while I was getting out of the shower. It frightened me. Made me queasy. But that was minor compared to what happened to your mom."

Julia finished her drink in silence as Jared absorbed a revelation no son should have to receive about an abuse no girl should have to endure.

"You OK?" she finally asked.

A single nod.

"I've always loved your mom, Jared. I'm just sorry I didn't do a better job protecting her."

"It wasn't your job to protect her."

"I know," she replied. "But I still wish I had."

"It was Grandma's job."

Julia quietly agreed.

"No. I'm wrong. It was Grandpa's job."

Julia looked in Jared's face. It carried the indignation of a fearless soldier encountering a blatant coward.

"He wasn't around," Julia explained. "He couldn't protect her."

Jared looked away, then back at Julia. "He should have been there. Daddies are supposed to protect their children."

She nodded to affirm the noble instinct.

"I hate him!"

"You never met him."

"I know. But I still hate him."

The conversation ended. Jared rose from the bed and collected Julia's half-empty mug before walking toward the kitchen. Julia sat reflectively, hoping she had done the right thing.

"Aunt Julia," Jared said, looking back from the door. He dithered for a moment. "Can I ask you another question?"

"Of course."

"If that man hurt Mom, you know, made her feel dirty, then why does she…" The right words didn't come.

Julia understood without them.

"I don't know, Jared. I don't know."

He exhaled through his nose, then inhaled with resolution. "I think I'll wait up, you know, until she gets home."

"I think that's a good idea."

Julia turned back toward her computer screen. She had time enough to reread each draft before making a final decision. The first version felt solid despite lacking the kind of scandal appeal Paul would prefer. The second would most certainly damage the Bright Spots proposal. But it also risked making her appear sleazy, like journalists who used tabloid-style dirt to sell papers rather than confirmed facts to influence minds.

Julia made her decision. Her finger lingered momentarily on the SEND icon. Another glance at the clock. No time for additional edits.

She tapped, releasing her final version of *The Breeders*.

A version absent the dirt on Kevin Tolbert.

CHAPTER FIFTY-EIGHT

The alarm went off at six thirty in the morning. Reaching toward the sound, Julia remembered the day. She had forgotten to change the clock to a more appropriate weekend setting, perhaps eight or nine a.m. As she rolled back onto her welcoming pillow she felt oddly rested, even refreshed. Then it hit her.

No dream!

For the first morning in months she could not recall any troubling images or night panics. It was as if a chronic toothache had suddenly been cured.

She spent several minutes mentally piecing together the clues.

For about eight months the nightmares had become progressively more intense and frequent. She had tried ignoring them as subconscious manifestations of insecurity, nocturnal echoes of her flailing career. Had completing a major news story finally released her? Finally killed the internal demon?

Dr. Moreland had suggested the dreams were somehow tied to her absent father. She had recommended Julia put a face on the man she couldn't reach. Had the conversation with Jared pricked a hidden boil? Daddies *are* supposed to protect their daughters. Why hadn't hers?

Or was Troy Simmons her angel? For the first time in her life a man seemed genuinely smitten *with* her rather than just aroused *by* her. Did his attention have anything to do with a night of unbroken rest? Might it bring more?

Whatever the reasons, Julia accepted the repose gratefully as she buried herself under the warmth of her blankets.

An hour later she awoke to the distant sounds of hissing and crackling. Then she inhaled the faint aroma of bacon summoning her to the kitchen.

"Morning, Aunt Julia!" Jared beamed at her from his perch beside the stove, where he was fulfilling his burnt-food-prevention mission.

"Good morning, Jared. What time did you go to bed?"

"About midnight," he replied. "Mom got home around eleven. We talked for a while."

"I'm glad." Julia placed her slumbering tablet in front of her usual seat. "Where is she now?"

"Getting juice from the store. Should be back any minute."

"Need help?" she offered.

"No thanks. Almost done."

"I'm back," Maria's voice sang from the opening front door. "I didn't know if you wanted grapefruit or orange juice so I got both." She noticed Julia. "Oh, good morning, sleepyhead."

"Morning, Sis," Julia replied. "You two seem to be doing better."

Maria kissed her sister's cheek. "Yes we are." She leaned close to whisper in Julia's ear. "I don't know what you said to him, but I appreciate it. You're the best."

Julia tilted her head toward Maria's to accept the sentiment.

"Let's eat," Jared announced.

"Looks fantastic!" Maria took her seat beside Jared, across from Julia.

A sip of juice and two bites of scrambled eggs later, Julia chose to indulge her curiosity.

"So, how was the date?"

Maria scowled. "I'd rather not talk about it."

Jared forced back a smile.

"Talk about what?"

"I said I don't want to…" Maria paused, glowering at her son. "You're enjoying this, aren't you?"

He nodded puckishly.

"Oh, why not?" she relented. "It's over with Fin."

Julia looked toward an obviously pleased Jared, then back at Maria.

"So you did end it?"

Silence.

"With or without leaving options open?"

Maria's eyes narrowed. "No options."

Julia and Jared each took another bite while waiting for more.

"He dumped me, OK?" Maria huffed. "He said he didn't think it was a good idea to keep seeing one another."

"Because of Jared?" Julia asked, pleased with the finality.

"No," Maria confessed. "Not because of Jared. Because of Beth."

"Who's Beth?"

"Ms. Cline," Jared interjected. "A new sub teacher. Really pretty."

Maria clucked while rolling her eyes, the sting of rejection apparently still tender.

"I'm sorry, Sis," Julia consoled while containing a grin. "But I'm glad it's over."

"Me too!" Jared added enthusiastically.

Maria's pout lifted. "Me too. I guess."

Julia accepted Jared's offer for seconds and thirds on perfectly turned bacon strips. When finished, she offered to clear the table and wash the dishes.

"I've got it," Maria insisted. "You just relax."

Julia liked the suggestion, grabbing her still-sleeping tablet and moving toward the sofa in the adjoining room.

Julia opened and reread the story she had forwarded to Paul ten hours earlier, zeroing in on the portion containing word-for-word quotations from Kevin Tolbert. It felt right including the comments even though she knew Paul would balk. The story hit the mark, effectively marginalizing critics of the Youth Initiative by associating them with extreme aspects of Breederville. And those elements did exist. Readers needed to know about them. Needed to be wary.

She even hoped her decision would salvage the possibility of continued friendship with Angie—or at least protect her and the kids from scandal.

As she scanned the final paragraph she thought of Troy. He would hate the story, would probably become angry over the potential harm it would cause to the Bright Spots proposal, not to mention his friend's political prospects. But it was far less damaging than it could have been. It was a version he might even be able to forgive.

"I nearly forgot to tell you," Maria's voice cut through. "Your phone started beeping with a new message alert last night around midnight."

Julia remembered placing her phone on the charging pad to let it recover from trip exhaustion.

"You might want to check it." Maria handed the phone to her sister. "It could be that handsome friend of Kevin's you told me about."

She tapped the screen to find a series of voice messages from a clearly troubled Paul Daugherty.

11:37 p.m. "You must be kidding me, Jewel. Call me right away. We need to make some changes."

11:51 p.m. "Are you up? We need to talk immediately!"

12:04 a.m. "My posting deadline is less than thirty minutes away, Jewel. You do remember we're running this story in the morning? I can't wait for you. I think I can make enough edits to salvage what you sent. Call if you get this message before twelve thirty. Otherwise, read my tweaked version in the *Weekend Journal* in the morning."

Weekend Journal? She looked at the time. Nearly nine o'clock!

Tweaked version? Millions of readers had already read the story while sipping their first cup of coffee. A version of the story she had never seen!

She grabbed her tablet to open the journal. There it was, the cover story title and byline plastered over an enormous image of baby pictures hanging on a wall.

THE BREEDERS
Their Alarming Agenda for Your Future
By Julia Davidson with Monica Garcia

"With Monica Garcia!" she shouted. "He didn't!"

CHAPTER FIFTY-NINE

Angie did her best to keep the kids quiet so Kevin could continue sleeping. Friday had been a long, eventful day. He had remained at the office until well past midnight putting finishing touches on the austerity proposal. He had promised Senator Franklin would receive a draft to review over the weekend in case the revised budget forecast went public on Monday. Franklin would want to call a press conference in response to the ensuing panic to gain support for a sensible plan by a decisive leader.

Angie didn't sleep well despite turning in early. That's why she nearly accepted Kevin's offer to handle Leah's early-morning whimper. But he looked even more exhausted than she. Besides, morning sickness would prevent her from drifting back into slumber. So she kissed his hand and insisted he get some well-deserved rest.

Sitting on the sofa in the living room, Angie watched Leah reach for one of Joy's plastic bowling pins while Tommy and Joy grinned at their favorite cartoon. Her mind picked up where it had left off while she tossed and turned during the night. How to tell Kevin about the pregnancy?

With Tommy she had taped a small love note to her positive pregnancy test and buried it in Kevin's sack lunch. She remembered holding her breath for much of the noon hour waiting for the phone to ring, waiting to hear his euphoric shout in her ear. The call never came. He instead showed up at the front door holding a bundle of flowers. They had never kissed more deeply.

For Joy she sent a cryptic text for Kevin to discover while checking messages between flights.

Three becomes four!

Two hours later she finally got her euphoric shout.

Leah had been less dramatic. They hadn't been trying to conceive, so assumed the morning nausea to be a flu bug just as they had this time. She bought a pregnancy test at the drugstore "just in case" on their way to Kevin's parents' house for a Thanksgiving meal a queasy tummy wouldn't let her enjoy. They sat beside one another in the car unable to believe their eyes while both children napped peacefully in the back. The momentary panic over the demands that would come with a third child vanished in the warmth of Kevin's virile embrace.

"Look Mommy," Tommy whispered, finally remembering Angie's shushing commands. "Baby Weah got the bowling pin!"

A clear stream of slobber had already begun dripping down the side of the toy, the hard plastic offering just the right friction to relieve Leah's teething gums.

"She sure did!" Angie said, joining the mini-celebration with faint enthusiasm.

As Tommy turned back toward the television, Angie mentally reviewed her imperfect options.

Should she wait to tell Kevin about the pregnancy until after he got past the austerity-proposal presentation? The tempest promised to get crazier before settling down, especially if

Franklin made Kevin the face and voice of the plan. She knew her husband could handle the spotlight in high-stress situations. But he had never been thrown into anything of this magnitude before. Besides, waiting a few weeks would mean she would have results from the genetic profile. Wouldn't it be best to have all the information first?

Or should she tell him right away? That's what she wanted to do. She wanted to share her unease, possibly draw confidence from his reaction. But his response could just as easily have the opposite effect. The slightest hesitation on Kevin's part would carry enormous, perhaps unintended, meaning. What if he searched her eyes for hints of her feelings before revealing his own? Could she make them glimmer with enthusiasm? Or would they betray her fears? And if so, would his eyes summon her away from those fears or reflect them back like a mirror confirming an unsightly blemish?

Don't be absurd! Angie chastised herself. She knew how hurt she would feel if Kevin withheld such a weighty revelation from her. *Of course he deserves to know right away*. She should tell him by the end of the day.

Whether due to resolving her dilemma or the grace of passing minutes, Angie sensed her nausea diminish enough for her to finally move Tommy's and Joy's cereal boxes from the table to the pantry. She noticed an unopened package of Saltine Classics. They might just settle the waves in her stomach. While swallowing her first cracker Angie searched the room for something to ward off another internal debate over whether and how to share the news. Her eyes settled on Kevin's tablet resting on the kitchen counter. It woke as she placed it in front of her chair at the table.

She tapped the daily news folder, where half a dozen options appeared. Passing over both the *Washington Times* and *Wall Street Journal* icons Angie selected RAP, hoping to find something of interest in the lifestyle section of the *Weekend Journal*. Aptly, an image of what must have been hundreds of newborn babies populated the screen.

She immediately noticed the byline.

Julia? She smiled, pleased to see her friend's work receive such prominent placement.

Glancing toward the living room to confirm that the children remained sufficiently occupied, Angie settled in to enjoy the rare luxury of reading a lengthy feature while chomping a salty treat.

But the moment quickly soured as she read the article's title.

THE BREEDERS
Their Alarming Agenda for Your Future

From the opening page Angie felt belittled. The most meaningful decisions she had ever made, even the decision that lay before her now, appeared part of a radical conspiracy against common sense.

People like Angie, the feature explained, clung to what they call "the marital covenant," a pious relic long since replaced by more inclusive and less rigid domestic partnership agreements. How quaint. How odd.

Those who embraced the benefits of medical science had learned to separate sex from babies, to eliminate the remote possibility of an unplanned conception. When sensible people considered parenthood they prescreened fertilized eggs before deciding whether and which they should carry to term. Religious radicals, by contrast, took a leap of faith every time they made love. Not that they did it very often since, in their view, sex was a necessary evil to be done in a manner that kept erogenous pleasure to a minimum.

Angie's brow creased at the description, knowing how much she and Kevin enjoyed intimacy. She in no way resembled the caricature, but felt indicted nonetheless.

Breeders, the feature continued, even opposed personal autonomy, as evidenced by their common hostility toward the popular Youth Initiative. If this radical group had their way, seniors and others would lose the freedom to transition wealth to younger, healthier citizens, leaving them no choice but to continue draining personal, state, and federal assets just when the economy needed them most.

And so it went, one stroke after another painting Angie's kind as either ignorant, reckless, or both. Even the ob-gyn highlighted in the story, Dr. Bryce Richert, came across as less appealing than his apparently noble life deserved. Angie found herself nodding in agreement with most of his comments, even as she blushed at his allegedly antiquated assumptions. *Her* antiquated assumptions.

About two-thirds into the article Angie swiped the screen to turn the page to where, to her surprise, she saw a large image of Kevin above text describing him as "the mastermind behind what several Washington insiders call an extreme proposal" presented during "closed-door meetings led by Senator Joshua Franklin" in which he advocated "so-called 'bright spot' economic policies that would put the government in the business of giving preferential treatment to those who choose parenthood."

A bit farther down Julia found a long quotation from Kevin. A rush of pride accompanied Angie's reading of the same words she had heard her husband craft in the car, at the kitchen table, in her bed, and in front of his mirror. Unlike Dr. Richert, Kevin came off as well-spoken and balanced. His argument in favor of bright spot strategies made complete sense, despite the hostile bookends to his comments, compliments of Nicole Florea and Trisha Sayers.

"Good morning, Daddy!" Angie heard Tommy and Joy leap to attention before rushing toward Kevin's slippers. He winked at Angie while relishing the attack.

She took another bite of cracker and offered a pinky wave.

"Hungry?" she asked.

"Looks delicious!" he lied. "But I think I'll just pour myself a glass of juice."

Her eyes followed Kevin into the kitchen, her hand gently touching his arm as he passed. She began to mention the article, but stopped short. It could wait until after he accepted Joy's wordless invitation to join her sitting Indian-style in front of the television. While Leah gnawed on Kevin's extended thumb Tommy made his way to the kitchen to refill his empty bowl of dry Fruity Pebbles.

Angie turned the page: speculation about Franklin's intentions and quotes from the usual opposing voices.

She swiped again, this time encountering images that stole her breath.

The first showed Kevin seated beside a gorgeous woman in a ritzy restaurant, her hand resting affectionately on his wrist.

Angie struggled to read the text, something about speculation of a romantic relationship between Congressman Tolbert and a Franklin aide.

The second photo showed the same woman standing on Angie's front porch accepting Kevin's help with her coat.

While trying to imagine any explanation but the obvious, she felt Tommy's body lean against her side.

"See, Mommy," he said proudly. "I told you she was a pretty lady."

CHAPTER SIXTY

Julia was livid. Paul hadn't merely tweaked her story. He'd sullied it with every ounce of mud Monica Garcia had managed to find and throw.

She spent most of the morning crafting and deleting notes to Angie. What to say?

The speculation about Kevin hadn't been her doing. It had been her editor's idea.

As if that would ease the pain of seeing those incriminating pictures.

The demeaning tone and scathing jabs didn't reflect Julia's feelings. They came from her younger, less refined coauthor.

Coauthor! she remembered angrily. *Paul had no business melding my story with Monica's drivel*!

But he had. Millions of readers had spent that morning nodding their heads in collective contempt finally given voice by a noted journalist. They would gratefully associate justification for their disdain with Julia Davidson: the same writer who had scoffed at the Peter Pan world of Guyland now granted permis-

sion to elevate the derisive label *breeder* from the gutter of snig-
gering whispers to the pinnacle of reputable condescension. A
new leper had been ousted from suitable society. Good riddance
to another small-minded subculture. Long live the civilized elite!

By noon Julia had left seven angry messages for Paul, none
of them returned. She declined Jared and Maria's invitation to
go out for pizza. No appetite. She opted instead to try settling
her fidgety mind and dulling her throbbing head by soaking in a
warm bath before lying down for a nap.

◆

"Its OK!" Julia heard Maria's shout at the same moment she noticed her own violently flailing arms. "You're home, in your bed.
Calm down, sweetie!"

The pace of her racing heart gradually slowed as Julia gulped
oxygen into lungs that had been ready to burst. Her mind finally
caught up with her waking body.

MAN
SHADOW
FEAR
ANGER

The nightmare had not retired. It had merely missed a shift.

"Are you all right?" Maria asked with concerned eyes. "I've
never seen it that bad before. I'm worried about you."

"I went under again," Julia explained breathlessly. "But I
couldn't resurface."

The memory prompted a shiver of dread.

Maria sat on the bed rubbing her sister's settling arm. Julia noticed Jared standing in the bedroom doorway anxiously looking
on.

"You OK, Aunt Julia?" he asked.

"I'll be fine. Just give me a few minutes."

They did.

Julia retrieved the notepad from her nightstand but immediately put it back. She closed her eyes, hoping for one last look at the frightening images before they faded entirely from her mind.

As before, she saw the fixed, shadowy image of a man extending his hand toward her as she drifted farther and farther away. She screamed toward him futilely. She felt the downward pull. Desperate for breath, she tried swimming away from the sadistic laughter bellowing upward from beneath.

Her eyes jolted open in reaction to something she had never noticed before. She closed them again, confirming what couldn't be.

Just when Julia had felt herself drowning she turned her eyes downward, away from the vanishing shadow and toward whatever dark destiny summoned below. That's when she saw the face. A boy. Someone she recognized but couldn't place, his expression fluctuating between stubborn anger and frantic terror at the same time his hands closed from beseeching grasp to defiant clench.

The snapshot of the face distinctly preserved, Julia scoured her mind for clues.

Where had she seen the boy before? A friend of Jared's? No. Too old.

What did he have to do with her haunting dreams? Anything? Nothing?

Had he also called out to the mysterious man?

Had Julia tried to save him before falling victim to his desperate grasp?

Why the looks of defiance and terror? Why the reaching and clenching?

And then it struck her. She *had* seen his face before.

She walked to the dresser and retrieved her tablet to hastily open the folder sent by Jeremy Santos. Two clicks later she stared intently at the picture of Jeremy sitting beside his mother and brother on the night before Antonio's transition.

Antonio Santos!

She opened Antonio's journal and began scrolling through pages before locating the final, unread entry. Antonio's final recorded words.

August 17, 2041: My final day alive. In a few hours I will finally leave the ranks of debits. Mom, I know you're upset. But I'm old enough to decide my own fate now, and this is what I want. I'm done. So are you and Jeremy. No more worrying about me day and night. No more of the humiliation for me or embarrassment for you. I appreciate all you've done. But I want you and Jeremy to enjoy your lives. Tell him I hope he gets past his anger at God so I can see him in whatever heaven exists. I know you'll get there after sticking with me through everything. You made life tolerable.

If you ever hear from Dad again tell him I said goodbye. And that I hate him. I know he's the faceless man in my dreams, the one who never reaches back when I call for help. I'm glad I won't have any more nightmares. They scare me more than I've admitted. They feel like I'm drowning, getting sucked down away from the life I was supposed to live. But that's over now. I don't want to think about what should be or could be anymore. I'm ready to go. Farewell cruel world. Have a nice day!

Julia sat staring at the page, trying to make sense of what seemed beyond comprehension. Antonio Santos had been haunted by the same dream!

She looked in the mirror to invite an explanation. Nothing came. She looked back, this time noticing the day of Antonio's final entry. It was a date that held significance beyond inclusion in legal documents describing the wrongful death incident. Something more personal.

Julia closed the file and opened her calendar to find any clues, perhaps an appointment record or a journal note suggesting something unique about August 17, 2041. Nothing of importance appeared.

A knocking sound interrupted her thoughts.

"Still doing all right?" Maria asked, poking her head inside the door.

"I think so," Julia began. "But I'm not sure."

She wanted to share details with her sister. But she hesitated, still trying to decide whether she had been yanked into a profound mystery or was simply losing her mind.

"Does the date August 17, 2041, mean anything to you?" Julia asked.

"Should it?"

"I don't know. I'm trying to figure something out. Something that might link to my nightmares."

The comment seemed to trigger a reaction, as if prompting a hunch. "Just a second." Maria rushed out of the room, leaving Julia alone with her thoughts.

Do I need to see a psychiatrist? Julia wondered. *Or should I call a priest?*

She remembered Angie's pastor. She wondered if he might have any experience unraveling the spiritual meaning of dreams.

Don't be ridiculous, she told herself. *There has to be a rational explanation. Maybe we both saw the same scary movie. Read the same horror novel.*

"I've got it," Maria said, bouncing back into the bedroom. "August 17, 2041."

"What about it?" Julia asked.

"I wrote a note in my diary on that date that might help.

'Julia woke up last night shouting. She had a pretty bad nightmare.' I think it was your first. At least the first one that ever woke me."

Julia felt the stun of realization. *I inherited the nightmare from a dying boy?*

"Does that help any?" Maria asked casually.

Julia's head bobbed up and down in dazed silence.

CHAPTER SIXTY-ONE

Julia couldn't recall a more chaotic two weeks. Even before she could absorb accolades from her weekend feature the floodgates flew open, bringing one big assignment after the next to her desk. The new owners of RAP clearly liked her work. But they also needed all hands on deck to handle the wildfire of coverage required after the congressional budget office released revised projections. A Monday-evening news cycle fed a Tuesday-morning market crash. Every sector of the economy known to Wall Street turned dramatically downward for six consecutive sessions. Neither the president's defensive fireside chat nor Senator Franklin's perfectly timed press conference had managed to quell the panic.

Despite the pervasive alarm, however, Julia felt grateful for the whirlwind of activity. It had kept her too busy to think about Angie. It also gave her a convenient excuse to decline Paul Daugherty's repeated requests to meet. The last thing she wanted to do was talk to the man who, despite salvaging her career, had lost her respect.

But she couldn't avoid him forever, and conflicts should be

resolved in person. So Julia accepted Paul's offer to take a seat across from his desk, settling in for what would likely be a weak apology buried somewhere within his self-satisfied boasting.

"We're back on top, Jewel," Paul began after insisting Julia accept his toast to her success. "Just yesterday Bobbie mentioned you, said you were doing stellar work!"

"Bobbie?" she asked.

"Roberta Grantwood. You know, the new editor in chief."

"You call her Bobbie?"

"Well, not to her face. *Ms. Grantwood* to her face. But I like the sound of Bobbie. More, I don't know, editor in chief–sounding."

Julia shifted in her chair while pretending to sip her drink.

"Come on, love," Paul said to fill the silence. "Don't tell me you're still upset about the breeder story. Look, I'm sorry, OK? But I did what had to be done."

She crossed her legs without a word.

"How can you be mad when what I did got you back on top? You and Monica both."

"I see it didn't do you any harm either." Julia perused the new office fixtures.

"What can I say? I struck while the iron was hot and everybody won."

The comment reminded Julia of why she had come. "Everybody?"

"Don't worry about Tolbert," Paul said. "He's a big boy. He'll move on. They always do. You've got bigger issues to consider."

She raised a single, curious eyebrow.

"I should say, bigger opportunities to weigh," he continued. "I've been asked to assign you the next big weekend feature. Another brewing scandal, this one much juicier than the last."

Her eyes sank.

"Do you remember the lawsuit story I tossed you before the breeder thing?"

Julia sat up at the mention.

"The one about the woman who died trying to stop her debit kid's transition," he added.

Julia winced, taking offense for a face she couldn't forget.

"Anyway. Rumor has it Franklin tried to intervene in the wrongful death case against NEXT Inc. Looks like he has financial connections of some sort. How would you like to obliterate the reputation of that budget-slashing Nazi before he becomes the most powerful man in the world? Monica's champing at the bit for this one. But I told Bobbie you're the best gal for the job."

"I'm a journalist, Paul," she protested. "Not a tabloid hack."

He cursed. "I know that, Jewel. But Bobbie loved the way you killed that bright spots nonsense before it saw daylight. She just wants you to aim a bit higher this time."

"Higher than what?"

"Higher than a freshman congressman fall guy."

"Fall guy?"

Paul covered his mouth like a boy realizing he had said too much.

"What do you mean by fall guy?" Julia demanded.

"Forget it."

"Paul," she pushed. "Tell me what you meant when you said Kevin Tolbert was a fall guy."

Silence.

"The pictures you sent of Kevin and that girl. How did you get them?"

He rose from his chair and moved past Julia to close the door. He turned toward her, lowering his voice.

"You didn't hear this from me. Deal?"

"Spit it out, Paul!" she said angrily.

"OK. OK." Open palms raised to block her line of fire. "Those pictures were staged."

"What? How? By whom?"

"Not sure. I think Franklin's office. You know, just in case things turned south with Tolbert."

"But they didn't turn south, at least they hadn't when the story broke."

"I know. But Monica used her magic to obtain copies. Don't ask me how." He returned to his seat. "Anyway, once they were in my possession I felt we owed it to the public to release them."

"But you said they were staged."

"I know that now. I didn't then. I made a judgment call with the information available at the time. So sue me."

"I'd rather kill you!" Julia confessed. "Do you have any idea...?"

She stopped short. It was futile to take the conversation any further.

"Never mind," she said calmly, placing her glass on the edge of his desk while rising to her feet.

"Come on, Jewel," he pleaded. "Don't be like that. No harm, no foul. Everything worked out great. Besides, you can write your own ticket now. You want to do more features? You got it. Prefer sticking with the weekly column gig? All yours. Whatever you want."

She turned toward the door.

"You know what they say, Jewel," Paul continued. "The end justifies the means. You might have lost your job if I hadn't pulled the trigger."

Julia looked back at Paul deliberately and spoke three frighteningly satisfying words. "Paul. I quit."

CHAPTER SIXTY-TWO

On her ninth attempt Angie's call again rolled to Kevin's voice mail. She felt her heart thumping in her temples, desperate to speak to her exiled companion, lover, partner, and heartbroken friend. Why hadn't she believed him? How could she have let him endure the humiliation of the past few weeks alone? Just when he needed her most she had trusted him least. Her regret deepened with each torturous ring.

"Why doesn't he answer?" she asked aloud, already knowing why. Angie had ignored Kevin's calls every day since he had started bunking with Troy after her emotional tirade. She hadn't wanted to hear another implausible explanation. She even ignored Troy's appeal to give Kevin a chance, to listen to his side of the story.

Kevin had left ten voice messages the day after their argument, which had gradually dwindled to one on day seven. It had been forty-eight hours since his last attempt. Apparently he was understandably convinced that Angie had meant the brutal words that now left a bitter residue in her mouth.

She had been strong.

She had been brave.

But she had been wrong.

"Hi, beautiful. Sorry, I'm tied up. Can't wait to talk to you."

Angie took some comfort in the fact that Kevin hadn't changed her unique greeting. A greeting she no longer felt worthy to receive.

"Hi, darling. I'm so, so sorry…" She couldn't continue, a deep sob overpowering her rehearsed script. "Please, please call me," she finally managed.

She looked back at the message from Julia.

FROM JULIA DAVIDSON: *Angie. Call me right away. I just learned that the pictures of Kevin and that woman were staged. Forgive me. I messed up bad.*

Julia had shared everything she knew over the phone. A colleague named Monica Garcia had given the pictures to Julia's editor. It was true that the girl in the photos had offered herself to Kevin. But Kevin had refused, end of story. The girl had had the pictures taken to use in the event that Kevin ever became a major player. As it turned out, she had amassed a stockpile of "evidence" on a wide range of Washington players as part of a sleazy small business selling dirt to tabloids and, when possible, major news outlets. Franklin's office had dug into the scam after reading Julia's story and dismissed the aide.

"What about the damage to Kevin's reputation?" Angie had asked.

"RAP will print a retraction next weekend," Julia explained. "But I'm afraid they've already left a stain that will be hard to get out."

Angie understood. Trisha Sayers had been asked to present the austerity plan in Kevin's stead. She barely mentioned the bright spots idea, holding her nose the entire time. What Kevin had intended as a game-changing strategy for economic growth got reduced to an embarrassing footnote in Franklin's larger strategy.

Any hope Kevin had had of influencing the growing controversy over the president's Youth Initiative seemed dead. Religious extremists weren't welcome on the national stage.

How hard the past few weeks must have been for a man who had known only success. A man everyone had once loved and admired. She could see the defeat in his eyes while watching Kevin on the television screen missing curve balls pitched by an invading press corps. Not one asked about his vision or dreams for America's future. They only wanted to know how his wife had reacted to the photos.

Angie thought what Kevin would never say. *She reacted like a naïve fool!*

Giving up efforts to call Kevin's phone, Angie decided to endure the embarrassment of again trying his office. She would gladly beg an acne-faced aide to make her husband take the call if it meant she could speak to the love of her life.

A voice answered after two rings.

"Troy?" *What a relief!* "I'm so glad I got you. Let me talk to Kevin!"

"Hi, Angie." He sounded surprised. "He didn't come into the office today. Third day in a row. He was still sleeping when I left the apartment."

"I'm going there now." She hung up, ignoring whatever else Troy was trying to say.

Five minutes later the kids sat strapped into three car seats, still wearing their pajamas. As the garage door rose she shifted into reverse and eased backward without bothering to look behind. That's when she heard the thud of Kevin's signature slap. Peering through the rearview mirror she saw the torso of a man holding a bouquet of her favorite flowers pretending the pain of a hit-and-run impact.

The flowers fell to the ground as Angie leaped into her husband's arms. He pulled her body tight as their lips locked stubbornly together.

"Daddy! Daddy!"

They heard Tommy yelling from the car, coercing their lips into mirrored smiles.

"You're home!"

"Hi, buddy," Kevin managed between kisses drenched in Angie's relieved tears.

◆

Angie accepted Kevin's offer to fix the family a gourmet lunch of peanut-butter-and-banana sandwiches. They both relished a ritual each had feared lost forever.

"Thank you for the food," Tommy led with clasped fingers.

"Tankoo da ood," Joy repeated.

"Thank you for baby Weah."

"Tankoo aby eah."

"And thank you for Daddy," he added. "Amen."

"Tankoo Daddy, men."

After eating they put the kids down for an afternoon nap, then made love in the shower before curling up in bed together, where Angie pressed herself as close as possible to the man she had hurt so much.

"Can you ever forgive me?"

"Of course I forgive you." He kissed the top of her head. "It wasn't your fault."

"I should have believed you."

"I should have told you about that girl's visit to the house."

"You did tell me. You said she stopped by with documents from Franklin's office."

"But I didn't say she made a pass. I should have told you that."

"Why didn't you?"

"I don't know," he said. "Maybe because it embarrassed me. Even scared me a little."

"Scared you?"

"It probably doesn't make sense. But when that girl began

coming onto me I felt like I had been grazed by a hunter's rifle shot. Like I had survived a close call."

"Were you tempted?" Angie asked. "Wait, don't answer that. I don't want to know."

They held each other without speaking for a moment.

"Were you?"

Kevin shifted his body to look Angie in the eyes.

"No, I wasn't tempted," he assured her. "But I was flattered. That's what scared me."

She nestled herself back into his embrace. "I think I understand. She's a very attractive woman. And you're only a man."

"It seems like political influence includes decadent privileges as part of the package. Like it's expected. Like it's no big deal." He paused and gently inched her chin upward so their eyes could meet. "To be honest, I'm kind of glad to know people take pictures like that."

"Glad? You can't be serious."

"There's nothing like knowing you'll likely get caught to keep you from doing something stupid."

She sat up and leaned against the pillow. "But it makes me so mad that they did this to you. I mean, you did nothing wrong and they destroyed your reputation while who knows who in this town does whatever they please without a scratch!"

"Don't worry about my reputation. As long as you know the truth, I'm a happy man."

She smiled back, then kissed his hand.

"I'll ask Troy to contact some friends in various news agencies to pressure RAP into a full apology."

"Julia said they would print a retraction next week."

"We'll try to get more than the usual buried correction," Kevin said expectantly. "Hey, where's your mom? I assume she came."

"Went back to Colorado yesterday. Dad insisted. He wanted the kids and me to join her."

"I bet he wants to castrate me!"

She laughed, then hugged Kevin again. "I'm sorry."

"You said that already."

A brief, wonderful silence.

"What do you think will happen now?"

"It'll all blow over in a few weeks. And if it doesn't, God has something else in store for us to do." He exhaled deeply, a man finally back home after a long exile.

Angie decided her moment had arrived.

"Speaking of what God has in store for us," she began. "I have some news."

He scooted up to join her in a pillow-propped position. "What kind of news?"

Disquiet reclaimed her expression. "Do you remember the flu bug I felt a few weeks back?"

He did.

"I never told you what the doctor said."

"Is something wrong?" he asked anxiously.

"No. Well, not exactly wrong. But he was a bit concerned about potential complications so he asked me to come back into the office next week."

He waited for more.

"Anyway, it looks like—no, not *it looks like*—I'm definitely pregnant."

She braced herself for Kevin's reaction, for the slight hesitation that never came.

"Pregnant?" he yelled.

"Shhh! You'll wake the…"

His pressing lips silenced hers before she could finish the warning.

"We're gonna have another baby," he said before planting his lips back onto hers. "Why didn't you tell me sooner?"

"I got a bit distracted by the possible end of our marriage," she snickered at the remark and the relief.

Kevin had already begun unwrapping the towel from Angie's body. His motions slowed as he deliberately positioned his face over her still-flat abdomen, then gently kissed his nameless child's nurturing cocoon.

It was without question the sweetest kiss she had ever received. But it also tickled, prompting a giggle of delight.

Kevin's need to know trumped his reluctance to interrupt the beautiful sound. "What complications?"

She didn't understand.

"You said you had an appointment next week, that the doctor was concerned about complications."

She hesitated.

"Please, babe, just tell me what's wrong."

"Probably nothing," she replied reassuringly. "He just thinks it would be a good idea to run a genetic profile this time. You know, in light of Leah."

"Why?"

She didn't answer, "*Just in case*" no longer seeming like a good enough reason.

"No," he said decisively.

"You don't want to know."

"No. I don't."

Nothing else needed to be said. They just hugged resolutely, thawing Angie's impasse in grateful release.

The door flew open, prompting Kevin to hurriedly cover his naked bride with the blanket.

"Hi guys!" he said to Tommy and Joy as they rushed toward the bed. "Jump up here and give your mommy a big smooch. She's gonna give us another baby!"

CHAPTER SIXTY-THREE

Julia scrunched up her face at the almost-but-not-quite-final paragraph. Jeremy Santos deserved better. Her mind ran through one last scan of the interviews recorded and journals read since the day she'd sat across the table his mother and brother had once shared. She found and typed what was missing.

There is much still unclear about the case of Sylvia and Antonio Santos. We know that their lives ended on August 17, 2041. We know that Antonio transitioned willingly, a path some call that of a sheep rather than a hero. And while many question the nobility of his decision, millions celebrate the result of his choice. One fewer debit on the books. One more estate freed for productive ends. A reasonable conclusion when formulating spreadsheets. A bit more complicated when reviewing photographs.

Julia felt her own approving nod grant permission to move to the kitchen. She noticed her nephew slouching on the living room sofa, staring at the television screen in his usual after-school-before-Mom-gets-home routine.

"Hi, Jared. Care to join me in a celebratory glass of"—she paused to eye the options on the refrigerator shelf—"grapefruit juice?"

"What are we celebrating?" he asked, approaching the kitchen counter.

"We're celebrating my success. I just finished a very important story ahead of schedule."

He flashed a puzzled glance.

"But I thought you were unemployed."

Julia winced. "I'm not unemployed. I'm an independent journalist."

"Right."

"RAP isn't the only media company in the world. People always need freelance writers."

"What's it about?"

She took a drink while considering the shortest answer. "A wrongful death lawsuit."

Jared stared vacantly.

"That's when someone claims one person did something wrong to cause another person's death."

"What other kind is there?" he asked.

"What do you mean?"

"Well, if you caused a person's death you must have done something wrong. Right?"

Julia smiled at the profoundly naïve statement.

"It's not quite that simple." *Or is it?*

Jared shrugged while taking a sip of juice.

"When will it run?" he asked politely.

"I need to find an editor willing to buy the story first." She tilted her glass toward his. "But that's tomorrow's challenge. Today, we celebrate my completion."

"Congratulations, Aunt Julia," Jared offered, the ding of touching glasses making the party official.

He stood a moment gazing awkwardly at Julia.

"Go back to your television show." She released him with a slim laugh. "Thanks for sharing my big moment."

She sat at the table to check messages, hoping to have heard back from at least one of the editors she had contacted. Everyone said freelance work could be feast or famine. Nearly a week since walking out of Paul Daugherty's office, she was still hungry for her first meal.

She opened the only message on her digital screen.

FROM TROY SIMMONS: *I don't mean to be a pest, but a noble knight never forgets his promise to treat a lady to the finest jelly-filled doughnut in the realm. Hope to see you soon.*

Moments later, Julia found herself searching airline ticket prices while trying to construct a plausible reason she was needed in Washington, DC.

June 2, 2042

Janet

"You look lovely today." Chuck mirrored Janet's smile at his thoughtful reassurance.

She had been looking forward to seeing Charles Kohl again. She only regretted wearing such an unflattering dress.

"I told you, Mom," Matthew said before turning back toward Mr. Kohl, who was taking a seat across from his timid guest. "We spent much of the morning trying to find her favorite necklace."

"Hush, Matthew," she ordered with a blush.

"Well, I'm glad you did," Chuck said. "It's delightful to see an attractive woman looking her best."

She beamed in grateful embarrassment.

Matthew kissed his mother's cheek to formalize the handoff. "Enjoy your conversation," he said supportively.

"I'm sure we will," Chuck said, gently patting Matthew's arm to alert the third wheel he needed to disappear.

"Bye, Son," Janet said carelessly.

"Goodbye, Mom," he replied after a heavy pause.

Janet's fingers fidgeted tensely with her necklace as she raised her eyes to the attentive gentleman's face.

"So, tell me how you're feeling about all of this," he asked.

Her lips pursed and eyebrows rose slightly as her head tilted to the side, a shy girl unsure of how to respond.

"Are you nervous?"

She nodded.

"I understand. It's normal to feel uneasy."

He looked away from Janet momentarily to glance at the clock.

"We have plenty of time together," he assured her. "Why don't we talk about you?"

She appeared momentarily confused, a vacant expression overtaking her forced smile. Then a change, as if willing herself to hold the present, pleasant moment.

"What would you like to know about me?" she asked.

"Anything you'd like to tell me."

Releasing the edge of her necklace, Janet lowered her hand to retrieve an object Matthew had placed on the table. The feel in her palm seemed to gird a lapsing composure.

"Do you have grandchildren, Mr. Kohl?" she asked.

"Please, Janet, call me Chuck," he insisted. "One grandson. He's about to graduate from high school. But I thought we were talking about you."

"I wanted grandchildren," she continued.

"Is that so?" Chuck asked without surprise.

"I had these pictures in my mind. You know, like pots and pans strewn all over my kitchen floor while my grandchild bangs a rackety concert using my favorite stirring spoon."

Chuck smiled like a man recalling his own grandchild's performance.

"I saw my granddaughter playing peewee soccer, me cheering on the sidelines when she made her first goal."

"Granddaughter?"

"I imagined her as a girl," she mused. "Of course, I would have been just as excited about a grandson's first goal!"

The realization forced Janet to smile.

"I had so many pictures. First communion. A middle school choir performance. Father Tomberlin giving a confirmation blessing." She paused. "So many pictures."

The door opened. Both Janet and Chuck looked toward a young man flashing an apologetic grin.

"I'm sorry for the intrusion," he whispered while tiptoeing toward Janet's chair. "Don't mind me. I'll just be a second."

"No worries," Chuck reassured him. "Go on, Janet."

She looked back toward her courteous host. "I know it's a silly thing to talk about here, with you. But it came to mind."

"Not at all," he said. "There's nothing silly about telling a friend about your hopes and dreams. Who knows, what we're doing today could make the possibility of grandkids more than faint pictures in your imagination."

"I hope so," she said flatly. "Did you know my son plans to become a professor?"

"He'll make a fine teacher."

"Yes, he will." She nodded. "Maybe after he finishes his education he'll find the right girl and..."

She couldn't finish the statement, because it either caused her pain or slipped her mind.

"Janet?" Chuck prodded. "Are you feeling OK? Are you comfortable?"

She looked toward the young man attending to the medical equipment beside her, then back to Chuck. She squeezed the object in her palm tightly before responding.

"I'm fine. Thank you. What was I saying?"

"You were telling me about your son. How he's going to become a professor."

"Oh yes."

They were her last coherent words. She gazed at Chuck for several minutes, her eyes seeming less and less able to focus until they disappeared beneath the falling curtains of eyelids eager to close.

On cue, the young transition specialist received the weight of her slumping form. He gently cradled her head to rest it on the back of her chair, then pressed a button that began its gradual recline into the horizontal position required for the organ donation procedure.

Janet's knees sprawled indecently in reaction to a final twitch of her reluctantly ebbing life. The young man bundled her legs to restore ladylike grace and shifted them sideways to place her cadaver in the prescribed position.

"She's gone," Chuck said while looking through the two-way mirror toward Matthew's tear-filled eyes.

Matthew heard the door open beside him as the protective blackness dissipated into unwelcome light. A middle-aged woman invited him to slip back into the transition room to say any final farewells before they begin what she called "the next stage" of the process. In a matter of minutes they would begin extracting useful parts from his mother's still-warm body.

He approached the spot where Janet Adams had entrusted her dreams to a near-stranger, to a man Matthew had convinced to provide the required secondary confirmation. His duties completed, Charles Kohl moved hastily toward the door, apparently eager to make a next appointment. He placed his hand momentarily on Matthew's shoulder. It was hard to tell whether he intended condolences over Matthew's loss or congratulations on his accomplishment.

"The receptionist will have your copies of the necessary documents," Chuck explained before slipping out of the room.

Matthew moved closer to his mother's lifeless figure to apprehend a moment he had imagined for months. He would touch her hand, the first his infant fingers had ever held. He would caress her cheek, the first his newborn lips had ever felt. Most of all, he would receive her silent thanks for freeing her trapped soul from a decaying prison. She had been resistant, even scared. But he had given her the resolve she needed to discard material form for a superior, purely spiritual existence.

He halted his approach two feet from the table. His limbs froze in what felt like fear.

You've damned her immortal soul!

"No. I set her free," he whispered back.

"Excuse me?" the transition specialist asked, turning away from his preparations.

"Nothing," Matthew replied. "I'm sorry. Carry on."

The young man returned to his duties, easing the corpse's wrinkled arm onto the bed that would soon become a butchering table. He noticed a sound that drew both sets of eyes downward, then knelt to retrieve an object that had apparently escaped the body's clenched fist.

"Would you like to keep this?" he asked. "Or should I put it with the rest of her things?"

Matthew reached toward the man's extended hand to accept an item he had so often placed in his mother's palm.

"Her rosary beads," Matthew explained. "They always brought her comfort when I had to leave her."

The man returned to his work without another word.

Rubbing the row of beads in his fingers, Matthew felt the form of a tiny attached cross. It was a symbol that had reminded his mother of another death, one she believed had taken place to pay for humanity's sin. His sin.

His body stiffened.

"Here you go," he said, handing the rosary back to the transition specialist. "Put it with the rest of her things. I don't want it."

The man accepted the object with a shrug as Matthew felt a surge of anger overtake his rising grief.

He left the room without touching his mother's hand or caressing her cheek.

He left slighted at the ingratitude she had shown.

Thirty minutes later Matthew approached his front door, his mind vacillating between thoughts of the life suddenly possible and thoughts of the death that had made it so.

While tapping his security code into the lock pad Matthew noticed a piece of paper wedged between the handle and the doorjamb. He unfolded it, recognizing the scribbled writing style from dozens of previous notes.

HI MATT

NOT SURE WHAT HAPPENED. ISN'T TODAY MY DAY TO SIT WITH YOUR MOM? CALL IF YOU STILL NEED ME. TELL HER I'LL SEE HER SOON.

DONNY

Matthew folded the note and shoved it into his pocket.

Then he sat down on the porch, placed his head in his hands, and wept like an orphan.

ABOUT THE AUTHORS

James Dobson is the founder and chairman emeritus of Focus on the Family and currently president and radio host of Family Talk, his internationally syndicated radio program heard on over 800 radio stations by millions of people every day. Dr. Dobson is also the author of over thirty books with 40,000,000 plus sold. He lives in Colorado Springs, Colorado, with his wife, Shirley. They have two children and two grandchildren.

Kurt Bruner is the best-selling author of more than fifteen books. For twenty years, Kurt worked at Focus on the Family where he served as Group Vice President over films, books, drama and other media. Kurt is president of HomePointe Inc., a network of churches driving home-centered faith formation. Kurt and his wife, Olivia, have been married for twenty-seven years and have four children. They live in Rockwall, Texas.

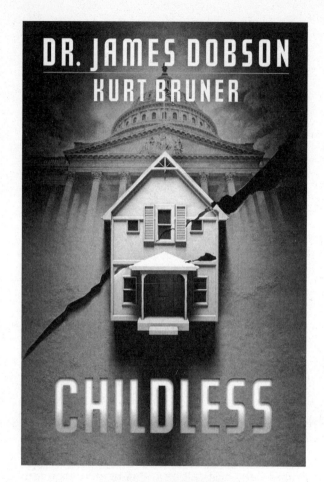

Fall 2013

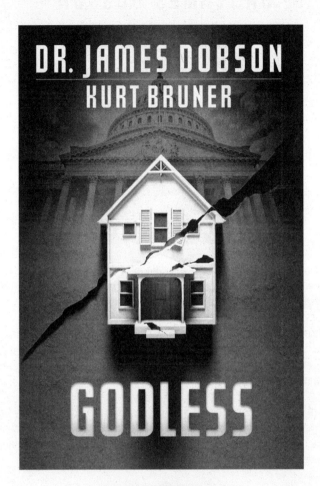

GODLESS

Fall 2014

DR. JAMES DOBSON

Dr. Dobson wasn't ready to retire when he left Focus on the Family in February 2010. He knew that God had given him a mission and a message many years ago, and that God had not yet lifted that assignment from him.

Dr. Dobson felt God directing him to start a new ministry, which he did in March 2010, to continue the important work of strengthening families, speaking into the culture, and spreading the gospel of Jesus Christ. He called the new organization *Dr. James Dobson's Family Talk*.

In July of 2012, Dr. Dobson filmed a new series titled **"Building a Family Legacy"** that combines new and relevant sessions with some of the classic presentations from his original film series recorded in 1978 and seen by over 80 million people worldwide. This timeless family resource will be available in 2013.

DR.JAMES DOBSON'S familytalk™

The voice you trust
for the family you love